Haven's Creed

by
Parker Williams

COPYRIGHT

DEDICATION

A huge thank you to all my friends who told me that I *could* write this book, even though it was something way outside my comfort zone.

Also, a thank you to the man with whom I shared many hours grumbling and groaning over a coworker's attitude, which inspired Haven. Thank you Ben Manske!

Praise for Haven's Creed

Grabs you by the throat – 5 hearts

I recommend this to those who love stories that pack a punch, a storyline that grabs you by the throat, characters that you can't help fall in love with, justice being delivered and an ending that is fantastic.

~~Pixie at MM Good Book Reviews

Couldn't put it down – 5 stars

I loved this story. Full stop, I couldn't put it down!

~~Molly Lolly at Molly Lolly, Reader, Reviewer, Lover of Words

A storyline that doesn't take shortcuts – 5 stars

...multi dimensional main characters...and a storyline that does not take shortcuts.

~~Mary – Reviewer at Molly Lolly, Reader, Reviewer, Lover of Words

A love story, but not a romance, it's not flowery or even pretty – 4.5 stars

I loved that Haven killed for all the right reasons and even loved the creative methods he used and the stories he told his marks before they died.

~~Jessie G. – Author of the Sizzling Miami and Devils Pride MC series

Haven's Creed absolutely captivated me – 5 stars

These characters—Haven and Sammy and the host of secondary characters—are so real.

~~Cate Ashwood – Author of the bestselling 'Hope Cove' series

Loved the premise of this story... - 5 stars

All together I really loved this book!

~~ Kara – Reviewer at Inked Rainbow Reads

HAVEN'S CREED

An act of violence destroys his family and ends the life he knows. To escape his haunted past, he joins the military, where, as a sniper, he is trained to kill with precision and detachment. When a covert organization offers him a new purpose, he becomes Haven, an operative devoted to protecting the innocent when he can and avenging them when he cannot.

After ten years of battling the evil in the world, the life no longer holds the attraction or meaning it once had, and he's ready to walk away. Then he meets Samuel, a young man forced from the age of twelve to work as a sex slave. If ever a man had a need for Haven, it is this one.

Yet nothing about this growing relationship is one-sided. Sammy gives Haven a stability he's never known, and Haven becomes the rock upon which Sammy knows he can depend.

When Sammy reveals something about the enemy Haven has been hunting for months, Sammy fears it will destroy what they've built and he'll lose his home in Haven's heart.

CHAPTER ONE

Decades of grime, caked and baked in the summer sun, crusted the filthy rooftop. I shuddered at the thought of what I might be crawling around in. Either way, considering the eddies of snow and ice swirling around in the bitter cold breeze freezing my exposed skin, I almost wished for the heat of summer now. Better to be up here sweating my balls off than freezing them.

Winds off Lake Michigan could be brutal, but they were even worse at the top of the building I'd selected. I'd chosen a tight spot, especially for a man my size. Still, it offered me the best possible vantage point. My muscles cramped as I slithered forward on my stomach, and the gravel bit into the skin where my shirt had pulled free from my vest. The edge of the roof held a myriad of pipes and ductwork. Great for cover, not so good for aiming. I pulled myself in between two pipes that gave me line of sight of the house where the deal would go down. It would be an awkward shot, especially given the weather, but I'd taken worse. My breath fogged the lenses of my goggles a bit, but not enough to matter. At least not to my target.

My fingers stiffened as I slid the chamber into the rifle, the fingerless gloves providing little protection against the elements. It reminded me why I didn't live in Chicago anymore. I hated winter with a passion. Give me my home in Florida or the one I kept in Arizona and I would be much more content.

The car pulled up a few moments later, drawing my attention back to my assignment. I glanced at my watch. Early. I hated when targets didn't stick to a timetable. It was very rude. The driver ran around and opened John Dunkirk's door, allowing the dead man walking to slide out of the backseat and step onto the sidewalk where he waited as Kenneth Alamo came out of the modest house. My fingers itched. Alamo had been in and out of prison for possession and distribution. His name should be next to Dunkirk's, but he wasn't my target. There would certainly be a reckoning for him at a later date. Maybe this event would set him on the straight and narrow. Unlikely, but in my line of work, stranger things happened.

While Alamo and Dunkirk exchanged handshakes and a brief bro hug, the driver closed the car door then pulled a case from the trunk, placed it on the hood and stepped away. I took note of the briefcase he carried and I tensed. The poison housed in the innocuous looking satchel was the reason I'd been sent. Twenty-seven people had died, that we knew of. Almost half of them were school kids, some as young as seven.

My employer frowned on that and had sent me to get the justice their families wouldn't have gotten otherwise. The fact Dunkirk had avoided prison was reason enough he had come to our attention and had gotten his name on a death warrant.

Dunkirk cracked the lid just enough so the other guy could look into it. I imagined the buyer being gobsmacked at the amount of crap crammed into the small case. Enough to make him a shitload of money, and at the same time, give people on the streets their last fix.

While they were both occupied, I took aim. No one noticed the red dot on Dunkirk's back. I squeezed the trigger in one fluid, practiced motion. The explosion of air that echoed off the rooftop announced his imminent death. The moment his chest exploded, chaos filled the streets. Men swarmed from the nearby building like so many cockroaches. The listening device I'd planted in Dunkirk's car allowed me to hear the barked orders to find whoever was responsible and deal with him. By the time they got their shit together, I would be back in the shadows and on my way home.

I pulled out my phone and tapped out a quick text message.

"It's done. Next?"

The reply came back a moment later. *"Police converging. Go now. Talk later."*

I slipped the phone back into my pocket. I could hear the sirens in the distance. They'd arrest the trash, but the man responsible for all the death through the poison he sold on the streets would never have been taken to prison. His lawyers would have guaranteed it, just as they had the last four times he'd beat the rap the government put together. Dunkirk had enough dirt on a handful of key politicians to ensure he'd live to spread his filth on the streets again. That was why they'd sent me in. If there was one thing I knew with absolute certainty, dead men told no tales and, in Dunkirk's case, sold no drugs.

Of course, I wasn't done with Mr. Dunkirk.

~

The smell of stale cigars clung to everything in Dunkirk's well-appointed office. Heavy burgundy drapes covered the double-paned windows. The furniture probably cost more than most people could afford in several lifetimes. I ran my fingers over the sofa, a thick luxurious fabric with what appeared to be gold-plated brass accents. On one side was a smaller love seat and on the other a single seat chair. It was ostentatious and extremely gaudy, with sunburst masks woven into the couch and pillows, but the damn thing felt like heaven. I made a mental note to check into getting one for myself, assuming I could find it with a less nausea-inducing fabric.

I picked up the remote from the garish monstrosity of an end table. Even through the gloves, I could tell the small wooden stand, with carved dragons blowing smoke as the legs, was another quality piece. I pressed the button and the opulent birch wood fireplace roared to life, bathing the room in a warm glow. I stepped in and allowed the crackling flames to chase the chill from my hands before I opened the doors, stepping back from the blast of heat. I didn't bother to close them again, because for what I had planned, the fire would come in handy.

I moved to the desk and marveled at the craftsmanship. If I had time, I'd love to explore it for hidden nooks and crannies, but soon this place would be buzzing with cops, firemen, and paramedics. I would, of course, be long gone. Moving the mouse brought the computer to awake mode. I plugged in the flash drive my handler gave me and quickly cracked the password. Dunkirk counted on his money to keep him and his secrets safe. If I was right, the cops would make sure the files never saw the light of day. Not all cops were crooked, but I was well aware of the number of men Dunkirk had on his payroll. I found the files I needed—shipment dates, ledgers, lists of names. Everything necessary to crush his organization. Apparently Dunkirk had never heard the adage about not putting all your eggs in one basket, because he left everything wide open. I copied it all to the thumb drive, then gave the computer a little virus that my handler had given me. Even if the computer survived, there would be nothing left to recover from the hard drive.

I took the device from my belt and placed it on the hearth. I toyed with the idea of letting everyone in the building fry, but I didn't hurt innocent people if I could help it. It was highly unlikely anyone associated with Dunkirk was innocent, but unlike my targets, I had scruples. With the timer set for five minutes, I had to leave quickly. Once outside, I headed for the rental car I'd parked down the street. As I walked, I sent my handler another message.

"*Set.*"

From the small box I'd put above the fireplace, a siren droned and lights flashed, in turn activating the other warning devices I'd dropped on my way in. Orders from non-existent cops were barked out over the speakers. Like rats from a ship, people came out of their hidey-holes and fled into the night. The area was quiet. I watched the time count down until it hit the thirty second mark. Then I started my engine and headed down the road. The fireball was spectacular as the building was consumed by an inferno of my making. Nothing would survive, and with the evidence I had on the drive, Dunkirk's organization was finished.

Chalk one up for the good guys.

And me.

~

I disposed of the car by leaving it in a predetermined place, where it would be picked up and stripped down to nothing. The parts would be spread around to various chop shops and destroyed, never to be found. The rental company would be out one car, but with the prices they charged, I found myself unable to work up much sympathy. I wasn't sure how the organization dealt with rental cars. Maybe they'd pay them, but I hoped not. I put my gear into the case I'd stashed in the trunk earlier, changed into something less militaristic, and took a cab to the airport, eager to return home where it was warm.

I boarded the plane, suffering with coach so as not to call attention to myself. Not that a guy who stood six foot two and had the build of a linebacker didn't attract it wherever he went, but in the confined space of the little tin box, people were a lot more wary. My rifle was stashed securely in the hold; no questions asked thanks to my very official-looking forged documents. One thing was certain: if I got caught, the government would disavow me, and I'd be as good as dead in their eyes.

I gave a brief nod to my pretty young seatmate as I grabbed the aisle seat. She looked up at me and her jaw dropped. She scooted as far as she could in the tiny chair, but my elbows still brushed against her when I squished myself into my seat.

As soon as we were underway, she loosened up. Might have had something to do with the four drinks the flight attendant gave her. She leaned up against me, rubbing her hands up and down my arms and flirting to beat the band. She whispered she'd always wanted to join the mile high club. I leaned over and told her I was a member and it wasn't worth the effort.

She gasped then gave a throaty chuckle. "Lucky girl," she whispered.

I had nothing against sex with women. A willing body was always welcome. In this case, I didn't bother to tell her it had been a dude who told me his name was Collin. I'd bent him over in the tiny cubicle that passed for a bathroom and banged the hell out of him. I'd fucked him hard, and he'd cried out so loud that the flight crew forced open the door to see what was wrong. We were taken back to our seats and that was where a different kind of shouting began. Collin hadn't bothered to inform me that he was on a honeymoon flight with his wife.

My seatmate had dozed off, allowing me time to think. Maybe I should reconsider her offer. Sex could be great stress relief, and I always needed to unwind after an op. I glanced over at her, and knew if I woke her, we could hit the bathroom, but after Collin, I had learned to be more circumspect. Drawing the wrong kind of attention to myself could be disastrous in my line of work. Still now that the thought of getting off was in my mind, it would be something to consider when I got home.

I weighed my options. A quick stop at Columns, the BDSM club about thirty miles from my house, would be sure to net me a thrill for the evening. I wasn't really into the lifestyle, at least not beyond a bit of tying up my partner so they couldn't move while I got off, but subs were generally a little more capable of handling my kind of rough sex. It was a good way to work out my frustrations, and they always walked away with a satisfied smile, even if they were a little bowlegged. But I was tired, and the thought of staying up the whole night had no appeal, so home might be a better choice.

After the plane touched down, I waited with the other passengers while our luggage unloaded. I collected my gear, including grabbing my rifle from one of the marshals, and stepped outside, the chill of Chicago being washed away by the dry desert heat. I breathed in a couple of lungsful, allowing it to permeate my body, then went looking for a taxi to take me home.

The driver, Kendrick, had balked at the length of the ride, but paying upfront, and throwing in a couple hundred dollars for the tip for the ride and a bit of silence, had him falling over himself to get me away from the bustle. I was grateful for the quiet and allowed myself to close my eyes.

Almost an hour later, Ken woke me to let me know we'd pulled up in front of my home away from home. Twenty-seven-hundred square feet of what might be called a frat-boy mancave. Wide-screen televisions in most of the rooms, a killer sound system that was piped through Bose speakers wherever I happened to be, even if it was outdoors. The nearest neighbor was well over a mile away, so I could be as loud as I wanted.

I unlocked the door and went inside, hanging my keys on the hook and then dropping my bag near the couch where everything would be put away in the morning. I glanced around and sighed. My homecomings were always kind of a letdown. While the house was opulent by many standards, it really was just a place I stayed. Though I'd been living here for several years, I had no attachment to anything in it, beyond the collection of top shelf scotches I enjoyed occasionally.

While I'd been gone, Kelly, my houseman, had restocked the bar. I ran my fingers along the rows of bottles to see if any new surprises awaited. As usual, the man didn't disappoint. I pulled down a fresh Chivas Regal Royal Salute and poured myself a snifter. I held it to my nose, delighting at the aroma. When I sipped it, the burn instantly warmed my insides and chased away the cold of February in Chicago.

I peeled off my shirt and tossed it onto the red leather sectional in front of the living room's massive television. A seventy-two inch monstrosity that had probably been used twice, and that was by one of the guys I brought home for an evening of no-questions-asked sex.

11

At the thought of sex, my cock hardened. I hadn't been laid in what felt like years. The blow job in the bathroom at Columns a few months ago didn't really count. The sub hadn't gotten his nut, just knelt there while I stuffed my cock down his very talented throat. I offered to get him off, but he declined. He seemed completely blissed out, so I sent him on his way.

The bedroom held one of my few cherished possessions, the Nerius I'd purchased. It was an incredible investment. Like sleeping on a cloud or fucking in cotton batting. It surrounded you, pulled you into its depths. It damn well cradled you. And it called to me. I decided to forgo the club. Despite dozing in the cab, I was tired deep to my bones. I trudged past the bed as I stripped off the rest of my clothes. I put my phone on the charger before I stepped into the glass cubicle shower and allowed the eight shower heads to massage away the aches. Thirty-one was too young to hurt this much.

My phone beeped and I knew it was my handler. He was probably sending me a message to tell me that my payment had been routed through the billions of subsidiary companies and deposited in my account. I didn't do this for the money, though. The fact I was helping to keep the streets clean was enough for me.

Of course the two hundred fifty thousand per hit wasn't bad either.

I lingered in the shower until my skin pruned, grateful for the warmth that relaxed my muscles. I stepped out, dried myself with a towel from the heated rack, then slipped into the artfully folded Luxe robe that had been placed on top of the side table. I'd have to talk to my handler. Kelly wasn't being paid enough.

I strolled back to the living room and picked up my phone. As I expected, it was confirmation of payment. After pouring myself another drink, I sat down on the couch and looked around the place. Kelly kept it immaculate and added his own little touches that were supposed to make it a little homier, but…well, it was a place. Not a home. The comforts were there, but nothing that made it more than somewhere to keep my stuff.

I downed the remainder of the whiskey, the slow burn warming me from the inside out, and walked around the house to see if, maybe, I could find a bit of myself somewhere in here. A game room, with all the latest things from

Xbox and Sony. It was here when I'd moved in, and I didn't think I'd ever used it.

The kitchen. I'd thrown together a sandwich or two, popped a pizza in the oven, and I think once I made breakfast for someone I'd brought back from the bar, but Kelly stocked everything and generally made the meals.

Room after room and none of it seemed at all homey. Sure, like the bed, I'd made my mark, but overall, it was Kelly who'd decorated it, kept it clean, furnished it, made it what it was.

I returned to the living room, glanced back at the bottle, and thought about pouring another drink, but I knew my limits, and I always kept my wits about me. I put the stopper back in then placed it on the shelf, even though Kelly would move it back to where he thought it belonged in the morning.

I trudged into the bedroom. I wasn't prone to melancholy, it never paid to not be focused on the here and now, but tonight? I let my gaze wander over the bedroom as I pulled back the comforter and made ready to slide between the silk sheets and wondered if I had made the wrong choices in life.

~

I was not a good man. Hell, there were many times I wasn't even sure I was a man anymore. I killed people for a living and made damn good money at it. I didn't do random chaos, though. That stuff was for amateurs. What I did was for a cause. The greater good, you might say. I was sure there were plenty who'd argue that fact, but they hadn't seen the things I had. They lived in their perfect little world where everyone was redeemable. Our penal system worked. The government was the bad guy. In some cases they were right. When they were wrong, that was where I stepped in. Either way, I did the things that needed to be done because others couldn't or wouldn't.

I had seen and done a lot of things in my life that would make most other people quake in fear or piss their pants. I was used to watching people move to the other side when they saw me walking down the street. Not because I was a hulking man, though I was big, but because I gave off the aura that I wasn't someone to be messed with.

When I was fifteen, I killed my first man. Every time Arnie, the guy my mother was shacking up with at the time, drank, he got it into his head she was cheating on him. He'd start slapping her, and that turned into full-fledged beating within a few months. When he was done, he'd start on my sister.

There were nights she'd crawl into bed with me, sobbing. For the longest of times, she wouldn't tell me what happened, but when I found blood on her pajamas, I knew. I'd tried to stand up to him, but he beat me badly enough that I couldn't go to school for two weeks until the bruises faded. But I got off lucky. The things he did to Chrissy gave me nightmares. I'd hear her cry out and knew there was nothing I could do but hide in my bed, my pillow covering my head. He was bigger, meaner, and stronger than me, and he reminded me of that fact constantly.

The old lady never said boo about it. She always forgave him and tried to justify what he did by telling me how much stress he was under. How he was a good man and didn't mean it. It was just the drinking, she swore. It was more like he was a bastard and she was his meal ticket.

I came home one night and found him whaling on her, my sister's body crumpled in a heap, her head smashed in. The son of a bitch had a gun in his hand, slick with blood, and he threatened to kill them both, screaming he wouldn't let her leave. She slapped him. It wasn't hard, but it shocked him enough that he dropped the gun. I picked it up. He sneered at me and called me a weak-willed fag.

I looked at the gun I held in my hand. The instrument of my revenge. The means to saving my sister.

"Give me the gun, you fuck. It's not a dick, you wouldn't know what to do with it."

The bullet I put in his forehead showed him how wrong he was. He lay on the floor, blood bubbling from the wound, and his eyes locked on mine as he took his last breath. I wanted that fucker to know it was the *weak-willed fag* who had done this to him.

The police and the courts ruled it justifiable. I had been protecting my mother, they'd said, from a situation that had escalated beyond my control. Not that it did me any good. My sister was never the same, even after multiple surgeries. Mom eventually dumped her in a state hospital because she couldn't care for her anymore. Then I came home one day to find out she'd bailed while I was at school.

It kind of sucked. The story got around about me killing Arnie, and most people went the other way when they saw me. Even my teachers were afraid of me. After a time, I decided I wasn't going to go back. I'd never told anyone my mom had left, and it was unlikely they'd come looking for me. I got myself a job to pay the utility bills and ate at McDonald's a lot. At least she'd left enough for the rent for a few months, which I suppose I was grateful for.

The next two years were rough, but I survived. I got my GED, knowing without an education I'd never get anywhere in life. Between work and study, I never went out. I was determined to make something of myself, to ensure that I became a person that would make Chrissy proud.

When I turned eighteen, I joined the Army, my sole goal to excel and move up the ranks. To become someone who earned the respect of people who had always looked down on me. Instead, I found something greater. I found a purpose.

My instructors were impressed by my skills on the rifle range. When I pulled the trigger, I didn't miss, because every time I took aim, it was the face of the man who'd started me on this path I saw in my sights. The one who took my world away from me.

Eventually they sent me to sniper training at Fort Benning. That was where I fell in love with killing my targets before they were even aware they were dead.

That was where I learned to murder.

Chapter Two

It wasn't long before my service record brought me to the attention of the people who would eventually become my employers. I was cocky, arrogant, brash. Perfect for what they wanted. It wasn't likely I would ever receive a promotion. My attitude had me scrubbing latrines quite often. And my overall hatred of potatoes might have been the result of hours spent assigned to KP duty. I may not have peeled them, but washing pots used to cook the damn things turned me off them completely.

One day, two years into my four year stint, I was pulled aside and told I was to report for a medical examination necessary for a special assignment. I snorted, because scrubbing the kitchen didn't require a physical. It seemed odd, but then again, in the military, everything seemed odd. They said a car was waiting for me and would deliver me to the doctor. Again, weird.

The *office*, for lack of a better word, turned out to be a warehouse. The driver tossed a bag at me and told me to get out. I was so full of myself that I figured I could handle anything they threw at me and went inside. Condemned would have been a step up for this place. Mold clung to the dingy gray walls and the air reeked of it. It started to appear that the whole thing had been a big joke on me.

In the end, maybe it was. The door burst open, six men poured into the building, and jumped me. Fists were flying, and the sound of flesh striking flesh echoed off the walls. I want to say it was a titanic struggle, and in the end, I was victorious, but honestly, it was over too quickly. Blood oozed from the corner of my lip, and the throbbing in my eye told me it was likely going to be black in the morning. An older man stepped up and peered down at me.

"This is what they're sending us now? Pathetic."

He nodded to the others who held me down while he pushed a needle into my arm. Fire rushed through my veins, then everything went dark. The next thing I recalled was waking in what I thought was a pitch-black room, I could see light filtered through a gauzy material. Turned out the fuckers had tied a sack around my head and I couldn't see anything. A breeze blowing over my skin told me I was naked, tied spread-eagle on what I assumed was a bed from the lumps under the fabric. I couldn't move my hands, but my fingers brushed against something solid, likely a wall. I was well and truly stuck.

A dozen scenarios went through my head, but none of them seemed viable.

"You're awake. That's good. Most men aren't able to rouse themselves as quickly. I'm going to remove the hood. You've got a mouth on you, and I don't want to hear it, so you're going to stay quiet and listen to what I have to say. If I deem it necessary, I'll gag you and you'll listen. Nod if you understand."

I didn't recognize his voice, and I hated not knowing what was going on. Tiny prickles of fear danced along my spine, but I nodded. When the hood was removed, the room was dark. The lights were raised incrementally, allowing my eyes to adjust. This room resembled more of a doctor's office. At least that was what I assumed it was. The antiseptic smell, the equipment, and the white lab coat on the man who stood over me gave me an indication, but the five uniformed men flanking him told me it probably wasn't the time for me to ask questions.

The man who'd been talking stepped closer to what I found was indeed a bed. A shitty bed, but beggars couldn't be choosers. I calmed a little at the concern I could see in his eyes. He spoke quietly, like you'd talk to a frightened animal, which I guess I was.

"We're going to loosen your bonds. I don't want to cut off your circulation too long. You're pretty much in the middle of nowhere, so don't bother trying to get out of here. No one is going to hurt you. We want to make you an offer that's going to change your life."

He cut the cords holding me down, and a wave of dizziness washed over me as I tried to sit up.

"Take your time. You're going to feel weak for a while, but it will pass."

Somehow I knew it wasn't a good idea to show weakness, so I forced myself to push through it. He handed me a gown, then pulled out a manila folder and flipped through the pages while I slipped it on, too stunned to care that my ass hung out. "No family to speak of. Mother deceased, sister under state care. No ties to anyone? Girlfriend or boyfriend?"

I hadn't realized my mother died, and finding out this way topped the scale of shitty ways to be told something.

"No girlfriend or boyfriend?" he repeated.

My mouth was too dry to form words so I shook my head. The doctor noticed and handed me a sealed bottle of water, which I gratefully chugged. He gave a quick jerk of his head and the other men left us alone.

"I get that you're probably scared," he said in a soothing voice. "I won't tell you not to be. After all this, it's pretty obvious you've got every reason in the world."

"Where am I?" My voice cracked from fear as much as dryness.

"At this point I'm not allowed to say anything. Suffice it to say, even if you somehow made it out of the building, you wouldn't get too far. There are guards posted everywhere and the location is so remote that you could walk for days and not see a living soul."

I sat up and slumped against the wall, every part of my body aching.

"Let me see your wrist," he said, grabbing my arm and running his fingers over the deep marks. "Bastards. I keep telling them not to put the zip strips on so damn tight."

There was a knot in my gut. I hated the idea that I was afraid, and every instinct inside me screamed that I needed to get the hell out of this place. The doctor tapped my shoulder to redirect my focus. "Hey, it's okay. Everything will be all right."

The words sounded hollow and his smile didn't meet his eyes. We both knew it was a lie.

~

They brought me some food, which I initially refused, but having not eaten since they locked me in…well, it wouldn't do me any good to get weak and lose my opportunity to fight back. My fear had turned to anger, which bubbled just under the surface. It would be foolish for me to act in haste, so I began to track the comings and goings of the guards—who, judging by their stance and posture, the close-cropped haircuts, and the crisp uniforms were obviously military—and noted their rotations. There didn't seem to be many people here, or, if there were, I hadn't seen anyone other than the men who watched me.

Nearly all of the uniformed men who came in greeted my questions with derision. They sneered at me, and one even slapped me across the face, then spat on me. It took everything I had not to launch myself at him and try to tear out his esophagus. I would be patient and bide my time. When I felt I could make my escape, I'd do my damnedest.

I watched them for days. The rotations were like clockwork. Every three hours there was a changing of the guard posted at my door. Every 0600, 1200, and 1830 they would bring me a meal. The spork and plastic knife would be of little use in a fight, but each man carried a Beretta M9 held in a Bianchi M12 holster. They appeared to be standard issue, so I guessed there would be fifteen rounds for each. Once I incapacitated the man who brought my meal, I would try to overpower the guard. That would give me two guns and enough firepower to take out most of the rest I knew about.

I waited two more days, channeling my nervous energy into exercise. Pushups, sit-ups, pull-ups at a bar in the attached bathroom. My muscles were loose and ready for action. At 1830 hours, the time finally came.

A young man, Corporal Kirkwood, the only one who'd shown me any real kindness when he came in, pushed the cart into my room. His looks would deceive most people. He appeared slender and effeminate, but his body was firm and wiry. The man who underestimated Kirkwood would find himself with a serious case of the deads.

He gave a wide smile as he entered. "Cook made something special tonight. Fried chicken and mashed potatoes with milk gravy. It's really good. I'd stay away from the dessert, though. I'm not really sure those crunchy things in the brownies are nuts."

I couldn't help but laugh. The man was a breath of sunshine in this dank place. I hoped I wouldn't need to kill him.

I decided to probe a bit. "How much longer are they keeping me here?"

He bit his lip and shook his head. "Please don't ask me questions I can't answer. You'll know when the time is right. That's all I can tell you."

He placed the tray on the table, and I leapt up, threw my right arm around his throat and squeezed hard while I grabbed his gun with my left. His baby blue eyes bugged as he clawed at my arm. His pale skin went red, then purple.

4

"I don't want to hurt you," I whispered to him. "Where am I? Are there vehicles I can use?"

He shook his head as much as he was able and I tightened my grip a bit more.

"You'd rather die, wouldn't you? That's dedication, soldier."

Kirkwood couldn't draw a decent breath. If I held him much longer, I'd probably kill him. Like an idiot, I wasn't expecting him to lash out and knock the tray off the table, though. At the noise, the door burst open and the guard—the man who'd spit on me—rushed through the door. I held Kirkwood's gun up and fired, a large red splotch blooming across the asshole's chest. He fell against the door and slumped down.

I pushed Kirkwood away, and he fell to the ground, clutching at his throat. I took aim and his eyes went wide. I pulled my arm back, knowing it would be useless to shoot the man. I stepped toward the door, taking a moment to deliver a swift kick to the ribs of the man who'd spit at me. I found myself in an empty hallway. No noises. No lights. None of the normal guards were in sight, which should have surprised me, but didn't.

A rhythmic thunking caught my attention and drew me forward. The end of the hall split into two more corridors. One of them had emergency lights dotting the walls, while the other was dark. The noises were louder down the lighted passage, so I took the darker one. As the sounds grew fainter, more light spilled into the corridor ahead.

When I finally made it to a doorway, I searched the edges of it. Nothing seemed out of place, so I cracked it open.

"Record time," came a voice from behind me. I turned and found the doctor who had been in the room with me upon my arrival. "Most of our recruits don't ever make it to this point."

I pointed the gun at him, then let it twirl on my finger, before I finally tossed it to him. "Useless without bullets."

His eyebrows went up. I gave a one-shoulder shrug and grinned.

"The weight was off. I figured it was blanks."

"So you knew McClendon wasn't dead?"

"Why do you think I kicked him?" A real smile lifted the corners of my mouth for the first time in days. "Nasty fucker shouldn't have spit on me. Now, are you going to tell me why I'm…wherever here is?"

"Not my job, but I'll take you to the man who will be overseeing you from now on. You can call him Rook." The doctor smiled. "Before you meet him, you might want to put on some clothes. Not sure if he wants to see your ass."

"Right now, he can kiss my ass," I snapped, but when Kirkwood stepped into the room with some fatigues in his hands, I took them and whispered thanks. He clapped me on the shoulder and gave a wink.

~

The hood was put back on and I was led outdoors. I could feel the sun on my skin and a breeze definitely too warm to be manufactured. They put me into the car and we drove about an hour. The doctor chatted amiably, saying how pleased they were that I completed the *interview*, and how he was certain, once I spoke with Rook, I'd sign on.

Some time later they removed the hood, and during the next hour, what I'd been told initially appeared to be true. We saw no one. No cars, no houses, no people. It was pretty eerie, to be honest. Kind of like a zombie movie, where they jump you and rip open your head to get at your brain.

The building we pulled up to seemed incongruous with the surroundings. A tiny saltbox alone in the middle of the desert. Dark green paint with cream-colored shutters, and flowerboxes that hung from the windows. If a place could be considered *cute*, this would be it.

The doctor pushed the door open, and a cool breeze wafted from the opening.

"No locks?" I teased.

The doctor rolled his eyes and ushered me inside. "Sit. Rook will contact you when he's ready. There are some sodas and waters in the cooler on the left."

"What about beer? Got any of that?"

He grinned. "Sure, when you turn twenty-one."

He turned and walked out, leaving me alone. My gazed darted around, taking in facts about the room. It appeared Spartan, but there were things that held my attention. The computer sitting on the desk was something brand new from Apple. It wasn't even on the market yet. The table itself, more a stainless steel shelf, was bracketed to the wall. The chair was designed for utilitarian use, and definitely not something you'd want to sit in for a long while.

The computer screen flashed as it powered up, displaying a military style logo, but not one I'd ever seen. A gravelly voice, obviously using something that made him...her...it sound akin to Darth Vader, echoed through the room. "Congratulations. You're one of the few who have made it here. That puts you in extremely powerful company."

"Thanks, I guess. Where is here?"

"In due time. We have things to discuss first. Have a seat."

"I'll stand, if it's all the same to you."

"It's not. Sit down."

Part of me wanted to rebel, but the other part, the smarter one, had me taking the chair, spinning it, and sitting down backward in it.

"I can see we're going to have problems," came the weary voice.

That told me I was being observed. Whoever these people were, they weren't to be taken lightly. Still, I always did have problems shutting up. "You kidnap me, drag me out to who the hell knows where, and put me through some kind of fucked up test, and you think we don't have problems?"

Rook sighed. "Okay, point made. You're in New Mexico, at a facility owned by your new employer."

"I think Uncle Sam already owns my ass...do I call you sir or ma'am?"

"Very subtle," came the droll reply. "You can call me Rook, and don't even think I'd believe you'd call me sir. You're too damned cocky for that shit. Anyway, as I was saying, your military record, along with everything else about you, has been expunged. You're a blank slate now."

I had to admit I was impressed. If it was true.

"It's true, you can count on that."

"You're a mind reader now?"

"If that makes you more comfortable. As of the moment, you don't exist. And that leads me to my proposition."

"I never put out on the first date."

"Oh, that's bullshit. We have pictures. Would you like to see?"

Laughter bubbled out of me. "High def, I hope."

"Complete with stereo sound. It's a good thing for Corporal Leonard that we don't care what you do on your own time, don't you think?"

That sobered me instantly. We had been so careful, gotten a motel room near the base, but far enough out that no one should have seen us.

"What do you want? I don't blackmail easily."

"You can unclench. We're not going to blackmail you. Hell, you don't have anything that would be of interest to us. In fact, we want to offer you a job. You're very good at what you do. Among the best in the world, in fact. What we want is to put you into service. A hired gun, if you want to call it that."

"Who is we?" I demanded.

"You wouldn't know if I told you, and believe me, it's better for all of us," Rook answered. "Let's just say you couldn't find us if you tried. We don't really exist."

"Ooh, mysterious. And what happens if I decline your generous offer?"

"We'll take you anywhere you want to go and drop you off. I wasn't kidding when I said you don't exist. We'll set you up with a new identity, and then you'll never hear from us again."

"And what's in it for you if I agree?"

"Like I said, you're among the best. You give us an edge that we need."

I was intrigued, but it all seemed too pat for me.

"If something sounds too good to be true—"

"It generally is. In this case, you're not going to get something for nothing. I'm going to explain it to you. If you decide you don't want to join us, no one will ever believe what I've told you, and you won't find us again. If you accept, your life starts new here."

"Okay, I won't deny I'm intrigued."

Rook went on to explain how they represented a branch of the US government that didn't really exist. The ones that cleaned up messes that couldn't be contained any other way.

"So you…exterminate the problem?"

"That's where you would come in. We have operatives that are specially trained to deal with certain situations. We offer you training far more intensive than the military would give you, and the means to get a job done."

"And what's in it for me?" I demanded.

"You'll do it because that's how you're wired. When you shot your mother's boyfriend, you did it to protect your sister, even if it did little good in the end. Your main dealings will be protecting kids from those who would prey on them. It's not going to be easy, and it sure as hell won't be pretty. Most cases can be handled through the courts, but when you get some bleeding-heart judge who lets a criminal off on a technicality, even when all the evidence presented is against them, that's where we come in.

"You'll also get a very healthy retainer of two hundred fifty thousand dollars per target and a certain latitude on how you want to deal with a situation. We care about the results, not the steps it takes to get there. Just remember, if you join us, you will belong to us. There are no contracts, but there's also no walking away from the training once you agree. If you start, you have to finish, and after that, we own you. We're going to give you time to think about it, if you want."

I pushed the chair away as I stood up. The picture of my sister, her head caved in, curled in the fetal position on the dingy floor was permanently etched in my mind. If I could spare one kid from that, no matter what I had to do, I was for it.

"I don't need to think about it. I'm in."

"Then say good-bye to your old life. The men outside the door will escort you to where the first phase of your training will begin. And just so we're clear, when I said your old life was over, I was serious. You are a man who no longer exists. We will be giving you a codename to use. This is the only name you will be known by."

The whole thing sounded like so much cloak and dagger bullshit, but from everything I'd seen, I took this man…woman…person. I took them very seriously.

"So what's it going to be? Maxwell Smart? Agent 99? Jack Bauer?"

"Very droll. No, your job is going to be one of protection. To bring the children to safety. Your new name will reflect that. We're going to call you Haven."

CHAPTER THREE

An old Army recruiting slogan talked about being an Army of One, which I had been told my new employer would mold me into. I had always heard the Marines were supposed to have the toughest training regimen in the military. I knew some Marines, and they would have given up within the first week or so of this training. My instructors insisted that physical fitness was a must. I had to be able to run a five-minute mile while carrying a twenty-pound pack. Then there were the chin-ups—sixty of them in twelve minutes. The tests were constant. Failure wasn't an option. At the end of the day, it was all I could do to fall into my bunk, but when the alarm bell rang at four in the morning, I was expected to be ready to go.

I trained at the first base for a year. It was weird, because I was the only trainee. Martial disciplines were stressed because many times we could not rely on weapons to get us out of trouble. Unarmed combat included aikido, jujitsu, and karate. I learned to drive a man's nose cartilage through his skull and into his brain. There was also training with swords, knives, guns. I excelled at all of them. By the time the twelve months were up, I could take down each of my instructors without breaking a sweat.

I was alone in my room, which was really nothing more than a pad on the floor, when someone knocked at my door. My senses were on high alert. The shuffling of feet indicated that there were at least two, possibly more.

"Who is it?" There wasn't an answer, and I hadn't been expecting one. "Hang on a sec."

I slipped through the window and dashed around the side of the building. I pushed open the door the smallest of cracks when a hard kick knocked me on my ass. The door was flung open and four men hurled themselves at me. I twisted to one side to keep myself from being pinned, and pushed to my feet. They were every bit as fast as I was.

"Let me guess… Training exercise. Probably a bad idea to kill you, am I right?"

Their mouths were set in a grim line as they danced around me, tagging me with quick hits. Alone they didn't amount to much, but they were repeatedly striking pressure points, and my arms started to go numb.

I leapt at the first one, wrapping my legs around his neck, and pulled him to the ground. He hit with a sickening thud. The second one tried for a roundhouse kick, but I blocked him, then delivered a knee to his crotch. I heard him squeak as he dropped to his knees, which earned him a swift kick to the side of the head.

The third and fourth men pulled butterfly knives from their pockets and began jabbing at me with them. My arms were still useless, and I was at a serious disadvantage. Opting to move to a locale more my style, I broke into a run, followed closely by them. I dashed inside the dojo and grabbed a bo staff. Even if there were better weapons available to me, this would give me some extra reach against my opponents, and was able to be wielded more fluidly with my now tingly arms.

The two stalked toward me from the door, nasty grins playing on their lips.

"We could call it a draw, guys. There's no need for anyone else to get hurt."

One of them snorted, but they both continued to advance. I twirled the staff between my thumb and forefinger.

"I'm getting the feeling back in my arms. You probably don't want to do this now."

One of them decided I had to be bluffing and charged me. A quick spin and a sharp kick delivered to his back knocked him face first into the training weapons. He groaned and collapsed, leaving me with just one last threat. This guy played it smart, keeping a good distance between us. He hadn't drawn a weapon and none of his colleagues had come back, so I was pretty confident this was a test, and I'd make damn sure to ace it.

By now, my arms did have feeling in them, but they were damned weak. I took a few steps toward my opponent, who deftly leapt back and waggled his finger at me with a cocky grin. He moved farther, until he reached one of the weapon stands and withdrew a polearm and removed the wooden sheath, showing the bladed naginata, which gave him the advantage in reach, as well as having a wicked sharp point.

11

We circled around one another, neither willing to make the first strike. Finally, he must have tired of the game, because he took a vicious downward stroke. I held up the bo, barely blocking his attack, then rushed back and jabbed my staff forward, clipping him on the hand, eliciting a pained grunt.

"Ooh, sounded like that hurt," I taunted him.

He stretched his fingers and winced. From that moment, he was a dervish. He spun and swung, parrying my attacks, then raking the blade across my chest, drawing a thick rivulet of blood. He'd upped the game now, because that shit hurt like a mother. I sucked in a quick, calming breath, then leveled my gaze at him. Beads of sweat skittered down his forehead. His advantage was gone.

Instead of trying to take him down, I kept him off guard. No direct attacks, but plenty of quick shots when the opportunity presented itself. His breath was ragged and his movements slowed and became jerky. By now, he was huffing like a bull, and I conserved my energy until I saw my opening.

My grip on the bo tightened, and when he made his last lunge, I turned it so the end faced him and slammed it into his chest, near his heart. Done right, so I was told, I could cause a myocardial infarction. I didn't want this man to die, but I think it'd stopped being an exercise to him. His eyes opened wide, then closed, as he collapsed to the floor like so much dead weight. As soon as he was down, the doors opened and the doctors rushed in and began tending to us.

The doctor wiped my chest with peroxide, then led me by the arm to the infirmary. It took thirty-seven stitches to close the slice the asshole had made, but I took it as a badge of honor that I'd survived it.

"How's he doing?" I asked, surprised to find out I really did care to know.

"He'll live," the doc answered as he snipped the ends of the threads protruding from my chest. "I have to know. Why didn't you go for the kill?"

"He hadn't done anything I wouldn't have. You're training me to be a killer, but I decide when to do it."

~

The tests were frequent after that. And each subsequent one, the parameters changed. Sometimes the men would start with weapons—knives, sticks, whatever—and sometimes they would attack while I was asleep. I learned quickly that I had to keep my eyes open, even when they were closed.

I trained a total of four years. I was twenty-three when they told me I was done. I was set up in this house, complete with service staff to care for the place while I was off on…business. My first assignment was to track down and eliminate a drug dealer who had beaten the rap three times, despite overwhelming evidence against him.

I was given a dossier and told by Rook that all of my assignments would start this way. I was to read it. To understand my target's ways. To act in haste would be trying to get caught. I had to know the person better than they knew themselves.

I skimmed through the pages. Each contained a ruined life. Emily Nesbitt, previously picked up on prostitution charges. When they found her this time, she was filled with enough drugs that she never noticed the men cutting her up, carving their initials into her skin.

Nancy Arroyo. Thirteen when she ran away from home. Not much older when this piece of crap swooped in and grabbed her off the streets. He had her turning tricks within a week. Not just any john, though. With her baby face, she drew the lot that liked to hurt little girls.

Annalyse Dandridge. Found curled up in the gutter, bleeding to death because she tried to get the baby, a little boy, out of her.

The file held details about all of them. Young girls who would never grow up.

I wanted this piece of shit.

It wasn't difficult to track him down. I found him holed up in a warehouse that was doubling as a meth lab. The place reeked of decay and the drugs they were cooking up. I tracked him for two weeks, finding out his habits, seeing who his associates were, and learning everything about him that I could.

Turns out the fat little bastard thought he was a kingpin of crime. He tried to dip his fingers into more pies than he ought to. He got a few prostitutes under his control and hooked them on his drugs, then turned them out to make him money. Every time I saw their faces, a rage rushed through me. Some of these girls were fourteen, tops. In every one of them, I saw my sister's face.

13

I made my move one night after he'd sent away his baby thugs, and I slipped into the bedroom, telling the girl to take a hike. She was fifteen if she was a day. I gave her a card for a halfway house and told her I would make sure she showed up, and heaven help her if she didn't. She was so scared I was surprised she didn't wet herself. Wisely, she took off. Not that I would have done anything to her, but I needed her to get help. And I would check.

The tables in the room were set up with all manner of kinky shit that probably made him feel like a man. He'd be alone tonight. He trusted no one when he was '*working*' with his girls. He'd stripped off his clothes before he threw open the door, growling about how she'd best be ready for him if she knew what was good for her. I lashed out, kicking the door shut, and pinning him against the wall, one hand wrapped around his throat, the other with a knife beneath his ear.

"So you're the big bad motherfucker who thinks he runs these streets," I growled.

"Back off me, punk. I'll gut your ass."

I jabbed the knife a little harder, not quite piercing the skin, but more than enough to show him that I was the one in control here. "Eddie Consaldo, also known as Eddie the Viper," I said, affecting a bored tone as if I were reading it from a card. "Drugs. Prostitution. Protection. Damn, kid…you got yourself a little empire in the making, don't you?"

"Damn straight. My boys get here—"

"Your boys are gone for the night. You never let them stick around when you're planning on a little *party*. Don't want them to see you don't have the balls to play with the big boys?"

"Fuck you," he snapped.

"Not with that little pig sticker," I retorted, reaching down and smacking him hard on the groin with the pommel of the knife.

"What the fuck, man?" he screamed. Then his voice turned steely. "You trying to take over? Is that what this is about?"

"Nah, dude. No one is going to be taking over for you. Once you're gone, your little house of cards is going to collapse. Ain't one of your lieutenants smart enough to fill the void. Once I get rid of you, they'll either be absorbed by the bigger gang that steps in, or they'll turn up in little chunks somewhere. Either way, you're not going to be a part of the picture."

His body shook as the knowledge I was here to kill him began to sink in.

"Man, we can make a deal… I can get you women. Lots of women."

"Wrong card, kid. I'm not into the chicks."

"Then I can get you some fag boys. Young. You'll like them."

I pushed the knife, slicing through the skin, and he yowled. I had intended to make his death quick, but he'd pushed my buttons the wrong way. I punched him in the face, knocking him unconscious, then picked him up and made use of the toys he was kind enough to lay out. The ball gag was the first thing. Didn't want to hear him talk anymore. I was already angry enough, no sense in waving the red flag in front of the bull.

I let my gaze run over the items on the table. I knew about BDSM, even thought I might dabble a little at some point, but some of the crap this little fuck had laid out scared the shit out of me. Metal bars with spikes that would drive onto a woman's tits, a neck collar with cuffs attached by steel links. It was like something out of Disney's *Hunchback* movie, but without any cute animals or songs.

This kid was a sadistic fucker. Nothing he had here was safe, sane, or consensual, I was certain. I hoped he enjoyed being on the receiving end. I locked the neck collar on, then cuffed him to the bed, attached a spreader bar to his ankles to hold his legs open. Being the pudgy thing he was, he had some man boobs on him, so the spiked tit clamps could have been tailor made for him. I think it was the shock of them digging into his skin that woke him up.

He thrashed on the bed, probably screaming threats, but the ball gag cut them off to a litany of muffled curses.

"So you get off on this shit, huh?" I asked, running my hands over a few of the toys. "Makes you feel like a real man, am I right? How many of these girls are here because they want to be? How many have been in the position you are because they enjoyed it? I twisted the clamp, forcing the bar to tighten on his boobs until he screamed. At least I guess it was a scream.

"Ooh, you liked that, huh? You are a kinky one." I turned the screws, tightening them more. His eyes went wide and his head thrashed from side to side.

"See, here's the deal, *Viper*. You pushed your shit to adults, I probably never would have been sent after you. But you brought kids into the

15

equation. Little babies who haven't yet had the chance to know what it's like to fall in love. To have their first zit. To get laid out of love, not because you forced them to. I can't have that."

I moved around the bed, using various instruments. A flogger with hooks at the end tore into his skin. A paddle with holes drilled through drew welts on the pudgy stomach. Tears streamed from his eyes. A lesser man would have been moved to pity.

"I'm not a lesser man," I whispered. I couldn't afford to let emotions cloud my mission. He was the bad guy, I was the…less bad guy. Still, I tried to hang onto a shred of my humanity. I didn't want to become what I hated.

By the time I finished teaching him his final lesson, the bed sheets were streaked crimson. Urine soaked through where he'd pissed himself. I tried to reach deep to find a shred of humanity. Something that would keep this shit stain breathing, and I came up empty. I sat on the edge of the bed and stared at him a few moments. The absolute terror in his eyes actually calmed me and made me feel better.

"Here's how this is going to end, Viper. I'm a firm believer in an eye for an eye. I know what you did to these kids. The rapes, the torture. You did things that make what I did to you seem like beginner shit. I'm not going to sink to your level, but you are going to die tonight. You'll never hurt anyone again, I can promise you that."

He struggled against his bonds, but he wasn't going to get loose. "You made your living off the shit you cook up here, so it seems only right that it should speed you on your way, right? This is the last time you're going to be seeing me, so if you got something to say, now's the time."

I tried to think of anything he could say that would put me off my mission. A promise to admit to his crimes? But he'd already been found not guilty. He would walk, and no one would remember his victims. I pulled the gag out, and he screamed invectives at me. Swearing to me that his boys would find me. I shook my head and pushed the ball back in, then went downstairs where he had his stash cooking. The meth was under pressure, so it wasn't tough to rig it to explode after I was well away.

I hadn't expected anything like the nightmare I saw. One by one buildings caught fire from debris that rained down on them. The news said before the fire department got it contained, three city blocks of empty warehouses were engulfed in flames.

It took several days to get it completely under control, as it turned out Viper stored a lot of shit in some of the abandoned buildings. Fortunately no one was hurt, though some firemen were treated for smoke inhalation and minor burns. When they finally got inside, they found the charbroiled corpse of one Eddie Consaldo. The reporter, a perky blond guy, went on to list the crimes Eddie was believed to have committed, but had never been convicted of.

That night he was convicted and found guilty, and the sentence had been carried out with all expediency.

My stomach clenched and I barely made it to the bathroom before I threw up. My mind and body were at war over his death. My mind knew it was right, but my body was sickened to have been a part in someone's murder.

This was war, though, and I had taken an oath to triumph over my enemies.

Despite the cost.

CHAPTER FOUR

Rook told me that the information I'd pulled from Dunkirk's computer had given him a treasure trove to sift through. There'd been enough stuff that would have had him imprisoned for life, if he'd lived to see the inside of a courthouse again. There appeared to be evidence that the judge who'd let him go had been on the take, and Rook didn't like that at all. He'd be dealt with at some point, I knew. Rook said he'd contact me if he needed me, but I knew it could be weeks before I heard from him again.

One of the things about my job was that there was a lot of downtime. That gave me time to hone my skills, whether it was on the gun range, or practicing martial arts at one of the studios in Phoenix. Even though I had to temper myself, it was a decent workout, and I made a few acquaintances. It also afforded me the opportunity to better myself in other aspects of my life. I even tried piano lessons…at least until I realized my hands weren't meant for such delicate work.

Strangely, though, I found my peace lounging by the koi pond Kelly had installed. Flashes of color as the fish swam lazily beneath the bright sun soothed me. I could watch them for hours and never be bored. I especially enjoyed touching them. Koi can be accustomed to human touch. They seek it out, floating near the surface, almost begging for you to stroke them.

I snatched a handful of their food pellets and tossed them into the water. Even at times when it should be a feeding frenzy, koi had a certain delicate grace to them.

"Would you like me to bring you something to eat?"

Kelly's voice reminded me of the fish—a delicate grace—but for Kelly it was backed by a steely reserve. I opened my eyes and found myself looking up my houseman's nose.

"You need a trim," I murmured.

He didn't even crack a smile.

"No, I'm not really hungry. Thanks anyway."

"Do you want to talk about it?"

"Huh?"

"You've been in a…funk for the last three months. Was your assignment that bad?"

"Nah. Standard in and out. Rook texted and said that with the files I got from Dunkirk's computer, they were able to take down some big names, including a state senator. I got a bonus out of that one."

"And yet you're not happy."

"So now you're my psychotherapist?"

"The company pays me well, so I dabble in all sorts of things. You know I'm the epitome of discretion."

"You know that if I told you and you blabbed, I have dozens of ways to kill you," I reminded him.

"That's a risk I take every day I wake up," he deadpanned. "Talk to me, Haven. Let me know what's going on."

I think in the years I'd known him, this was the first time that Kelly and I really talked about my work.

"It's the house," I blurted. "There's nothing of…me here."

"Then change it. I only bought the furniture so you wouldn't be sitting on the floor. If you want, I'm happy to go out and get you some beanbag chairs."

I thought he was joking, but with Kelly you never could be certain. His trim figure, salt and pepper hair, and thin mustache made him appear almost grandfatherly.

"How old are you?" I probed.

"Sixty-one on my next birthday."

"Do you want to do something other than keep house for a…for me?"

"For an assassin. You can say it, you know. Nothing shocks me. And like I said, the company pays me well. Is that what's bothering you? Your job?"

Thoughts exploded through my head. How could I answer that question when I didn't even know for sure myself? A warm hand rested on my shoulder and Kelly almost smiled.

"You're very good at what you do. You've kept countless people safe, even at great personal risk. But this life isn't for everyone. It's lonely, because you can't simply say, 'Honey, I'm going to be gone for a while. I have a man who needs to die tonight.'"

I could never tell with Kelly if something was meant to be funny, but I laughed anyway.

"If you think this life isn't for you anymore, then maybe it's time to consider a new direction? You're thirty-one now. You've given eight years to this, and maybe now is the time to try something new."

"Yeah, right. I don't think my particular skill set would translate well in the corporate world. Besides, I take the phrase backstabbing pretty literally."

He gave me one of those looks like a dad would give, then stepped back.

"If you're not happy with who you are, only you can make the decision to change it. You wouldn't be the first person to leave the company and explore new options in life."

"They *let* people quit?"

Kelly rolled his eyes and frowned. "This isn't a spy thriller. There isn't a contract out on you if you decide to leave. I believe Rook told you that you couldn't find them, even if you looked. It's true. It's done for their safety as much as for yours. If you want to walk away, do it. Let Rook know that you're done, and that's it. The world won't end if you decide to do something for yourself."

Without another word, he turned and headed back toward the house, leaving me alone with my thoughts. Could I walk away? I glanced down at my hands and saw the metaphorical blood all over them. Even if I quit, it would always be there. It was for the greater good, a mantra I'd adopted over the years, but one I sometimes found hard to reconcile.

My phone gave a little tone I knew well. I wanted to leave it, grab some stuff, and get the hell out of here, but I picked it up and what I saw chilled my blood.

Case failed. New target. Needed to be handled with expediency and utmost prejudice. Files will be available by 0800 tomorrow. Expect call at 0900. Warning - This one is bad.

Ants crawled beneath my skin. For Rook to say it was bad meant it was going to be one of those that sank hooks deep into me and would never let go. Those types always cost me a bit of myself. Still, if it kept one kid safe, then that was all that mattered.

I gazed back at the koi, swimming idyllically in their own little world, then tore myself away and headed for the house, knowing my decision had been made. Eventually I would be carted off with a self-inflicted bullet through my skull. It was the only way anyone ever left this life.

~

Kelly had breakfast laid out when I woke up. Oatmeal with sliced berries, a few strips of turkey bacon, a glass of freshly squeezed orange juice, and, most importantly, a travel mug filled with coffee. Like with most days, he was already somewhere in the house doing his duties. On the rare occasions I saw him, he was like a blur, zipping from one task to the other.

For everything I was thinking about at the moment, I might as well have been eating sawdust. The food had no flavor, but I continued shoveling it in. What was it about this one that had Rook worked up? And when the time came, would I be on top of my game, ready to tackle it? Or would this be the mission where I'd finally meet someone faster than me and wind up dead?

A few moments after eight, Kelly stuck his head into the kitchen to let me know it was time. He trailed behind me as I went down the stairs to what I considered my war room. He stood back as I punched in the code on the touchpad then gave a thumbprint identification. The heavy oak door swung open and allowed us access. Lights went on automatically when we stepped in.

I fired up the computer, entered the twenty-seven digit passcode, then the sixteen character password, followed by answering a litany of questions. The mail opened on a picture of a corpse. A young girl, no more than twelve, her body thrown into a refuse container. Sightless blue eyes implored me to avenge her.

Page after page, picture after picture. Boys and girls, cast away like garbage. A sea of names—Anna Monroe, Allan Thompson, Courtney Delachamp, Tyson Gleason—made my chest ache. It was several moments before I noticed that Kelly had one hand on my shoulder and a box of tissues in his other.

"This is what tells you that your heart hasn't hardened," he whispered, swiping away a tear from my cheek.

What he didn't realize was they weren't tears of sadness. The rage was a potent, almost living thing. It took everything in me to keep from lashing out at Kelly, taking every ounce of frustration that welled up inside of me and bringing it down on him.

The computer chimed and the voice of Darth Vader echoed through the room.

"Have you looked at the files?"

"Who did this?" I growled.

"Sit down, Haven."

"I hate it when you tell me what to do." But still I sat.

"In all the years we've worked together, I have never run into something like this. There is an organization to it. A hierarchy that is protecting the person at the top. Her name is Valérie Masonnareu. When she came to this country, she went by Valerie Mason. We've known for years that she was the one who directed this cabal, but no one would ever turn evidence on her.

"She has her fingers in every pie you can imagine. Drugs, prostitution, racketeering, blackmail, extortion. If there is money to be made, she's dabbling in it. We've finally decided we can't wait any longer. She needs to be taken out, but—"

"But? You never say but."

"This isn't a loose-knit group. She rules it with an iron fist. She handpicks only the best to be part of it, and each of her underlings is in charge of his or her own territory, even if she is the one they report to."

"So I kill her and that's it?"

"No. I wish it were that simple." I could hear the unspoken plea for me to let Rook get through this. "Each part of her organization is an entity unto itself. Even if we took one out, another exists. We can't break them fast enough, because she's got someone else in line. So it's been decided we will no longer act defensively and try to shore up the reserves. We're going to take it directly to her. Several of our operatives are going to simultaneously take out a majority of the weaker elements. It won't stop anything, but the disruption will give you time to take out her network and, finally, her."

"Why not kill her first?"

"We want her to know that we're coming for her. We want her to sweat it out and, hopefully, make a mistake. There are so many people she's suspected of having taken or killed, and we don't have a clue where to start looking."

"I'm in."

"We will pay you for each target you eliminate, of course."

The pictures of the children she was responsible for killing were on an endless loop in my head.

"I'll do this one for free," I told him, my jaw tightening enough to crack. "As long as I get the kill shot on this bitch."

"She's all yours. There isn't anyone else we could give this assignment to. I have to warn you, though…you might not be prepared for what you're going to see. Bits of information have come to us, and these pictures aren't the worst of it. Each of her people has a kill mark on them, Haven."

"Fine. No problem."

Then why were my hands shaking so badly?

~

Rook sent me everything he had on Valerie and her cronies. The files were startlingly thin, all things considered. Still, my eyes ached by the time I got through them. I sipped at the jasmine tea Kelly had put on the table beside me. It must have been hours ago, because it had gone cold. My stomach rumbled, even though the thought of food made me sick. I opened the refrigerator and found a bowl of soup with a note attached.

Microwave this for two minutes. Grab a roll from the refrigerator and put some ham and cheese on it. Then sit down and eat.

The soup smelled awful. It was some kind of a greenish broth with unidentifiable chunks floating in it. That shit went straight down the disposal. I took one of the artisan rolls from the bag and slathered it with mustard before slapping on some turkey. I stuck my tongue out in the direction of Kelly's house. I knew he'd check tomorrow to be sure I ate, but I wasn't going to give him the satisfaction of having what he said.

A lassitude swept over my body as I finished the last of the sandwich. It was nearing three a.m., and if I didn't get a bit of sleep, I would be useless come the morning. The thought of my bed enveloping me was tantalizing, but it seemed miles away, so instead I curled onto the couch and allowed myself to sleep.

23

Nightmares were a common occurrence in my line of work. Faces of those I'd *helped* off the planet. I couldn't give a number, but I remembered every one of them. Their expressions when they'd realized they were about to die. They pleaded and begged, tried to absolve themselves of guilt by pointing fingers at other people, offered me wealth or power. In each instance, it did them no good. Rook provided ironclad evidence of their crimes, and there was no questioning it at all.

I sat up and groaned when the clock told me I'd only been asleep an hour. I went to the war room computer again, deciding to scan through the documents once more. It paid to know as much as I could before I took on a case. The crimes these…people had been accused of turned my stomach. I liked to think I maintained a tremulous link to humanity, something that separated me from them, but peering at the faces of the children—both dead and those who would probably take their own lives by the time they were eighteen because of what happened to them—threatened to push me over the edge into insanity.

Six of the pictures held my attention. A collection of before and after images Rook had gathered. How could the man live with himself, knowing what he saw on a daily basis? I shook the thought away and forced myself to memorize everything I could about these kids. These six would be the ones that pushed me forward and made it okay to do what I was about to.

I noticed that over the years, I'd developed a certain style of going about my assignments. Something I'd said to *Viper* was true. I was a very firm believer in an eye for an eye. As I read the story of these children's lives and deaths, plans began to form in my head about how I would go about seeking retribution on their behalf.

The buzz of the computer startled me. I glanced at the clock and groaned. It was only four thirty.

"You don't sleep either, do you?" I said as I started up the program.

"I'll sleep when this bitch is dead," he growled.

In all the years I'd been working with Rook, I'd never heard him lose his temper. If anything, he was the one who kept me calm. The way his voice trembled gave him away, though.

"Wanna talk about it?"

24

He was silent for a moment then inhaled sharply. "Do you know I have a family?"

Very few things surprised me. This was one. "How does that work out in our line of business?"

"My kids are the reason I do this job. My story isn't so different from yours. I'm not going to give details, but my daughter could have been your sister. Way too young to play the hand life dealt them. What they did to…my daughter still wakes me up with night terrors. She has such strength, more than me. I want to make damn certain that every one of those sorry bastards know pain before they die."

"So this is a revenge thing for you?" I probed.

"No, this is a justice thing for me. Revenge is messy and serves no purpose in life. Justice ensures that someone else's daughter is going to wake up tomorrow and go to a school she hates, flirt with the boy who makes her tingle to her toes and dream of being married to when she grows up. And she will grow up because of people like us. Those who are willing to damn their souls in order for innocent people to have a real life."

"Is your daughter okay?"

"She survived. I don't know that she'll ever be okay, but she can make it through each day, mostly on her own, and that's more than the doctors had ever hoped for."

"And what happened to the person who hurt her?"

"The courts dismissed his case due to lack of evidence. He leered at my daughter as he was taken out the door. It took two weeks, but I finally got up the nerve to confront him. He told me that she'd asked for it…begged him to do it. She was ten years old.

"I took out the gun I bought off the street and told him to beg me for his life. He laughed and said I couldn't touch him. I shot his dick off. You've never heard a man scream like that before. He fell to the floor, cupping his groin and begging for help. I was seconds away from calling an ambulance then I remembered the way he looked at my daughter and the way she cried herself to sleep each night. Instead I bent over and forced the barrel of the gun in his mouth, then emptied the chamber.

"The police detained me, of course. Someone ensured I had an alibi for the time in question, because I didn't have one. I hadn't even given a thought to surviving after I killed him. They pulled me off the street one day and brought me into the fold. I've worked here for…a lot of years."

"Fighting the good fight?" I prompted.

"Like I said, fighting to make sure someone lives to enjoy life." He was quiet for a few moments. "Good night, Haven."

Rook disconnected, and I turned off the monitor. I was left in the dark to think on his story, realizing that my soul was a small thing to give up if someone else grew up happy.

CHAPTER FIVE

A testament to our motivation was the fact that it normally took months of planning before we were ready to move on a mission of even half this scope. Everything was planned down to when people would have time to take a crap. Not this time. Our teams were deployed in twenty-one days, spreading out across the Midwest to fight an enemy we could not allow to win.

More information came to light about Valerie's people. It was secondhand, from a mole that Rook had in the group, but our guy wasn't part of the inner circle and couldn't get much useful intel. Many of the players had been on the periphery of Rook's radar for years, but the local police seemed to be doing an adequate job of keeping them under control. With one crack opening, others formed, and soon we were able to start putting together pictures of an organization larger than we'd ever suspected.

Rook hadn't been wrong. They were tightly structured. They had resources to withstand any close examination of their dealings, at least at local and state levels. Apparently the government didn't consider them enough of a threat to send in the feebs. Then a thought skittered across my mind. Maybe that was what my group was, a branch of the FBI. I quickly pushed it aside. Stray thoughts made you sloppy.

It wasn't difficult to locate my first target. Edmond Rouland was a big, big man. His doctor's files listed his weight at close to four hundred pounds. He enjoyed living high on the hog at the expense of others. Rouland distributed drugs for Valerie—highly sought after strains of designer drugs. One of the big sellers was a benzodiazepine derivative. The file had all the specs on the shit. Worked in less than fifteen minutes. Undetectable by conventional means. Victims didn't know they'd even been raped.

Rouland had made a name for himself with the club crowd as someone who could provide the kids with everything they needed to fly. What they didn't know was that Rouland would cherry pick some of them and turn them into *movie stars* by filming them as they were unconscious and used by any number of men.

Rouland would take the ones no one would miss. He liked the younger ones because they were more pliable. Courtney Delachamp was suspected as having been one of his. She was a sweet girl who got herself into a jam she couldn't get out of. Rouland probably played on that fact and got her hooked.

She was sixteen when they found her body. The coroner report said that there had been multiple instances of penetration, both vaginal and anal, with a variety of items, including bottles. Broken glass had been found embedded deep in her vagina. Three tests indicated the presence of semen, and the men were questioned, but got turned loose because of *insufficient evidence*. They'd said the girl claimed she was eighteen, and they'd paid her for kinky sex. There were indications that she'd been arrested for prostitution, something that further proved their claims of innocence. The one sticking point? Rook couldn't find any such arrest record. He did find proof that a large sum of money had been transferred to the judge's bank, though. While I wanted all of them to suffer, Rook promised he'd see to it. Those bastards would be someone else's target. Rouland was mine.

~

I found him in the High Hat, a private sex club whose main clientele were upwardly mobile and thoroughly obnoxious guys who thought they shouldn't have to wait for good things to come to them—women included. Guys like these didn't mind using the shortcut Rouland offered.

Rouland lounged in a corner booth, a young girl on either side of him, stroking their fingers over his chest, giggling at his comments, and snorting cocaine with rolled-up bills, probably hundreds. I had to wonder if they cared that this douche would have them on their knees soon. I sat at the bar, sipping a tonic with lime, and kept my eye on the man. My stomach rolled as I watched him paw the kids. I wanted to put a bullet in his brain now and be done with it, but this was too public. I would have to bide my time and wait for the right moment.

I had the bartender ply him with this club's version of top-shelf booze, and saluted him with my glass when, after the sixth shot, he finally looked over at me. I had long ago aged out of his preferred group, but when he pointed out the girls to me, I raised my eyebrows. He smiled, slid his fat carcass out of the booth, and waddled over in my direction.

"They're pretty cute, huh?"

I shot a look at the table and saw the girls rubbing one another, probably in an effort to get Rouland's new friend 'hot.'

"I'll say. How'd you score some fine ass like that?"

I would be scraping my tongue tonight from all the bullshit coming out of my mouth. Still, Rouland ate it up with a spoon.

"Those are my leftovers. You should see my main squeezes. They're superfine and they love this," he said, cupping his crotch.

It took every ounce of my willpower not to end his miserable existence and quell the headache escalating behind my eyes.

"Maybe I can help you find some fine little things like them," he said, tossing a friendly arm over my shoulder. I winced as the acrid scent of stale sweat hit my nose.

"Naw, man. I do all right."

"Can you score with those kinds? They're seventeen, man. Ripe for the picking. For the right price, one of them could be yours for the night."

I snorted. "What if I want both?"

Every roll on Rouland's stomach jiggled when he threw his head back and laughed.

"Cocky little rooster, aren't you? I like that."

I signaled the bartender who brought down the bottle of Johnnie Walker single label and poured Rouland another snootful. When he insisted I drink with him, I had a shot. Compared to the Chivas back at the house, this was total crap. It was like being used to having silk on your skin, then switching to sandpaper. It tore the hell out of my throat as I drank it. Not nearly smooth enough, but I forced it down.

"Why don't you join us?"

Everything in Rouland's file indicated he was into girls only, but the way he touched me had me wondering if he'd make an exception in my case. I held back the snort at the mental image of me stabbing him with the knife hidden in my pants leg if he so much as got naked in front of me.

He kept his arm over my shoulder as we walked to the booth. The girls slid out, then surrounded us both, allowing their hands to run over me like

29

they'd known me forever. It creeped me the fuck out, but I had to keep Rouland talking. I needed to know about Courtney's last minutes of life, this man's involvement in them, and just how pissed off he was going to make me.

~

The home was palatial by almost any standard. It was also pretty fucking tacky. The man apparently loved purple, because the drapes, the carpeting, and the furniture were all variations on a theme. He encouraged me to take a seat while he poured us some drinks. More of the rotgut we'd had at the club. It took everything I could muster to choke the garbage down.

The girls had gone home not long before we left the club, begging off when Rouland told them he'd book the four of us a private room for an 'all-night party.' I got the feeling the girls knew something seemed off, and they decided the excitement they'd come looking for had become much more than they could handle. Rouland had been insistent to the point where I'd thought he was going to spike their drinks. If he'd done that, it wouldn't have mattered what else occurred, the man would have met a tragic end before he'd made it out of the club. They'd gone, despite his pleading, and finally he said fuck it, and we left alone.

After we went to the living room and lay back on the overstuffed eggplant-hued couch, Rouland started talking about the fun he had in this house. The number of girls he'd banged, the rooms he'd done it in. He seemed proud of the fact that a majority of them were underage and that he'd been the one to 'pop their cherries.' Every utterance from his mouth was another nail in his coffin.

The hardest part about all this was acting like I was into what he was saying. I rubbed my crotch when he talked about the kids, like it was something that made me hot, but the thought of those poor girls had my balls shrinking back inside my body.

"Man, you live the life," I ground out. "All the pussy you can handle and being able to break in some cherry ones at that."

"Not even the tip of the iceberg, man. You should come by one night when we have a party. We get one of the girls up here to take care of the guests. At the end of the night, we take her down to one of the rooms and film the…after-party."

The liquor had obviously loosened him up. The file on Rouland said he'd been interrogated by the cops more than once and always left with a smile on his face. Or maybe it was the fact he saw something in me that lowered his guard. Either way, it was time I pressed my advantage.

"I don't know, man. I don't want my wife finding out I'm on film with a kid. I barely made her believe the girl lied last time. I would have lost everything. The wife took the kids to her mother's house for almost a week, before I had a buddy lie and swear I was with him. I can't take a chance of any evidence."

"Nah, we edit out the dude's faces. All you see is the chick. Just think of it, man. You get your choice of the hole you want to plug and there's no whining about you being too big or her being a virgin. She's quiet and compliant all night, like a chick should be."

"And no one will know about it?"

"There are a few guys who don't mind their faces being seen. When the video goes online, they send the links to their friends. Sales shoot through the roof. We net at least a quarter million per movie."

It seemed appropriate I'd make the same amount off this job. I kept topping off his whiskey, and he kept downing it. His slurred words were getting more excited as he rubbed his own crotch. In my mind, I wondered how far I would go to get this job done. Would I jack off with him? Would I have sex with him? The thought repulsed me, but I had to get this information. I needed to avenge Courtney, yes, but I wanted to make sure that no one would ever get to see her last moments of life. She deserved that much. I would do whatever it took to ensure she was at peace, and I made a vow to her that this fucker would pay.

"You could get in on the ground floor," he continued. "We're always looking for new talent. Your kids have got to have some friends you could bring around."

Immediately my mind went to Rook's daughter. Was that how it was for her? My fingers tightened around the glass I held until I thought it would shatter.

"Maybe," I answered through clenched teeth. I berated myself because I knew if this guy were sober, there was no way he wouldn't notice my anger.

He unzipped his pants and reached inside to stroke himself. "I'm partial to blondes," he whispered. "Brown eyes are a plus." He laid his head back and closed his eyes, tugging at his cock. "So eager to please. They'll do anything with the right persuasion." He raised his head and peered at me through slitted eyes. "Go ahead, take it out. We don't need the chicks to have a good time, as long as you don't mind playing."

"Nah, I don't mind at all," I whispered, convinced my dick and balls had beat a retreat and that I'd never see them again. "But I need more...visual stimulation. I usually have someone take care of my hard-on for me."

He sat up and his dick flopped to the side. "Yeah, I know what you mean. Maybe...maybe we could watch a movie together. You could see what I'm offering."

"That's the ticket," I exclaimed, standing up to follow him. My heart raced, because I was hopefully about to see exactly what I needed in order to allow this son of a bitch to know why he was going to die.

He walked unsteadily up a flight of stairs, me at his back. The room he led me into was like a mini theater. The seats were crushed velvet with cup holders built into the arms. A fully stocked glass-fronted refrigerator stood to one side. I could see probably a dozen varieties of beer, as well as bottles of vodka, gin, and mixers. Beside that was the remainder of the alcohol. No expense had been spared to create the lavish setting. Except for the cheap booze.

"Have a seat. Best view is in the middle."

He moved to the back of the room and opened a cabinet. I could see hundreds of jewel cases and my anger threatened to consume me yet again.

"You got anything with a young girl, maybe fifteen? Long brown hair and dimples? I love chicks with dimples."

I was pressing my luck, but revenge drove me to protect kids like Chrissy and Rook's daughter. To make those who hurt them suffer as much as I could make them. My target's pain gave me focus, too. In their eyes, I could see the fear the others felt. Their cries gave voice to those who were no longer able to do so. And I hoped their deaths would bring peace to their souls.

"Yeah, yeah. I got exactly what you want. She came to us last year. She was the prettiest little thing. Horny as all hell, too. We had a group here, maybe six guys, and this chick let them do whatever they wanted."

He traced a finger over the cases as he muttered off the names. "Here. I think this is her. She said her name was Courtney and she liked cocks, so I titled it Courtney Cocks and Friends."

He laughed, but when he turned around, his laughter caught in his throat. I stood over him, glaring down. I reached out and snatched the disc from his fat little sausage fingers.

"Who else has seen this?" I demanded, shoving him down to the floor. The time for pretense was over, and Rouland was about to pay for his sins.

"What the fuck man?" he bellowed, trying to stand up. One punch to the stomach told him that was the wrong choice to make. It also made him throw up a lot of the booze and food he'd consumed.

I grabbed a fistful of hair and dragged him away from the goo and threw him against the seats, causing the backs to break off a couple. I stalked over to him, drew out a pair of handcuffs I used to ensure he wouldn't be going anywhere, and watched as the blood drained from his face. He was afraid, but not as much as he needed to be.

"Who else has seen this video?" I repeated.

"Just the guys who are in it. This one wasn't as popular and we didn't think it had market value. Little bitch just laid there."

I kicked him in the ribs. "She has a name. Courtney. Use it."

"Okay, fuck man," he gasped. "Her name was Courtney. What's the big deal?"

I kicked him again, certain I heard a bone snap. "I want to be sure I have your attention," I growled. "Let me tell you a little story, 'kay? You can let me know if I get any of it wrong. There was a young girl named Courtney Delachamp. She was a good kid. Got great grades in school, was well liked by her peers. When her parents told her they were getting a divorce, it rocked her world. Her grades slipped. She started skipping class. She fell in with the wrong crowd. They brought her to you.

"Now, the way I figure it, you offered her some kind of sick stability. You probably showered her with attention, gave her the affection she craved. Then you started her on soft drugs. Maybe marijuana. As time went by, you got her hooked on harder things. When you had your claws in her well and good, you let her know what the cost was going to be.

"You started pimping her out. She didn't like what you were making her do, but her body needed the drugs, so she did it anyway. And you kept her high most of the time. But when people stopped asking for her, the money dried up. So you started to rent her out for your parties. A couple hundred bucks a head and no limits.

"One night, a party got out of hand. The men got rougher than normal, and Courtney died from being all cut up inside. She bled out and you had people toss her body into an alleyway. How am I doing so far?"

The man was sweating bullets. He kept glancing toward the door, and I could see he was trying to work it out in his head if he'd make it.

"You won't," I assured him. "Even without the cuffs, I would drop your fat ass before you made five steps."

"What do you want?" he whined.

"Justice for Courtney. And for all the kids like her that you got hooked on your shit over the years and used them up until there was nothing left. Then you tossed them aside, like they were garbage."

"I didn't do anything, I swear."

"You helped these men rape her. She died because of you."

"I only filmed it. I didn't touch her. I wasn't into her that way."

My blood boiled as I glared at this pathetic excuse for a human being. He'd set up a *party* for friends where they'd snatched a young girl off the streets and passed her around. He'd watched them and collected money for it.

I stepped in closer. His breathing hitched. His eyes went wide when I pulled the gun from my jacket's inside pocket. He was moments away from begging for mercy, but he wouldn't find any. Not from me.

"Tell me why I shouldn't kill you."

"I didn't touch her. I swear," he babbled.

"Did you film them?" He started shaking violently, tears streaming down his face. "Did you?" I roared.

"Yes. Yes, I filmed it. I can give you the copies. It wasn't released, I swear," he whimpered.

That was all I needed to hear. Rouland no longer rated a bullet to the brain. That would be too quick. I pushed the gun back into my pocket and pulled out a rag that I then stuffed in his mouth. His eyes went wide.

"Courtney had been a good kid, and you took everything from her. Her hopes and dreams were destroyed because of you, and instead of helping her, you let them steal her innocence. To you it was business, but to me it's so much more. It's why I'm here, to hopefully let her rest."

As his muscles strained in an effort to move away from his fate, I took my thumbs and pressed them against the lids of his eyes. It felt like I was pushing against marbles made of jelly, the way they slid, popped, and undulated beneath my thumbs. I squeezed harder. His cries of pain would have caused a weaker man to buckle. To have mercy. They simply made me press more. They gave under the pressure, squishing into his skull. Blood spurted, running down his mangled sockets. He sobbed in agony.

"You only watched," I whispered, not even sure if he could hear me over his wails. "Let's see you do it again."

I left him quivering on the floor and texted Rook, knowing he'd understand my reasoning. Someone would find Rouland and get him to a hospital. He wouldn't die, even though every fiber of my being screamed for me to finish it as I'd planned, but I realized he was more useful to me alive, for now. If I killed him, his body would be disposed of, and no one would know what happened to him. This way, word would get back to his people, and it would hopefully send them running for protection.

And Valerie would know I was coming for her.

CHAPTER SIX

"Our sources say that Valerie isn't overly concerned with this loss," Rook told me. I could hear papers shuffling through the speaker.

"She's already replaced Rouland, who's going to live, by the way. The police questioned him, but he shut up tight. I don't know for sure, but I would hazard a guess that he's got a target painted on his back and will be taken out at some point. Valerie doesn't like loose ends, and as much as you rattled his cage, I think Rouland is definitely that. Even though you didn't kill him, we believe you made the right call. Your standard fee has been deposited into your account, though personally, I think you should get a bonus for your...creative flair.

"As far as his *collection*, we confiscated and destroyed it. I've got people working to take down the images and videos from online retailers, but you know that nothing can ever really be made to disappear from the net. Still, even though Rouland may not have shown the men's faces on video, he kept meticulous records of all transactions, including payments made to his actors and received from purchasers. It won't be long before we track them all down."

I sighed as Rook droned on. It had been two weeks, and he had yet to give me the go ahead on my next target—Manny Ramirez. I wanted to press forward, use any advantage we had, but Rook nixed the idea, saying we needed to use strategy, because brute force wouldn't work. I knew patience, but the longer this played out, the more kids would be hurt.

Manny was a vicious fucker. He ran a dog fighting ring and made Michael Vick look like Mother Teresa. Allegedly he not only killed the dogs, he fed their bodies to his others. He claimed it toughened them up. As much as I cared about animals, they weren't the first thing on my mind. That spot belonged to a young man named Jaime, thirteen, dark hair and eyes. A good-looking kid. His would be the image that stayed in my head while I took the sick bastard down.

Jaime had told the police about Manny's activities. Unfortunately he'd told the wrong cops and ended up mutilated for his troubles. The words of two fine, upstanding citizens against one street urchin who was a member of a gang? No contest. Rook had paid for Jaime and his family to get away from Manny, but I knew Jaime would be looking over his shoulder for the rest of his life, wondering if someone would find him and finish the job.

"Are you even listening to me?" came Darth's exasperated growl.

"Not in the least," I answered truthfully. "I figure when you've got something important to say, like giving me the go ahead on Manny Ramirez, then my ears will perk up."

"We've discussed this, Haven. We want Valerie to sweat—"

"And is she?" I snapped. "You've already said she's replaced Rouland, so it's back to business as usual. I think we need to move faster. Take out more of her group and she'll know what it means to worry."

"The other teams took out four targets we considered to be lynchpins for her organization. We thought that if we did that, the organization would begin to collapse in on itself and make her vulnerable. It didn't. She is far more adept than we anticipated, and that's cost us the lives of three agents."

That was news to me. People in our line of work died, but Rook never spoke of it.

"Agents Stonewall, Chaperon, and Bulwark were killed when they went in ahead of their teams. Somehow, she knew we were coming and was prepared. The only thing I'm thankful for is that none of them felt any pain. This is why we're not moving faster. We thought we understood the game. We figured we could approach it like every other operation, but this changes everything. We need to adapt to her rules, then use them against her."

"Did they have families?" I asked, grateful I wouldn't have to be the one to tell them.

"No. But you knew one of them. You trained with him. Bulwark was the one who gave you the scar across your chest."

The wind was sucked right out of my sails. I had no love for the guy, but I had a shit ton of respect for his skill. It might have been my military mentality, but the man was a brother to me, and that was one more debt Valerie would owe when I found her.

"So what do we do? I'm not big on patience."

"I've been speaking with my superiors and they're willing to give me carte blanche to handle the problem. They want to throw men and money at it, but I want to do something different. It's true that a full squadron failed, but maybe if one man went in and started eliminating her people, she'd use resources trying to track him down. Kind of like avoiding a charging bull, but still getting chewed up by the mosquito."

"Let me guess, I'm the mosquito?

"You are definitely the best pest I know," he replied without any humor at all.

"So how will this work?"

"We're thinking that if one man can get in, do the job, and get out, she'll see that we can get to anyone we want. In and out. No way to predict where we'll strike. No pattern. Nothing to keep us from hitting her when and where we choose."

I thought about it. A large group of men was easy to prepare for. I was good at getting into places unseen, doing a huge amount of damage, and slipping back out. It'd worked well when I started a turf war between two gangs that had killed a young family caught in their crossfire. Many of them killed one another, never aware that I fed both groups various information that ended the turf war permanently.

"Please tell me I can start with Manny."

"You have permission to do whatever you think is necessary. Our original goal is still the same. We want her on edge. The parts have to be taken out before the head, so that there is no chance of them filling the void. While we don't believe any of them would be as much of a threat, they still would have access to the funds, weapons, and personnel."

"So start wiping out all of them from behind the scenes. I like that idea."

~

It had been a good number of years since I had seen my sister last, at least beyond my nightmares. I rarely even thought about her anymore. The night I found her bludgeoned was the night she died, as far as I was concerned. Becoming a ward of the state and being transferred to a hospital where she would live out the remainder of her life never knowing who I was, was more than I could handle. Yes, I was a coward. I won't use the fact that I was a teenager to justify anything. I mean I killed a guy, so I'd grown up pretty damn fast.

I sat in the living room with my memories of Chrissy. The two of us could hardly be more different. Her golden hair was nothing like my dark brown. She had the prettiest hazel eyes, where mine were lighter, more like cognac. Had she grown up, she would have been an absolute stunner. When we were kids, she used to tell me she dreamt of being a fashion model, because they'd pay her to wear pretty clothes. Her only flaw was a slight bump in her pixie nose where it was broken when she was tackled from behind while running with the ball.

She was such a dichotomy. She would rough and tumble with me and the neighborhood boys out on the football field, but then turn around and put on a dress and look nothing like the kid who had just ground a boy's face into the dirt. When her nose got broken, she jumped up, blood dripping down her face, and tackled the boy, telling him he played dirty, before she beat him up.

Now I sat thinking about her. What was she like? If I went to visit her, would we recognize each other? I snorted as I poured another drink and sat down again. I didn't know what brought about the melancholy I was experiencing lately, but I found myself wishing for the life not lived. The one where Chrissy grew up to realize her dream of strutting across the catwalk. Where she'd have a family with nieces and nephews I could spoil mercilessly.

I sipped my brandy and it burned like acid. I wanted my life back. I needed my sister to tell me it was going to be okay. Even my mom hugged me on occasion. Now? No one did. To even think it was a sign of weakness that others could exploit. I again considered going to the club, but I wasn't in the mood for company. Even a quickie in the bathroom seemed like too much effort for me right now.

Maybe I was getting old. When I had been a sniper, I never once doubted my job served the greater good. Hell, up until last year, I never doubted what I was doing. I had the occasional twinge of regret, but that was more for me than for any of the people I'd taken out. Now? It seemed like my heart wasn't in the job anymore. In the eight years I'd worked with Rook, I'd eliminated nearly two hundred people who had done some god-awful things, and while I never reveled in it, I at least took comfort in the fact that I was doing good.

39

This thing with Valerie shook me to my core, though. How could I think what I was doing made a difference? There were always going to be a string of people out there who made their lives on the death of others. Nothing I did changed that one bit. Maybe Kelly was right, and it was time to walk away and make a life of my own. This job belonged to a younger man. One with the ideals I used to have. One who thought he could go out and change the world, not one who knew for certain the world had moved on without him.

I got up and rinsed my glass, then placed it into the drying rack. I glanced around the place I'd lived for almost a decade and never felt more alone in my life. I trudged into the bedroom, stripped, flicked off the light, and crawled into bed. Sleep refused to come for me, though. I reached across and tugged the pillow to my chest, imagining someone's body cradled in mine before I finally drifted off.

~

First light hadn't even broken before the sound of the vacuum cleaner roused me. I sat up, still holding the pillow, and glared toward the door, where I could see Kelly with a set of headphones on and dancing around the living room doing the cleanup. I cursed at him, despite the fact it was a lost cause. I got out of bed and padded to the bathroom for a quick shower. When I returned, Kelly had laid out my clothes, and placed my Desert Eagle 50AE on top. It might not have been the most powerful handgun, but it had...sentimental value.

"They found Manny," he said from the doorway.

"Where?" I asked, not even caring that I stood buck naked in front of the man.

"Detroit. Your plane leaves in four hours."

Not a lot of time, but for this, I would make it work. I ran through the files one more time to ensure I knew everything there was available about my target. Manuel Ramirez had quickly worked his way up Valerie's organization. His cruel and sadistic streak would make strong men throw up. At twenty-three, he was known for violent outbursts that would end up with someone dead over a perceived slight.

His dogs didn't fare any better. Beatings, electrocutions, and death weren't uncommon for those that didn't perform. Manny wanted his mutts to be as psychotic as he was. Jaime had been lured in by promises of money, power, and the respect that went with it. What kid didn't want that? And who better than someone you figured you could trust? Manny started him out slowly. Deliveries and pickups were the only thing he had to do. And that was fine with Jaime. He got spending cash and was able to afford stylish clothes. Girls flocked to him when he spread the wealth.

Then Manny called him to come to a warehouse in a neighborhood that no sane person would venture into. Still, at thirteen, Jaime thought he was tough and no one would mess with him. He got to the designated spot and found Manny stomping a dog to death. Then Manny forced Jaime to dispose of the body. Jaime buried the dog and went back, where he found dozens of other dogs, malnourished, violent, and being made to fight. He fled and went to the police where he was directed to the men who would ultimately betray him to Manny.

Detectives Meyer and Johansen looked the other way in Manny's dealings in exchange for hefty bribes. When Jaime told them what was going on, they promised him they'd look into it. They gave Manny a call shortly after Jaime left, then had him picked up.

They assured him everything would be okay, then they dragged him kicking and screaming back to the warehouse where Manny proceeded to tell Jaime how disappointed he was. How he'd expected better of him. While the detectives held him down, Manny forced Jaime's mouth open, grabbed his tongue with a pair of pliers, and sliced it off.

The three of them then dragged Jaime out of the warehouse, and severely beat him, while Manny screamed that they were no longer brothers. They dumped him in an alley, then went off with Manny laughing about how much fun it had all been.

From somewhere deep within him, Jaime found the strength to drag himself to a nearby street where a homeless man found him and used Jaime's cell to call 911.

Rook wouldn't tell me how he got involved, or where Jaime and his family had gone. All he said was that Jaime would be okay. His terse reaction told me there was a story there, but I thought it best to let it go. When I asked what happened to the detectives, he told me they were no longer in the picture. I didn't ask for details. Whether we took them down or Manny thought they were a liability and took care of them himself didn't matter. They paid for failing this kid.

~

Years ago, Detroit was a thriving city. Automakers had made it a place to live, to raise a family, and people flocked there in droves. Then the recession came and the jobs dried up, instead going overseas where cheap labor was plentiful. Things went downhill quickly after that and never recovered. Gangs sprung up, enticing young kids with the thug life. Violence became a way of life for many of these disenfranchised youths.

I didn't feel one bit sorry for them. My own story could have ended like a lot of these, but I refused to give up. I had made something of myself. Even in my current frame of mind, I knew it had been the right decision to make at the time.

My dossier told me that Manny had his headquarters in a refurbished apartment that he owned. He spent his waking moments training the dogs, arranging fights, and taking care of problems that cropped up for him or Valerie. I tracked his movements, waiting until the time would be right.

Manny was a conundrum. There was little doubt he was a complete psychopath. What he'd done to his brother proved that. Yet he worked hard to maintain an air of respectability in his neighborhood, trying to appear as a savior. He volunteered at a soup kitchen, bought Girl Scout cookies, and even donated money to various animal shelters. As fronts went, he had created a good one, but I knew the truth about what went on in his mind. The image of Jaime, taken not long after he was mutilated, wiped out any attempts Manny might make to absolve himself of the crimes.

For two weeks, I camped out on a rooftop adjacent to Manny's apartment complex, tracking the comings and goings of his associates. I determined that there were no other tenants in the building, and that despite the numerous people who visited the place, Manny lived there alone with his dogs. While he was out one day, I let myself into the place. Housekeeping wasn't high on the man's list. Dogs lived in filthy cages with gates controlled by a winch near the door. It opened up into a room converted to a crudely made arena, spattered with blood.

The dogs went nuts when I walked in. Slavering, throwing themselves at the gates. Chewing on the barbed wire mesh until their mouths bled. I stepped closer to the pens, speaking in a low, calm voice, but nothing helped. I could see the dogs before Manny got hold of them. Likely someone's loving pets, taken out into the yard one day and gone when the owner came back. Forced into this dump and beaten, mistreated, underfed, until they turned mean. Then trained to fight for some sick sons of bitches' pleasure.

I took pictures of the place and sent them to Rook. I focused on the dogs, but I also grabbed some paperwork on a crappy desk in what appeared to be his office. Ledgers of wins and losses of dogs, harsh red lines drawn through some that I assumed hadn't given him a return on his investment.

After I found everything I thought might have some value in taking down Valerie, I let myself out of the place, knowing it was only a matter of time until I went back in to handle the situation. It was strange, when I had downtime, I found myself dwelling on my life, but in the here and now, while on assignment, I was laser focused on my objective.

And while I was in Motor City, my whole being was committed to bringing down the sack of shit who'd tortured his brother. The one whose only concern had been for the safety and wellbeing of the dogs.

My guts clenched as I pictured the scene in my head. The big brown eyes gone wide as Jaime realized what was about to happen to him. A panicked gaze trying to convey to his brother how scared he was in hopes Manny would pull back at the last minute and tell him it was all a joke.

Then the terrifying prospect of death at thirteen as the person you looked up to, the one who should have guided you into the world, severed all ties with the stroke of a knife.

That was the man I was ready to face.

CHAPTER SEVEN

Apparently Friday night was a fight night. I watched from the roof across from Manny's place as men filed inside, many shepherding snarling dogs. As soon as the streets were clear, I took some time to reconnoiter the area. Dozens of vehicles surrounded the building, some with metal cages locked to the floor in the back of a van. If I had brought a rocket launcher with me, I would have taken out every last one of those bastards. One incendiary charge lobbed through the window, and the resulting explosion and fire would take out most of them. But as much as I wished otherwise, Manny was my sole target tonight.

I returned to my perch on the roof, pushing down my anger. Through the open windows, I could hear the cheers and jeers of the crowd as the fights commenced. With my binoculars, I could see the dogs, all teeth and claw, tearing at one another. The sounds of wounded animals in their death throes tore at my heart. Yeah, I was a hard man, but I had a soft spot for kids and animals. I slipped my iPod from its pouch on the side of my bag and put in the earbuds, cranking up Def Leppard as they begged to have some sugar poured on them.

Eventually boredom overtook me and I dozed against the stairwell door. Finally, at about four in the morning, the noise on the street kicked up and I peeked over the edge. The men were heading for their cars and leaving, some now no longer in possession of the dogs they'd arrived with. Whether they'd lost them in a bet, or the dogs had died in the fight I wasn't sure.

I waited until the streets were quiet for an hour before I grabbed my gear, then hit the stairs and exited the building. I popped the lock on Manny's door, a cheap piece of shit considering how much money he'd invested in the building. I worked my way up to the dogfighting room and slipped inside. The dogs began growling and barking, not quieting when Manny shouted for them to shut the fuck up. Several of the pens were empty, and many of the dogs that were still in theirs were streaked with blood.

Manny sat at a desk, his nose buried in a ledger of some sort. Piles of cash were stacked next to him. He rubbed his eyes, then grinned as he picked the money up and began thumbing through it.

"Good night?" I asked, shocking Manny and causing him to leap up out of the chair. I held my gun on him, making the fact that I was aiming directly at his face as obvious as possible.

"Who the fuck are you?" he snarled.

"Sit down. You and me are going to have a conversation."

"Fuck you. I don't talk to no one."

I lifted my hand and fired a round over his head, through the window behind him, causing it to explode outward. The loudness of the gun caused the barking of the dogs to reach a fever pitch, and I had to raise my voice to be heard over their rage. "Imagine what this would do to your pretty face," I intoned as I rubbed the handle. I approached cautiously and grabbed the chair, dragging it a few feet to the edge of the fighting pit. I waved my gun toward it and he took a few tentative steps. Another round through the next window had him moving faster.

"Sit," I ordered.

He paled a bit and stumbled back into the chair. I kept one hand on the gun as I rooted in my bag for a roll of duct tape. I went over to him and pushed the barrel of the gun to his forehead.

"One move. Please. Just make one."

"I'm going to gut you, man."

I gave a dark chuckle as I began to tape his hands and legs to the chair. "Let's be honest here. We're both smart men. I'm fairly confident you know how this whole thing goes. I mean you've been where I am plenty of times, right? But I bet the ones who you had here begged for their lives, am I right? For the moment, I want to tell you a story, and I just want to make sure you're going to stay seated for the whole thing. After I'm done, then we can figure out what to do with you."

"Fuck you," he growled.

"See, that kind of attitude is what got you in this mess to begin with," I answered, checking to ensure he was bound tight. "I have to tell you, I don't like you. I don't like what you're doing. I think you're a piece of shit."

"You one of them animal rights bitches?"

I scratched my cheek and sat on the edge of the desk before I looked him in the eye.

"I guess you could say that. But I know there are times when an animal needs to be put down for the safety of everyone."

"So now you're going to take my dogs? Won't matter. I'll have all those kennels full again by tomorrow."

"Maybe. Maybe not. The end of the story we're going to share hasn't been written, so I can't say one way or the other how this will all play out."

Seeing pictures or watching him from a distance didn't prepare me for the reality. Manny was a handsome man. Dark hair that had been slicked up by some product, big brown doe eyes that twitched, probably from nerves. In my mind, I had built him up to be a monster, but the reality was he was just a sick fuck who got off on hurting others.

"I've been asking about you," I informed him. "Just a few folks here and there. Nothing to raise suspicions. The people around here speak so highly of you. They say you're a credit to the neighborhood. I bet they don't know what it is you're doing here. Or the things you've done in the past. I have to be honest with you, no one had anything bad to say. I'm a very thorough man. I need to know everything before I finish an assignment."

Manny grunted as he struggled against the bonds. I glanced over and saw hatred burning in his eyes. I smiled, then reached out and patted him on the cheek.

"Sorry about that. Sometimes I ramble. Anyway my story begins a year or so ago. There was a young man who wanted more than anything to be someone. Poor, but there had been a lot of love from the parents. The kid went to school, got mediocre grades, though he applied himself as much as he could. He knew that he was stuck in the same dead end that his father was, but his brother? Not him. He got out. Made something of himself, and the boy wanted to escape the grim reality that he felt trapped in.

"He begged his brother to take him along when he left. There had been another huge argument with their parents, who pleaded with their son to think about his younger sibling and stop doing bad things. The older brother ruffled the kid's hair and said that he'd be back for him. Promised him. And then walked out of his life. What happened to the older brother after that is kind of a mystery. He fell in with a bad crowd, obviously, but he got money and power. True to his word, he contacted the kid and gave him a job as a delivery boy. The kid was awed by the amount of money he earned for delivering packages.

"He'd go to school in shiny new clothes, all designer labels, which earned him some kind of faux respect amongst his peers, but the kid ate it up. He had girls who wanted to date him, and he loved the hell out of that. He was going somewhere with his life. He figured he might actually make it out of this hellhole. Then the penny dropped."

Manny sneered, his thin lips curling in what I could only call disgust. "Yeah, fine. You're talking about me and my snitch of a brother, I get that. Do you know where he is?"

"No, I don't. And if I did, I wouldn't tell you."

"I *made* something out of that little bastard. He would have grown old and died here like our parents, but I gave him the means to get out. I find out where he is, I'll finish what I started."

And that was all I needed to hear. I took a knife out of my bag. It had a wicked serrated blade that would do some serious damage to flesh. Manny struggled and shouted as I gripped his silk shirt and sliced through it like butter. I was surprised by the amount of chest hair he had. I figured he'd be smooth, but dark, curly hairs graced his chest and stomach. He was definitely not what I thought. I gave a mental shrug, then moved to cut off his pants and underwear.

"What the fuck, man? What are you doing?"

"I'm writing the end of the story and making sure that someone has a happily ever after. Here's a clue. It probably won't be you."

His struggles intensified, and for a few minutes, I worried he might break the chair. The dogs yowling reached new levels at his shouted expletives. I thought about cold-cocking him, but I wanted him awake for what I planned.

I pointed the gun square at his chest. "Calm the fuck down, or I swear I'll blow a hole through you they could drive a truck through."

He continued to stress against the bonds, but I was confident he'd stay put. I took some alcohol wipes out of my bag and dragged them over the blade to sterilize it. I had no idea why I did it, but it gave my hands something to do while I talked.

"Your brother is going to be okay, you know. I wasn't lying about not knowing where he is, but he and your parents are somewhere you'll never find them."

"I got people looking for him," Manny barked.

"That's good to know. I'll make sure that information gets to the proper people. My concern now is you. Do you have even an inkling of regret for what you did to him?" I asked as I leaned forward and drew the blade across Manny's chest. A rivulet of blood dripped into the fuzz, matting it to his skin.

"Man, are you fucking crazy?" he screamed.

Another line, this one a bit deeper. Manny grunted, cursing me and my parentage. Yeah, that was real original. "I'll kill you, man. I swear to God."

"I asked you a question," I gritted out. "Jaime. You left him to die in a fucking alleyway. Do you feel any remorse at all?"

"He was a bitch," Manny shouted, his tone defiant. "He went to the cops and told them everything. I don't play that shit. Got what he deserved."

"You cut out his fucking tongue," I roared. "Thirteen years old and you cut out his tongue because he couldn't stand to see you hurting the dogs." A haze of red clouded my vision. I wanted nothing more than to plunge the knife into the bastard's neck. Instead, I calmed my nerves by continuing to make slices ever deeper on his brown skin. I let my mind wander. Tic-tac-toe patterns. Circles. Triangles. Each deeper than the last. Each eliciting a pained shriek. "He would have died if someone hadn't found him. I'm going to give you the same chance."

I jabbed at his dick with the blade tip, and he wailed as the blood seeped out. "No, man, you can't do this," he whimpered, his defiant tone gone.

"Sure, I can, Manny. But I'm not an inhuman piece of garbage. I won't leave you like you left Jaime." A deep slice across his neck and blood oozed out. "You won't die from this. If someone finds you, you're gonna be fine," I assured him, wiping the blood off my gear before I stowed it in the bag. "Take care, Manny. So you know, your brother is going to be fine," I repeated as I turned to leave.

"Hey, man, you said you wouldn't leave me alone," he gurgled.

"Oh, I'm not." I slowly walked to the door and stopped near the button to the pens. The snarling pits and Rottweilers threw themselves against the wire mesh, their voices adding to the cacophony of Manny's pained cries.

When he saw what I was about to do, Manny's eyes widened. "They're going to be destroyed anyway. They're a lot like humans. Once you teach them to kill, there's no going back. Beg them like Jaime pleaded with you. Maybe *they* will show you mercy."

I opened the door, pressed the button, and pulled the door shut behind me. I could hear him begging me not to leave, to save him. Then the screams as the dogs exacted revenge. He might survive it. I wouldn't want to be him if he did. That shit was gonna be ugly.

~

I texted Rook when I got to the airport. I gave him my status update on Manny and let him know that there were people still looking for Jaime. He assured me the family would be safe. As my plane readied, he told me that he'd be in contact when I arrived home.

It was well after midnight when I walked through the door. The house smelled of lemon furniture polish. Kelly had obviously been busy while I was gone. It occurred to me I had no idea what the man did from day to day. He cleaned and stocked, but beyond that, I didn't have a clue. I made a mental note to ask him.

The refrigerator was crammed with goodies, but I went to the freezer and pulled out a pint of Chubby Hubby ice cream, my guilty pleasure. I took it into the computer room and flipped on the system. It wasn't but a few moments later that Darth came on.

"You are a sick and twisted individual," the dark voice informed me.

"And?"

"Nothing. Just wanted to make sure you knew we were aware."

"Did he live?" I asked, spooning a big scoop into my mouth.

"You're kidding? One of the techs almost got sick when he found the…leftovers. Those dogs did a number on him. But Manny disappeared last night, and we took another of Valerie's players off the board."

As Rook went on, I scanned through the files, searching for the person who was next on my list. I wanted one of the bigger players this time. Someone that Valerie would take note of. Manny was barely a blip on her radar. He was basically a well-paid errand boy.

"Arianna Martella," I blurted out.

"Okay…" Rook answered, obviously waiting for me to continue.

"She runs a prostitution ring. People can get anything they want, for the right price."

"I know who she is. I put the files together."

"She brings in a lot of money, right?"

"I'd say. Everything is filtered through shell companies, but we estimate she brings in several million dollars a year. And that's a conservative estimate."

"I want to let Valerie know that no one is out of our reach. Big fish, small fry, everyone is a target. It should keep her off balance."

"Okay, what do you need from me?"

I pulled out the file I had. Arianna was considered by our organization to be one of Valerie's lynchpins. She made cheating seem almost respectable as she entertained clients when they came to Dallas. Her worth was estimated at nearly seventy-five million dollars, at least the money we knew about. She ran one of the largest prostitution rings in the country, with places in all fifty states. There were thousands of people employed by her, but many more that had been forced into sexual slavery. People who rebelled disappeared, and even Rook wasn't able to find out what happened to them.

"A ticket to Dallas," I grumbled. "Leaving tomorrow."

"Don't you think you should—"

"Tomorrow," I stated firmly. "You said you wanted her off balance. That means her people have to be taken out in quick succession. After this one, I'll wait a few weeks and let her wonder when the next hit is coming."

"You know, if I ever decide to retire, they're going to tap you for my job," Rook mused.

"Nah, not my thing. I'm more hands-on."

"If I were twenty years younger, I might be in the field."

"If you were in the field, I wouldn't have someone like you watching my back."

"If I was in the field, you wouldn't have been picked," he informed me. "I chose you, based on everything I had available to me. My superiors thought you were too much of a loose cannon and not to be trusted. I staked my reputation on your ability to get the job done. I'm proud to say, you haven't ever given them reason to question your abilities."

I had to ask. "Why me?"

"I told you, we're a lot alike. Both single-minded in our quest for justice, both lost family to violence, and both willing to do what has to be done to get results. Beyond that, you're wicked skilled. I've never worked with anyone who had your qualifications."

"Kelly needs a raise," I sputtered.

"Um…okay."

I ran a hand over the back of my neck, trying to get rid of the prickles that kept cropping up. "Here's the thing. I'm not sure how much longer I can do this. I'm not a young man, and I don't know that I feel the same now as I did when I started. Manny was scum, I can't deny, but I can't help thinking if we had pressed the agencies responsible…" My voice trailed off.

"Haven, if you want out, that's fine. The organization was here long before either of us, and it will go on. We're, none of us, irreplaceable. I'm going to ask, though, as a personal favor to me, can you wait until we bring Valerie down? She's hurt a lot of people, more than we'll ever know. The police can't—or won't—prosecute, and she just keeps on going."

Images of Rouland and Manny assailed me. Their pleading tore into my heart in a way it hadn't before. I was tired deep into my bones. I wanted to stay home and find a hobby. I'd always wanted to paint. Or maybe just lay out by the koi pond.

"Yeah, okay. I don't think I could walk away yet anyway. I need to see this through."

"Here's something for you to think about before you make any decisions. First, you're not old. I could almost be your father, but I get that it's hard for you. Think it over for a while. Maybe you're right, and it's time to walk away. Maybe you just need a break. We could always route your assignments through other agents."

"Yeah, maybe," I answered, not wanting to commit to anything.

"You did good work. Get some sleep. I'll have a ticket ready for your trip to Dallas tomorrow morning. Okay?"

"Yeah, sure."

If only I had known what was going to happen in Dallas, what was going to be there when I arrived, I don't know if I would have rushed there, or stayed far away.

CHAPTER EIGHT

Morning found me in the gym working off some frustration. Kelly had added the equipment a few years ago to keep me from getting soft, he'd said. While I enjoyed using the public facilities, my setup was every bit as good. Kelly knew his gear. Barbells and free weights on one side of the room, leg machines on the other. A lifting rack within easy access of everything in the room was the centerpiece. It meant I could do my exercises without the need for a spotter.

Sweat streamed down my chest as I finished my reps of back squats. The aches in my muscles told me I needed to work out more. It was a good kind of sore, but I'd feel it for a few days. I finished my circuit and headed back to the main house to down a protein shake and get ready for my flight.

Kelly stood in front of a table laid out with a box of oils and liniments next to it. He stepped back and gestured for me to lay down.

"Is there anything you don't know how to do?" I murmured as I stretched out.

His hands were strong and insistent. My muscles melted under his touch. "I told you, I dabble in many things." He paused for a moment, then continued. "Do you think it's wise to go again so soon after you got back?" Kelly wondered.

"I think it's necessary. I want this job over with. I have decisions to make, but I told Rook I'd finish the assignment first."

"Don't rush. It makes you sloppy. If you're having second thoughts about your commitments, it makes sense not to take this job."

"Aw, I didn't know you cared," I teased.

He gripped the muscle in my shoulder and squeezed hard enough for pain to shoot through my body.

"Don't make jokes," he growled. "Promise me you'll be careful."

"I'm always careful," I reminded him.

He smacked my left side, where a bullet had grazed me a few years back. It still left a pretty interesting scar along my ribs. "Yes," he replied drolly, "I can see that."

"Is it wrong that I want a normal life?" I knew it wasn't, but I needed the validation from someone.

"Do you even know what normal is anymore?" he asked in return.

"I… I'm not sure," I admitted. "Maybe something where the job description doesn't entail sneaking around on a rooftop, waiting for someone to show up so I can put a bullet in his brain. A job with regular hours, where I know what's going to happen on a day-to-day basis. Some kind of consistency in my life."

"Is this still about the house?"

"No, the house is a symptom of the bigger problem. I'm becoming increasingly aware I don't know who I am anymore. This morning while I shaved, it took me ten minutes to remember my real name. I haven't heard it in so long, I almost forgot it myself."

"You know what's best for you, so I won't try to give you advice—"

"Would you? I'm alone in my head most of the time. It'd be good to hear someone else's thoughts for a change."

Kelly wiped the liniment from his hands and helped me sit up. I slipped on a T-shirt, enjoying the warming sensation of the lotion he'd used on me.

"We've chosen a life that, to people on the outside, seems exciting. The chance to play Punisher, taking out the bad guys, is like a video game wet dream for most kids. The reality is we live in a separate world, one where there are no shades of gray. You're either a good guy or a dead guy. There's nothing wrong with wanting to live in that other world, but you have to realize that you'll always be a part of this one.

"Let's say you leave the organization and go ahead and take up residence in the 'real' world. You're out at a shopping mall one day and you see someone snatch a child from his mother's arms and rush toward the exit. You see security after him, but you know there is no way they'll reach him in time. What do you do?"

"I go after him," I said, confident in my answer.

"Okay. You're highly trained, so you catch him. You see his face and realize that he'd been in the papers as a suspect in the kidnappings and killings of several small children. You saw the parent's crying on television, while begging for the safe release of their child. But you know the truth. The man had gotten away with it once. Who's to say he won't again?"

My gut clenched at the thought. Could I allow this monster to walk free? I claimed to want a normal life, but was that really what I wanted?

"The thing about our lives," Kelly continued, "is our actions become a part of us. We come to a point where we can no longer separate who we are from who we wish to be."

And that was the moment it hit me. "You used to be an agent."

Kelly gave a coy smile. "I was about your age when the operation went bad. Half of my team died, the other half wished they had. We thought our intel was solid and that we had the drop on these guys. We didn't know someone betrayed us and that they were waiting with a lot of men. By the time we escaped, they'd broken twenty-seven bones, some of which never set right. It wasn't that I didn't want to go back, I couldn't. Medically I was no longer capable of being an operative."

"So what did you do?"

"Told Rook I quit. He got me this job, taking care of agents and their wellbeing. So don't ever think I don't care, because I was in the same place you are."

"Do you miss it?"

His laugh was rich and warm. "No. I'm happy with my life now. I don't talk much, but I listen. I see and hear things, then move to try and correct them if I think they'll go tits up."

I needed to know. "So do you think I should stay with the organization?"

He bent down and began putting his liniments away. "You're missing the point of the story. It doesn't matter if you stay with them, because they'll always be a part of you. Even if you walk away, and that is something you need to decide for yourself, those instincts to save will always be engrained."

He clapped and stood up. "You need to get moving. Your plane leaves in three hours."

Though it didn't calm the mental storm brewing in my head, I still appreciated what he'd said to me. "I...well, thank you."

"Anytime. Oh, and do you remember telling me you had dozens of ways to kill me? Keep in mind that I know how to counter every one of them, plus I still have a few moves of my own."

"Like trying to poison me with some nasty tasting soup?"

His expression grew grim. "That was not nasty. I work on your meals for hours, just to ensure you have decent food."

"You obviously didn't taste it," I told him.

"That was my grandmother's recipe," he informed me.

"So you like it?"

"Well, no," he admitted. "I just figured my version had to be better than hers."

"It's not. Never make it again."

He laughed as he packed up his gear, then his expression turned serious. "Haven?"

"Yeah?"

"There's nothing wrong with wanting something more."

"Did you ever?"

"Maybe, once upon a time. But for me, this was more than a job. It was… It *is* my life. The two worlds don't mix well."

"Rook seems to handle it," I reminded him.

"Is that what you heard?"

I answered hesitantly. "It sounded like it."

"Don't tell anyone I said this, because Rook wouldn't be happy. After Rook killed the man who hurt their daughter, things changed. Rook became obsessed with revenge. It consumed every waking moment. The agency tossed a lifeline and gave Rook something to focus on after the divorce.

"He still keeps an eye on his daughter. He's paranoid about her safety, because he wasn't there to stop her from being hurt. She lives at an assisted living center, but is fiercely independent. Every time she goes somewhere, there is always someone who follows her to ensure she's safe. He can't ever go back now. He knows too much to walk away from this life. Rook will die long before he ever gives up.

"So in answer to your question, our two worlds coexist side by side, but I'm not sure we can ever stay in that other one. We've seen too much, done far too many things, to ever feel comfortable there for long."

"I think I understand."

"It's a good dream, but I'm not sure if it's attainable. Our lives are finding a happily ever after for other people. It's not likely we'll ever have our own."

It was a sobering thought. Listening to Kelly, I wondered if I could walk away from this with even a fragment of my soul intact.

~

Dallas had one of the busiest airports in the world. Flights arrived and departed day and night, bringing people in for thousands of reasons. As I grabbed my bag from the carousel, I wondered how many times an assassin had been through there before me.

Kelly had booked two hotel rooms, as standard procedure dictated. Both would be under an alias, but they were necessary. For my assignment, he'd provided me with identification, giving me the name Chester Mayfield. I groaned at the moniker and his fucked up sense of humor. That would be another one that I owed him.

I checked in at the desk, clenching my fingers to avoid throttling the clerk who chuckled when she saw my ID. Kelly was so going to pay. As I made my way to the elevator, another agent, who had checked into a different room, slipped me a keycard. This would be my safe house if something went wrong, which it rarely did.

I opened the door to Chester's room and stepped inside. It was a pretty standard suite for a high-end hotel. Two rooms, one with a king-size bed and the other a living area complete with an in-room office, it definitely didn't rank among the worst places I'd stayed. I tossed my bag into the corner and pulled out my laptop, ready to get to work.

Arianna ran legitimate escort services throughout the country. In fact, I often saw her billboards inviting married people to have an affair. The underbelly of her organization, though, was where the money poured in. She had an exclusive list of high rollers who paid tens of thousands of dollars for her to procure someone special for them, even for a single night. She rarely disappointed a client.

This arm of Valerie's organization was one of the most high profile. Everyone knew of Arianna's Affairs, or had read about it. She made money hand over fist setting up people who were bored in their relationships with something spicy that had no strings attached. While a lot of people thought it was sleazy, me among them, she'd taken cheating and turned it into a lucrative business.

I dialed the number Kelly had provided me, not surprised when it was answered mid ring.

"Arianna's Affairs, this is Amber, how can I service you?" came the coy voice on the other end of the line.

"Good afternoon, Amber. My name is Chester Mayfield. I believe you've been waiting for my call."

"It's nice to hear from you, Mr. Mayfield. I understand that I'm supposed to treat you like family. What can I do for you?"

Arianna was to be in Dallas today, and Rook had said he'd placed a near impossible request for so short a time.

"Arianna was to…uh…procure something special for me. I wanted to see how that went."

"Oh. Well, your request was quite specific, but Arianna said she's never failed a client, and had no intention of starting now. She will pick you up from your hotel at six and take you to your…date for the evening."

It was supposed to be unlikely she could find someone who would meet the specifications Rook had asked for. Young, male, receptive to kinkier things, and especially fond of being tied down and used. He was to have flawless skin without any marring at all.

"She was able to get me what I asked for? That's impressive."

"Arianna's Affairs has a long list of satisfied clients, Mr. Mayfield. Arianna was intrigued by your request, and for the fee you offered, she said she would handle it personally."

I could feel a trickle of cold sweat run down my neck. I hadn't thought they would be able to find someone and that Arianna would convey apologies. How far would I have to go to ensure the job was done?

~

The concierge phoned at six on the dot. Arianna's limo was waiting to pick me up. I gave myself one last check in the mirror. I'd done my hair in short spikes, poured myself into tight leather pants, a black T-shirt that stretched across my chest, and a worn, tight-fitting leather jacket which covered my bulletproof vest, then added in a few fake earrings, and a shiny diamond nose ring to complete the look of a young internet mogul who enjoyed kinky sex.

I swaggered through the lobby, not at all oblivious to the stares I received. When I stepped out into the hot, dry air, a perky young blonde stood next to a sleek black limousine.

"You must be Mr. Mayfield. I'm Amber. We spoke earlier."

"You're a busy woman. Answering phones, picking up clients. Where do you find the time?"

"I'm Arianna's assistant. She asked me to convey her apologies. A meeting she was in ran late. She's going to meet us at our destination. If you're ready to go, we can be on our way."

I gave her the once-over. She was sexy as hell. Her hair flowed over her shoulders like strands of gold, and her hazel eyes actually fucking sparkled. The angelic face, appearing so innocent, completed the picture. The black uniform she wore showed off a tease of cleavage, but left enough to the imagination that you wanted more. A long skirt, slit up the side, showed flashes of leg whenever she moved. This woman was stunning, and if the gun she hid in the holster tied off at her leg was any indication, she was also pretty dangerous.

I sat in the back of the limo, taking in the sites of Dallas. Amber answered questions about landmarks, but didn't offer more than cursory replies, nor did she attempt to engage me in conversation. We drove for about an hour before Amber turned off into what seemed an older residential area. The streets were fairly quiet, and the houses seemed to be mostly two-story saltbox type homes, older but well maintained. We pulled up to one that sat at the end of a no-through street. My muscles tensed. This had setup written all over it.

"Where are we, Amber?"

"Arianna is waiting inside for us. Please come with me."

"You know, I'm not so sure this was a good idea. Maybe I ought to go back to the hotel."

She turned and pointed the gun at my chest. "I'm afraid I have to insist. Step out of the car, please."

There were at least five ways I could disarm her from the backseat, even with my limited mobility. She opened the door, keeping the pistol trained on me. I slid out and stood up straight, making it obvious I towered over her.

"What's going on? I don't understand."

"Once we get inside, it'll be explained."

As she herded me toward the door, I took in the features of the house in case I needed a quick exit. The upstairs windows were four panels of glass held in a wooden frame. Not so difficult to get through, but high enough that jumping would probably result in broken bones. I couldn't be sure how many people waited inside the house, and it was suicide to go into the situation without any knowledge of what I'd be facing. I stopped and turned toward Amber, doing my best to seem confused.

"I paid you a lot of money. Please," I pretended to plead. "I didn't do anything wrong."

The door to the house opened and a tall, curvaceous redhead stepped out. Her face had graced many billboards.

"Mr. Mayfield. A pleasure to meet you. I'm Arianna."

She held out a slender hand with artfully decorated nails. I took it and gave it a quick shake.

Since fearful didn't work, I tried for indignant. "What the hell is going on here? I paid damn good money, and I don't know if this is how you normally do business, but—"

"You can stop now, Mr. Mayfield, if that's really who you are. I don't know how you got your name onto our special guest list, but considering the master copy is kept with me at all times, it wasn't too hard to figure out you'd done some fancy hacking."

I'd been with Rook for all these years and never once had it come up where someone questioned my credentials. This was new and exciting. Adrenaline rushed through my veins as I weighed my options.

"Okay, fine. I hacked into your system. I heard rumors about you being able to provide anything, and I wanted to test that. I have the money, and I do want what I ordered, but I didn't want to wait. I guess you don't really have what I asked for," I said, giving my best sullen voice.

"On the contrary, we have exactly what you asked for. He's waiting inside. You should come in and meet him. I think you'll get along with him very well."

My skin tingled, and every fiber of my being screamed not to go into the house, but if there was a kid in there, I wouldn't leave him.

"Amber, you can put your gun away. I'm sure Mr. Mayfield is exactly who he claims to be."

Without hesitation, Amber slid the gun back into the holster. I walked up to the house and we went inside. There were four men waiting for me, and I got the distinct impression Arianna didn't for a minute believe I was Chester Mayfield.

CHAPTER NINE

A s soon as I entered, they stalked toward me. It was evident their intentions weren't a group hug, and also, standing together like they were proved they were complete amateurs. When the first one lunged, I twisted and pushed him into another, taking note of them collapsing in a heap, then shoved the palm of my hand up into the next guy's nose. If Kelly could have seen that move, he would have berated me for being sloppy. Properly done, it could kill a man. As it was, I only shattered his nose and left him disoriented.

The first two regained their footing, but by now, I had my gun out. Two quick shots became two quick dead men. The last guy had retreated into another room and taken a defensive position behind a couch of all places. One shot blew the stuffing out of the cushion and out of his chest.

Arianna and Amber had disappeared in the ensuing fracas, and if I guessed right, Arianna would be on the phone to Valerie very shortly. I texted Rook and let him know what was happening, then decided to explore the house to see if they did have a person in there.

I found a room in the back of the house that appeared to be some kind of fallout shelter from years when the threat of nuclear war was a reality everyone lived with. I pulled open the door which scraped on rusty hinges and stepped into the darkness.

Small slivers of light shone in the basement. Barely enough to see by, but I couldn't take the chance of turning on the lights. I pulled a small Maglite from my belt and shined it around quickly. In the corner, I caught a glimpse of something moving. I resisted the urge to shoot. I was never one for kill them all and let God sort them out. It was my responsibility to make sure they suffered for their crimes before they received their final rewards, whatever those turned out to be. And if I got to have a little fun along the way, so much the better.

The prone figure whimpered when I got closer. He tried to draw back, to scamper toward the crates behind him, but he was tethered to the floor. I knelt about ten feet away, looking at the long, stringy brown hair matted to his face. He smelled overpoweringly of shit and piss. His eyes glinted in the beam of my light, and I could see them sparkle with tears. He shrunk back when I moved a little closer.

"Please," he begged. "I can't do it again. Please don't."

He trembled when I reached out toward him. When he knew he couldn't move away any farther, he dropped his hands to his side, all the urge to flee seemed to seep out of him. I could see abraded skin, worn to blood in some areas.

"Please, please..." he kept whimpering.

"Don't be afraid. I won't hurt you. I only want to help you, if you'll let me," I promised, setting my gun on the floor. I touched his face, caked with grime, and he pressed against my hand as if he'd never felt a gentle touch. I was a hard man, one of the worst you would ever meet, yet the fear on this young man's face, the terror in his eyes, made my heart hurt.

"What's your name?" I asked, my voice a harsh whisper that echoed in the dark.

He was quiet for a moment, then he peered up at me, his lips trembling, but his expression changed. I saw hope there. "Samuel Morin," he squeaked. "Do you have a name?"

I tried to comfort him with a smile. That was something I probably shouldn't have done. The terror in his eyes was back.

"Sorry. I'm not used to this," I admitted. "Call me Haven."

A gasp from Samuel had me looking over my shoulder. It seemed that Amber hadn't left after all. The gunshot shattered the silence, slamming into my back, tearing through my favorite jacket. Without my vest, parts of me would have been painting the walls. I grunted and fell forward. Samuel cried out and began chanting, "No, no, no." He tried to cover his face, but the ropes that held him didn't allow it. I didn't want him to see what was about to happen, but there'd be no way to avoid it.

I grabbed the gun from the floor, firing as I turned. Amber screamed as the bullet entered her chest and exited through her back, then she fell to the floor, dead. I lunged for Samuel and he cried out as I unhooked him from the ropes that bound him.

"We have to go," I told him. "I want you to put your arms around me and hold on tight, okay?"

He wrapped thin arms around my neck and held on with a death grip. I headed up the stairs, peering around corners as we made our way out of the house. A quick check confirmed the car was gone. I put Samuel down and told him to stay put, then went back into the house. The man whose nose I broke lay in a pool of blood, whimpering. They just didn't make tough men anymore.

"Where's your car?" I growled.

He gave me a pitiful look, and when I put my gun to his chest, he started babbling all sorts of interesting information. Amber had hired him and his slug friends at a bar. She promised them money and a night they'd never forget if they helped her with a problem she was having. My guess was that was me. I had to admit, for having such a short time, she got things together very quickly. I hoped that Arianna's next assistant would be as helpful.

He told me they had parked down the street, a blue Escort, and gave me the keys. Then he started blubbering, begging me not to kill him. I bopped him on the nose, which caused him to cry out, and reminded him that he could have very easily been as dead as his friends today.

When I got out of the house, Sammy was nowhere to be seen. Panic shot through me, thinking perhaps Arianna had still been close by and grabbed him. When I heard ragged breathing among the hedges, I realized where he was. I knelt down next to the bushes, and in as non-threatening a voice as I could manage, asked, "Hey, you wanna come out?"

"Are you going to shoot me, too?" he whimpered.

I had promised to help him, but after seeing me shoot Amber, I could understand his fear. "Aw, no, definitely not. You're safe with me, I swear. We're going to get you some help. I know people who can—"

He shot out of the bushes and threw his arms around me again. "No, please. No one else. I don't want anyone but you. Please don't make me."

He buried his face in my neck, and I could feel the warmth of his breath and tears. What he was asking was impossible, but I whispered to him and promised I'd help him.

~

For all the looks I had received when I'd left the hotel, the ones I was getting now were even more incredulous. I literally carried Sammy through the ostentatious lobby while he clung to me. He refused to even look up as we walked past throngs of people. He trembled as we stepped into the elevator. The woman who had been inside, fled the moment she caught sight of him. Or maybe it was the smell.

I opted to use the second room, something I'd never done before, and closed the door behind me, making sure the deadbolt was thrown. Even though Amber probably never had Chester's room number and had met me out in front of the hotel, I wasn't going to take any chances with Sammy's life.

The room looked almost identical to the one I'd gone to previously. I made a mental note to have someone pull my gear from that room and have it brought to me. For now, though, I had other things that needed attention.

"Hey, it's okay. You're safe now," I crooned to Sammy. He loosened his grip and slid to the floor, eyeing the room warily, and not moving from my side.

I pointed toward a door that was slightly ajar. "The bathroom is in there, if you want to clean up. I think there's a robe hanging in there, too. Use it until we can get you some clothes. Those things you've got on wouldn't even qualify for rag status."

He nodded mutely and shuffled into the bathroom, not bothering to close the door. He stripped out of his clothes, completely unconcerned that I was nearby. He was painfully thin. There were bite marks from some kind of insect dotting his body. I tried to be clinical in my examination as he stepped into the shower, but rage poured through me.

"Sammy?" I called out. "Or do you prefer Samuel?"

"I like it when you say Sammy," he answered, his soft voice muffled by the water. "Can I stay in here? I don't know when I had a shower last and it feels so good."

"As long as you'd like. Can you tell me what happened? Why were you in that house?"

He gasped and I felt like shit. I had just rescued him from some kind of hell, and I was already dragging him back there mentally.

"How about if we discuss that later? What do you think about something to eat? I could have room service bring you something up." I opened the guest service directory and glanced at the menu. "What about a cheeseburger? How does that sound?"

"Um…okay."

"Do you want it with French fries?"

"I don't remember if I like them," he answered quietly.

Rage continued to bubble beneath the surface. I needed to know his story, to see what had been done to him. I'd learned more from my government trainers than how to shoot a man. I know which ribs to push a blade through to pierce a heart, where to shoot a person to make it hurt, but not kill, the creative use of poisons, plus finding some of my own ways to bring the end of a man's life.

For the most part, I used to love my job. I lived on the edge, stepping over it regularly to get my assignment done, but always pulling back at the last moment. It was heady. My targets were always the worst of the worst. In many instances, you could take down a leader and the organization would wither, or infighting would cause them to self-destruct. Some though, like Valerie's, were so well organized that a vacuum would always be filled. The lower echelons were kept honest by money, bribes, and, if they got too full of themselves, a death that would be a lot kinder than what I'd dole out.

Sammy stepped from the shower and ran a towel over his body, whimpering as he patted himself dry. I noted his pruned skin, the long brown hair, no longer matted, which now hung down, draped over his incredible green eyes and covering his slightly protruding ears, the divots on his arms, the gouges that raked across the freckled torso.

Valerie's death would be slow. She would not go quickly. If I had the power, I would kill her, bring her back to life, and start all over again. Sammy's—why the hell was I calling him Sammy—eyes were haunted. I was right. They were dark like jade and had flecks that twinkled as if stars were formed in their depths.

"You don't need to be afraid," I whispered. "I promise I won't hurt you."

He threw his arms around me and squeezed for all he was worth. I barely felt it, but I couldn't deny the warmth that flooded me.

"I'm not afraid of you," he said, his voice firm. "I could never be afraid of you."

God, if this kid only knew.

~

The knock on the door had me at full alert. I glanced toward the bed where Sammy lay sleeping, covers pulled to his chest. When he had laid on the bed, he let loose with a moan that vibrated through me. "It's so soft," he whispered, right before he fell asleep. I took the opportunity to study him closely. He was a beautiful young man, almost painfully so. Now that he'd showered and removed who knows what kind of filth, he no longer appeared to be so frail. Though he was just a half-step beyond skeletal, I could see him as he'd look once he'd seen a doctor and gotten some meat on his bones, and it sent a shiver of desire through me.

I peered through the peephole, my gun within reach. The server in his black jacket with a pencil-thin mustache was glancing over the booklet he held.

"Leave it at the door, please."

"I need a signature, sir. I can slide the receipt under the door if you'd like."

"Yeah, thanks."

A moment later, a slip of paper appeared under the door. Two hundred seventy-three dollars. If it made Sammy happy, it was well worth it. I signed it, added a hundred dollar tip, and returned it to the waiter. He let loose a small gasp, said thank you, and almost ran down the hall. I checked the cart at the door—opened the box beneath the table which held our meals, searched the underside of the flip-up leaves, the legs. Some might say paranoid, I say survivalist.

I rolled the cart into the middle of the living room, and placed two chairs nearby, before I walked into the bedroom. Sammy was curled up beneath a couple of blankets and seemed to be totally at peace. I hated to wake him, but he needed to get some food into him. I placed my hand on his cool skin and gave him a shake, fearful of frightening him when he woke, but he opened his eyes and gave a yawn, then smiled.

"You're not a dream," he said, a touch of awe in his voice.

"Not even close. Food is here, if you want to eat."

He threw back the covers, his robe flying open. The kid had no modesty that I could see. I went back to the living room, took the plates from the warmer and placed them on top of the table. Sammy's eyes went wide as he came in and saw the amount of food laid out before him. He began to grab bits of everything, but slowed when I cleared my throat. "You need to eat slowly," I informed him. "If you eat too quickly, you'll get sick."

He slowed down, taking one of the chairs, and nibbled at his food. Each bite was an experience for him. The facial expressions alone told me he enjoyed everything he tasted. When he sipped the banana-chocolate shake I ordered, he gasped. "What is this?"

The simplest of questions and anger slammed into me. "How long were you there?" I demanded, expecting him to shrink away.

Instead, he met my gaze with one of his own. "Arianna has owned me for the last twelve years, I think."

"What the fuck do you mean 'owned?'"

He shrugged and continued eating. "I was given to her when I was eleven. She told me I wasn't wanted."

He said it so matter of fact that it frightened me.

"Can you tell me what happened to you?"

That brought him up short and he appeared to shrink in on himself again.

"Whatever Arianna told me to do, I was expected to make sure got done without complaint. When I was younger, she would give me to people for a few hours or a night. They always did…things to me. Some of them hurt a lot. Others were really nice. One of them said he was going to talk to Arianna about buying me, but he never came back.

"As I got older, I was requested less and less. She kept me tied in that place when I wasn't being used."

And again, he spoke like all of this was natural.

"You know what she did was wrong, right?"

A wan smile crossed his face. "Even when I was a kid, I knew men weren't supposed to do the things they did to me. But it wasn't just me. She had a bunch of us that she would send out. Most of them I'd see for a few weeks, then never again. That woman, the one you…hurt, she told me that they hadn't listened, so they were sent away."

I needed to make him understand he wasn't safe with me either. He needed to let me get Rook to find him help. "I didn't hurt her, I killed her."

"I know," he whispered. "She deserved it."

"Why do you say that?"

"She did stuff. Really bad stuff. One of the kids I used to see…she said he'd done something wrong. That he was going to be an example of what happened to children who didn't listen. Then she shot him."

He said it so dispassionately.

"His name was Eric, and he was my friend. At least as much as we could be friends. Even after the others were gone, she kept me there. I don't know why."

"Did you ever hear anyone mention the name Valerie?"

Sammy grew agitated. His gaze darted around the room, and his breathing came in heavy pants. I rushed to him and drew him into my side.

"It's okay, I have you."

He sucked in heavy lungsful of air, and fear that he was having a panic attack clutched my heart.

"Breathe with me. Deep breaths in, then out. Do them in time to mine."

Slowly, he matched my pace, calm washing over him, easing his tense muscles.

"Yeah, I've heard of her," he whispered.

"I wouldn't ask, but it's important. What can you tell me about her?"

"Well, for the first eleven years of my life, I called her mother."

A moment of shock, then an insane rage slammed into my heart. I started to stand, but Sammy pulled me back down, and this time, he held me to him. "Let it go. I did. It took me a few years, but once I realized she wasn't coming back for me, I got over it."

No matter what the circumstances, I always tried to project an outward calm. I found it rattled people when they couldn't fluster me. Even when I was seething inside, I had an icy exterior. This time I wanted to tear the room apart, break every piece of furniture, shatter the windows, stalk the halls, and beat every person I saw. Instead, I was being held by someone I had just pulled out of a horrible situation, and heaven help me, I liked it.

"Tell me everything you know," I asked, my voice cracking.

"I can't recall much of it. Everything I know, Arianna told me. I think it amused her to see me cry. When I was eight, Valerie started a new job. She was a secretary for some big shot who she was apparently drawn to. She started working late at night, then sometimes overnight. She'd take long trips and be gone for weeks. It would be me and my father alone, but that was okay. I don't really remember much about her anyway.

"One night, I think I was about ten, she came home all agitated. I could hear loud voices in the kitchen. My dad was shouting at her about having a family, and what did she think she was doing? She told him he could give her everything my father couldn't. The voices continued to rise, and I got scared. I ran and hid in my bedroom.

"She moved out a few days later, leaving us alone. A few weeks before my eleventh birthday, my dad was reading the paper and became upset, but he wouldn't tell me why. He called Valerie and said he knew what she did, and that she wasn't going to get away with it.

"Not long after that, he had an *accident*. A drunk driver ran him down. The police didn't seem to care much about it, and of course they let Valerie take me. Twenty minutes after we were in the car, she was pulling up outside this big building. She took me inside and that was where I met Arianna.

"That was where she gave me up to her."

In my head, I planned Valerie's death about three hundred times before Sammy finished his story. There were so many options for how I was going to kill that woman.

CHAPTER TEN

Sammy wasn't able to fill in many more details. After Valerie abandoned him, Arianna turned him into a prostitute, and he never saw his mother again. He'd gleaned bits and pieces from conversations between Arianna and Amber, but nothing that really added to what we knew. After he finished his dinner, I told him to get some sleep. He didn't argue, instead allowing me to return him to the nest he'd made for himself.

I stepped out of the bedroom and closed the door behind me. Pulling out my phone, I tapped the screen and dialed Kelly. He answered on the first ring with a cheery, "Okay, you're not dead. That's a start."

Instead of laughing, I put him on speaker, praying Sammy was a sound sleeper, and then placed the phone on the table, knowing I'd likely break it if I had it in my hands. After I'd explained what happened and gave him the short version of who Sammy was, I proceeded to tell him what I needed as I paced around the room, trying to rein in my anger.

"Contact Rook. I want a safe house for Sammy. And I need you to find some men's shops in the area and order him some clothes. Right now he's got pretty much nothing. Have them deliver the things to the hotel. And someone needs to pull my stuff from the other room."

"I'm sorry, I didn't know I was your servant," he huffed.

Heat rose in my face. "I apologize. I'm angry. If you had heard what they did to him—"

"I wasn't serious. You've never used your safe room, so I understand the situation. I'll take care of it now. Do you know what size he wears?" A moment of hesitation, then a sigh. "How tall is he?"

"I don't know. Maybe five foot seven or eight. Not too tall. And he's skinny, but there's a bit of muscle tone that hasn't gone away."

"Okay, size medium. Should I even ask about the size of his feet?"

An embarrassed mumble was my only answer. How could I expect Kelly to know what to do, when I wasn't even sure myself?

"I wear a size eleven," came a voice from the doorway. "And why do I need a safe house?"

He was squinting at me, small crinkles in the corners of his eyes gave me the distinct impression I was about to get reamed out by a twig of a young man.

"I have a job to do, and you need to see a doctor and let them take care of you."

His eyes went wide and he began to shiver. "I want *you* to take care of me. Please. Don't make me go. I-I-I can't go out there again. I just can't, not without you. You make me feel safe. I haven't felt like that in so long."

He threw himself into my arms and clung tight. His eyes shimmered with tears and he turned his face up toward me.

"Please, Haven," he whispered. "I want to stay with you. I know I'm only safe with you."

Every instinct told me to extricate myself from his grip and step away, but instead, I put my arms around him, marveling at the way he fit against my body.

"I can't stay here. I need to work, and that means I have to go."

"I'll stay here. I swear I won't move from this room. I'll do anything, just don't make me go back out there." He tucked his head next to my armpit.

Under the circumstances, I could understand his fear of being found again, but I needed to go make sure that didn't happen. I didn't want to tell him why I was leaving, but—

I tucked a knuckle under his chin and lifted until he met my eyes. "Sammy, I have to work tonight. I need someone to watch you. Do you understand?"

"Yes, I know what you're going to do," he answered, his voice strong. "I also know that I can't be out there. Among people. They...hurt me, and looking at them reminds me of it. When Arianna... When I was with her, I used to beg her to let me go, and she laughed. Then she'd bring in some man, and he'd use me. Afterward, she'd come in and remind me that's all I was good for."

"Hey, it's not true. You're good for a lot of things." I hoped he didn't ask me what, because I had no idea. It was amazing how this young man had brought out my instincts to protect him so quickly.

"It's nice that you think so," he replied softly.

"May I make a suggestion?" came the disembodied voice. Holding Sammy in my arms, I'd completely forgotten Kelly on the phone.

"Who's that?" Sammy demanded. I swear I detected more than a hint of jealousy in his voice.

"You can call me Kelly, Sammy."

"Samuel," came the frosty reply. "Only Haven can call me Sammy."

"Very well, then. Haven, I could be to Dallas in about four hours if I can get Rook to pull some strings. I'll bring Dr. McQuade with me, and she can examine Samuel in your absence."

"No!" Sammy shouted. "I don't want to see anyone else."

"Hey," I said gently, cupping his chin. "Kelly is a good man. One of the best you're going to meet. I trust him with my life, and I need you to trust him, too. I know it's hard for you, and I think we all may understand some of the reasons, but I swear Kelly won't hurt you, and I need the doctor to check you out. I've worked with them for years. She's patched me up more than once, and I promise you that they'll only help."

He was quiet for a moment before he nodded.

"Tell Rook I owe him one," I told Kelly before disconnecting the call. I took Sammy by the hand, which caused butterflies to burst into tap dancing in my stomach, and led him to the couch. I sat and patted the seat next to me. He sat gingerly and folded his hands across his lap, looking so prim. He sat quietly for a few moments before he scooted a little closer and took my hand. He gave it a squeeze that I returned.

"Once they get here, I'll go…work. For now, we can just sit and talk. Would that be okay with you?"

His lips quirked into a grin. "Sure. Where do you live?"

"I have a few houses. My main home is in Arizona."

"Is it nice?"

"It's not bad. It's big, kind of empty."

"Tell me about it."

I leaned back and told him about the house, bringing up all the minute details that I could remember. As I talked, I noted that he didn't let go of my hand, instead twining his fingers with mine.

72

"It sounds nice," he murmured. "I've never been to Arizona. Do you think I'll like it?"

The question jolted me. I hadn't considered that he thought he'd be coming with me. "Look, I know you're grateful that I got you out of there, but you can't expect to come with me. I'm not your white knight here."

Now he full out grinned, his teeth surprisingly clean. "I don't look at you as a white knight. I understand that you got me out of there, and I'll always be grateful, but trust me when I say I see something more than the man who rescued me."

His voice held such conviction that it startled me. I looked at him, and I didn't see a victim. He owned what had happened to him. He took it and made it a part of himself. He had a strength of character I rarely saw. But questions still niggled in my mind.

"How do I know you're gay? What's to say this isn't something you're doing because of the life you led?"

He laughed. "When I had been brought to Arianna, she tried to send me on calls to males and females. I...um...couldn't get it up with women. I knew I liked guys from the first time Jeff Blakely kissed me on a dare when we were eleven. He sputtered and spit. Me? I loved it. After the first few, let's call them disappointed customers, she sent me exclusively with men."

He'd surprised me once more. I'd believed Sammy had been damaged. He'd needed protection. But the man before me? He had a depth I didn't know could be there. His strength shone through, and I shuddered at the intensity.

He tilted his head and leaned forward, his lips puckered.

"No," I said flatly.

He drew back and gazed up at me. "You don't want me to kiss you?"

I wasn't the kissing type. Intimacy wasn't a part of my world. You fucked and you moved on. Sammy stood and straddled my legs, his engorged dick jutting obscenely in front of him.

"See, here's the thing. After all these years, I'm good at reading people. I could tell when a guy came in if he was going to be nice to me or if he was going to hurt me. I don't know that you could ever hurt me. I've seen what you do, and I think I know what you are, but I'm willing to bet you won't stop me if I lean in and kiss you."

And he did just that. It wasn't a forceful kiss. It was…sweet. Chaste. Just enough pressure to let me know he was there and that he controlled the kiss. When he pulled away, he smiled at me.

"See? That wasn't so bad, was it?"

I shook my head. I knew what Sammy had been through, but the young man sprawled across me didn't seem to be the one who'd undergone years of abuse because of that bitch, Arianna. This one seemed completely unaffected by the trauma.

"I would think you would be afraid of me," I murmured. "Why aren't you?"

"Honestly? I don't really know. Every man who ever…was with me scared me. You're different, and I know that. With you, I'm not afraid at all. I feel alive for the first time in forever."

Intellectually it made no sense. That kind of trauma didn't just go away, but Sammy didn't appear at all concerned by what he was doing as he leaned forward and pressed his bare chest against me, resting his head against my shoulder.

"I'm still afraid," he whispered. "The thought of going out and being around people scares me to death. I don't want to see anyone but you, because you're the only one I've ever met who didn't frighten me."

I barely contained the snort. No one I'd ever met in my life wasn't at least somewhat afraid of me. Yet the young man who I now held in my arms was completely unaffected by the bubble I'd surrounded myself with that kept others at arm's length. Instead, he snuggled against me and made himself comfortable.

We sat there for what seemed to be a pleasant eternity, Sammy dozing, his head on my shoulder, and me tracing my fingers over the terrycloth robe he wore. I was shocked by how comfortable I was having him in my space. His breath on my neck was warm and sweet, and strange urges filled me. I wanted him protected, but couldn't imagine anyone else doing it. I'd never wanted anything for myself, but for this brief moment, I did.

A knock on the door had Sammy scrambling for the bedroom and slamming the door. I peered through the hole and relief washed over me as I opened to let Kelly in, his arms laden with bags, including my gear, which I stowed in the closet. Dr. Lilah McQuade followed close behind him.

"I had the cab driver stop on the way over. I picked up a few essential items—shirts, socks, pants, underwear, deodorant, toothbrush, toothpaste, a comb, and a handheld video game. Then I stopped at the desk and told them I'd forgotten my room key, and asked if they could let me in. They were very accommodating...Chester."

I grimaced at the name, but gave him a grateful smile. "Thank you. I appreciate it."

"Wait until you see the bill," he said blithely, patting me on the back and noticing my wince. "You got shot again?" he asked incredulously.

"Shut up. It's just a bruise. It'll be fine. The vest did its job, though I think my jacket has had it."

"Let Lilah take a look at it."

"It's fine, Mom. She's here to check on Sammy."

"Where is the young man?" Dr. McQuade asked, rolling her eyes.

"Sammy? Can you come out here, please?" I called.

Silence was the only reply. My palms grew damp as I waited, but after several moments, I went to the door to find it locked.

"Sammy?"

"Are they gone?" he called out, his voice cracking.

"They're not leaving. You need to let them in. You said you trusted me, so I need you to believe me that they're only here to help you."

There were a few moments that I thought about kicking the door down, but eventually he opened it a crack. "You promise they won't hurt me?"

Gone was the seductive young man of a few hours ago, and in his place was the timid person I'd gotten out of that house.

"I swear on my life that they won't hurt you. Please, let them help you."

Kelly handed me a bag that I passed over to Sammy. "Here are some clothes so you don't have to walk around naked.

"And here I thought you liked me naked," Sammy whispered, before taking the things and closing the door again. My face heated at the thought of his nude body pressed against mine, and I found myself wishing Kelly had waited a little longer before showing up.

"Haven? A word?" Kelly said, taking me by the elbow and pulling me to the other side of the room. Dr. McQuade began digging around in the items she'd brought with her as Kelly led me to the other side of the living room. "Are you sure this is a wise idea?"

"He won't go to a safe house," I informed him.

"You know he's at risk being with you, right? As you are with him. I told you, things like this make you sloppy."

"Things like what?" I snapped. "My job is to protect people. Why the hell is my name Haven if not to offer a safe spot for everyone?"

Kelly took my sleeve. "I'm not saying you were wrong for what you did, but will he understand what he's getting into? Our lives aren't meant to be shared with others."

"He's seen what I do," I replied. "He knows I shot Amber."

Kelly sighed and scrubbed a hand over his cheek. "Then I guess he'll be coming with us."

"What? No. Absolutely not."

"He's seen your face. He knows what you do. He could identify you to the authorities. Even though the agency would be in no jeopardy, we would not want to lose a good agent. It's either that, or..."

"Or what?" I snapped. "There have been others who have seen me when I went on assignment. Or did you forget that?"

"No, but those people didn't spend hours sitting with you either. They caught a glimpse of you. This young man has seen too much to allow him to go off—"

"What the hell are you saying?"

"Do you want me to spell it out? Fine. You put him in danger. Knowing what he does, he's a link to you. If Valerie's people were to get hold of him, do you think they wouldn't find out more than you're comfortable with them knowing? Even a safe house isn't secure now. He's become your responsibility."

"I told him that, too," came Sammy's voice. It quivered when he spoke. His eyes were wide and filled with fear, and I wanted to pull him to me again.

Kelly turned and flashed a smile. "It's good to meet you, Samuel. I'm Kelly. This," he said, pointing to Dr. McQuade, "is Lilah. We're associates of Haven and we'd like very much to help you."

"Haven said I could trust you, and I promise I'll try."

Dr. McQuade led Sammy back into the bedroom to begin her examination. I grabbed my case from the closet and began to gather the items I needed to track down Arianna.

~

D r. McQuade was very thorough in her job. She'd seen me often enough that I trusted her with my life, and Sammy's. The organization paid her well and she took her patient privilege very seriously. When I asked her about Sammy, she glared at me.

"You should know better," she chided.

"It's okay. You can tell him," Sammy said quietly.

"Fine. Judging by the coloration in his nails and brittleness of his hair, he's malnourished and at least fifteen pounds underweight. I'm a little concerned about the bug bites. Based on what you told Kelly about the conditions Samuel was kept in, infection is a very real possibility, and that worries me more than anything else right now."

"What about…um…"

"I won't know the *um* until all the test results are back. The initial test came back negative, and Samuel said that the one thing his captors were good about was insisting that condoms be used at all times. That doesn't negate the possibility of some form of sexually transmitted disease, but it does lessen the likelihood significantly. For now, I'm going to give Kelly a prescription for some antibiotics, both oral and cream for the bites. He'll also pick up some multivitamins. It will help bring his levels up to where they should be over the course of a few days…

"That said, I want to encourage you to seek someone for him to talk to about his ordeal."

"I don't *need* to see anyone," Sammy hissed. "I came to terms with what happened to me a long time ago. I won't ever be in that position again, I can tell you that."

"We'll keep it in mind, Lilah," I promised. I checked my watch. "Okay, I have to go. I have an appointment that needs to be crossed off my calendar."

Sammy put his arms around me and stretched up to kiss me on the cheek. "Be careful," he whispered in my ear.

~

A rianna had her offices in the Maxwell building. She'd kept the penthouse suite for the last fifteen years, and with the money she made, she had no problem affording it. There were a few challenges I faced; the lobby was guarded twenty-four hours a day, and so was the reception desk. I stopped and asked for Arianna's office and the demure young lady behind the counter told me I could find her on the sixty-second floor. The whole fucking floor. Maybe if I decided to quit, I could take over the place and call it 'Haven's Hotties.' I chuckled to myself as I moved toward the elevator.

There was no one sitting outside the door when I arrived. A quick glance at my watch made me think that the staff was long gone. I slipped my electronic passkey into the lock at the door and waited a moment while technology did its magic. A few moments later, the door popped open and I strode in like I owned the place.

Rifling through the desk revealed nothing, but the click of a gun to my right brought me up short.

"I gather if you're here, then Amber's position needs to be filled."

"Well, her chest was open, so I think it's a safe bet."

"I admit I wasn't expecting you to show up in my office."

"I admit I wasn't expecting you to be here either, so I guess that's a gotcha on both of us."

"Who the hell are you?" she demanded.

"Chester Mayfield, remember? We met earlier. I came by to find out if you filled my order."

"Cut the bullshit. Who the fuck are you?"

"Do you kiss your mother with that mouth?"

She raised the gun and pointed it toward my face. "I'm willing to bet your Kevlar vest won't stop a bullet to the brain."

"Actually it's graphene, but I think the same principle applies."

She was a cool one, I had to admit. She held the gun rock steady, but she was too close to stop me from kicking her hand and forcing her to twist to avoid dropping it. Before she could steady herself, I had her on the ground, my gun aimed squarely in the middle of her forehead.

"So let's talk about Valerie, shall we?"

"I don't know who you're talking about."

She tried for bravado, but this time her lip quivered and her eyes darted away from me.

"Dumped you, didn't she?"

"No," she snapped. "She wouldn't—" I grinned at her and her eyes went wide. "Fuck you," she snarled.

"Sweetheart, if it wasn't for what I know about you, it would have been a pleasure. I bet you're a wild ride."

Her lip quirked up. "I am. You'll never find anyone who can rock your world the way I can. We could go into my office; there's a nice couch in there. It pulls out into a double bed."

"Funny, you seem more the type to want to be bent over the desk and taken from behind."

"I'm flexible," she replied, stroking her fingers through her hair.

"Maybe after," I told her.

"After what?"

"We find out if you survive."

CHAPTER ELEVEN

Her hazel eyes went wide and her hand dropped to her chest.

"Yeah, I'm here to kill you. You don't have to say it. Life isn't fair, I know. You have things to do. More kids to corrupt. It's just that I have a problem with that."

"I didn't—"

"Please don't insult me by playing innocent. You had Amber set me up, tried to get four douchebags to jump me, then you sent your flunky in to make sure the job was done."

"But Valerie—"

"Dumped you. I'm guessing she knows the heat is on and left you to twist in the wind. And that works for me. She'll hear about your death, and she's going to know I'm coming for her. See, it works for me no matter how you score it."

She tried to move back, the fear on her face marring the pretty features.

"You can't do this."

"Actually I can. I'm kind of like 007, you see. I have a license to kill. But I'm willing to give you a chance. I'll give you a thirty second head start. You get away from me, I'll walk away and let you live."

"How do I know you're telling the truth?"

I frowned at her. "Does this look like a face that would lie? You know the building inside and out. Getting away shouldn't be any trouble at all. Get up and put your cell phone and the gun on the floor."

She dropped the items, then stood rather shakily. I kicked them several feet away, then bent over to retrieve what she'd left behind. I stole a glance at my watch before I gave her the sweetest smile I could muster. "Your thirty seconds starts now."

Her eyes went wide and she rushed out of the office. I counted to thirty—by tens—then went after her. I saw the door to the elevator close and moved toward it. Then stopped. That was too easy. Arianna wasn't stupid, and she didn't get where she was by playing the fool. My guess was that she'd called it, but knew it wouldn't get there in time to save her.

I glanced at the door leading to the stairs and hurried that way. As I opened it, I could hear footsteps and heavy breathing leading up, so I followed them. The roof door was locked, and there was no one there, so I gathered she had a key. Kicking it open was a possibility, but I wanted to avoid unnecessary noise. I picked the lock, a cheap thing that wouldn't hold up to a baby. Well, a baby with a bit of skill.

The roof was set up as an oasis in the city. Overhead panels covered a large area, tables and chairs placed throughout. Potted palms even swayed in the warm night air. There were plenty of places someone could hide here. I took one of the chairs and jammed it under the door, ensuring that Arianna couldn't get away without me knowing it.

"You know, if you had hit the stairs down instead of coming up, you probably would have gotten away. Nah, who am I kidding? You wouldn't have made it. You might have the survival instinct, but I have the skill. I promise you that tonight you're going to regret what you've done to the kids. To the parents who loved them."

"Why are you doing this?" she screamed.

I turned in the direction of her voice. "Death comes to all men," I called out. "I'm just moving the clock ahead a little."

Like a rabbit trying to flee a fox, she ran, but there was nowhere to go. I continued to stalk her, forcing her toward the edge of the roof. When she could go no farther, I still advanced. She picked up a discarded can and hurled it at me, but it was easily batted away. She tried to climb the ledge, but it was precarious at best.

"Please, don't do this. I'll give you anything you want."

"You don't have anything I would ever need," I replied, moving right up next to her. She tried to move away again, but this time succeeded in tumbling over the edge of the roof. She was damn lucky I grabbed her. Balanced sixty-two stories in the air was enough to make most anyone find their version of God.

"Please, please, please. I'm sorry. I'll make it right, I swear. I'll tell you everything I know about Valerie. I'll give you anything you want. Please, don't let me fall."

I gripped her wrist and she relaxed a smidgen.

"Thank you," she cried. "Thank you so much."

"For what?"

"Saving me. Pull me up, please."

I glared down at her and all I could see was Sammy, huddled in the corner of the shelter, reeking of his own excrement, afraid of everything...but me. The trust in his eyes when we were at the hotel room gave me the strength to do what had to be done.

"You have that wrong. Do you know the young man you left in that house where you jumped me? Samuel? He's with me now, and he told me a lot of interesting things about you and his mother. See, I'm the kind of guy who believes that the punishment should fit the crime. Now obviously I can't turn you into a prostitute. But Sammy said something to me tonight that made me think, and the more I pondered it, the more I realized how appropriate this all was."

"What do you mean?"

The fear in her voice caused my pulse to race. I think it was dawning on her that she was about to breathe her last.

"Please don't do this."

"Sammy said he begged you to let him go, and you laughed at him. I'm going to do for you what you never did for him."

And I let her go. Sixty-two stories straight down. I think her scream cut off somewhere around the fortieth floor. Then I turned away from the roof and forced myself not to throw up as I texted Rook to let him know we'd need a cleanup crew on the street below.

~

I marveled every time I saw what Rook was able to accomplish. When I got off the elevator from the offices, I found the security staff was outside trying to control the chaos, and the young lady at the counter came running in from the street and headed into the bathroom.

It had only taken a few minutes for me to reach the lobby, and by that time, Rook had his people swarming the streets, moving bystanders away from the scene and setting up a situation that would explain Arianna's death. My job was done, and sticking around was a bad idea. I happened to see Arianna's body as I walked by. At least what was left of it. She'd landed on top of a Cayman green Ford Escort, shattering the windows when she crushed the roof.

None of Rook's people made eye contact with me, instead interacting with the police, rescue squads, and the like. They knew the risks of drawing attention to me, and after so many ops together, always had an exit available. They scurried around like ants, ensuring they eradicated any potential link to the organization. Some had entered the building, where they'd remove or plant important information using her computer before they'd allow the police to have access. Their federal government badges would keep anyone from asking questions, and by the time the cops were allowed inside, there wouldn't be anything beyond what Rook wanted them to find.

I took a cab back to the hotel, where Kelly had my bags packed. He'd tried to pick up a ticket for Sammy, but a lack of identification proved to be a problem that couldn't be solved with one phone call.

"You'll be driving back to Arizona," he informed me.

"What the hell?" I growled.

"Rook said he can get Samuel some ID, but it will take time that we don't have. I had a car dropped off at the hotel, so we won't have to worry about that."

Sammy sat on the couch, his eyes down. "I'm sorry," he muttered.

I strode over to him and scooped him into my arms. "Not your fault. It's fine. We'll have a nice trip, and you can see some of the sights. For now, why don't you go ahead and make sure you have all your things."

His demeanor brightened considerably, and he scrambled toward the bedroom, which gave me a few moments to have a conversation with Kelly.

"You and Lilah go ahead and fly back," I told him. "No sense in all of us making that trip."

He smiled and clapped me on the shoulder. "I didn't say *we* would be driving back. Lilah's already heading for the airport, and I stayed to keep an eye on Samuel. Now that you're here, I'm gone, too."

"Bastard."

"Bastard who is flying first class," he teased.

I glanced over my shoulder to ensure Sammy hadn't returned before I asked the question I needed answered. "What about Arianna?"

"The investigators will find she was skimming money from the company to pay off some bad investments. It will look as though a noose was closing around her neck. They'll question her boss, Valerie, and how can she deny it without allowing scrutiny into her own dealings?"

"I'm glad Rook is on our side," I muttered in total awe of the man's capabilities.

Kelly picked up a few bags and walked to the door, then stopped. "Samuel's a good kid," he said softly. "I don't know what they did to him, but he's goddamn strong. I mentioned it to him and he told me that he gets his strength from you. He's got it bad for you."

"Because I got him away from that bitch," I spat.

"Maybe. Maybe not. When you were here, the young man I saw had been strong, belligerent. Yes, he's nervous around people he doesn't know, but after what you told me, who can blame him? When you walked out of the door, it was like someone had turned the power off. He was listless and nervous, kept asking when you'd be back. Lilah had mentioned giving him a sedative, but he went back into the bedroom and closed the door. He's not a victim. Okay, wait. He is. But he's not letting it run his life. He is, however, drawing strength from you. After so many years, he needs someone he can depend on."

That had been how I saw it, too, but overall it changed nothing. "It's been a few hours. As soon as the fear subsides, I'm sure he'll be ready to move on."

"When I met my first girlfriend, I knew it was love within the first fifteen minutes," he said with a wistful sigh. "She was perfect. Long brown hair, eyes like chocolate milk, and a laugh like tinkling glass."

"She sounds great," I told him. "Did you marry her?"

He snorted. "We were six. I fell out of love when she pushed me down on the playground. What I'm telling you is that feelings don't subscribe to a timetable. Will he still feel the same way in a week? A month? A year? Who knows? For now, though, be mindful of the fact he worships you. Don't hurt him, or I'll kick your ass."

I glared at the man. He'd told me we didn't have relationships like other people, and yet here he stood, pushing Sammy at me. "You said things like this could never work out."

84

"I'm allowed to be wrong once in a while," he said, pulling the door handle. "Look, all I'm saying is if an opportunity for happiness presents itself, you should grab it tight. My flight leaves in two hours, so I need to get a move on. See you soon." With that, Kelly headed for home.

A few minutes later, Sammy came bounding from the bedroom like a puppy on crack, his game unit gripped firmly in his hand.

"I'm ready," he informed me, bouncing with unbridled enthusiasm.

"Do you have your things?"

"Your friend said he'd take everything back to our house."

That one brought me up short. "Sammy, this is only temporary. When the situation calms down, we'll find you a more permanent place to live."

He grinned enigmatically, but said nothing. And that worried me.

We hauled my things down to the lobby. I'd traveled light, but that still required several suitcases to ward off suspicion. Sammy pasted himself to my side, which made it very difficult to walk, but if I so much as attempted to take a step away, his breathing increased and he made little squeaking noises, until he was once again touching me.

The *car*, for lack of a better word, was crap. It had to have been Kelly's idea of a joke. A lime green Chevy Spark, for God's sake. I'd be scrunched in the goddamn seat all the way back to Arizona. And it was barely enough space for me, but I had to fit Sammy and the luggage in, too. I glanced down at him, and he had a grin that had to be five miles wide on his slender face.

"We're really going to be driving in that? It's so great."

I bit my tongue to avoid saying anything to the contrary. After I got Sammy situated and stuffed the bags in any open spot they'd fit, I climbed into the driver's seat. Sammy touched everything—the dashboard, the steering wheel, running his hands over the fabric of the seats.

"I can't remember the last time I went anywhere," he whispered. "At least not somewhere that I wasn't going to *entertain*. Can we drive slow? I don't want to miss anything."

His voice broke my heart and lessened any regret I had over killing Arianna. No one should be treated the way Sammy was, and when I finally went after Valerie, my revenge would be for him and his lost childhood.

I put the car in gear and pulled out of the lot. Sammy's excitement was something to behold. He pointed at everything, asking what it was, wanting to know the minutest details. I began to enjoy myself as I saw the world through his eyes, which despite what happened, were filled with wonder and innocence.

We'd driven maybe five hours, when I heard soft snores coming from the passenger seat. Sammy had somehow brought his legs up and tucked them underneath him, almost rolling himself into a ball. My back ached looking at him, but he seemed surprisingly comfortable. When his stomach growled loud enough that I heard it, I pulled over to a restaurant and went inside to get us some food.

As I waited in line, a trucker came in and asked if anyone was with the young kid in the green car outside. I told him I was. He leaned over and whispered in my ear, "You might want to get out there. I think he's having a seizure or something."

I ran out the doors to find Sammy frozen in his seat, his head thrown back, eyes squeezed shut, screaming my name at the top of his lungs. I ripped open the door, and he tumbled out into my arms, clawing at my chest hard enough that it hurt.

"Haven! Haven!"

"Hey, I'm here. It's okay, you're safe. I'm sorry. I went to get us some food."

"Don't leave me alone. Please don't. I'll be good, I promise," he begged, withdrawing from me, his eyes brimming with tears.

I dropped to my knees and held my arms out. He pushed out of the car and leapt at me, knocking us both to the ground.

"I'm sorry, I didn't think. I won't do it again," I told him, squeezing him tight, and rubbing light circles on his back. "If I have to go, I will always tell you where I'll be, okay?"

"Promise me you'll never go away again," he whimpered.

"You know I can't make that promise. I have a job to do, and it requires that I might be gone, sometimes for a long while. This is why I want to find you somewhere you'll be safe."

He purred as he nestled against me. "I'll never be safer anywhere other than here," he informed me. "Get used to it, because you're stuck with me."

Kelly's comment about Sammy getting his strength from me was just talk. Sammy didn't know me. He knew nothing about who I was, but I got the distinct impression he saw me better than anyone ever had.

I helped him back into the car and told him I'd be back in a few minutes after I got some food. With a shy smile, he asked if he could have another shake. They didn't have it on the menu, but twenty bucks to the kid behind the counter, and it suddenly appeared in front of me, along with onion rings, mozzarella sticks, two burgers, and some hot apple pies.

Sammy dug in with gusto. Everything he sampled came with a moan of delight as he licked his fingers, then his lips, chasing every last crumb.

"I remember some of these things," he told me. "My dad would take me out to eat on special occasions. We didn't have a lot of money, and he wasn't home much after…well, after she left. He worked two jobs to support us. He was an amazing man. When people used to ask me what I wanted to be when I grew up, I always told them I wanted to be my dad."

A scab on my heart was torn off with his story. I never knew my father. He could have been any number of drunken fucks my mother engaged in. I used to pretend he was someone important, and that his job took him away, and that was why he didn't come for me. Eventually I outgrew the fantasy and learned to live in the real world. Sammy was similar to me in a lot of respects, but the time would soon come where he'd have to understand that the fantasy he was building couldn't include me.

~

We stopped for the night at a small motel. The room was clean, if not tacky. The plastic sheets on the bed threw me for a loop, but I guessed it was better than bedbugs. Sammy quirked an eyebrow when I parked the car outside the door and walked with him to the room.

"Two beds?" he questioned.

"Yes, one for me, one for you."

"We could have shared, you know."

I closed the door behind us and turned to him. "I don't know what you think this"—I gestured between us—"is, but I assure you it's nothing like what you might be thinking. I don't have any interest in you like that."

Liar.

87

"Please. You think I can't keep my hands to myself?" he asked, stepping closer and running those same hands over my chest.

I gripped his wrists and gently pushed him back.

"Apparently not," I replied.

"Why? Do you think you're too old for me? I'm almost twenty-four."

I wanted to tell him I'd fucked men younger at the club, but his pout was disarming to say the least.

"No, it's nothing like that. I'm not going to take advantage of our situation. It would be wrong for me to have sex with you because you feel grateful to me."

He laughed, a bitter sound. "You talk like I don't know my own mind. Gratitude has nothing to do with it. I want you because…well, because I want you." He gave me that Cheshire cat grin again. "And believe me, I'm going to have you. Maybe not today, or tomorrow, but soon. And often. You can count on that."

With the heated gaze he ran over my body, my dick jumped up, suddenly very interested in the conversation. This young man was going to be the death of me.

CHAPTER TWELVE

I seldom fell into a deep sleep. The phrase sleep with one eye open was one I'd lived with for the last twelve years or so. It had to be close to one in the morning when I heard the crinkle of the plastic sheet on Sammy's bed, then felt the dip on mine as he crawled in next to me. I was ready to jump up and send him back to his own bed, but he startled me when he wrapped an arm around my chest and snuggled in, quickly falling back to sleep. It was warm and oddly comfortable, so I let him stay where he was.

The next time I looked, it was after eight, and I was lying on my side, Sammy spooned behind me, his arm wrapped around my stomach. His breath was warm on the back of my neck, and his morning wood poked me in the back. I tried to pull away, but there was only so much room on the bed. When I made to get up, he sternly said, "Stay," and I melted back onto the bed and relaxed in his embrace.

It had been twenty-four hours, and somehow Sammy had turned my world upside down. He'd kissed me and made me like it. Now, he held me tight in his embrace, and though I knew I shouldn't be here, I couldn't think of anywhere else I'd rather be. He moved in a little closer, pasting himself against my back, and stroked his fingers across my chest, tickling the hairs. It was…different. I found this level of intimacy to be totally alien to me, but it somehow felt right with Sammy.

We lay there for another hour or so, me completely awake and him dozing, but never releasing his hold on me. When he shifted and sat up, I was waiting for him to make excuses about why he'd come over to my bed and how he was sorry.

"See, I told you we could have shared one," he said, smiling like the cat who'd gotten the cream.

"You know you shouldn't have done that."

"You're at least four inches taller than me, and outweigh me by maybe eighty pounds. I think you could have moved away if you'd really wanted to. But you didn't, did you?"

I couldn't look at him. My body heated in an all-over flush as anxiety washed through me. I could have moved, but didn't. I wasn't sure why. Sammy lay back down and put his arm over me.

"Do you see how we fit? Like we were meant to be? There's a reason for that, you know."

"Oh?" I said, as cocky as I could, even though I didn't feel it. He was right; he did fit next to me in a way no one ever had.

"You can deny it all you want, and I'm going to keep proving you wrong. You need me every bit as much as I need you. I think we complete one another."

"You don't know anything about me," I snapped, instantly regretting raising my voice.

"I know you're lonely. You live alone in a big house and you do a job that weighs on you, but let me tell you something. You're a good man."

That comment brought out a snort so loud, I'd be surprised if the neighbors hadn't heard it.

"You are. I don't know the why about how you got involved in your...line of work, but I could tell after you came back yesterday it hurts you. Let me ask you a question. Last night, when I was in the bed with you and holding you, what were you thinking about?"

A thousand things filled my head. Any one of them would have been a better answer than what I told him. "You."

"And that's what you need to focus on. You'll do what you have to, and then you'll come home to me, and I will hold together those pieces you think you're going to lose."

"I can't do this," I argued, trying to sit up, but he held me in place. "Being with me could put you in danger."

"I'm not Mary Jane," he said gleefully.

"Who?"

"Mary Jane Watson? Spider-man? He always told her that they couldn't be together because she'd be targeted by his enemies. This is real life, and I'm in danger everywhere I go. I could be hit by a car, fall out of an airplane, eat

90

something and have an allergic reaction that kills me. But through it all? The one thing I know with absolute certainty is that a life without you in it isn't worth living."

"I can't love anyone," I whispered.

"No, of course you can't. Love makes you weak, right? Knowing that after going out and doing your job, having someone to come home to, someone who understands you, won't judge you, and loves you without hesitation would be awful, wouldn't it?"

"We don't know each other well enough to declare love," I said, this time more certain of what I was saying.

"I don't deny that. Love takes time to build, but if you push me away, then you're wasting that time. Your head is so full of what-if, can't be happy, have to be alone, that you're cutting yourself off from the possibility. Have you always pushed people away who tried to get to know you?"

"I don't push people away," I growled.

"So you have tons of friends, right? People who know what you do for a living? Or do you show them a mask?"

That made me angry. I pushed off the bed and spun to face him.

"What the hell do you know about me? Nothing. You can't know a fucking thing, because…because you've been held captive for almost twelve years."

"It doesn't make me stupid. I told you, not everyone who I was sent to hurt me. Some were just lonely men who wanted someone to talk to. There was a guy who I got sent to several times a year. He said his name was Tim. He never touched me, just asked me to stay with him for the night. He'd tell me stories about his time in the Navy, about how his family didn't know he was gay, and he could never tell them, the fact he got married and his wife died, and he could never fall in love again.

"And that's the kind of loneliness I feel from you. All-encompassing, like something weighing you down."

"Fine. I'll take you to Tim. Where does he live?"

Sammy's smile faded a bit. "He's the one who said he was going to buy my contract and never came back. I don't know what happened to him. Maybe it was another one of Arianna's games to break me, to show me I wasn't worth love. She's wrong, though. Everyone deserves it, even stubborn men who don't think they need it."

I stood stock-still, breathing heavily. He brightened and crooked a finger. "Come here," he said quietly.

I took a step toward the bed, then two. I couldn't resist. When he patted the bed, I lay down beside him again and he pulled me back into an embrace.

"Tell me how this feels to you."

I was at a loss. In all my years I could count on one hand the number of times someone had held me and I'd still have five fingers left.

"Talk to me," he insisted.

"I can't," I said with as much force as I could muster.

"We're not leaving this bed until you do."

I couldn't see his face, but I knew the son of a bitch was grinning.

"You like it. Just admit it. You enjoy being held and not having to think about anything else. Back at the hotel, when I was on your lap, I could see in your eyes how much you wanted this. I don't know that I've ever met someone as stubborn as you, though."

He reached farther up my chest and tweaked my nipple, causing sparks to zing through my body.

"Hey, check it out. Goose bumps. I guess you liked that," he chattered happily.

"No, I didn't."

Even to my own ears it sounded like a lie. Of course Sammy would pick up on it.

"You probably won't believe me, but I'm a patient person. It's one of the skills I learned while being locked in a room waiting to be brought out for someone. I'm not going to push you on this little fabrication of yours, but I want you to know that I realize it's going to be in the back of your head. One day, probably sooner than either of us think, you'll realize how badly you need me."

He was smug and wrong. I never needed anyone. I went in, did my job, then got out. I had a decent life, and I had Kelly who was kind of a friend. I glared at Sammy, wanting to tell him how wrong he was, but he lay there, his head resting on his hand, and smiled at me.

"It's okay to want something, you know. Everyone does. For twelve years I wanted my freedom, but now that brought you to me, so I have to ask myself if it was worth it. I won't lie. I would rather have been like everyone else, living a normal life, but we play the hand we're dealt, and after meeting you, I'd say I hold the best one."

"How do you know all this stuff? For someone who was locked away for years, you know way more than you should."

He sat up, his pale skin dotted with freckles. I could see where the bones in his shoulders protruded, could count his ribs, but his smile made him the most beautiful person I'd ever seen.

"I went to school until I was given to Arianna. Even then, she provided newspapers and a modicum of lessons. There weren't too many calls for drooling idiots, and I was expected to be able to talk to people, so I needed to be smart. And I learned things from Tim. He taught me to play chess, which I never got the hang of. We snuggled on the couch and watched movies on occasion.

"But there were rules even when I was with him. No going out of the house. Arianna told him she'd have people watching, and if he didn't follow the rules, there would be no more visits. One night, the night he told me he was going to talk to Arianna about buying me, we snuck out and played mini-golf. Have you ever played it? It was my eighteenth birthday, and I begged him to take me out and do something I'd never done before.

"I think she did have people watching, and that was what kept us apart after that. She didn't want me thinking I'd ever get away from her, and that was what Tim represented. Freedom. Thing was, I didn't love Tim. I liked him, a lot, but there was no spark there. Still, he was a good friend, and he made me feel human, even if he was *renting* my time."

I made a mental note to see if I could find this man. If he tried to get Sammy away, there was no way that Arianna left him alive where he could go to the cops. This would be another one I'd owe Valerie for Sammy.

"We should get going," I murmured, avoiding his gaze. "We still have a long way to go. We can shower and get dressed, then head out and pick up something to eat along the way. Go ahead and shower, I'll grab some clothes from the car. You'll have to make do with something of mine." It dawned on me then. Kelly had purposely taken Sammy's things, probably with the intention of forcing me to deal with the situation. That would be another one I owed him for.

"Yes, because the stuff you wear will fit me. I showered yesterday, so I should be okay for now. You go ahead, though." Then in a teasing whisper, he added, "If you want, I'll scrub your back, or, you know, anywhere you want."

His chuckle followed me as I opened the door and stalked the few feet to the car, where I moved the luggage to grab some clean clothes. Of course, the only suitcase that had anything in it was buried at the bottom of the pile. I picked out what I needed, then went back to the room where Sammy sat, his grin still wide and annoying as fuck. I ignored him as best I could, then put the clean clothes on the bed.

"So that's a no to joining you, huh?" He waggled his eyebrows, and I had to bite the inside of my cheek to keep from laughing.

"It's definitely a no," I answered. I stepped into the bathroom and closed the door, locking it behind me. I heard Sammy's voice hitch. "Please, leave the door unlocked. I promise I won't come in, but... Please?"

I pushed the button again, unlocking the door, and heard the whispered thanks. When the door jiggled, but didn't open, I could only assume he slid down and sat outside of it. I heard a heavy sigh, then turned the water on, hot as it would go, before I stepped into the shower. The water was tepid at best, but having it sluice down my body as the soap rinsed away always went a long way to relaxing me after an assignment...until today.

Knowing that Sammy was outside the door made me uncomfortable. Not in the way that he might see me naked, but more in the way he'd attached himself to me. It wasn't healthy, and I had to make him see that. Once I was finished with Valerie, he would have a life he could get to. Rook would set him up with a new identity, I was certain.

The towels were scratchy as hell, in part, I assumed, to keep people from wanting to steal them. I finished drying and wrapped the towel around my hips, then opened the door.

"Hey, nice view from down here."

It took a lot to startle me, but the little shit did it. He was laid out on the floor, looking up my towel. I refused to let him know he'd rattled me, and went to the bed and grabbed my clothes, then purposely dropped the towel and spun around.

"Take a good look," I told him. "This is the last time you're going to see it."

He was practically drooling as he eyed me. His gaze wandered down to my crotch and he smiled. "It's like an all-you-can-eat special. I just don't know where to start."

I stepped into my pants and hiked them up to my hips. "How about you start by getting ready to go."

"I'm not in a hurry. I could enjoy the view all day."

A thought struck me. "Is this how they taught you to talk to men? Do you think this is what turns them on? This isn't a porno, Sammy."

He got up off the floor, stepped in close and ran his fingers over my chest, plucking at the hairs.

"Of course not. If it were a porno, we'd already be ready for some action. I told you, I'm patient. I'll wait until the time is right, but that doesn't mean I'm going to let you forget I'm watching."

"Is this how you behaved with other men?" I dreaded the answer, though I wasn't really sure why.

"You don't need to worry. When I was sent to be with someone, I usually kept my mouth shut and did what I was told. In rare instances, like with Tim, I got to talk about things going on in the world. I didn't miss out on as much as you might think."

I put my hand up and grabbed his long hair. "Yes, because this is a look you chose for yourself, right?"

I let go, but he caught my hand and held it to his head. "Feel it," he instructed me.

It was shiny, soft, and silky. I found myself stroking it gently, enjoying the feel as it slid through my fingers. Realization struck and I yanked my hand away.

"I'd like a haircut," he announced. "I want to look… I want to look like someone other than the person I was. Does that make sense?"

I nodded. "If you want, we can stop at a barber along the way."

"No," he said quickly. "I want you to do it."

"I don't know how to cut hair."

"Oh, how hard can it be? Let's try it."

I wanted to refuse, I *should* have refused, but I agreed. I borrowed a pair of scissors from the office and went back to our room. Sammy sat in the chair, a towel draped around his neck. The trust he showed was remarkable. The haircut much less so. When I finished, there was a pile of hair on the floor, and clumps of various lengths attached to his scalp.

"Well," he said, grinning as he looked at himself in the mirror, "I said I wanted to look different. I can say this definitely qualifies."

"I told you I didn't know how to cut hair," I shouted. "Why didn't you listen to me?"

"Because this was a lesson for you."

"For *me?*" I gasped.

"I wanted you to know that I trust you. Even when I know it's going to go bad, I know you'll do the best you can for me."

Words escaped me at that moment. I looked down at him, his eyes wide and shining with something I couldn't identify. People didn't trust me, unless it was to send me out on an assignment. Maybe it was possible he had the wrong idea about my line of work.

"Sammy, what do you think I do?"

"I think you protect people like me," he said simply.

"I'm not a good man, you know."

He cocked his head. "Why do you think that?"

I sat at the edge of the bed, trying to find the words that would make him understand why he shouldn't get attached to me.

"I can't tell you everything, but the people I work for? They send me out to find people who are beyond the reach of the law. Their solution is to put them down permanently."

He sat staring, an earnest expression on his face. "Okay."

"Okay?"

"Half my life was lived as someone's property. I saw you kill Amber, and I told you she deserved it. I know the world isn't a good place, and people like you are needed to separate Amber, Arianna, and Valerie from people like me. You're our safety zone. I do understand, and it's important that you do the job, because not everyone can be strong."

Though I'd never tell him, my heart swelled, and I thought I might have fallen in love with him just a little.

CHAPTER THIRTEEN

The remainder of the drive home was spent watching Sammy's eyes widen as we drove through New Mexico, with some of the most beautiful natural flora you'd ever see. Brilliant hues burst everywhere we looked, and Sammy's head bounced like he was watching a tennis match, trying to take it all in.

"It's so beautiful," he said, his voice filled with awe. "I've never been out of Dallas, and you don't see things like this in the city."

"If I hadn't built the house in Arizona, I would have gotten one in New Mexico. I still might. It's one of my favorite states."

"Where do we have houses?"

Again with the *we* stuff. When the time came for Sammy to move on, I hoped that he'd finally understand it was for the best.

"The main house is in Arizona. I have other places, but they're mostly small houses I can stay at when I'm in the area. There are places in Boca Raton, San Francisco, Chicago, and Hawaii. I pay people to do the upkeep for me, so the places look lived in. I haven't been to the ones in San Francisco or Hawaii in five or six years."

"Could we go one day? To any of them. I think it would be incredible to be able to visit them."

"Sammy—"

"Sorry, I said I wouldn't push. So can I ask you a question?"

"Yeah, sure."

"Is Haven your real name?"

I paused. Beyond Rook and Kelly no one knew my name. It was meant to be a secret because the less people knew, the more unlikely they'd come after me. But Sammy had shown me a level of trust I'd never known before. I opened my mouth to answer him, then closed it. This was my most closely guarded bit of information.

"No," I finally answered. "It's—"

"Stop," he blurted out. "I was wondering if it was your name. I don't think you're ready to share yet. When you're completely comfortable with us, then we'll share secrets."

I glanced over at a bright smile. He was so full of life, despite everything that happened to him, while I was afraid to open up just a little and let his light in. I didn't want him to see the ugly that was inside me. Yes, he'd seen me kill, but it was a quick, clean thing. When he found out the things I'd done in the past, and those I would undoubtedly do again, he'd come to fear me and see me as a monster, and for some reason I didn't want that look he had whenever he saw me to fade.

Sammy leaned and put his head on my shoulder, sighing. "You know, I never thought I'd actually live to see the outside again. I expected Arianna would use me until no one requested me anymore, or until she needed another target for her *lessons*. I fully expected I was going to die when she had me, and no one would even remember me.

"Then you came in, larger than life—literally—and turned everything inside out. I know you think it's about appreciation, and I really do appreciate you, but there's more to this. I can't explain it so you'll understand it, because it barely makes sense to me. When you knelt down by me, you radiated such kindness. I admit your smile needed a bit of work, because I can see you don't use it often, but from the moment I saw you, I knew I was safe for the first time I could remember.

"And it wasn't just my body. My heart was safe, because I knew you'd never hurt it. I can't explain it any better than that. I know you don't feel it like I do, and that's okay for now. But I know that one day you'll see the same thing. When you give me your heart, I'll hold it next to mine where it will always be safe."

That same heart he spoke about was hammering at my chest, aching for what he offered. As much as I told myself that it would never work out with Sammy, I wanted it badly. To feel normal, finally, after all these years. To know love in all its glory. He had them all and was offering them up on a silver platter, but I couldn't take that step and stayed quiet.

~

It was late by the time I pulled into the garage. Sammy had been asleep for a couple of hours, nestled into my side, an arm threaded around me.

I should have nudged him over, but he wasn't in my way, so I let him stay where he was. The door to the carport opened and Kelly came out to help with my things even though he should have been home asleep by that point.

"He looks so innocent," he whispered to me. "Except, what the hell happened to his hair?"

"That's because he is innocent," I replied. "As for the hair, don't ask. Just tell me you can fix it."

He gave me a look that screamed 'duh.' "Where should I put him?"

I had to think. Any of the rooms would work, and there were enough of them available. "Put him in the room next to mine. That way I'm close if he needs something."

"Well, I lost that bet with Lilah."

"What bet?" I demanded.

"I said by the time you got home, you'd want him in your bed with you. She said no."

"What the fuck? Why would you think that?"

He rolled his eyes. "For someone who is known for seeing the smallest detail, you're pretty damned blind about this. He adores you, and he won't want to be away from you."

"And? I'm not taking him to bed."

"So you say. I'll make *you* a bet. Fifty dollars says that, before the end of the night, you'll find him in your bed."

Remembering the night at the hotel, it was a bet I wasn't willing to take. I wanted Sammy to be comfortable, and my bed was certainly big enough for two. Just because we slept in the same room didn't mean anything would happen between us.

"Fine. He can sleep in my bed, but only until he feels comfortable sleeping alone."

"Right. That's going to happen. I think you should be the one to take him in. He's anxious with everyone else. By the way, Lilah called back. He needs to put on at least thirty pounds to be at a good weight. I've filled the prescriptions for his antibiotics. I also picked up some multivitamins. She wants him to take the pills every day and get out in the sun. She also said he's clean of any diseases, but she wants to retest him regularly. All things considered, it could have been worse than it is. He's quite the man, Haven. I'm not sure you'll find better."

"Are you *trying* to get me together with him?"

He stepped closer and put a hand on my shoulder. "You've known me for a lot of years, and I'm not given to flights of fancy. You can deny it all you want, but you're already together with him. I've seen some of the guys you've brought home with you, and Samuel is different from any of them. And you're not the same with him either. Those were bodies to you, a means to a release. Samuel is a person, one I think you want to keep."

"I don't want to keep anyone," I said, not sounding convincing even to myself.

I shook him, but Sammy didn't wake up. He simply curled up tighter until I lifted him off the seat. Then he wrapped his arms around my neck and relaxed into my embrace.

"We're home," I whispered.

"I know where home is," he mumbled sleepily. "It's in your arms."

~

I explained to Rook that I would be taking several weeks off before I went after my next target. He agreed it was a wise decision, especially considering Valerie definitely knew she was targeted by now. He also agreed that my priority at the moment should be helping Sammy.

He blossomed before my eyes every day. After a healthy breakfast, we'd go work out. Tai chi to limber himself, weights for muscle, and floor exercises for stamina. His body transformed slowly. He wasn't frighteningly skinny anymore. Instead, he was lithe and moved with a kind of grace that I envied. It wasn't all roses and rainbows, though.

Sammy would go sit out at the koi pond, dipping his toe in the water, and be fascinated by the fish. The bright sun gave his skin a healthier glow, though I had to remind him often he needed to wear sunblock. The only sticking point was his fear of other people. Even Kelly, who he saw every day, had him inching closer to me.

"You know Kelly won't hurt you," I reminded him often.

"I try to tell myself that, really. When you're here, it isn't so bad, but if I can't see you, I get nervous. I try to tell myself everything is okay, but my body wants to bolt."

"I'm here. Don't worry about it. And if I'm not, I swear to you that Kelly will protect you with his life."

I gave him credit for trying. He bluffed his way through conversations with Kelly, even as he kept me in line of sight at all times. Even though it was incremental, he began to relax a little around Kelly. When he was certain I wasn't going anywhere, he explored the house. He found the room with the game systems and was enthralled with them. When he was a kid, *Legend of Zelda* was high on his list. Now the game graphics were much better, and he loved watching the cut scene movies. He grew bored quickly, though, preferring to stay near me.

At night, we'd go into my room, and he'd build himself a fort out of the blankets, saying he felt safe there. As the evening wore on, his walls would fall and he'd move in closer to me. I tried to move away at first, but finally decided that he was only seeking comfort, and it wasn't as if I didn't enjoy the sensations, too.

True to his word, he never pushed me. Many times I found myself almost wishing he would, because that would have made things easier. I would put up a token resistance, then succumb to him, allowing him to suck me or to throw his legs up around his ears while I took him. That was fantasy, though. The reality was I wanted to snuggle with him. I realized I had something in common with the fish in our pond. I'd grown accustomed to his touches, a brush of his fingertips against mine, his slender arms wrapped around my waist, the feel of his breath as it ghosted over my neck.

There was little doubt in my mind, I had become addicted to Sammy. I found myself looking for ways to get him to touch me, because it seemed to ground me in the here and now. He never disappointed either.

We were in our fifth week when Kelly came outside and whispered to me that Rook was calling. I got up and started for the house, Sammy close on my heels, and went to our war room. "You'll have to stay out here," I told him. "This is business."

"I understand. I'll make you some dinner."

I grimaced. Sammy's cooking skills were definitely lacking, but it brought him such joy when I ate what he'd made that I didn't want to disappoint him, even if Kelly's soup would have been tastier.

He turned and hurried back up the stairs. "When are you going to stop playing around and tell him?"

I gave Kelly my attention, noting the expression of happiness. "Tell him what?"

"You love him."

"Bullshit," I snapped. "I have a job to do. I don't have time for love."

"Everyone has the time. And time is something we all have so little of. You could die tomorrow without ever telling him."

"Rook is waiting," I reminded him.

Kelly put his hand on my arm. "Don't wait too long. Things don't always go like we plan."

I shrugged him off and keyed into the war room. I hadn't even gotten inside the door when Darth started in.

"Haven, I need you ready to go immediately. There won't be a lot of time for briefing, but I'll give you the basics."

I was gobsmacked. Rook never sent me on a mission without giving me all the information I'd need.

"A source has informed me that they just found a mass grave of young girls, ranging in age from six to twelve. There hasn't been an official autopsy yet, but it appears as though they were brutally beaten and their bodies dumped in a quarry. There were dozens of them, some estimated to have been there for years.

"The suspect is Eric DeMarco, a businessman who runs a delivery company. We have reason to believe he's in Valerie's pocket and is her link to child slavery markets in the poorest areas of Asia, Africa, and South America, where parents often have no choice but to give up a child if they want the family to live. We believe he brings the girls here and ships them out to buyers throughout the world. To date, no one has been able to bring enough evidence for an indictment against him. The grave they discovered has yielded no clues to tie him to it, but we know he's as dirty as they come."

Blood pounded in my ears as Rook continued, clinically listing the injuries suffered by some of the children. Whoever this DeMarco was, he had vaulted to the top of my list.

"What time is my flight?" I ground out.

"There is no flight. He's here, Haven. In Arizona."

103

~

Dusk had begun its descent. The purples and golds of the sun as it dipped below the horizon were an awe-inspiring thing of beauty that I'd have to show Sammy one day. He'd show me how gorgeous it could be, but right now, amidst the ugliness of my thoughts, they reminded me of a bruise on the sky.

Rook's information had been on the money, as always. A warehouse owned by DeMarco on the outskirts of the aptly named Paradise Valley—one of the richest areas in the country—had delivery trucks parked outside. An examination of one of them netted me a child's bracelet wedged inside the back of one of the truck beds. I clutched it in my hand for a moment, then slid it into my pocket.

I hid in the foothills outside of the area, sipping water and nibbling on granola bars as I observed the comings and goings of numerous men. It seemed that the place was busy twenty-four seven, which would complicate matters, but not enough to save DeMarco.

Sitting on the hard-packed dirt, I spied on the compound through a pair of high-powered binoculars. DeMarco waddled through an office on the second floor. He had several people stop in to see him, which seemed to frustrate him, based on his gestures. He also made a lot of trips back and forth from the coffee maker. I counted eight cups he'd drained. If that was regular, I didn't think he'd be sleeping any time soon.

I pushed thoughts of Sammy out of my mind. I needed total focus on my assignment. Still, he'd pulled me into a hug when I told him I needed to go, not even asking any questions. He'd said he understood and how proud of me he was. His praise gave me the strength to calm the raging anger in my heart.

As I watched over the next several hours, the workers moved about like ants, and I had to decide if I was going to take out the whole lot of them, but the fact there might be children inside stayed my hand. The place was sprawling, covering nearly eighty thousand square feet. No way could I get to the kids if Demarco's men discovered me. This had the potential to turn ugly very quickly if I wasn't careful.

I kept a close eye throughout the night, noting delivery times, the transfer of shifts, the guards who walked the perimeter every thirty-five minutes. Eric

DeMarco certainly ran a very tight ship. I admired it, even as I was about to sink it.

At just past four a.m., I decided I couldn't afford to wait any longer. The number of people thinned out, giving me an opening I had to take advantage of. I moved toward the building, as stealthily as I could. The rusted door creaked, which sent a shiver through me, but no one seemed to notice or care.

I hid in the shadows, working my way through the warehouse, ducking behind anything large enough to hide me. They'd packed the place with vehicles, boxes, barrels. If I didn't know better, I would agree that this was a simple garage. The thing of it, though, we did know better, and it was my job to make sure it ended tonight.

DeMarco would hopefully still be in the office on the second floor. I didn't want to alert anyone to my presence, and dealing with the workers would delay me needlessly. Fortunately the sounds of engines and working men was loud enough to cover my steps.

Voices to my left forced me to duck behind a column and wait until two men passed by. The stairs to the floor above were in the back of the building, out of sight enough I would be able to climb them without drawing attention. The number of men here still concerned me. There were more than we'd anticipated, and I hated not being prepared.

The office was dimly lit, the shadows not receding even after I opened the door. That worked for what I was about to do, because I did like to work in the shadows. I stepped inside and took a half second to note my surroundings. A thick coat of dust covered everything, which made the place appear even shabbier. The carpet, couch, television, and desk were so banged up they could have easily come from a thrift store. For a man who made a lot of money on someone else's despair, he seemed to be pretty damned frugal with it.

Eric DeMarco sat hunched over the desk, pounding away at an ancient desktop computer. "Close the goddamn door," he said, his voice gruff. "Fucking don't need this shit. These bitches should have been out of here yesterday."

My grip tightened on the worn leather handle of my favorite knife. The rumors had been right. DeMarco was shipping young girls to other countries

105

to be part of the slave trade. He never moved from the computer or looked up. Big mistake. I slid through the room quietly, moving behind DeMarco, and stood there, casting a shadow over the monitor.

"For fuck's sake, what do you want?" DeMarco spun in the chair, the spindly thing groaning under his weight. "Who the fuck are you?" he demanded.

I gave a casual shrug. "I might be interested in your merchandise."

DeMarco moved to snatch something from a drawer, but I was faster. I jammed the knife down, pinning his hand to the desk. DeMarco shrieked, and I tensed. I didn't want to attract any additional company. I didn't give a damn what happened once I was sure if there were kids here, that they were safe, but until then… "As I was saying, about your goods."

DeMarco whimpered until I yanked the blade up, which elicited another anguished cry. "Take 'em. I don't care. There's plenty more where they came from." DeMarco moaned and cradled his bloody hand.

I shook my head. "There's always more, isn't there? You're a parasite, preying on young girls who don't have any other options in life. I'm guessing you go to their parents with a promise that you'll help them find a better life. You pay them, probably pennies on the dollar, because you know they're so desperate they'd take just about anything. You smuggle the girls into the country and bring them here.

"Now I could be wrong, so you'll have to fill in any gaps that I might be missing. The young ones, you try to sell off to people who'd pay an arm and a leg to adopt them. They get the decent life you promised. Except you might not be able to find someone to take them, and you're stuck with your *merchandise*. Easier to cut your losses right there.

"Then we get to the older ones, kids no one will adopt, and that's where things get dicey. You offer them the world in exchange for your protection. Then you get them hooked on drugs, or you threaten to send them back to whatever hell you dragged them from, and they're so scared, they do whatever you tell them. You use them up, then pass them on to your buyers who pimp them out until they're of no use. Then what? They kill them?"

DeMarco pushed back in the chair and eyed me.

"What are you? One of those bleeding hearts who thinks they're going to come in here and throw around a few bucks, figuring you'll take the girls out of here and they'll drop to their knees and suck your dick to say thanks? That won't happen. They need to understand their place now. It doesn't matter how old they are, these bitches need a firm hand."

I pulled back and slapped DeMarco so hard I heard the crack of teeth. "Oh, I have a firm hand. I don't think you have to worry about that."

CHAPTER FOURTEEN

My patience had worn thin. He'd refused to answer the most basic questions about his operation. His stubborn streak would be the death of me. Or him. I put the tip of the knife blade against his throat, maybe pushing a teeny bit harder than I needed to in order to get my point across.

"I'm tired," I told him. "I've been roasting out in the sun, watching you all day, then freezing my ass off when it got dark. I'm really not in the mood for your bullshit. Here's what you're going to do: I know you have a way to communicate with your crew. You're going to call them, yell to them, or whatever, and tell them they have the rest of the day off."

"Like fuck I am," he snarled, even though he'd gone pale a long while back.

"This knife I carry has been sharpened by a professional," I lied. "I can slice clear through bone with no more effort than I'd cut butter. I figure if none of your men heard you scream earlier, they're not going to hear you when I start to carve you up. I wonder if I paid them, would they like to watch? Or do they only murder little girls?"

His gaze shifted away from me, and I grabbed his greasy hair and yanked his head back, putting the blade of the knife directly across his throat.

"One way or the other, I'll find the girls. You can help me, and maybe you live to see the inside of a prison cell, or I'll fucking filet you right here and now and leave you to bleed out. And bleeding out? It's a bitch of a death. Blood rushes out of your body through the artery in...let's say your leg, and soaks into the floor. You'll watch as it does, unable to stop it at all, no matter what you do.

"You'll get tired, but you won't be able to sleep, because your lungs will begin to collapse, and you'll choke on your vomit as you try to catch your breath. It's a horrible way to die."

It wasn't true. As ways to die went, bleeding out wasn't the worst. He'd lose consciousness and wouldn't wake up. But it scared him enough for what I needed. Chubby fingers scrabbled for the microphone on the desk. I put the tip of the blade behind his ear and reminded him how sharp my knife was.

"I have a client coming," he bellowed. "He's an important man, and I can't have him seeing any of you. I want you to close up shop for the day. Lou, give the second and third shifts a call and tell them to take the time off, but be here for their shifts tomorrow."

A few moments passed before I heard machines being powered down. It took all of thirty minutes for the place to empty out.

"I'll give you the girls," DeMarco rasped.

"I'm taking them anyway," I informed him. "I'm shutting you down today."

He puffed up his chest and tried to appear menacing. "You got nothing. Cops have been in and out of here at least a dozen times. They know I'm clean."

"We both know you're a piece of shit. One who deserves to rot away in prison for the rest of his very short life. I'm giving you a chance here, and that's probably more than you've ever given anyone else. And don't think about trying to run. I have a lot more weapons than a knife, and I can drop you from a hundred yards at a dead run."

He shook so badly I kind of thought he'd have a heart attack, and I needed him to show me where the girls were. He led me down the stairs and through the building to a spot near a grease pit. He moved some equipment away to reveal a hidden trapdoor in the floor.

"Let me guess, the cops never bothered to look here." Then it hit me. "Or you paid them to look the other way."

At first, DeMarco didn't answer, but when I jabbed the knife in his back, he screamed and opened up. "The police don't come around here. They file reports that say they've checked the place, but no one ever shows up. We pay them good money to stay away."

I made a mental note to let Rook know what had been said, then forced him to open the door, which was nothing more than a flimsy piece of metal. Even a child could have moved it out of the way easily enough. I realized, though… He had said there were three shifts. Where exactly would a kid go, even if they were able to get out?

He lifted the lid and insects flew up and out in a hazy cloud, scattering when they hit the open air. Then came the smell. Rancid, choking. Like rotted meat. Instinctively I knew what I'd find when I went down in the hole, but I hoped to hell it wasn't what I dreaded.

"What the fuck is that?" I demanded, my stomach clenching. DeMarco flushed and turned away. I grabbed him by the back of his arm and jerked him until he faced me. "I asked you a question. What is that smell?"

"S-s-sometimes we g-g-get girls who don't follow the r-r-rules…" His voice trailed off and a veil of red fell over my vision. I shoved the fucker away from me and stormed down the stairs. What I found went beyond anything I'd seen before. There were at least two dozen naked bodies, in various states of decomposition piled on one side of the room. In the farthest corner were maybe six or seven girls huddling together, clinging to one another.

"I'm sorry," I whispered to no one in particular. My mind flashed to Sammy. This could have been him, or any of the other kids that Arianna had turned out. I want to say I don't recall what happened next, but the memory is burned into my mind. I knelt by the girls, who whimpered and began babbling something I couldn't understand. There was nothing I could say to calm them. I didn't know where they were from or the language they spoke. On every face, I saw Sammy. Except these babies had their innocence ripped away from them by the filth upstairs.

I turned away and raced for the stairs. DeMarco was gone, but I was fairly certain he couldn't get far. He might have been a big, scary figure to the girls, but to me he was a scared rabbit. I glanced up toward the office and knew he didn't go there. He'd run, try to get as far away from me as possible. That wouldn't happen.

I did a quick scan of the area and found what I needed: a twenty-four inch length of black metal, with a wicked curve to one end. The crowbar was likely used when they worked on the trucks, but I had a better use for it. I said a small prayer to any power that might exist for the girls in the basement. I texted Rook and told him to hurry and bring along a lot of people for this one, because it needed to be a torch job when they were done.

110

I put my phone away and began to stalk my prey.

~

Even with a five minute head start, DeMarco hadn't gotten far at all. I found him trying to conceal himself behind some barrels of chemicals used for cleaning machine parts. I took the bar in my hand and whacked the side of one of them, causing him to cry out.

"You sick, twisted fucker," I snarled, as I advanced slowly. I wanted him to know fear. I wanted him to quake with piss-your-pants terror.

"You s-s-said you were going to give me a chance."

"You're right. I did. Stand up."

I could hear his knees knocking as he stood, this pathetic piece of shit who lorded his power over tiny innocent children. My temples throbbed, and my vision narrowed to laser focus. I'd killed before, but I couldn't think of anyone who deserved it more than DeMarco. I knew those poor girls in the basement would never be the same, and this fuck had caused it all.

Once again I thought of Sammy. He'd been a pre-teen when they'd taken him. He was strong. The kids DeMarco had? I could scarcely imagine what their lives would be like. Though I couldn't change what happened, I could make sure the man responsible paid.

I drew my arms back and swung the crowbar like a baseball bat, slamming him in the gut so hard he was knocked backward. He tried to scramble away, but I brought the bar down on his shoulder, grinning when I heard the satisfying crack of bone.

"I thought about it," I rumbled. "Then I thought about those kids you stole the lives of. The ones who will never be able to overcome what you've done to them. What I'm about to do to you, it's for them."

And with that I hit him in the face with the crowbar. His nose shattered and blood ran freely. Then I hit him again. And again. And again. His screams were cut short as he passed out at some point, but that didn't stop me. I beat him without mercy, rejoicing in every broken bone, every piece of flesh torn from his body. Nothing was left untouched. His face, his legs, his torso. Every part of him was bloody. Finally, I stopped and stepped back, witnessing what I'd done. Revulsion hit me like a wave.

I'd killed before, but never like this. I'd never savaged anyone the way I had DeMarco. The coup de grace, though, was when one puffy eye opened, blood streaming down the side, and in my mind, he looked up at me and whispered, "Help me."

Every fiber of my being exploded with rage once again as I pulled out my gun and put four bullets in his head, causing it to explode like an overripe melon. I was caught in the spray of blood and offal, then suddenly I was numb. I felt nothing.

~

At some point, Rook's men entered the warehouse and relieved me. Several people, men and women, broke down crying when they found the girls. I had to get out. I needed to be away from that place. I couldn't say how I got home. It was a three-hour trip, and I don't remember one bit of it. Dawn had broken at some point, but it didn't really register. I stumbled through the door, DeMarco's blood splattered on my face and hands. Sammy saw me enter and rushed over to where I stood.

"Haven? Are you okay?"

I opened my mouth, but the words wouldn't come. Sammy gripped my forearms, checking to see if any of the blood was mine. Before I'd met him, none of my jobs had ever had an effect on me. Now? My hands trembled. I saw those little girl's faces in my mind and I sagged in defeat. Sammy tugged me up and stripped off my clothes, not caring what I was caked in. He led me to the bathroom and turned the shower on. In a few moments, the bathroom filled with steam. Sammy shucked his own clothes, then guided me under the hot water. Grabbing a cloth from the rack, he squirted a spicy scented soap onto it and began rubbing his hands over my body. The tension drained out as the red ran down the grate.

It took a few minutes of Sammy's gentle touches before I realized he was singing to me. His voice was soft and sweet. I could feel the tears as they ran down my cheeks.

"He killed them," I whispered, afraid to say it aloud. "They were just commodities to him. When they became too much trouble, he snuffed them like a candle. He left their bodies in the room with the other girls so they'd know what happened if they didn't do what they were told."

Sammy turned off the water, dried me with one of the bath towels, and then wrapped me in his arms. "Come on. Let's put you to bed."

He took my hand, his touch grounding me in the moment, and led me to the bedroom. He laid me on the bed, a soft smile on his face.

"I'll bring you something to eat," he whispered.

I shook my head and he stopped. "Hold me? I need you to chase away the memories for a while." I sounded pathetic, even to my own ears, but my mind was fractured. Visions of dead children intermingled with the deaths I'd caused. DeMarco's face, a bloody pulp, was seared into my thoughts. I believed I could handle anything, but now I was falling apart. Sammy lay beside me and pulled me into his arms.

"Okay. I'm going to help you forget everything but me," he said softly, stroking his fingers over my chest.

"Promise?" I pleaded. I was embarrassed by my need for him, but I had to have what he was offering.

"Always," he swore.

I shifted in bed, and he snapped, "Lie still. I don't want you to move. I want you to close your eyes and focus on my voice and touch. Nothing exists beyond that. Do you understand?"

My voice trembled when I answered him. "Yes."

"What scares you?"

No one had ever asked me that, and I tried not to give it much thought. DeMarco terrified me, though, and I knew why. "Failing someone. I couldn't save my sister, and I couldn't save those girls."

I couldn't help myself; I bolted from the bed and fled to the bathroom where I clutched the toilet bowl as if it were my god. I expelled so much I couldn't possibly have had anything left. Sammy stood behind me and stroked my hair, murmuring softly.

I trembled when I stood. He didn't say anything, simply flushed the toilet, had me sit on the seat, grabbed a washcloth, and cleaned me up, even going so far as to brush my teeth. Then he led me back to bed. He pulled the thick curtains over the windows, plunging the room into darkness.

There was a knock at the door and Kelly called out my name.

"Not now," Sammy shouted.

The door opened a crack. "Is he okay? Rook is asking for him."

Rook. I had completely forgotten to report in, but I couldn't let him see me like this. I needed to be strong when we talked, to tell him why I'd done

113

what I had, and not let emotions cause me to break down into the sobbing mess that I knew lay beneath the surface. I opened my mouth, uncertain what to say, when Sammy put a finger to my lips and shook his head.

"Haven?" came Kelly's voice again.

Sammy leapt off the bed and stalked to the door. "I said not now. I don't want anyone bothering him today. You tell Rook he can wait. Until I say so, Haven isn't leaving this room."

I recoiled at the vehemence in Sammy's words. Kelly would go ballistic on him, and that anger would send Sammy rushing back to my side for protection that I simply couldn't provide for him right now. Still, I'd promised to take care of him, and I would do what needed to be done. I staggered out of bed, intent on making sure Sammy wouldn't be afraid again.

I heard Kelly chuckle, then his voice was a stage-whisper. "You're exactly what he needs. I'll be doing my duties if you need anything."

When Sammy turned toward the bed again, he found me rooting through my dresser, nearly dressed in blue jeans and a western shirt. He growled. "Back to bed. Now."

"Rook needs to talk to me."

"Rook can goddamn well wait until you're able to talk about it without throwing up. I made you a promise that I was going to make you stop thinking."

He moved closer to me and put his hand on the side of my neck, pulling me toward him. I was six inches taller and outweighed him by nearly eighty pounds, but I couldn't stop my forward movement. His lips touched mine and everything in the universe froze. I couldn't think. Couldn't move. Didn't *want* to move. His tongue tickled the seam of my lips and I automatically opened to him. Never before had someone else been the aggressor. When his body pushed against mine, I groaned. His hands stroked my chest through my shirt while his lips sucked at my neck. There would be a hickey. I didn't care. I wanted him to mark me over and over.

"Sammy, please," I hissed.

I grabbed his head and held him firmly against my neck. He responded by sucking harder. I ached. Fire and ice warred in my veins. When his hand brushed across my groin, I shot so hard I wondered if I could die from pleasure.

114

"Take off your clothes," he ordered. "I want to see all of you."

Wordlessly, I began to strip off my shirt, followed by my pants. Sammy's keen gaze raked over my body. He was completely different than he had been before. Gone was the mouse, and in its place was the hawk. It took everything I had to keep from snorting at my sudden shyness. This small man, sexy as he was, made *me* shy. It was ludicrous.

He took a seat near the window and, in a very husky voice, said something that left me with no doubt he had taken control. "Take them off slowly. I want to watch you."

My hands stilled. Sammy smiled at me and I melted. I wanted to please him. I pulled off the remainder of my shirt and felt my body go warm under his scrutiny.

Sammy sat back in the chair, the tip of his finger ghosting over his lips. My cock hardened. I had problems getting my belt open because I was so flustered.

"Do you need help with that?" he asked, his voice husky.

I nodded, unable to think of anything else.

"Come here then."

I closed the gap between us. His hands worked their way across my stomach, raising goose bumps. He leaned forward and tongued my belly button. I heard the buckle clink open.

"Strip the rest of it off."

I slid the pants down, my cock snapping up.

His voice was light with humor. He stood up and ran his hands over my body. "Commando? Why am I not surprised? Lie down."

I splayed myself on the bed while he opened the nightstand then knelt next to me, his hands seemingly everywhere at once. He made my body sing, wanting everything he was demanding.

"Spread your legs."

I flinched. No one topped me. When I went to bed with someone, they knew I would be the one who did the screwing. Yet, when he said it, my body reacted on its own to his command. My legs went wide, knees spread.

"Beautiful," he murmured. He ran a finger over my throbbing cock. "Every inch of you."

He leaned over and licked the engorged head. I arched my back, wanting more of the delicious heat. He chuckled and backed off.

"We'll get back to that, I promise."

He lifted my legs, giving him better access. I heard a snick and closed my eyes tight as the cool fluid drizzled down my crack. His slender fingers twirled around, spreading the goo. "You look so good like this. Open your eyes."

I couldn't resist. My gaze met his and I trembled. I'd never had anyone look at me like that. I knew what was going to happen, and God help me, I wanted it.

Sammy gripped my shaft. His touch set me to trembling. God, I ached so bad.

"I'm not going to be gentle," he murmured. "I don't think you'd appreciate that."

I wanted to insist this wasn't how it worked, but I shook my head harshly. "No, don't..."

He slid up farther on the bed and touched my hole with the head of his cock. In one deft motion, he pushed all the way inside. I felt like I was being split asunder, but Sammy continued to talk to me, forcing me to focus on him. The pain dulled to a hollow ache as he slid in and out. The feel of his balls, low-hanging and big, bouncing against mine was so incredibly hot.

"Keep your eyes on me, Haven. Don't stop looking at me."

The look on his face was a mixture of awe and possession. It was fucking hot and comforting at the same time. I gave into it fully.

"Fuck me, Sammy. For the love of God, please fuck me," I ground out.

His lips drew into a satisfied smile before he slammed hard, causing me to gasp. "Like that?" he asked.

I let out a small whine.

"Hold your legs," he told me.

I locked my fingers around my thighs and held them open. He put his hands on the bed and began deep thrusts, each one pushing me against the headboard. I'd never known a feeling like this.

"Only with me," he muttered. For a minute, I thought he had read my mind. Then I realized I didn't care. Sammy was the only man who'd ever topped me, and I couldn't imagine anyone else ever doing it.

116

"Yes," I agreed. "Only with you."

Sammy continued to drive into me. I was so fucking close. He was going to make me shoot before I even touched myself.

"Do you want to know how you feel around me?" he rasped. "Hot. Slick. Intense. Like a thousand fingers grabbing me and massaging every point on my dick."

He was so shy. So awkward. Yet seeing this side of him propelled me to new heights. And his dirty talk was the icing on the cake.

"I'm going to come. I'm going to fill you, Haven. If you don't want that, you need to tell me now."

"Yes." I moaned. "That's what I want."

A few more thrusts and a strangled cry ripped from him. His blue eyes went dark; he bit into his lip so hard I thought he'd be bleeding. Through it all, he never once stopped looking at me.

"Come for me," he whispered.

One last thrust and I blew my load everywhere. It was fucking intense, and it took every ounce of energy not to scream his name. I lost my grip on my legs and they flopped onto the bed. Sammy slid out of me and I felt empty. He collapsed across my chest, nearly weightless. He continued sucking at my neck, nipping here and there. I was still painfully aroused, but sated in a way I had never been before.

"Mine," he purred in my ear. His words were so soft and were followed by light snores as he fell asleep atop me. I ignored the mess that stuck us together, pulled up the covers, wrapped my arms around his waist, and held him while we slept.

CHAPTER FIFTEEN

The light streamed into the room, forcing me to cover my eyes.

"You can't sleep all day," Sammy said. "And we need to talk."

At first, I thought it had been a dream, but the ache in my ass reminded me of the reality of what had happened. I noted that he'd wiped me down while I'd slept. I didn't know why that made me feel so…cherished, but it did.

I started to sit up until Sammy put a hand on my chest. "Stay there. I want you to be comfortable." His eyes twinkled in the bright light. I'd never noticed twinkling eyes before, but with Sammy it felt right.

"Are you feeling better? Ready to eat something?"

The enormity of his question shook me to my core.

"I don't know if I can do this anymore." I whispered the words as if saying them out loud would give them weight that I wasn't ready for.

"Tell me why." He stroked my arm and I found it comforting.

I had no idea where to start. "I was a sniper in the military. I'm trained to kill, but what I do now is different. When I shot a target from a few hundred yards, it wasn't personal for me. I had a detachment I was able to maintain. What I do now is very personal. I know the people. I know their victims. Sometimes I'm able to take the shot from a distance, but the way I do it now makes me feel like I'm giving the victim the final word and letting the person know why they're about to die."

"Is that what you did with Arianna?"

I nodded.

"And you did it because of me?"

"Mostly," I mumbled. "She hurt a lot of people. You, the kid she shot, and a lot of others we may never find out about."

"And what happened last night?"

My heart began to race at the thought of DeMarco, his brains spattered across my clothes and body, and still I continued to shoot.

"They were just little girls. They were naked and holding one another, taking comfort where they could. H-h-he kept corpses in the room with them. He said they didn't always follow the rules. I was too late to save them."

Tears stung my eyes and rolled hot down my cheeks. Sammy drew me into his arms and held me, rubbing small circles on my back. It reminded me of me doing the same to him when we had been on our way to Arizona. The reversal of our roles should have sent me running from the man, but my body knew it needed him. I allowed myself to soak up his warmth, which helped to chase away the chill of the memories.

"I thought about my sister. I haven't seen her in a long time now, but I could see her face and yours everywhere I looked, and that fucker had to pay for what he did to them."

I began hiccupping, trying to draw a breath. Sammy's voice finally cut through me.

"Enough." He stood and cupped my chin, forcing me to look into his eyes. "You did what you had to. No one will dispute that. You do a job that I don't know anyone else could do, but you can't rescue everyone. There's only one of you, and you're mortal. Remember that. If you want to stop what you're doing, we can go somewhere and start over. But, Haven, you have to know how important your job is. Without you, Arianna would have continued to hurt more people. I would have died. DeMarco would find more girls that had no champion."

I broke my connection to Sammy when I looked away, and immediately regretted it. I shivered, not from cold, but the darkness of remembered emotions seeping back inside. The rage and fury that drove me, the thought that any of these bodies could have easily been Sammy. The satisfaction as I blew Demarco's brains out.

"Whatever you're thinking, stop now. I want you to focus on me, let me know what's going on in your mind."

I sucked in a calming breath. I glanced back toward him, and saw he continued to watch me. "I think there were six still alive. But there were at least two dozen he'd killed."

"Focus on the six. On me. We're your wins. Every person you've saved owes you their life, even if they never realize it."

"And you're here because you're grateful?" I hated the question, but I had to know.

He smacked me lightly on the back of the head. "I'm here because I want to be. I don't ever want to hear you question that again."

He had to hear the ugly truth. I needed to be sure he understood what being with me meant. "I nearly beat him to death. Then I shot him in the head."

"I don't know that I could have made that call, but I'm grateful to you for having made it. He was a monster and he had to die."

"I have to kill your mother," I reminded him.

"I think she killed my father. She gave me away. She might be many things, but she's not my mother. Not anymore. You'll do what you have to, and I know it'll be the right choice."

"I've noticed the last year or so that the jobs hit me hard. Every time I come back from one, I feel like I've lost a piece of myself. Killing a man isn't easy. It takes something away, a part of your soul you'll never get back."

"I don't doubt it's not easy, but sometimes we do things because they have to be done, not because we want to."

"So you think I should keep doing it?"

He lay on the bed and pulled me down, putting my head on his chest. I could hear his heart thumping slow and steady and I focused on that. I had to get my headspace clear again.

"I'm not going anywhere," he told me. "Whether you keep the job or don't, I'm going to be with you. If you stay on, I'll make you a promise: if you ever think you've lost your way, you'll come to me and I'll find you again. I know you thought you were alone, but it's not true anymore."

We lay there for a long while, neither of us speaking. Sammy ran his hand up and down my back, tracing my spine. It felt so good, but I still needed to talk with Rook. I tried once more to sit up but he held me tight.

"Don't be in a hurry to go anywhere," he said, a light tease in his voice. "I've got you where I want you now."

"I have to give Rook my report," I reminded him.

He let loose and we both sat up. "Do you feel better? Because if you don't, Rook is going to wait until you do."

I thought about it for a moment. I did feel better than I had in a long time. "Yeah, I do."

"Wanna know why?" he asked playfully, running his fingers over my chest.

I grinned at him. "Do tell."

He kissed me on the neck, raising goose bumps yet again. "Because you know you've got someone who cares for you now. Someone who is going to be in your corner, no matter what."

I finally asked the question I'd been dying to know. "After everything they put you through, how can you be this strong?"

"Because I had no choice. I refused to think of myself as a victim, though. Yeah, I was scared shitless, but every day I told myself that if I got free, I would never let myself be in that position again. And I grew stronger. Not enough to get free by myself, but I did get out. And no one will ever break me again."

The fierce determination on his face emboldened me. If Sammy could be strong, so could I. I could do my job and do it well. Then I could come home and know that he would take care of me.

~

"What the hell did you do?" Darth's voice intoned.

"What I had to," I replied, though my voice quivered slightly.

A sigh, likely one of exasperation, resonated from the speakers.

"Haven, he was pudding. In the years we've worked together, I don't think I've seen you be so...brutal."

"I got the job done," I growled. "Since when is this a problem?"

"A problem? Wait. You thought... Oh God, no. We gave you the okay to deal with it any way you felt you needed to. I'm only concerned that you're okay. I wanted to let you know we found six girls alive and recovered the bodies of the rest. We'll be sure they're given a proper burial."

"And what about the girls who survived?"

"That's a tougher thing to deal with," Rook admitted. "We've taken them to Lilah. She said they were in bad shape physically. They'd been beaten, starved, and two of them appear to have been sexually assaulted. They're going to need a lot of help coming to terms with what happened, but I promise we'll utilize every available resource."

"What about their families?"

"To be honest, we have very little hope of finding them. None of the girls speak English, and the translator we brought in said they don't know where they're from. Two of the girls, one who lived and one who later died, said someone hurt their parents and took them away. We've contacted some families who have helped us to care for abused children in the past, and they're going to take them in."

My stomach burned as I paced around the room. As bad as my life had been, I would never compare it to those little girls. "And what about the *men* who did this?"

"The men who did this are going down. I have people covering the warehouse, and they'll be arresting anyone who shows up. I've also made overtures to the Justice Department, and there will be an inquest into the failures of the police department to follow up on complaints. I couldn't tell them everything, of course, but enough for them to know what to look for. The only good thing to come out of this, besides the girls you rescued, is we found some files on the computer that will help us bring down some major players in a multi-national slavery ring."

"I'm sure the dead kids will feel so much better then," I said bitterly.

"Yes," Rook said slowly, then he coughed. "We wanted to suggest you take some downtime. A few weeks at least. We know this mission was hard on you."

I thought about it for a few moments. Sammy and I had formed a bond, and I wanted to explore it, see where it would lead, but the truth of the matter was, after this, I couldn't rest until Valerie's organization had been burned to the ground, preferably with her inside.

"No. I still have a schedule to keep."

"We believe Valerie is now aware of your activities. This many deaths in such a short span has to have registered on her radar. Our sources tell us she's been calling on her people demanding to know what's happening and what's being done to stop you."

I snorted. "She's impatient. I'm willing to bet after the next target is eliminated, she holes up somewhere."

"Don't be so sure. Valerie isn't like the people you've dealt with before. She's brutal and has no problems ordering an execution or doing the job herself. She's always very careful, of course, to keep her hands clean, but she's an example of why the female is considered the deadliest of the species."

"I'm not worried," I told him, though deep inside I had a gnawing in my gut. Sammy said he understood that I had to kill her, but when push came to shove, did he really? If I had to choose between him and finishing this assignment, could I step away?

"So how are things with Samuel?" Rook asked.

"What? Why would you want to know?" I fired back.

"What's with you today? I'm just curious how you're both adjusting."

"We're fine," I informed him. I shot a look at the other man in the room. "Has Kelly said anything different?"

The bastard leaned against the wall, folded his arms over his chest, and grinned at me, showing every one of his pearly teeth. They had to be false. No one his age had teeth that perfect.

"I assure you, I said nothing," Kelly said, giving me a cocky grin.

"Haven?"

"Everything is fine," I muttered.

"If this isn't working out, we can find him a safe house. I know it's not an ideal situation for you."

My ass clenched tight, reminding me where Sammy had been just a few hours before. I reached behind me and rubbed my left cheek, which, naturally, Kelly saw.

"I think the situation has improved tremendously, or am I mistaken?" Kelly mocked.

I gave him the one-finger salute, which caused him to burst out laughing. "Sammy is fine. There's no need to find him anywhere else to stay."

"If you're sure."

"He's sure," Kelly answered for me. "Samuel fits here. I can't think of a better place for the young man."

"Okay then, when you're ready to take on your next assignment, let me know the details. And Haven? You did good."

Rook disconnected and I turned to Kelly. "Spill it."

"Whatever do you mean?" he asked, fluttering his eyes at me.

"You tell Rook and I'll kill you," I threatened.

"What's there to tell? You finally found someone who makes sense in your life. He's it for you. I've watched the two of you together, and he's hopelessly devoted to you. And whether you want to admit it or not, you are to him. That's love and everyone should be lucky enough to have it in their life. It's not a secret to be hidden away, unless you're ashamed of him for some reason."

I wasn't ashamed of Sammy at all. Quite the contrary. He was amazing, and I got butterflies when I thought about him.

"I never thought I'd see the day," Kelly said, beaming a wide smile.

"What are you talking about?"

"You're in love. And it looks good on you. I have some work I need to do," he said.

Kelly patted my shoulder then left the room. The realization that he was right, that I was in love with Sammy, smacked me between the eyes. I pushed a button and the door slid closed. I tapped a few keys and Rook came back online.

"Yes?"

"I love Sammy," I blurted out.

"Oh, it's about goddamn time," he shouted.

"What do you mean?"

"You've been dancing around it for weeks. The way you are when you talk about him is like a teenage girl with a crush on a rock star. Frankly, it's embarrassing."

"Fuck you. I'm not embarrassed."

Rook's laugh, sounding like Darth Vader, was chilling. "I didn't say you were. I said I was embarrassed. I was afraid I'd have to explain the birds and bees to you before you'd finally get your head out of your ass." He was quiet for a minute. "Do you want to quit? Is that what you're telling me?"

"No," I said, surprised by the surety of my answer. "Sammy... We talked. He told me he understands the job I have to do. Even if it means killing Valerie, he wants me to keep at it."

"Are you sure? This job could jeopardize your relationship, and something like this doesn't come along very often for people like us."

I thought for a moment, trying to form my answer before I gave it to Rook. "Part of the reason that Sammy is with me, or so he said, is because

I'm the strength for people who don't have anyone to look out for them. I don't know that he'd feel the same if I walked away now."

"You know, I don't really appreciate being spoken about like I'm not here," came a voice from behind. I spun to find Sammy, hands on hips, an expression of annoyance marring his normally cute face.

"How did you get in here?" I demanded, which was apparently the wrong question.

"For your information, Kelly gave me the access code and programmed my thumbprint into the database. He said I'd want to be here, and he was right. And you're an idiot. I'm going to be with you if you keep this job or not."

"Samuel, I assume?" Rook's amused voice carried over the speaker.

Sammy startled and glanced around, but recovered quickly, his eyes locked on the computer. "And you must be Rook."

"Kelly told me you said I would have to wait to speak to Haven after his assignment." Rook's tone gave no indication as to his thoughts.

"Yes, I did." Sammy's, on the other hand, was strong and full of certainty.

"You do realize he's my employee."

"You do realize that some of his time belongs to you, but his heart, body, and soul belong to me, and I'm the one who is going to make sure they stay in one piece after I let you *borrow* him."

"You know, I have something to say on the subject," I growled, understanding now how Sammy had felt being kept out of the conversation.

"Unless it's 'Sammy's right,' no, you don't."

I glared down at the young man in front of me attempting to show strength and determination. He stared right back at me. The weird thing was, I blinked first.

"Sammy's right," I mumbled.

He smiled and twined his fingers with mine. "See how much easier it is if you just agree with me?"

"I like him, Haven. He won't take any shit from you."

"Or you," Sammy reminded Rook.

"So since you control his calendar," Rook continued, obviously amused, "I'm trying to get him to take a break. Spend some time with you and unwind. These last few assignments have been difficult, and if it weren't for the fact that three of our top agents were killed, we'd have forced him to take an extended leave."

"Haven is strong, and he can handle it. When he needs a break, we'll let you know."

We was an innocuous word, but the weight behind it meant more to me than I ever could have realized. I'd always had Kelly in my corner, even if it wasn't something I let myself believe until recently. But Sammy? His words left no doubt. He claimed me to Rook, and probably Kelly.

"I love you," I whispered.

Sammy's gaze snapped to mine. "What?"

For a moment I wasn't sure if I had spoken too soon. Maybe he wasn't ready for the words yet. Then he tucked himself into me and wrapped his arms around my shoulders, pulling me down until we were face-to-face. "I love you, too."

He cocked his head and brought our lips together. He devoured my mouth; that was the only thing I could call it. He consumed me with just his lips, dragging me down into the depths and banishing the darkness, then soaring skyward and shining over all. It was as if he was declaring himself the center of my universe.

"I am so glad I didn't turn the camera on," Rook said, which I knew was teasing since I'd never seen the man. "You…have fun." Then I heard him disconnect.

I tried to pull back, but Sammy held me where I was and continued the kiss, his tongue touching the crease of my closed lips, which instantly opened and allowed him to delve inside. Our tongues tangled together as though locked in a life and death struggle, which I was quickly losing.

Sammy pressed on my shoulders and had me sinking to my knees in front of him. I could see the outline of his dick pressed against the chino pants he wore, and I licked my lips. I glanced up and saw Sammy staring at me, a cocky grin on his face. He rubbed a hand over his groin, and waggled his eyebrows. I reached out and gripped him through his pants.

"You can have it if you want it," he whispered.

And, God, how I wanted it. I fumbled with the zipper, drawing it down as quickly as my trembling fingers would allow, until Sammy grabbed my wrists.

"Might wanna be a bit more careful," he teased. It was then I noticed he had no underwear.

"Fuck, that's hot," I murmured, fishing his cock out.

His smile widened. He let go of my wrists, grabbed my head, and nodded toward his dick. I took the hint and drew him into my mouth, pleased with myself when his grip on my head tightened, his back arched, and he moaned.

Sammy held my head tight as he began to rock back and forth, feeding me his cock. Each thrust went a little deeper, until he was knocking at the back of my throat.

"Can you take it all?" he asked, his voice a harsh whisper. "I want you to have my cock in your throat. Can you do that for me?"

Sammy's cock wasn't long, maybe a bit more than average, but it had a thickness to it. His voice was insistent, though. He was letting me know what he wanted, what he needed me to give him. On his next push, he wedged his cock in my throat, crying out when his balls rested on my chin.

"That's it. Take it," he moaned.

For a few minutes, he fucked my face, slow but insistent, and I stayed on my knees, letting him take his pleasure. When he pulled back, I looked up, finding his gaze locked on my face.

"Stand up," he told me.

He pulled me up and pushed my pants down around my ankles. "I want you to bend over the desk," he said, a wicked gleam in his eye. He whirled me around and bent me over the desk, before he knelt behind me and spread my cheeks. Without hesitation, he dove in, and began rimming me. I hissed as new sensations rocketed through me. Then he stood and put his hand on the small of my back. He rubbed his cock along my crack, seeking the place it would bury itself, and I waited.

It wasn't long before I felt the burn as he began pressing, giving himself entrance. With just the spit, it burned, but Sammy didn't go easy on me. Before long he was hammering my ass, shoving me against the desk with each thrust, eliciting a grunt from me. When his hand found my cock and wrapped it in a tight grip, I knew he was close.

"I want you to come first, Haven. I want your ass to milk my orgasm from me, to drain me dry. Come for me now."

And I did. Spurts coated the desk, the computer, and Sammy's hand. He stayed hunched over me for several moments before he drew out, causing me to wince. He looked at his hand, then held it out to me. "You made a mess. Clean it up."

I grabbed his wrist and licked the warm cum from him, sucking each finger into my mouth. Afterward, he stepped back and smiled at me.

"Do you know why I did that?" he asked, arching his eyebrows.

At first I didn't understand the question, so shook my head.

"This is the place you get your assignments. Where you do your work. It's just a room. It doesn't matter what you do in here, because no matter where you are, I'm your home. Remember that."

And with that, he slapped me on the ass cheek then opened the door and left the room, leaving me with my pants pooled around my ankles, his cum running down my leg, and the realization I'd just been claimed.

And enjoyed it.

CHAPTER SIXTEEN

The dichotomy with Sammy intrigued me. He was forceful when we were alone, never letting me forget the fact he'd laid a claim on my body, but he was hesitant and painfully shy around Kelly. Despite repeated attempts to draw him into a conversation, Sammy recoiled when he couldn't see me nearby.

I offered to take him out one day, go shopping, buy him some things he wanted for the house, something that would make this his home, but he insisted he couldn't leave. The terror in his eyes at the thought of being in public had him literally shaking and seeking comfort in my arms.

Instead, we shopped online. Sammy had eclectic tastes. He loved bold prints when it came to fabrics for the bedroom, but the bathroom things he picked out were soft, almost feminine with their flowery design. I laughed as he pointed out things he wanted us to have, delighting in his excitement.

"Why don't I give you my credit card? Pick out what you think would make this into a place we both want to live. Make it into a home."

"Seriously?"

I took his hand in mine and peered into his eyes, which shimmered with excitement.

"Haven told me that this doesn't feel like a home to him," Kelly called from the other room. "He said there's nothing of him here."

"You're a shit psychotherapist," I growled. "What happened to doctor-patient confidentiality?"

"My advice was free, and I told you, I only dabble, so it's not like I'm going to be getting paid."

"And the advice was worth every penny," I muttered, before turning my attention back to Sammy. "He's not wrong. I never had a home. There are houses, places to stay when I need them, but if I didn't see them for five years, it wouldn't be like I was missing them. This place was the closest I ever had to a real home. But since someone informed me, in no uncertain terms, that he was my home, I want to make it one with him."

Sammy launched himself onto my lap and kissed me hard. "I can stay?" he asked, when he pulled back long enough to catch a breath.

"Wait. Now you mean to tell me I have a choice?" I asked, keeping my tone light so he knew I was joking.

"Nope. You were mine since the moment we met. I'm just glad you finally figured it out. So I can really buy anything I want?"

"Whatever makes this into a place for both of us, yeah."

He grinned, and I suddenly felt like I'd made a huge mistake.

~

I took my next assignment, despite the fact it felt off. It kept me away from home for almost two weeks. As the days went by, I became more irritable because Sammy wasn't there to keep me calm. I couldn't risk contacting him for fear of someone tracing the call. I was paranoid about his safety, but the need to hear his voice nearly overwhelmed me, and my temper frayed more each day.

My target, one Josiah Day, ranked so low on my list I barely knew he existed. He wasn't even worthwhile as a courier, but suddenly he held a position of importance to Valerie, and that made him important to me. Seemingly overnight, he'd been bumped up and given a lot of authority over several smaller bits of the organization. The man I tracked could barely tie his own shoelaces, let alone oversee millions of dollars in gambling money.

Josiah was a nervous, twitchy man. He constantly peered over his shoulder, chewed his nails, or hid in darkened corners of the establishments he frequented. Every movement telegraphed a terrified man who would eventually draw attention to himself. Which meant this was a trap.

Instead of being the mouse to the cheese, I opted to play cat. I began to toy with Josiah. I'd let him see me constantly. My presence in the restaurant where he ate, at the theater he went to, or at the casinos he operated began to unnerve the man.

I took great pleasure in making my presence known to Josiah. Oh, I was careful. I never stayed anywhere long enough for anyone to pin me down to one place. The first few times I would approach him where he probably thought he was safe, then sidled up to him and whispered, "You're next," before melting back into the crowd.

After that, a grin or a nod would be enough for the sweat to break out on his brow. Then I'd disappear into throngs of people and return to my perch, watching as he made a string of phone calls, gesturing wildly as he pleaded with whomever he was talking to. He was a man on edge, and I was about to push him over.

He lived in a dump of an apartment. Definitely not something one would expect from a high roller. The carpet, which I could only assume had been white at some point, was dingy and frayed, worn to the floorboards in some places. His couch had rips in it, and the cushions were torn and had stuffing hanging out of the holes. I began to leave presents for him, always in a spot where he was sure to notice. A bullet on his pillow? That one I thought was inspired.

Then I'd head back out into the night and keep an eye on him from my perch. I wanted him to know he wasn't safe anywhere. I wanted him to panic and run to Valerie. But on Thursday night, my second full week from home, I became anxious. I made my way to Josiah's building and popped the lock on his door, allowing myself entry into the shithole apartment.

"She said you'd come," he gloated from the couch. "She knew you'd take the bait."

He tensed as I got closer to him. His eyes shut and he began shivering violently. It was then I notice the wires strapped to his chest.

"What did she do to you?"

"She said I was supposed to keep you here until she showed up."

My eyes drifted over his arms and hands. In his right hand, he held the dead man trigger. In my head, the entire thing played out like a movie. I knew exactly what was going on here.

"You think this is a game," I ground out. "This display is supposed to make me piss my pants in fear while we wait."

He smiled, but it was weak and watery.

"She told you that if you kept me here, you'd be rewarded. She said that they'd strap a fake bomb to your chest, and that I'd be too afraid to move, right?"

His smile wavered.

"The thing is, that harness has a real bomb, and if you don't keep your thumb on that button, you're going to blow yourself sky high."

The panic in his eyes had me stepping back toward the door.

"She swore it wasn't real," he whispered.

"Yeah, she's a lying bitch, ain't she?" I countered. I did a quick examination of the apartment, trying to ascertain the most likely exit. It was then I noted the glint from the roof across the street. Someone was out there with a sniper rifle. I turned and hauled ass out of the room, diving for cover in the hallway as the bullet shattered the window and hit with a solid thud into Josiah. The explosion rocked the building, no doubt blowing Josiah to hell and back.

Plaster rained down on me, and my ears were ringing like a beast. I scrabbled out of the building and ducked into an alleyway, keeping a close eye out for anyone who might think my moment of stupidity and ego would be enough to get the drop on me. When no one showed, I made my way to the airport and headed for home.

But Valerie's message was delivered. My days were numbered.

~

"You can't go after her now," Kelly growled.

"The hell I can't," I bellowed. The argument was going nowhere.

Both Kelly and Rook were telling me I needed to back off and let things cool down. I disagreed. Valerie knew the pressure was on, and she wouldn't relax her guard. If anything, it was likely she would start stepping up her operations to draw me out.

"I agree with Kelly," Rook said. "We'll come up with a new plan and—"

"And nothing. She already knows I'm coming for her. I want her to feel helpless as I continue to take out her men. There aren't many left on my list, and now I know she's sweating."

"Do you think Sammy will agree?" Kelly demanded.

"What? What difference does it make? Sammy isn't my boss."

I went cold when I heard him clear his throat. "Is that so?"

I glared at Kelly who had a big smile on his face. I made a mental note to leave the stained sheets on the bed the next time Sammy and I fucked.

"Good afternoon, Samuel."

"Hi, Rook," Sammy replied, moving to stand beside me. I glanced down at him and a shiver ran through me at his expression. He was pissed. I tried to take his hand, but he brushed me off. I didn't know why, but that hurt. Sammy was tactile. He liked to touch, and I found I enjoyed it when he put his hands on me. Plus the look of anger and disappointment damn near tore me apart.

"Sammy, I—"

He waved a hand in my direction. "I'll leave you guys to discuss whatever you're talking about. Haven, when you're done, I'd like to see you."

He turned and stalked out the door, despite my attempt to call him back.

"Someone's gonna get it," Kelly crooned.

"Fuck you," I snapped, jabbing my finger in his chest. "You had to start shit, didn't you?"

He smirked at me. "Yeah, pretty much."

"I have to go talk to him."

"We need to discuss—"

"Later," I snapped, cutting Rook off with a click of the disconnect button.

Kelly tried to say something, but I hurried out of the room and rushed after Sammy. I found him in our room, pacing and gesturing. I stopped at the door and thought about trying to back away. Then I snorted. I was bigger. I knew how to kill a man in dozens of creative and fun ways. There was no way I was going to be cowed by someone I could snap like a twig.

When he found me at the door, he pointed to the bed, and goddamn if I didn't sit down. It struck me then. Sammy *was* in charge. Somehow he'd crept into my life and set himself up as if I was his submissive. He fucking topped me, for God's sake. And while that bit of knowledge should piss me off, or make me want to prove my masculinity, and how I was in control, I knew I wasn't. For years, I'd been falling apart, the job taking a heavy toll on my mental health.

Then this snip of a man walked into my life and turned it upside down. He held me while I cried. He dragged emotions out of me that I had suppressed for so long, and through him I was stronger than I had been in years. Sammy probably wouldn't see himself as a Dom. He obviously had no formal training, but he had strength of personality. He overcame things that would have anyone else in an institution.

I was stronger physically, but he had me beat in many respects, and I had to acknowledge that fact. Was I his sub? I doubt we'd label it like that, but I needed his support and depended on him to keep me together. In the years I'd visited the club, I knew that it took a strong man to submit to another.

"I'm sorry," I said. "They made me angry, like I don't know how to do the job. But I should have discussed it with you."

He didn't say anything, just continued giving me a look that screamed disappointment, and I wanted to get that gone right away.

"I'm not used to someone else being a guiding influence in my life. Since you arrived, I've noticed I'm a better person. Stronger. More certain than I have been in a long time that I was doing the right thing. That's all because of you."

He stepped over to me, stood between my legs, and took hold of my hand. "It's important that you know how much I love you," he said. "When I say something, it's for your own good."

"I'm not a child," I snapped then instantly regretted it.

He placed warm hands on my face. "No, you're not. You're an amazing, wonderful, strong man who needs help to stay on his path. If you don't want me to be that person, just tell me and I'll back off."

My heart thumped erratically. The thought of Sammy not being there when I came home from a mission, not reminding me that my job was important, and being my strength would have me cracking within a month. Was I his sub? Fuck if I gave a shit. I needed him to care for me.

"I need you," I admitted. "I've never said that to anyone before, but I fucking damn well need you."

He bent down and kissed the top of my head. "That's all I wanted to know. Now, what's going on?"

"Rook and Kelly think I should back off and wait to see what Valerie does. I don't agree. Backing off would give her time to regroup, run, or hurt more people. I think by pressing my advantage, I can wear her down until she makes a mistake."

It took a few moments before I remembered this bitch was his mother, but he didn't say anything about it. He was silent for about five minutes, rubbing his fingers through my scalp, then he whispered, "She needs to be put down. You've been doing this job a long time and know better than anyone else what needs to be done."

His praise meant the world to me. I grabbed him by the hips and pulled him down on top of me, kissing his neck. "Thank you."

He chuckled. "For what?"

"Believing in me. Helping me to believe in myself again."

"Let's go talk to Rook."

He pushed up and grabbed my hand to help me stand. He held my index finger and led me back to the war room. Kelly was still there and had been speaking with Rook. He glanced at our joined hands and grinned like a loon.

"Haven's ready for his next assignment," Sammy told them, his voice strong and clear. It dawned on me that when he was standing up for me, he was fierce, like a bear protecting its cub. It was when he wasn't focused on me, on my needs, that he was hesitant and uncertain.

"We don't think it's a good idea," Rook told him.

"And *we* say it is. Haven knows what he's doing, and I trust him to get it done. If you don't trust him, then maybe we're not needed anymore."

We? It wasn't the first time he'd used the word, but he was throwing down the gauntlet and backing it up with proof that he had no intention of walking away.

It was quiet for a few moments, then Rook chuckled. "Remind me never to piss him off, Haven. I get the feeling he'd give as good as he got."

"Better," Sammy shot back. "I don't understand why you don't trust Haven to complete this assignment. He said you gave him permission to do what he thought was best, but now you're saying he can't go forward. What's up with that?"

Rook cleared his throat. "I understand that you care about Haven, but you've only known him a short while. Kelly and I have worked with him for years. We've had people die on us before, and if I thought it was necessary, I'd ask for someone to do it again. We don't want to lose Haven any more than you do. There are other battles to be fought."

"I appreciate the sentiment," I cut in. "My mind is made up."

Sammy cleared his throat and pinned me with a stare.

"Sorry, *our* minds are made up. The mission proceeds as we planned it. I don't want anyone to have time to pull in their assets. She's finally learned that she's vulnerable, and I intend to exploit that. There are only a few more people on my list. They're her lynchpins, and once I remove those, her entire structure will collapse in on itself, and leave her vulnerable."

"Why the fuck aren't you listening?" Rook roared, followed by a slam, which I could only assume was him hitting whatever his computer sat on. "She. Is. *Never*. Vulnerable. She's like an animal. If you back her into a corner, you'll find out she's that much more dangerous."

"And you're not listening either," Sammy said, his voice dead calm. "Haven knows what he's doing."

"So what the hell? You *want* him to end up dead, kid? You're not in the will yet," Rook snarled.

Sammy's lip turned up into a sneer and he growled, a sound that sent shivers up my spine.

"You listen to me, you sorry sack of shit. This man has risked his life more in the last few months than you probably did in your entire life. No one would blame him if he walked away, because not one of you ever took his needs into consideration. It's a little late for you to be acting all worried. I'm here now, and I'm taking care of him. If he says it's time to act, then it's time."

Sammy's chest puffed up as he spoke. The authority in his voice was clear, and he wouldn't back down from anyone right now. He'd do anything to protect me, but he also knew when I had to work.

"We've *always* worried about Haven. Don't think you're going to come in here and things are going to change. Haven is our operative. He takes orders from us. If we say go, he goes. If we say wait, he waits. It's simple enough to understand."

"Then you're on your own. Haven and I are through."

"Haven, don't—"

I grinned when Sammy gripped my wrist. Rook was right, he was a tough fucker in his own right.

"Sorry, Sammy says we're done, so we're done."

CHAPTER SEVENTEEN

In all my time spent with the agency, no one had ever gotten the better of Rook. It was fucking epic to listen to him sputter as Sammy led me from the war room and to our bedroom.

"I can't go," I told him sadly.

"I know. You have to finish this job."

"Maybe after…we can leave, start a life together." The words sounded false, even to my ears. The job was a large part of me, and I couldn't walk away from it. The thought hit me before I could think. If I had to make a choice between the job and Sammy, which one would win?

Sammy lay back on the bed, his arms folded behind his head. "We both know the only way you'll leave the job is if you can't physically do it, or if you're in a pine box. Trust me, I know you better than you think."

"Can I ask you a question?" I blurted, finally not able to stand it any longer.

"Anything you want."

"Why is it that you'll face down Rook, but you have problems being in the same room as Kelly?"

Sammy's brows drew together as if he was trying to find an answer.

"People scare me," he admitted. "Every time Arianna brought a new person to meet me, I was never certain what they'd expect. There were rules, of course. No leaving permanent marks, no broken bones, no sex without a condom, but beyond that, not much else was forbidden. And I was expected to be good and accept it, no matter what *it* was."

He took a breath, then graced me with a lopsided grin.

"Frankly, some people are fucking freaky. If I told you some of the things they did to me, you'd probably insist on hunting them all down and killing them. There's a few I probably wouldn't mind, but beyond that…

"You're different. With you, what I see is what I get. The day you found me, I looked into your eyes and I saw nothing but concern for me. It was the first time ever. I knew then that you were the person I needed to be with. Each time I had to go with someone, I swore that when I was free, no one would ever hurt me again. I'd be the strong one. With you, I found someone who needed me to be strong. You needed someone to care for you, even if you didn't think so."

I frowned at him. The fact he saw me beyond the exterior thrilled me, but frightened me to death. He must have seen something in my expression, because he rolled his eyes and continued talking.

"You told me you were badass, and don't get me wrong, you are, but there is a side of you that needs to be taken care of, to be loved. I'd like to think that, with me, you're getting the best of both worlds."

I stood at the door a few moments, desperately trying to decide what I should do. Fortunately Sammy took the choice from my hands.

"They'll come for you, I promise. For now, take your shoes off and relax."

I toed off my sneakers and lay on the bed beside Sammy, who immediately stood. I eyed him curiously, and he smiled at me. He walked to the end of the bed and pulled up my socked foot, digging his thumbs into the arches. I admit I moaned.

"Feels good, right?"

"I'll give you until tomorrow to stop," I whimpered.

"So now that you're at my mercy, tell me about your sister."

The question was like a splash of cold water. I tensed, but Sammy appeared oblivious. He just kept rubbing my feet, until I melted into the bed. I didn't want to talk about her, not to Sammy. Even though I hadn't seen her in so many years, she was still my weak spot.

"You know that you can tell me anything, right? I'll never judge you."

"How do you know about her?"

"Sometimes you talk in your sleep. We hold conversations, and you'll answer questions if I ask. You murmured the name Christina so many times I finally asked you who it was. I didn't even know you had a sister."

Her name rolling off his tongue was sweet. It was as if there were no harshness associated with it.

"If you wanted to know so badly, may as well pick my brain while I was asleep, right?" I asked, much more harshly than I'd intended. It was the thought that he could plumb my secrets while I was unaware that didn't sit right. It also showed my comfort level with him, if I slept that soundly.

"You can be such a prickly thing," Sammy said, digging his thumbs into my arch. "I only wanted to have a conversation with you. I could insist we talk, but I'd rather you felt like you had a choice in it."

He said it lightly, but the words spoke volumes. We both knew if he told me to talk to him, I would. I could never deny him anything. Haltingly at first, I began the story, about my mother's drunken escapades, not knowing who Christina's and my father had been, or even if we shared the same one, and ended it with being drafted by the agency. Through it all, he never spoke, just rubbed and listened.

"We should go see her," he said after I was quiet for some time.

"No, I don't want to see her that way. The brain damage was so extensive, I doubt she'd recognize me, and that would kill me."

"I think you're killing yourself, wondering what might be. We can't let past regrets ruin our futures. Every day I remind myself that I have to let go of what Arianna did to me, because if I don't, it will destroy me. You can't keep letting your sister and the memory of what happened drag you down."

He was right, but without that rage that simmered in my belly, what did I have left? Then I peered up into the face that smiled at me, the eyes twinkling, and knew. Sammy gave me a reason to go on every day. Pleasing him, being taken care of by him, gave me a sense of purpose. The thought I was submissive to him wended its way into my mind, but was dismissed just as quickly.

"I don't even know where she is."

Sammy laughed. "You work for an agency that has a finger in every pot. Don't you think, if you asked, Rook would find out for you?"

"After our display? I'll be lucky if he doesn't have them force me out of the house at gunpoint."

"Won't happen," he informed me. "Rook cares about you. Deeply. It may seem weird, but he wants you safe, at least as much as your job will allow. If you had even the slightest bit of hesitancy about going forward on this job, I would have sided with him. But I trust in you. Your abilities. I know you'll do what you need, but you're not stupid. You'll do it safely, because you have a home to come to now." He let go of my foot, straddled my legs, and pinned my wrists to the bed.

I could see the look of concern on his face. It shook me to my core, knowing that I'd become weak enough to depend on another person, even if it was Sammy. Still, I couldn't deny my need for his touch.

Sammy reached for the lube and dropped it onto the bed and then lay next to me. I turned on my side as his arm wrapped around my stomach and drew me close. I soaked into the feeling, warm and comfortable. No pressures, nothing to think about other than what Sammy told me to. To simply be. No other person had ever been able to draw that from me. I wasn't sure what power Sammy had, but he definitely had it over me.

"You're a good man, Haven," he whispered.

"I kill people," I countered. I pictured the blood on my hands from countless assassinations. Yet I wouldn't stop. After what happened to my sister… No, now wasn't the time to think about that. I needed to focus on Sammy. What he was doing to me. How his hands drifted over my chest and abdomen. How his fingers lingered on the scars.

"I can't tell you how sexy these are," he whispered.

I snorted. "They're fucking scars. It means I let someone get too close."

Sammy pressed his erection against my ass cheeks. "You mean like this?"

A shudder went through my body. He was right. I was too close to him. He would eventually hurt me when he left, but right now I needed him so badly.

"I want you inside me," I murmured.

Sammy tossed the lube back onto the nightstand. "No, I don't think you do. I get the feeling you just need to be held."

I wanted to protest, but goddamn if he wasn't right again. As amazing as sex with Sammy could be, the comfort and safety he offered were so much more enticing at this moment. His fingers scratched lightly at my skin. Not painful, but pleasant in the feelings. The moan came from deep inside me.

"Let it out, Haven. Let me hear you. What is it you're keeping locked up so tight? Why can't you let me in?"

Chrissy's face flashed into my mind. Not the one I loved, the one that proved to be the only good thing in my young life, but the bloody and beaten one. The one that stared up at me with blank, vacant eyes. The gun in my hand and Arnie's fucking sneer, reminding me how weak and pathetic I had been. His death, so richly deserved, and the emotion I couldn't dredge up. The expression of every person I'd killed, when they realized I had come to end their lives. What about their families? Did they grieve? Had I taken something from them that could never be replaced?

The thoughts slammed into my head, and I couldn't shut them out. For every person I saved, had I caused someone else to suffer as I had? What kind of a monster did that make me? How could Sammy bear to look at me?

And the dam burst. I blurted it all out as I sobbed like a baby. I hated myself for this. I hated Sammy for making me do it. He held me through it all. I didn't know if he said anything else, because all my attention was focused on his fingertips and my cries. My mother. My sister. I'd never cried over either of them. I was stronger than that. Nothing would ever hurt me. Yet this young man holding me had broken through every defense I had like it was nothing. He pulled every fucking emotion out of me, even those I'd kept buried for years.

When my tears finally subsided, Sammy leaned over and put his lips near my ear. "Sleep, love."

And I drifted off while he held me.

~

The knock on the door several hours later woke me, but didn't seem to surprise Sammy. The conversation had drained me, and I didn't have the energy to move. He still lay next to me as he continued to run his hand over my body. He glanced over his shoulder and called out, "Come in."

The door opened and Kelly entered. His expression was grim, and my heart thumped so loud I was afraid everyone would hear it.

"Rook gave his blessing for you to continue on the mission," he said. Then he leveled his gaze at Sammy. "He wants to speak to you. Alone."

"What? Why?" I demanded.

"You know Rook. He didn't say. He wants to talk now, though."

Sammy grinned and chuckled, which seemed to jack up Kelly's attitude. "Let him know I'll be there when I can find the time, but not to wait for me."

"You can't—" Kelly sputtered.

"Can and did. I don't work on Rook time, I operate solely on Sammy time, and right now that means I'm hanging out with Haven, because he needs me more."

Kelly reminded me of one of the cartoon characters Sammy enjoyed. His jaw dropped open, eyes bugging out, and he pointed between us and stuttered incoherently.

"Was there anything else you wanted?" Sammy asked, his voice dripping with honey.

Without another word, Kelly turned and stalked out, slamming the door behind him.

"You are such a troublemaker," Sammy teased.

"Me? How am I involved in this?"

He scooted closer and wrapped an arm around me. "Because you need me to hold you now."

He was magic. That was the only thing I could call it. He knew what I needed and gave it to me. The heat that pooled in my stomach at his touch, featherlight, warmed me all the way through.

"I love you," I whispered.

"Yes, you do," he teased, nipping my ear.

"I can't make it without you," I admitted.

"Good, because I have no intention of going anywhere. You amaze me, you know."

A chuckle bubbled out of me. "Oh?"

"You've been alone for so long. Between the job you do and the weight you carry on your shoulders, I'm stunned you're still so strong."

"I'll tell you a secret. I'm not. When I started, I used to be. I was young and cocky, certain of my place in the world. The assignments I took were for the good of the people, to serve and protect. It was like my job in the military, but on steroids. Year after year, though, I lost my taste for it.

"When I shot the asshole who hurt my sister, my mother was covered in his chunks. She was repulsed. She puked and screamed. Me? I was fascinated by the power I held in my hand.

"But killing a man is never as easy as they make it look in the movies. You can't just twist a man's neck and break it. You can't punch through his chest and rip out his heart. Death takes skill and planning. And it moves along at its own pace. A knife to the heart might kill someone instantly, but more often than not, he'll lay on the floor and bleed out. Death is seldom clean. Gunshots don't leave tiny holes. They rip through flesh like a hot knife through butter. They only stop if they hit something or tear out an exit point. Shoot a person in the head and the entry wound will be small, but the hole it makes on the way out will leave a splatter trail over everything. Bone, bits of gray matter, blood, it all comes out.

"I prefer the long distance for that type of kill. That shit sticks to you no matter what. For my assignments, I draw the worst of the worst. Most of them were people that Rook wanted dead ASAP. Some, though, were so horrid that I decided they needed to suffer. In the beginning, those were my favorites. I wanted to see their eyes as they experienced the terror that their victims felt. To know that no one could save them. For them to beg for their lives. Then end them."

Sammy shuddered, and I thought he was repulsed.

"Wow. Eye for an eye, huh? Yeah, I can see that. I think sometimes a person has to know why they're about to die. I don't know why, but it seems to me that it's closing the book on their lives. I can see why you were so upset earlier, but you have to know that people don't change overnight. The ones you have to take down? It's because they escaped justice. You get no joy in it, which I'm guessing they probably did. The fact it eats you up should prove to you that you're nothing like them. If you didn't care, it wouldn't hurt."

Sammy's words washed over me, and made me think. He hadn't been put off at all. In fact, he sounded proud of me, and that soothed my jangling nerves. "I thought I didn't have the stomach for it anymore. I assumed that I was done, but wouldn't be able to walk away. When Rook told me I could, I swore to myself that this would be my last job. That after I was done with this assignment, I'd turn around and not look back. Then I met this man, and he showed me a different way of looking at things. Proved to me that I wasn't like the people I killed.

"He opened my eyes and I saw the world around me for what it is. Filled with good people who need someone to stand between them and the ones who intend to harm them. It's a long trip back, but I think I'm making it. At least I can see the light at the end of the tunnel. I might never regain the enthusiasm I had, but I know I can keep at it."

"And why is that?"

I leaned closer and kissed him. "You. It's all you."

He grinned and patted my cheek. "You're learning."

~

It was two days before Sammy went to speak to Rook. Despite Kelly's sputtering, Sammy simply smiled and went about his business. When he announced he was ready, I walked him to the door, intent on being with him, but he placed a hand on my chest and reminded me that he was supposed to go alone.

"You'll tell me what he says," I demanded.

He flashed his trademark grin. "Maybe. If you're good."

"I'm serious, Sammy. I want to know why he insists on talking to you."

"Don't worry about it. Everything will be fine, I promise." He paused. "Do you know who you're going after next?"

"Yeah. This one isn't part of Valerie's group exactly, but he reaps the benefits. This guy, everyone refers to him as Lanny, had dealings with Arianna. She—" I stopped, not wanting to dredge up memories for Sammy.

"Go on," he prodded.

"It's nothing. I'll take care of him."

I turned to leave and his hand gripped my arm.

"You have something to tell me, so do it." His voice was stern, and I knew that any attempt to dissuade him would be ultimately futile.

"He hurts boys," I whispered. "According to the records we pulled off Arianna's computer, he received the boys who weren't needed anymore. He was allowed to do with them whatever he wanted, but then it was up to him to dispose of them. It looks like some got sold off, but others…"

"Others, he killed."

I nodded. "They believe some of the bodies they located were his victims."

"Okay, so what will you do when you find this guy?"

I hadn't decided yet how I was going to confront him, but he was definitely an up close and personal job. The information we'd gotten was sketchy at best and required a lot of connect the dots, but the team that worked for Rook was the best. If they passed it over, it was as good as gold in my book.

"I'm not sure," I answered.

"Do me a favor?" he asked, his eyes boring into me.

"If I can."

He gripped my arms and pulled me down to eye level. "Make it hurt. A lot."

I chuckled. "Yeah, that I can do."

Chapter Eighteen

I sat at the table, going over the dossier we had on Lanny. He was important to Valerie somehow, I knew it. The boys were a side payment, something she allowed, but for the life of me, I couldn't figure out why. Everything we'd gathered, and I wouldn't deny it wasn't much, showed she kept a tight ship. Lanny didn't fit into the mold, and I wanted to know why.

"Hard at work? Don't let me interrupt."

I'd been so intent on the files, I hadn't noticed Sammy leaning against the doorframe until he spoke. I pushed back the chair and rushed to him, running my hands over his body as if I was going to find some wound.

"What did he want? Are you okay?"

"It's fine. I told you it would be."

His tone said everything was not fine.

"Sammy," I growled.

"I'm glad you're worried, but there isn't anything wrong."

"Don't bullshit me," I shouted. "Your body language, your tone, the way you won't meet my eyes. Every one of those facts tells me that Rook said something to you, and you're going to tell me now."

He dipped his head and quirked an eyebrow. "Oh, really? Seems to me that you talk, I listen. That's how it works."

I grabbed him by the front of his shirt and twisted it in my fist. I put my face close to his and snapped, "Not this time."

He was still for a moment, then he burst out laughing, pushing away from me. I was at a total loss as to what the hell was going on. After he caught his breath, he brushed his hands down the front of his T-shirt, smoothing away the wrinkles, then he put his hand on my arm and walked me back over to the table. "Sit," he said, his voice low. Of course I turned my chair around and sat.

"I want you to take a deep breath. You're agitated, and I need your head clear."

He was speaking to me like you would a child, and it was beginning to piss me off.

"I need you to trust me that everything is okay. Rook only wanted to talk, nothing more. Okay?"

"No, it's not. You wouldn't accept that from me, and I'm sure as hell not going to let you smile and say everything is fine when it's goddamn well not."

Sammy straddled my legs, pressing our chests together. "Haven, I swear to you, if something was wrong, I would tell you. There isn't."

"Then why won't you talk to me?" I hated the petulant tone, but I needed to know what was going on.

"Seeing you all protective like this is a turn-on, you know," he said, pushing his crotch together with mine.

I gritted my teeth. "You're not going to distract me. I'm trained to keep my focus."

"Really? Can we test that?"

He leaned forward and ran his tongue over my neck, which brought up goose bumps. Then he sank his teeth into the tender flesh, sucking hard.

"What are you doing?" I gasped.

He leaned back and smiled at me. "Marking things that are mine. I want to make sure anyone else who finds them knows that they're already claimed."

His grip tightened and he pressed his erection into my stomach. I was losing this battle so quickly it wasn't even funny.

"Please," I moaned.

"Please what? Tell me."

"I have to know what Rook wanted."

Sammy stilled and leaned back, a lopsided grin on his face.

"You're right. You *are* focused."

He stood, his bulge tenting his pants obscenely, and stepped back. I licked my lips, and he chuckled, wrapping a fist around his engorged cock. "If I said you had a choice between knowing what Rook said and having this, what would you say?"

I tore my gaze away from his crotch and glared at him.

"Right. You'd choose that." He sighed. "Fine. Let's talk about Rook."

147

He sat at the table across from me. "Rook wasn't happy with me contradicting him. He tried to explain to me that I was new and didn't know what the protocols were for agents. He listed the rules, and there are a shit ton of them, then told me that he needed you to follow the ones he set. He said it wasn't a good idea for you to go off on your own, and that I was risking your life by saying it was okay."

I was on my feet before I realized it. I stalked toward the war room, intent on ripping Rook a whole new asshole, but when Sammy shouted, "Stop," I froze in my tracks, cursing myself for letting him do that to me.

"You are *not* going to go off half-cocked," he warned.

"Oh, it's going to be the whole cock, believe me," I said, regardless of how stupid it sounded. My fingers clenched into fists, the urge to hit something overwhelming me.

"No, you're not going to say anything at all. You're going to come back here and talk to me. You'll listen to what I have to say before you do something you'll regret."

"I'm not going to regret this," I promised.

"And I'm going to make sure of that. Come back and sit down."

I cast a glance down the hall, then huffed a sigh. "Fine," I groused.

After I took my seat, Sammy stretched his arms out and forced my fists open so he could take my hands. "Rook had some good points. He's been taking care of all his operatives for years before I showed up. He is certain he knows what's best, and he's cautious, especially about you, because you're a valuable asset to him."

"That doesn't give him the right to—"

"Dial it back, Haven. It gives him every right. If Rook didn't worry about you, I'd drag your ass out of here and hole up somewhere, just the two of us. But he *does* care, and that makes all the difference to me. After he finished, I asked if it was my turn to talk. He agreed to let me say something. I told him I appreciated what he said, and we were on the same page in wanting to keep you safe, but Valerie isn't going to play by his rules, so we can't either.

"I know she killed my father, and I'm sure she killed her ex-boss so she could take over his operation, and she turned it into an empire on the backs and blood of people like me. Rules of engagement don't apply here, no matter what he thinks. If he wants the job done, he's going to have to let you do it your way. He gave you all the leeway you'd need, and he can't take it away now.

"I promised him that I'd look after you. That we would look out for each other. He's not happy about it, and that's fine, he doesn't need to be, but he does accept what I said. Now do you understand why I didn't want to tell you?"

"Yeah, I guess," I grumbled.

"Good. Now, you caused a problem that needs taking care of. I'm going to get a glass of water. I want you to go into the bedroom, strip off your clothes, lie on the bed, and put your hands on the headboard. Don't move or touch yourself until I get there."

A shiver ran through me at the huskiness in his voice. I practically ran for the bedroom, his chuckle following me.

~

Baltimore was a beautiful city, but like everywhere, it had the neighborhoods that you didn't want people to see. Rundown buildings that were probably inhabited by more rats and cockroaches than human tenants. It surprised me that people lived here, but it wasn't far off from where we'd lived when we were kids. Of course there was always that house that everyone envied, too. The person didn't have to have a palace, just a nice house. Lanny Davies had that house. It was an enormous old Victorian style. A sprawling yard with a lot two to three times the size of those that surrounded it.

From the outside, it was a pretty place. There were topiaries of cartoon characters in the front yard. I had no idea who they were, but Sammy probably would. It disturbed me, because it gave the house an appearance of innocence, and if what we believed went on inside actually did, it was a perversion of the childhood many kids would never experience.

Lanny was different from the others I'd stalked. He was nervous, almost insanely so. His house had a security guard that sat in a side room, presumably watching camera feeds on monitors. My notes didn't mention the guard, and I had no desire to hurt a potentially innocent person, so there would need to be a different approach on this one. I'd let Rook know about the guards, because I had to wonder if they really didn't know what their boss was doing.

An abandoned house down the street from Lanny's became my base of operations. Lanny rarely left his home, and a few people I spoke with knew next to nothing about the man, except he was always very generous when it came time to hand out Halloween candy. The kids loved him, everyone said.

It turned my fucking stomach.

I stayed at my post for four days, watching the times the guards switched off. There were four of them that worked six hours each. When one arrived, the one on duty would tour the house. He'd be gone for three hours, and upon his return, he'd leave for the night. They never deviated from their schedule. Everything was run with such precision that it wouldn't be hard to throw them off with a few ill-timed problems that cropped up.

My opening came late one afternoon when one of the men found himself inexplicably off schedule. Well, that might have had something to do with the fact that I tracked him to his house, then screwed up his car so he wouldn't be able to get to work on time. That meant either the guard watching the cameras would have to leave them unattended, or there would be no tour. I could work with either situation.

I watched as the guard took a call, his gestures showing how unhappy he was with the situation. He hung up and flipped a few switches, then stormed off to do his rounds. As soon as he was out, I slipped into the house, put the cameras on a playback loop, and disconnected the emergency call light. As long as no one did any in-depth check, they'd never know I'd been in the building.

Mindful of the guard, I crept around the house, taking note of the decor. Lanny was a man of money, apparently. The furniture was all modular, distressed-looking teak. Very snazzy. I loved the way it flowed throughout the house; from bookcases to futons, each piece had been carefully chosen to complement the rest of it. Maybe I'd compliment him on his decor before I killed him.

I used the time the guard patrolled the outside to search the upper level and main floor of the house without finding anything useful. Raised voices outside alerted me to the guard returning as the other one made it to work. They entered the house together, as the one who had done the patrol complained about the other one being late. They spoke quickly and agreed Lanny didn't need to be informed, as nothing ever happened anyway.

I grinned and wondered what they'd say if they knew I'd hidden in an alcove, tucked away, but still able to see and hear everything around me. Unless the guards were standing right in front of my hiding spot, they'd never notice me. When the first guard returned to the office, and the other moved upstairs, I headed toward a door I assumed would lead me to the basement, the only place I'd yet to check out, and where I assumed I'd find Lanny since I hadn't seen him leave.

The door was heavy wood, maybe oak. It could keep someone out for a good while, unless they came prepared with a battering ram, which I must have left in my other bag. I tried the knob, and found that while the door was sturdy, it didn't seem well secured. I slipped my knife through the crack and popped the lock, a simple hook, then stepped inside and started down the stairs.

Some kind of neoclassical piano music drifted up from below. It was a piece I wasn't familiar with, but the dark tones seemed appropriate for the house. I hadn't heard it from upstairs, and wondered about the soundproofing of the lower level. Given what we suspected Lanny had been responsible for, it would make sense he wouldn't want anyone hearing what was going on.

At the bottom of the stairs, I paused to take in the layout of the place. The room I was in appeared to be a living room. The teak furniture dominated here, too, but this time had leather coverings as opposed to the fabric of the stuff upstairs. A well-stocked liquor cabinet stood behind a small portable bar, which had an assortment of glasses and a built-in icemaker. What caught my attention, though, had to be the bookcase near the corner of the room. A few inches shorter than the eight foot ceiling, it stood on a swivel base, which allowed it to turn freely. There were kid's books on the lower shelves, and slightly less than pornographic books up higher. On the opposite wall stood a door where I could hear the music playing.

After about ten minutes, the music stopped, so I hid behind the bookcase and waited. A few moments later, a door opened, and out popped a man's head. He glanced around a few times, before he stepped into the room. From the pictures in his file, I knew I'd found my guy.

Lancaster Davies was a short, squat man. If the gay community wanted a troll, Lanny was definitely the poster boy for the part. Shaggy dark hair drooped below his collar, his eyes reminded me of a possum's. They were dark and beady and creeped me the hell out. He poured himself a snifter of brandy and sat on the couch. He sniffed the alcohol, then hummed appreciatively, before sipping it.

I tried to look into the other room, but the angle I was at made it impossible to see much beyond the doorway without showing myself. Finally I got fed up. Hoping to spook him, I cleared my throat. Without even checking, the little rat bag rushed into the room and pulled the door behind him, the lock clicking in place. Definitely an antsy bastard.

I strode to the door, stood to the side of it, in case Lanny had a gun, and knocked. "I'm guessing you're in there pushing your panic button," I called out. "Won't work. I disabled it before I came to find you."

There was silence for a moment, then a scratchy voice asked, "What do you want?"

"I'm sorry, how rude of me. My name is Haven. I'm here to kill you."

~

For someone who was such a worried little shit, Lanny's doors weren't built to withstand a good solid kick. And a gunshot. Or two. It made me wonder if Lanny realized his soundproofing would make it so no one could hear him, either. I burst into the room to find him desperately punching the phone's panic button.

"Told you. No one is coming for you. Right now, it's just you and me." I cast my gaze over the area. A finely appointed leather chair with a dark-stained teak table sat in the middle of the room, allowing a good view of the gas fireplace. Above the mantle were crossed twin swords. The feature pieces in this little house of horrors, though, were cabinets that filled most of one wall. Lighted top sections contained floggers, whips, and other sundry items, all displayed with loving care. The bottom halves were drawers I found myself afraid to open. Directly across from them, in perfect view of the soft sofa, stood a metal table, similar to what you'd find in a doctor's office, but this had clamps spaced evenly along the edges, where a body could be displayed in any number of positions. There was little doubt what Lanny did here.

"Why not have a seat? We've got time, so we should be comfortable."

His eyes went wide, but he sat. Seeing some rope in one of the hutches, I took the lengths and ignored the rest while I tied Lanny to the chair. He didn't struggle, simply dipped his head in resignation.

"I knew you'd come," he said.

"Oh? Go on."

"Valerie said you would find me. She told me she wanted me to kill you."

I laughed at that. "You? Kill me?"

His eyes blazed.

"You're a mousy little bastard. You wouldn't last against me."

"Tell that to the people I've killed," he snarled. "You might think you're untouchable, but Valerie will find out who you are, then no one can save you."

I laughed at his pathetic display. "You're her assassin? Wow. She must have gotten you pretty cheap."

He flushed and averted his eyes.

Lighted cabinets held a variety of toys, but nothing you'd find in any BDSM club I'd ever visited. Even with my knowledge, limited though it was, I knew most of this stuff wouldn't be allowed in a legitimate club.

I started opening drawers, pushing aside ball gags, spiked cock rings, electric prods, and machines for penetration, with huge dildos on the ends. What I found when I got to the highboy dresser sealed Lanny Davies's fate. Pictures. Hundreds, maybe thousands, scattered in the drawer, a testament to his disregard for their lives. Young boys, eyes wide with fear, cheeks stained with tears.

This man didn't play, he tortured. He kept photographs like trophies. The sick fuck would hook kids to these machines and sit down with his glass of wine to watch them suffer. My stomach clenched at the thought.

"She paid you in kids," I whispered. "You'd kill for her, and she'd offer up the boys for your sick games."

"She said no one wanted them," he protested. "They wouldn't be missed."

I turned and sneered at him. "Guess you were wrong there, Lanny. You said you've killed for her. Who?" I demanded.

He was quiet, defiance shining in his eyes. I went over and grabbed his hair, jerked his head back, pressed my gun against his head and gritted my teeth. "Spill."

He began stammering, calling out names I'd never heard of, but would tell Rook about. Then he said, "Her husband. One of her former employees who someone ripped out his eyes. Some guy she said was trying to blackmail her into letting a kid go. Plus a few people who got big heads and brought too much attention to her operations. A few weeks ago, it was some guy named Josiah."

"See how much easier it is when you work with me?" I asked, as I slid the gun back into the holster. My mind reeled. Sammy's father. Rouland. No doubt the blackmailer was Tim, the guy who tried to get Sammy away from Valerie. The attempt on my life. How many others had he taken out and how many kids lost their lives to him in payment?

A calmness I hadn't known in years swept over me as I pulled one of the gags from the drawer and forced him to open his mouth, shoving the thing as far in as I could. He screamed, shaking his head from side to side.

I walked toward the fireplace and pressed the button, satisfied when it roared to life. I pulled one of the blades from the wall, tested the heft and smiled at the obvious craftsmanship. Whoever the maker was, they were more than competently skilled.

"Now see, this is a fine weapon," I murmured, stroking a finger lightly over the blade. "An obvious forgery, but overall not too bad. It's got good balance, but it's too shiny to have been anything other than a reproduction."

I shot a glance toward Lanny, hoping to convey without words what was about to come.

"Usually I'd never sully a blade this nice, but it seems more appropriate than a bullet between the eyes." I jammed the blade into the fire, then turned my attention back to Lanny.

At that, muffled cries from behind the ball gag burst forth. I shook my head, surprised that the man had invested in such cheap toys. Or... then it dawned on me.

"You *wanted* to hear them scream. Those boys you brought down here, the ones who begged you to take them back home before you beat and sodomized them were meant to scream, weren't they? The gag was...for what? To keep them from biting through their tongues? I guess I can understand that. I mean, I don't approve of what you did to them, and rest assured, I'm going to see you pay for it. But I don't want it to be over too quickly, so I see the wisdom of the gag."

He began to struggle as realization finally set in.

"You're not going anywhere, I promise. Maybe you and I have something in common," I admitted, though it caused bile to churn in my stomach. "I don't necessarily *like* pain, but I know how to inflict it well enough."

I pulled the sword out of the fire. Even through the grip, I could feel the heat. I strode across the room, each step making Lanny more keenly aware of what was about to happen. I could have felt bad, but I pictured the children in my dossier. The wounds that would never heal from the cold, dead flesh. I shuddered involuntarily. I was an evil son-of-a-bitch, but I didn't hurt children. And I didn't give a tinker's damn about those who did.

I stabbed forward with the sword, blocking out the screams as it pierced the tender flesh on his side, which sizzled as the blade made its way through and charred the skin.

"Are we having fun, Lanny?" I shouted, wanting desperately to be heard over his agonized cries. "Is this what you did to those poor kids? Tortured them. Made them fucking wish they were dead? Made them cry out for their mom and dad?"

I yanked the sword out, causing him to shriek in pain. The more I thought about those little kids, the more his suffering was music to my ears. I looked quickly at the mantle clock. Another two hours before the guard made his way back to this side of the house.

"We've got a long time left to play, Lanny," I muttered, stroking the blade in the flames once again. "How long do you think you'll be able to stay conscious? How long before *you* beg for death? I'm a lot more merciful than you. When you beg me for it, I'm going to let you have it. I'm not inhuman, though. You make it through the next couple hours, I may just let you live." I pulled the sword from the fire once more, the blade glowing a wicked red. "Okay, let's get started."

I gave him thirty minutes, tops.

CHAPTER NINETEEN

"Twelve minutes," I told Sammy. "He passed out after that. I hadn't even gotten a good start."

I lay on my stomach as Sammy stroked his hands down my back.

"Did you at least have fun?"

I waited for a moment before I answered. "I don't know that I'd say it was fun, but it didn't bother me as much as it did six months ago. I...found out a few things. They're not pleasant."

"Okay. Tell me."

I rolled over and tugged him down onto the bed, then wrapped my arms around him. He'd been the one to hold me when I cried, so I owed it to Sammy to be there for him.

"He killed your father and Tim."

Sammy's breath hitched, but he made no outward expression that he'd heard me.

"Sammy?"

He drew in a deep breath, then smiled at me. "Thank you. It helps to know."

"It's okay to cry," I told him, echoing the sentiment he'd said to me.

"I did years ago. I cried myself to sleep almost every night. To be honest, I don't have anymore tears left. I knew my dad was dead, but now I know that he was murdered. And Tim? I feel bad about what happened. If he hadn't been trying to protect me, he wouldn't have died. But I can't change any of that."

Even if he didn't want to cry, I still held him. He wrapped an arm around my waist and snuggled up against me.

"I appreciate what you're trying to do," he murmured against my chest, "but I'm okay."

"Then stay here for me," I told him.

A knock, then the sound of a door opening had me on full alert.

"Are you guys decent?" Kelly asked.

"Haven't been since I got here, why start now?" Sammy replied.

Kelly walked in and closed the door behind him.

"Rook informs me that the police located Lanny's stash of photographs and…paraphernalia. They've got a bulletin out for his arrest."

"Won't find him," I assured him. "The guard fled the home when I confronted him, demanding to know what happened to my son. Then the cleanup crew came in and removed Lanny, plus pulled the files from his computers."

"Are you sure it was wise to involve the authorities?"

"Normally I wouldn't have, but I wanted them to see what was going on under their noses. Maybe next time they won't be so quick to dismiss it when a kid turns up dead."

"I think it was a great idea," Sammy said, throwing his legs over the end of the bed. He stood, the globes of his ass pale in the bright sunlight. Kelly didn't even flinch when Sammy bent over to retrieve his clothing.

"You do know that out here you can sunbathe in the nude, right? Might help to get rid of those awful tan lines," Kelly said, shielding his eyes as if there was a glare.

Sammy turned to him and chuckled. "You're just looking for an excuse to ogle my ass, aren't you?"

"What? No," Kelly sputtered.

"Haven, tell Kelly why my ass is so nice."

I coughed, shocked as hell that he was playing with Kelly like this. Then I saw the cheeky grin and knew he was trying to ruffle the older man.

"They're two perfect pillows," I began. "Soft to the touch, but with a firmness that makes you want to squeeze them like melons. The light dusting of hair tickles when it brushes against your cheek as you—"

"Okay, I think you've had your fun," Kelly snapped.

"I don't think Kelly's into the boy bits," Sammy stage-whispered, slipping into his clothes.

"At his age, I don't know that he's into any bits," I replied.

"You can both go to hell. I have a very active sex life, thank you."

"Masturbation isn't sex," Sammy reminded him.

"It certainly is. As someone once said, 'it's sex with someone I love.'"

The room was quiet before we all broke up laughing. It was needed to relieve the stress and tension that floated in the air. In an effort to keep the mood lighter, I turned to Sammy.

"So, what happened to your shopping spree? It's been a couple months and I haven't seen anything different. Nor have I gotten my credit card back."

Sammy gawped. "You didn't notice the changes?"

My stomach clenched. He sounded hurt, and his eyes closed.

"Samuel, don't tease him. He's very sensitive."

"Fuck you," I snapped at Kelly, who only laughed. "Sammy, I'm sorry. What did I miss?"

He gave me a stupid grin that melted me on the inside. "I went online and bought some scented soaps that I thought you might like. I picked up a few new towels, something a bit bolder than the boring white ones you had. There are new blinds in the bedroom, and new curtains in the living area."

I blinked. "That's it? I gave you my credit card to go wild, and that's all you got?"

He sauntered over to me and wrapped me in an embrace. "Like you said, it's just a place. It doesn't matter what it looks like, only that we're in it together."

He'd made some romantic comments before, but he opened my eyes to the house in a way I'd never seen it. When I came back from a mission, I wasn't coming to the house, I was coming home. To him, to Kelly, to a place where I'd finally started to feel like I belonged.

"Oh."

"Is that a good oh, or a bad oh? Sometimes with you, I can't really know."

"I have a home now," I muttered, still reeling from the shock of my realization.

"See," Kelly said. "I told you eventually it would sink in. He can be rather thick."

Sammy busted a gut. "You've been watching him naked, too?"

Kelly spluttered then schooled his features. He walked over and placed a hand on my shoulder, smiled, then drew me into a hug. "It's been an honor working for you," he whispered.

I stepped back and grabbed his wrist. "What the hell are you talking about? You're not going anywhere."

He glanced over at Sammy and then his gaze drifted back to meet mine. "You have your family now. Samuel said he would take care of the home."

"What the hell? No one is going anywhere," I roared. "You don't move," I shouted to Kelly, "and you"—pointing to Sammy—"tell me what's going on."

"It was my decision," Kelly said. "The two of you work. You don't need another person in the house."

Sammy eyed Kelly and shook his head. "I'm not sure which of you is more stubborn. At least with Haven I can probably spank it out of him."

My face heated at his comment, but Kelly didn't seem to notice.

Sammy turned to me. "I told him you wouldn't let him go. He mentioned it just before you got back that he was thinking about moving on. I said he needed to stay for you...and me. I'm not sure when or how it happened, but he's become a part of my life, too. I'm not as afraid as I used to be. At least not of him. When he asked if we would be okay, I said I could take care of you and the house if I had to."

"You hear that? You're our family, too. We *need* you. Is that what you wanted to hear?"

Kelly's eyes were watery. I'd never seen the man show much emotion beyond laughing at my misfortune, but now it appeared he was having problems reining them in.

"What brought this on?" I asked softly.

Kelly shrugged. "I'm not really sure. I just thought maybe you'd be okay without me. I talked with Rook and he said he could reassign me."

"Bullshit!" Sammy shouted, pointing at Kelly. "You wanna go, then you man the hell up and say so. Don't tell him what I can do. Can I take care of him? Yes. Do I want to? Yes. Do I think I can do it without your help? No. I spent the last dozen years of my life as a fucking sex slave. I can figure out how to clean house, and I can hold Haven and keep him whole, but I don't know anything about cooking or maintaining a home. So if nothing else, I need you for that.

"Haven needs you for more. You've been his friend for ten years or more. The two of you have a bond I won't ever be able to share with him. He

159

doesn't want you to leave. I don't want you to leave. So the only person who has to make a choice now is you. If you're going to go, then take responsibility for your decision."

"You know, he can be kind of an asshole," Kelly grumbled.

"Sometimes we need an asshole to set us straight. He's right. If you don't want to be here, then just say so."

Kelly bit his lip as his gaze flitted between me and Sammy. I'd never seen him nervous before, and I couldn't understand his hesitation now.

"What's this about?" I asked, my voice even.

"It's stupid," he replied.

"I've no doubt about that," I teased, which earned me a smack from Sammy.

"Apologize," he snapped.

I gritted my teeth and said I was sorry. One day he was going to push me too far. And somehow that thought earned me another smack.

"What the fuck?" I whined.

"The expression on your face told me you needed another one."

"My God, you two are like children," Kelly said on a laugh. Then his expression changed and I could see the sadness there.

"Okay, spill. What's going on with you?"

"Children are supposed to outlive their parents."

"I'm confused. I didn't know you had kids."

"You can be such a dumbass," Sammy groaned then wrapped his arms around Kelly's shoulders. "He's talking about you."

I stood there in shock. Sammy had never touched Kelly. Barely allowed Kelly to be within a few feet of him, but now he willingly got into the man's space. Sammy said something I didn't catch. "Say what?"

Sammy hugged Kelly tight. "Kelly, tell me if I get this wrong, okay?" Then he turned to me. "He's trying to say he thinks of you as a son. He's worried about this mission, and he's afraid you won't be coming back from it."

That hit me right in the feels. I joined the group hug, pulling Kelly and Sammy to my chest. "It's going to be fine," I promised.

"You can't know that," Kelly whispered. "I have a dream where Samuel calls me and says you're not going to be coming home, and I wake drenched in sweat with a feeling that my heart stopped. I tell myself it was just a dream, but it takes me hours to believe it. Something bad is going to happen, I can feel it."

~

Kelly's admission rattled me. Sammy took him into the other room and the two of them were deep in conversation. I slipped into the war room and turned on the computer. Rook answered almost immediately. He listened politely and when I finished, he laughed. "Samuel is right. You *are* a dumbass. How could you not know how Kelly felt?"

"Because he never said anything?"

"One of the reasons you make a great operative is your ability to read your targets. To know what they're going to do, or how they'll react in a situation. It seems that once you're out of the field, you turn that off completely. Kelly's discussed missions with me several times. He's insisted on changes to the parameters so that you would be safer."

Was I really that blind? Obviously I was, if Sammy and Rook both saw it.

"Do you want to know what I see?" Rook asked.

"Sure, why not? Seems everyone knows me better than I do."

"After you lost your family, you pushed people away. You were always intense and had a laser focus about your missions, but outside of that there was a shell you built up. We always thought it was damn near impenetrable. Then you met a young man and he shattered what you encased yourself in. Now you're dealing with all of the things you didn't see for the last umpteen years. People care for you, and it's finally sinking in."

The new knowledge swirled in my mind. I'd locked myself away and made sure no one got close enough to hurt me the way I had been when…

"Can you find out where my sister is?" I asked.

Rook was too quiet for a minute.

"Or do you already know?"

I heard a deep sigh, then Rook answered. "Yes, we know. Christina died not long after you joined the Army. She went peacefully in her sleep."

My stomach clenched and temples throbbed. How long had they known? Hell, how long had they been lying to me? "Why didn't you tell me?" I demanded.

"You blamed yourself for what happened to her. What would have happened if you knew she died? I wanted to tell you, but Kelly said you weren't ready to hear it."

"Kelly said? Fuck that. He had no business sticking his goddamn nose in my life."

"He's been doing that for years," Rook informed me. "He's been running interference for you ever since I assigned him to you. Normally we don't let our operatives and their staff stay together more than a few months. We want to avoid emotional attachments, but Kelly seemed to be the perfect fit for you, and since you were our best operative and seemed to be attached to him, we kept you together. He appeared to be a stabilizing influence for you, and when you met Samuel, Kelly thought maybe you didn't need that anymore."

Thoughts filled my head. The fact that Rook and Kelly knew all this time that my sister was dead and never thought to tell me. I knew that the agency was secretive, but when it was something that affected me, it pissed me the fuck off.

"I don't need him," I snapped.

"Then you'll be okay with me reassigning him?"

I ground my teeth as anger overwhelmed my common sense. "I want him out of here."

"No, you fucking well don't," came a sharp rebuke from behind me. I turned on my heel and found Sammy stalking toward me. One day I would figure out how Sammy was able to sneak up on me so easily. "Private conversation. Later," he said, then clicked the button, cutting Rook off. "What in the ever loving hell is your problem?" he demanded, poking me in the chest.

"You can't possibly be serious. He's known for years that my sister was dead. He let me carry the guilt all the time he's known me. Fuck, I expect that kind of stuff from Rook, but not Kelly."

"I wouldn't have told you either," he informed me.

It was like I'd walked into a funhouse version of my life, and everyone I thought I knew was suddenly someone different.

"You weren't ready to hear it," Sammy continued. "Kelly knew that you didn't want to know. He waited for you to ask, but you never did. Why is that?"

The acids in my stomach burned. All I saw was a haze of red.

"What difference does it make? I'm a grown goddamn man, and they shouldn't be keeping secrets from me. Especially not when they're *about* me."

"Sit down," Sammy said, pointing at the chair.

I looked at the chair, then turned my attention back to Sammy. "No."

I gave him credit, he didn't even bat an eye at my refusal. He lifted his head and jutted out his chin. "You want to do this standing, we can do that."

"We're not talking about this," I retorted. My anger was building, and I needed to get away from Sammy. I didn't think I would ever hurt him intentionally, but there was enough rage that I couldn't be sure I wouldn't do it accidentally.

I turned to leave and he grabbed my sleeve.

"We're not done talking."

"Yes, we are." I jerked my arm away and headed for the door, intent on grabbing Kelly and dragging him from my house.

Sammy's next words brought me to a screeching halt. "Michael Patrick Phelps, you bring your ass back here and sit down."

CHAPTER TWENTY

I grabbed him by the neck and drew our faces together.

"Who the fuck told you my name?" I demanded. Possibilities stretched out in front of me and I didn't like any of them. The worst one was that Sammy was some kind of a plant sent in by Valerie, but it wasn't possible. There was no way she'd known we were coming.

"So I have your attention," he wheezed. "Might want to loosen your grip a bit, Chief."

I let go of him and he stood and smiled at me.

"Wanna sit down now?"

All the energy was sucked from my body. I'd never been in a situation before where someone I loved could hurt me like this. I staggered to the chair and sat, uncertain of what else I could do.

"How did you know?"

"I've known your name for months. Remember when I said you talk in your sleep? We've had interesting conversations, you and I. I know the first boy you ever let blow you was named Henry, and that when you were sixteen, he let you fuck him. I know you fucked your commanding officer when you were in the Army, and that's freaking awesome, even for you. And I know I'm the only man who's ever made love to you."

"Don't you mean fucked?"

He sat on my lap and wrapped an arm around my neck. "No. What you did with everyone else was fucking. What you and I do? That's making love."

"I've got a sore ass that begs to differ," I grumbled, even as I wanted to sink into his warm touch.

He laughed and reached around with his other arm to pull me into an embrace. "What I'm trying to say is that sometimes we know things we don't tell people for their own good. I know a lot about you, but I knew if I told you what I know, you'd worry about me."

"It's not the same," I told him.

"No, it's not. It's not fair that they knew something that important and didn't let you know. But you've been carrying this hurt around for so long, it became a part of you. It was your driving force. Kelly was afraid that if you lost it, you wouldn't recover. But he's also seen how much different you are now."

"With you," I supplied, even if it wasn't necessary.

"I wanted to wait until you were ready to talk to me yourself. I wouldn't have said anything, but your anger was about to get the better of you. You were going to throw away a friendship that I don't think you would ever be able to forgive yourself for, and I wouldn't allow you to hurt yourself."

"Me? He hurt me. He could have told me years ago. Maybe I could have—"

"Could have what? Come to terms with it?"

"Maybe," I said hesitantly.

"You're right. Maybe you could have. But Kelly didn't want to take the chance. I wouldn't have either. I think you know you weren't ready for the truth. As for what Kelly did? He was willing to risk you being angry to protect you. That's what a friend…what family does for one another."

My head pounded so much it hurt. My instincts told me I should throw Kelly out of the house, but they also told me I had to trust Sammy. Everything was all jumbled up inside. "I don't know what to do," I whispered, hating the uncertainty I heard in my voice.

"What you'll always do. You'll let me take care of you."

He hugged me, and it calmed me to hear his heart thumping a steady rhythm.

"Kelly also did something else. He wanted to be sure Christina would be remembered. And he did it for you."

I felt about two inches tall. In my anger, I wanted to lash out at him, but he'd done something so that Chrissy wouldn't be forgotten. Even if I died on a mission, he'd guaranteed her memory lived on. "He was looking out for me."

"Always. Just like I do. We're family, you have to keep reminding yourself of that. I know where she's buried. It's not far from here. Kelly wanted her to be close for you," Sammy murmured in my ear. "We could go if you wanted to."

I shook my head. "I wouldn't know what to say."

"When the time comes, you'll know," he promised. "Maybe we can go tomorrow. It's going to be nice."

"And you'll come with me?"

"I think Kelly would come, too. Do you want to ask him?"

My anger had bled out in the last few minutes, leaving behind a cold numbness in its place. Kelly and Rook were wrong for what they did, but I understood their reasons. I wasn't ready to handle the news, and I'd reacted badly when I found out the truth. But it wasn't anyone's fault. Before Sammy, I couldn't have handled it. The only way for me to deal with it was to keep a tight rein on my emotions, which Sammy had stripped away, leaving me able to feel again for the first time in years.

"I hurt," I admitted.

He tightened his arms around me. "I know, but that's the beginning of healing."

"She would have adored you, you know."

"I wish I could have known her." He sniffled and I looked up. Tears were streaming down his face. He hadn't cried for his own father, but thoughts of my sister made him weep.

We went out to the living room to find Kelly sitting on the couch. He looked older, or maybe I'd never really noticed. Sammy sat on one side, and I on the other. We wrapped him in a hug and he held us both as I thought about my sister's life and death.

It was painful, but cathartic. It was almost time for me to let Christina go and live in the present with the family I had built. The ones who had my back now.

Rest in peace, sis.

~

The cemetery wasn't anything like I'd imagined it. The sign said it was a private cemetery, something I hadn't heard of. Kelly told me that he had convinced Rook to purchase the plots to bury agents who lost their lives in the line of duty, then he'd had Christina moved here. He showed me where Chaperon, Bulwark, and Stonewall were buried, giving me a few moments to pay my respects to my fallen comrades. Then Sammy took me by the hand as we followed Kelly into the corner where a tree covered in purple flowers hung over a single mirror-polished gravestone with the words Christina Michelle Phelps, May 12, 1987 - October 15, 2001.

I knelt at the grave and ran my fingers over the stone, then stood up and plucked a flower from the tree to place on the grave. "Chrissy loved purple," I said to no one in particular.

"I know," Kelly said. "I had every piece of information I could find about her pulled so I could get to know her a little. I wanted this to be a place she would have liked. The tree is called a purple orchid. It's a specialty tree that we found in Phoenix. I also took the liberty of reserving the spot next to her, if you're interested."

I was surprised that Kelly had thought that far ahead. The gesture touched me, but I wasn't sure if I could spent eternity here without… Sammy squeezed my fingers. How he always knew the moment I needed something escaped me, but I was grateful for it.

"Tell us about your sister," he whispered.

He drew me close when I stood up, holding me tight. "As I was growing up, Christina was my best friend. We shared secrets in the night, including stories about who we thought our father might be. Each tale was more fantastic than the others. He was in turns a spy, the president, a Navy SEAL. There were so many wild stories, but never once had we admitted we thought he might have been some no good drunk our mother had gone on a bender with.

"She once said she thought maybe we didn't even have the same father, owing to the fact we looked nothing alike, but I told her that she was my sister; no one would ever be able to tell me different. She hugged me and I knew she loved me. I was never afraid to tell her how I felt. She was the center of my world, and when I lost her, the edges frayed and the center couldn't hold it together. Then I met Sammy and he showed me I had built a family. It's pretty fucking non-traditional, but I love it."

Sammy let me go, but laced his fingers with mine. I held my breath for along moment, then turned to Kelly. "Thank you for doing this."

"You're welcome."

"I'm sorry about…" We both spoke at once, then chuckled.

"Go ahead," he said.

"No, you."

"I'm sorry I kept it from you. I thought I was doing the right thing, but I can easily see how you would see it as a betrayal. That wasn't my intention at all. Samuel talked to me and I tried to get him to understand that I wanted to protect you, but he told me that wasn't my call."

"Sammy said he would have done the same thing, and I hate to admit he would be right. I wasn't ready to know. I'm not sure it's really hit me yet either."

"When it does, I'll be there," Sammy promised.

Kelly looked away, and even though I hadn't let go of the hurt, I had let the anger slip away. I took the three steps that separated us and put an arm over his shoulder. "What about you, old man? Are you going to be with us?"

He blinked several times, then nodded. "If you still want me there."

Sammy let go of my hand, reached over, and smacked him lightly on the back of the head. "You're family. Sometimes we make mistakes, but we're there for one another."

Although I knew his comment was meant to be confined to those of us who gathered beside my sister's grave, what did that mean for Valerie? She was his mother. Could he forgive her for what she'd done to him? Could he forgive me for what I had to do to her?

"I'm going to head back to the car," Kelly told us. "I figure you might want a little time alone."

"You can stay," I replied, but he just gave me a sad smile and walked back toward the gate.

"I'm going to go, too," Sammy said.

"No, please."

"You need this, so I want you to talk to her." He reached out and squeezed my hand, giving me the strength I needed. I knelt by the grave and Sammy nudged me. "Tell her."

I was confused. "Tell her what?"

"Anything. Everything. You know you want to say something."

I almost told him I didn't, but then I realized I did. He patted me on the shoulder and wandered off toward Kelly. I looked down at the grave and sighed. I didn't believe in heaven or hell. I was not a subscriber to any theology or religion. I didn't even know that I would consider myself a spiritual person, but I wanted to believe that somehow Christina would hear me.

Chrissy hated the fact we weren't the same height. I used to tease her about being short. The memory made me grin as I knelt in front of the grave. "I want to say I'm sorry," I began, looking at my reflection in the stone. "If I hadn't been late getting home from school that day, I might have been able to protect you and Mom. I think that failure is my biggest regret. There are so many times in my life I look back on and wish I could talk with you again. Say something that would make you laugh, because that always melted my heart. When you died, I grew cold and angry at the world that took you from me."

The urge to move hit me. I stood up and paced, before I noticed a flower that had fallen. So delicate, but strong, just like my sister. I picked it up, then leaned against the tree. I ran my fingers over the petals, focusing on the texture, the scent, before I let spill what I'd kept in for so long.

"When I killed him, I felt nothing. No pleasure or anger or even satisfaction. To be honest, I don't know if I felt many emotions that weren't dark since then either. I think you'd probably be disappointed in what I've become, but I know you'd forgive me like you always did. There was so much pain inside me that it festered and became like an infection. If I hadn't met Sammy, I don't know that I'd be alive now either. He's helped me so much."

When I looked at my hands, I saw I'd crushed the flower I held. Instantly I set to smoothing out the petals. I couldn't bear to hurt anything associated with my sister. I did the best I could, but it wasn't enough. I looked up and I could see Sammy smiling at Kelly. I lay the flower atop her grave and continued.

"I think you'd like him. He's sweet and considerate and such a bossy little fucker. Pardon my language. But he's taken away a lot of the choices I used to stress over. He takes care of me, and though I don't know I'd ever say it to another living soul, I need that. My whole life has been the result of a series of decisions I was forced to make before I was ready. I got by, but it was only because I grew up fast. Sammy… I don't know how to explain it. He allows me to just feel. I don't have to think when I'm with him. It seems that it makes my head clearer when I'm on a job, because I know he'll decide what's right.

"I used to think that being submissive to someone was only about sex. At least that's how I thought of it. I'm giving up a part of myself to him that he's holding onto and keeping together. At first it freaked me out to think that someone else had control over any aspect of my life, but with Sammy it's different. He... I don't know how to explain it. He centers me and giving up some choices to him grants me more freedom than I've had in years.

"I miss you every day, but the hole in my heart that kept me separated from everyone might be healing. I'm not saying I won't miss you, because I think we both know that wouldn't be true, but with Sammy's help, I'm pretty sure I'm ready to move on with my life. I'll come visit again and next time I'll bring some lilacs." I took a deep breath, then exhaled slowly, tracing my fingers over the etching of her name. "I love you, Chrissy. You were one of the only good things in my life, but I think I'm finally ready to let go of the pain of losing you and live again. You're always going to have a spot in my life, and that's never going to change." I glanced in Sammy's direction again and smiled. "Our family has grown now, Sis. None of us will ever forget you."

When I finished, my heart seemed lighter than it had in years. Even if she wasn't able to hear me, being able to say the words that I'd held in for so long finally allowed me to let them go. With a final glance at the grave, I turned and went to where Sammy stood with Kelly. Sammy wrapped an arm around my waist and held me close.

"Are you okay?"

For the first time in a long time I didn't even have to think about the answer. "Yeah, I am. Thanks."

"Did you want to stay a little longer?" Kelly asked.

I gave him a smile and said, "No, it's time to get on with my mission. I have places to go and people to kill. And there's no time like the present."

~

It had been two weeks since our visit to the cemetery. Things between Kelly and I were still somewhat tense, but the strain was no longer there. Sammy made good on his threat to spank it out of me, and I will neither confirm nor deny enjoying it.

Rook had gathered every scrap of information he could pull on my next target and found out a few interesting things. Sammy, Kelly, and I stood huddled around the war room table where I'd rolled out the map I'd printed. My next target distributed drugs for Valerie. He had a good trade going in Miami, selling in impoverished areas to young kids as well as sending them into more affluent areas to distribute his shit. The problem for me was the fact that he cut his garbage with dimethocaine, otherwise known as bath salts. The formulation had killed more than one person by inducing heart failure, but the one I focused on was sixteen-year-old Alex James.

Alex had been one of the drug mules for Herman Spiers, Valerie's lieutenant and, if intel was correct, her sometimes lover. This was the one I hoped would push Valerie over the edge, make her sloppy, and allow me to finally end this.

"So she shacks up with that, huh? Big step down from my dad," Sammy said, his voice flat and emotionless.

"You don't need to be here," Kelly reminded him, apparently picking up on the same vibe I was getting.

Sammy shrugged and stepped away from the table, but stayed near me. "It doesn't bother me. I let go of the hurt and anger years ago. It made me a stronger person, so I guess I should thank her." He ran a hand over my arm. "Or maybe you can thank her for me. Show her how much I appreciate her making me the man I am today."

It chilled me to hear him talk like that. Sammy was a good man with a decent heart. He wasn't like me, and I didn't want him to be. I wrapped my arms around his shoulders and he laid his head against my chest.

"Is this where you tell me I'm better off now?" Sammy asked, looking up at me, a frown I hated seeing marring his face.

"Are you?"

His frown faded and was replaced by the trademark grin. "If you take me back to bed, I'll show you how much better off I can be," he answered, his hand sliding down my stomach toward my crotch, which reacted to his playfulness.

Kelly coughed and glanced around the room.

"You can watch if you want," Sammy told him. "I don't think either of us would mind an audience."

"A whole world of no," Kelly grumbled. "Are we done here?"

"In a hurry?" I asked.

"I want to bleach my eyes and scrub my brain."

Sammy chuckled, then gave me a pat on the ass. "You guys go ahead and figure it out. I'm going to go play online. Did you know Facebook has games?"

Kelly groaned. "He's lost to the dark side."

"You have a Facebook account?" I asked, concerned about his privacy.

"Fake name, fake information, no pictures. Nothing to point anyone in my direction. Rook okayed it." He added the last bit hastily, probably knowing I was concerned. "He also monitors my friend requests and keeps tabs on any messages I receive."

That allowed me to relax a little. "Okay, have fun."

He scampered down the hall, leaving me with Kelly, who turned to me, concern evident on his face when he said, "We need to talk."

CHAPTER TWENTY-ONE

Kelly sat heavily on one of the couches in the war room. "I'm concerned about Samuel."

"Why?"

"He's going to be twenty-four in a few months—"

"Really? When's his birthday?" The thought of giving him a gift filled me with pleasure.

Kelly sighed, apparently none too happy with my interruption. "December 23."

"How did I not know this? That's gotta suck, having it so close to Christmas. I think we should do something special for him. Maybe a car."

"Can he drive?"

"Okay, maybe driving lessons then a car."

"Haven, can you listen to me?"

I stopped planning and gave Kelly my full attention.

"Samuel isn't…" He paused and glanced up at me. "He's missed out on his childhood. He had it taken from him and there are so many things he never got to experience. Does he have aspirations? Maybe he wants to go to school and learn a trade. What are his talents? I don't want him to regret anything he hasn't experienced."

I remembered the car ride. A simple thing I took for granted, but to him it had meant so much. Then I let my mind wonder about other things he'd never had the chance to explore—a first date, his first crush, the sweetness and nervousness that came from the first real kiss, or making love for the first time, and I could see Kelly's point.

"I can't give those back to him."

"No, you can't. They're gone forever, and I think it bothers him. But maybe he needs to move on." He stood and moved closer to me.

"What the fuck? *You* were the one who insisted I bring him here. *You* told me that I needed him, and now that I admit it, you tell me he needs to move on."

Kelly stared dispassionately. "Are you through? Samuel is right, you are prickly. What he sees in you is beyond me. What I'm trying to say is he needs to take control of his life. When you're gone, he doesn't leave the house. He sits on the computer and plays games."

"And?"

"It's not right. He's young and needs to meet real people. He should be going out and building a life."

I opened my mouth to protest, but he held up a hand.

"I'm not saying separate of you. Well, yes, I guess I am. Even a homemaker has friends who aren't words on a screen. He needs interaction and stimulation. He should go to school."

"Aw, it's nice that you want me to get out and make friends, Mommy."

Kelly's chin drooped to his chest. "I hate it when you do that."

"And I hate it when people talk about me while I'm not around." Sammy leveled his gaze at me. "The computer is frozen. Can you fix it?"

"Sammy, I—"

He held up a hand. "Hold that thought." He stalked over to where Kelly stood. He appeared annoyed, but not angry. "Thank you for worrying about me. I do appreciate it. I can't be upset when I told Haven he couldn't be. But it's been four months since Haven rescued me. I'm not ready to go out. I might never be ready, and I accept that."

"Well, I don't," I cut in.

"Excuse me?"

The hairs on the back of my neck stood on end when he pinned me with his gaze. *Now* he looked angry.

"Kelly is right. You need something more in your life. I'm not saying you should dive into the deep end, but maybe take a few classes. Isn't there something you want to learn? What about how to drive? Then you could go places and see things."

"So let me see if I get this right. First, you don't want me out in public, reminding me all the time that it's too dangerous. Now, you're trying to get me out there."

"Not right away. After I… After this is over."

"When she's dead, you mean. You can say it. The bitch who took all those things you listed off that I missed out on, but guess what?" He brought his hands up and cupped my cheeks. "Yeah, I wish it had never happened, and I swear to you I will spit on her grave, but it brought you to me, and as much as those things hurt, having you makes them bearable. You told me I give you strength, but you do the same for me."

"Then why are you so afraid to go out?" Kelly asked.

Sammy spun on him, his face contorted in rage. "Gee, I'm sorry if I have this fear of people. Silly me, I should deal with having been whored out and abused by running into public and making nice with everyone, right? I dealt with it by becoming strong. I won't ever let anyone take advantage of me again."

He turned to me and I could feel his gaze burning into me. "Haven gives me something to focus on. He needs me to be strong for him and I need to take care of him. So I'm not ready to deal with the real world. I might never be ready, and that's okay with me. I'm happy with what I have right now. I'm sorry if it's not enough for you. For either of you."

He turned and stormed out of the room. I'd never seen him so angry that his face flushed and he trembled.

Kelly's chin dropped to his chest. "I have got to learn to stop interfering in people's lives," he muttered.

"It's fine. I think Sammy needed to explain why he won't go out. I'll be back in a while. I think he needs me more than he knows about now."

It wasn't hard to find him. He'd gone into our room and stood at the windows, staring out at the desert.

"It's beautiful," he said softly. "No people for as far as the eye can see."

"Are you really that afraid?"

Sammy stiffened when I laid a hand on his shoulder, then slumped into the chair by the window.

"It's not logical, I know. With you, I'm in control. You let me bend you and shape you any way I want, but my own life is a disaster."

"No, it's not. Kelly and I were wrong to push. Maybe Dr. McQuade was right. It wouldn't hurt to see someone."

"No," he growled, pushing my hand away. "I don't need to see anyone."

It shouldn't have hurt, but it did. He must have realized what he said because he stood up and pulled me against him. "Except you. If it was you and me for the rest of our lives, I'd be happy."

"It might not be a long time," I reminded him, nuzzling his hair, which smelled of vanilla. "I could die tomorrow or the next day. My job doesn't equate to a long life expectancy."

"You'll live. I'll come kick your ass if you don't."

"I'll trade you. I'll promise to come back, if you promise me you'll see someone."

"Why is this so important to you?"

He tried to pull free when I put my arms around him, but this time I refused to allow him to put me off.

"Because *you're* important to me. I want you to be able to go out and see the world. I want to buy you a car so you can tool around and look at all the pretty people. I want us to be able to get on a plane and take a trip to Hawaii, to spend a month playing in the sand and surf."

He sucked in a breath. "You make it sound better than I would have imagined."

"You, me, and a private beach. Have you ever seen the ocean?"

He was practically salivating, the excitement rolling off him. This was the Sammy I wanted to see. The happy one who I could share new experiences with and, yes, build a life with.

No," he answered.

"Water nearly as blue as your eyes and almost as nice to sink into. Sand so warm you will dig your toes in and never want to stop. We could take a scuba class and dive down to see sunken ships or fish in all colors of the rainbow."

I slipped my fingers into his hair. "But we can't do any of that if you can't go out. Do you see what I'm saying? There's a life there that you should be living. People to meet. Classes to take, if you want."

"You're not trying to get rid of me, right? Not planning on changing the locks when I go out?"

His tone was teasing, but I could sense the underlying fear beneath it.

"Never. You told me you were here forever, and I plan to make sure you keep that promise. But I want more with you. There's a whole world out there, and I want to see it with you. Give that to me, okay? Promise me you'll see someone."

His eyes closed and he swallowed hard. "When this is over, we can talk about it again."

I needed to know. "Why are you so resistant?"

His body language told me he was uncomfortable. I tugged him close and whispered to him, trying to prove to him he was as safe with me as I was with him.

"When I turned fourteen, I hit puberty. Arianna made me shave all my hair off. Anything to keep me looking like a little boy for her clients. She did everything she could to keep me weak and helpless. But strength comes from within, and I built mine up. Yeah, I was never going to be strong enough to get away on my own, but I wouldn't let anything she did break me. It's why I—"

He stopped and opened his eyes, staring straight into mine.

"Why you need to be in control," I finished for him.

He nodded. "If I give that up, I'm going to go back to being afraid all the time. Every sound in the night will terrify me, because it will make me think someone is going to come along and take it all away. Seeing someone who will try to get inside my head, bring all those things back out? I'm afraid I'll lose myself in the process."

"Maybe they can bring all the parts together," I murmured. "But your core, everything that makes you who you are? That will never change. You're strong now, and I think you always will be, but if you bring in all the pieces you think are broken and slap a little duct tape on them, it's only going to strengthen them."

He snickered. "Duct tape?"

I put my hands on his cheeks and pulled him up to face me. "Never doubt the power of duct tape."

"What if I do this, and you don't like who I become? What if I decide I don't want to be with you or that this isn't the life for me?"

If he had ripped my heart out and showed it to me, I wouldn't have been as surprised. He'd burrowed under my skin and taken up residence in a heart I thought long dead. Could I let him walk away? Yeah, I could, if it would make him happy.

I collapsed into the chair and scrubbed a hand over my chest to soothe the ache. "Then I'll help you find a home and a job. But I need you to know something, okay? If you do leave, we can never see each other again. It would be too dangerous for you. Kelly and I would be moved somewhere else."

His gaze turned steely. He grabbed my hair and tugged. Not enough to hurt, but he sure as hell had my attention. "What part of forever are you not listening to? It doesn't matter what I become, I will always want you. I like the fact you need me. I love the fact you're mine."

He leaned over and kissed me then. It was brutal and would leave marks, but I didn't care. I opened for him, allowing him to take whatever he needed. He pulled back, hunger in his eyes. He yanked my head to the side then latched his mouth on my neck, sucking hard on the skin, marking me for all the world to see. I hoped that any moment he would bend me over and slam into my ass. I quivered with anticipation.

"Stand up," he growled.

My hands fumbled with my belt as I stood, and he stilled them. "I don't want you to move. Stay where you are and close your eyes. Breathe for me. That's all you need to do."

He stripped off my belt and let my pants slide to the floor and pool around my ankles. He knelt in front of me and nuzzled at my cock and balls. I was so hard I ached. Sammy licked the head of my cock and I groaned involuntarily. I cut it off, figuring he hadn't wanted me to make noise, but he chuckled. "I want to hear you, Haven. Give that to me, please."

Then without another word, he opened his mouth and plunged down onto my dick, taking me to the root. I cried out, wanting to grab his head and keep him there forever, but he held my hands down by my side. Even when he was on his knees in front of me, I was reminded he was still in charge.

He sucked hard, then switched to featherlight licks. He teased the slit, then gobbled me down again. I had no idea what he was going to do next, and it was maddeningly delicious. I heard the zipper on his pants and realized he was likely taking his cock out, but I didn't look down. I lost myself in the overwhelming sensations he was causing. He was incredible. He'd learned his skills in the worst possible way, but he owned them, and I was the recipient of his talented mouth.

178

I could feel my balls tightening up and knew I couldn't hold back. He released my hand and stroked my crack. When he pushed in a finger, I lost it and shot into his mouth, grunting in time to the spurts as he swallowed. He stood and claimed my mouth in a kiss, allowing his tongue to share my flavor with me. I reached out and slid my hand over his cock, noting the sticky remnants of his cum.

He propped me up as I slumped against him, panting hard.

"That was fun," he whispered, sucking my earlobe into his mouth. My cock gave a valiant twitch, but after that orgasm, there was no way I'd be getting up again right away. I glanced down and noted that we were both still fully dressed. Even though we were in the bedroom, it was hot and more than a little dirty. A blow job in the bathroom of the club seemed tame by comparison.

"I think I need a nap," I informed him. "You sucked all my energy out."

"A nap sounds good. Count me in." We finished stripping our clothes, then took a quick shower to wash off the sticky mess. Sammy took me by the hand and led me to the bed. He pushed me near the center of the mattress and wrapped himself around me, warmer than any blanket.

"Remember your promise," he whispered as he drifted off.

In all the years I'd been working for the organization, I never had something to come home to. In the last few months, my life had shifted and gone off in a direction I never would have expected. I'd had no dreams of a future for myself. I lived for the moment, knowing in the back of my mind that any mistake I made would likely be my last. Now, I saw a future that called to me and made me want it with everything I was.

"I will," I replied, even as his light snores lulled me to sleep with a contented smile on my lips.

~

I woke alone. Sammy's side of the bed was cool, so he must have been up for a while. I glanced at the clock and groaned. Already after three. I sat up and listened for sounds in the house, but heard nothing. My heart began to beat a little faster. Since Sammy had moved in, the house was never this quiet, and that alone made me nervous. I pulled on some clothes and got my gun out of the locked cabinet where I stockpiled my weapons.

A quick run through the upper level of the house confirmed my suspicion. There was no one here. I checked the war room, koi pond, garden, and each place I ticked off had my nerves ratcheting upward into the stratosphere.

I pulled open the door to the garage and found that one of the cars, a black 1969 Boss 429 Mustang, was missing. It wasn't the coolest car in my collection, and definitely not the most expensive, but it was the first one I bought. It got me started on my love of cars, and the idea that someone took it pissed me off, but more, it frightened me that Sammy was missing.

I stepped outside, pulled my phone out, and dialed his number, grateful I'd gotten him a cell in case he ever needed me. It rang four times, then went to voice mail. I dialed again and nearly sagged in relief when a familiar voice answered.

"He's a little busy right now," Kelly said, his voice strained.

"What the fuck is going on?" I demanded.

"Slow down," he pleaded.

"Kelly?"

"For the love of God, Sammy, stop."

"Kelly!"

I heard a laugh in the background and a screech of brakes which sent shivers through me.

"That's enough. Get out of the car," Kelly snarled then hung up the phone.

My mind was going a million miles a second, trying to think of what the two of them were doing that had Sammy laughing and Kelly begging. Then it dawned on me, and I relaxed, heading to the garage to get the cleaning supplies Sammy was going to need to get the car back in mint condition.

Kelly pulled in, his eyes wide with fear. Sammy was loose and relaxed as they got out.

"I didn't do *that* bad."

Kelly shook a finger at Sammy and sputtered, "You're a demon, that's the only excuse. You were *trying* to give me a heart attack."

"Want to clue me in?" I asked, struggling to keep from laughing.

Sammy came over and wound himself around me. "I drove," he said proudly, breaking free and bouncing on his heels.

"He went in a straight line. At ninety miles an hour."

"That's all? Rumor has it that car can go up to one seventy-five."

Sammy's jaw dropped. Kelly tossed me the keys. "You tell him that shit, and you're taking him out."

We watched as he stormed into the house, leaving Sammy giggling in his wake.

"So what brought this on?" I asked.

He flushed a little, then smiled and averted his gaze. "I wanted to see if I could do it. Kelly taught me how to shift and stuff, but I wanted to... I don't know. I wanted to move. I wanted to feel the speed, the freedom. It was incredible."

"So does that mean you'll see someone when this is all over?"

He averted his eyes and bit his lip, before he turned to me. "Yeah, I think I will. I don't want to be locked away forever. I want to see the world with you."

And at his words, the blood roared through my veins faster than any car would ever go.

CHAPTER TWENTY-TWO

There was something almost magical about Miami when it got later in the year. There was a lot of tourist trade, people who wanted to get away from the colder climates. Things like that were good for the drug business. The prevailing wisdom was that younger folks were the ones who kept drug dealers hopping, but most ignored the fact that kids couldn't afford the price tag that came with the higher-end stuff. So while Biff and Muffy were out smoking some pot they'd picked up on the street corner for ten bucks, Mom and Dad were in the basement doing fancy named drugs that cost them several hundred or more in the short run, and in some cases their kid's college funds, their marriages, or their lives.

Herman had his hands in all of it. Reports showed he bragged to his cronies that when they got kids hooked early in life with the mild drugs like pot—laced with something a little heavier—they eventually graduated to more hardcore drugs as they were sold cheaper shit that didn't give them the same high.

Case after case had been thrown out due to lack of evidence or failure to read the suspect his rights or some other bullshit. Rook said that from his research, most of these investigations ended when large untraceable deposits got made to people's accounts. The fact that it was so easy to buy people's silence sickened me.

And Herman was nothing if not careful. No one got in to see the man without knowing someone who could vouch for them. Still, despite his wealth and what he did for a living, he carried himself as a regular Joe. No dogs. No fences. One bodyguard, but Herman kept him at a respectable distance when they when out and at night. He stood about twenty feet from Herman at all times while they were club hopping. The perpetual glower on the man's face seemed to beg for someone to start trouble.

This was going to be almost too easy. Or so I thought. The truth was, he was never alone.

I watched him for eleven days, which wasn't a hardship. I could see why Valerie would bed him. Early thirties, trim, but his suits gave him an air of power, and he knew it. He didn't walk so much as swagger. His dark hair and shocking green eyes were a lethal combination. More than one woman, and a fair share of men, tried to get his attention. He never lacked for companionship of either sex.

His daily schedule took him around the town, stopping at clubs where he was a part owner. Though most of them were legitimate businesses, Rook suspected some were points that Herman's mules would stop for their supplies. I gathered enough information to confirm his suspicions, and texted him to let him know. Plus I asked him to tell Sammy I was thinking about him.

As the sun set on the twelfth day of being away from my home, the ache in my chest intensified. Sammy would be asleep soon, nestled in our bed. Would he hold my pillow, thinking about me? Or would he simply fall asleep, knowing that I was thinking about him? None of this was fair to either of us. I craved his touch. The way he held me while we slept. The simplicity of a brush of fingertips that conveyed his thoughts without a word.

Melancholy began sinking in again. I needed him, and I was stuck stalking this sleazy bastard. It would have been so easy to go in, put a bullet in his head, and hurry home, but I hoped that Valerie might make an appearance and I could kill two birds with one stone…or really big bullet. A tingle in my leg told me I had an incoming text from Rook. I pulled out the phone and there was a picture mail of Sammy holding up a placard with the words, 'Focus on your mission, or I'll kick your ass!' I laughed. Of course he'd know. There didn't seem to be anything I could do that would come as a surprise to him.

I slipped the phone back into my pocket, grabbed my binoculars, and settled in for a night of watching a walking dead man.

~

Herman pissed me off. There wasn't any other way to put it. He may not have been aware of the fact that I was tailing him, but the constant nights of clubs, picking up a different man or woman each night, then taking them back to his place wore on my very last nerve. The partners he chose always stayed the night, which made it difficult for me to get close to him without someone being around. I had no desire for witnesses, and killing an innocent person, even if they had questionable tastes, was a definite no-no in my book.

I hadn't heard from Sammy or Rook again, but that was okay. Late in the evenings, after the lights in Herman's place went out, I pulled out my phone and stared at Sammy's picture. I thought about masturbating, but it seemed wrong. I didn't need Sammy's permission to come, but I liked the huskiness in his voice when he told me to do it. I was so lost on him it wasn't even funny. And it was about time I finished this job and got my ass back where it belonged, under my lover.

The night finally came two days later. Herman picked himself up a twinky little thing who hung on him all night, touching him, stealing kisses, and allowing Herman and his entourage to cop a feel every now and again. As the night wore on, and I continued to suck down warm tonic with a limp lime twist, the kid excused himself and went to the bathroom. I followed.

He stood at the mirror primping himself. A thin layer of eyeliner, a little blush on his cheeks, and a slide of fingers through his hair to give it an unkempt, just out of bed look. He reminded me of the subs at the club, someone you'd use for a few hours of pleasure, then push them out of the house.

"Hey, kid," I drawled, affecting a bad Texan accent. His eyes flicked up, and he caught my gaze in the mirror.

"Hey, yourself," he replied.

"I'm Andy. What's your name?"

"Trevor."

"What's say you and me get out of here? I got a nice hotel room, a bottle of Dom Pérignon chilling, and a gourmet meal for two waiting for us."

He bit his lip, and I knew he was thinking about it, then gave a deep sigh. "I can't. I'm already here with someone and we're heading back to his place."

I reached into my pocket and pulled out my wallet. I flashed two hundred bucks in his face and his eyes went wide. "You sure about that?"

His hand flew out and grabbed the money, then he sidled up next to me. I wrapped my arm around him and kissed him on the cheek, working hard not to make a face at the taste of his makeup.

"I'm staying at the Chatsworth Inn. Do you know where it is?"

He nodded and I gave him an extra fifty. "Hop a cab and head there. Stop at the desk and tell them you're there to see Mr. Peterson. They'll give you a keycard to get into my suite. I want you undressed and waiting for me when I walk in."

He grinned. "Whatever you say, Daddy."

I winced. *Daddy?* Fuck that. Sammy would laugh his ass off when he heard that. The kid pulled me down and kissed me, and in my head, I apologized to Sammy a thousand times. His lips parted, and I wanted nothing to do with it, so I just patted him on the back and sent him on his way.

I made my way back to the bar and watched as he left, then sent Rook a quick text, letting him know what he needed to do regarding the hotel. I knew he'd handle it. The kid hadn't done anything wrong, and I didn't want him being questioned in case the front desk staff had issues with him showing up to a hotel I wasn't even booked in. The crowd thinned, and Herman must have finally realized that his date for the evening hadn't come back from the restroom. He waved over one of his people and nodded to the bathroom. The big guy lumbered to the john, then came back and shook his head. Herman slammed his hand down on the bar. No doubt about it, he was pissed off.

He stormed out, and I was close behind him. He got into his car and peeled out of the lot. I guess he wasn't the kind of guy you stood up. At two in the morning, about the only people you'd find on the streets in Herman's neighborhood were prostitutes, and he didn't seem the kind who would be willing to pay for sex. He parked his car in the underground lot, then a few minutes later, his lights came on. I could see his silhouette as he stripped off his shirt, and I knew he'd be in for the night. Well, as long as he had left. I opened my bag and pulled out my supplies, then made my way to the front door.

I will never understand why residential places have such crappy security. The front door should be able to keep intruders out. A quick pop of the lock and I was in. No cameras in the corridors, no alarmed exit doors, but at least they had fire pull stations. Those would come in handy later.

I paused at the door, listening to Herman shouting at someone. From the conversation, it was obvious he was on a phone call. My heart sped up. Maybe this would be what I was waiting for after all.

185

"I don't give a fuck," Herman shouted. "We aren't exclusive. We both agreed to that. You want me home when you call, then you better damn well start pulling me in on the bigger jobs. I'm tired of this penny ante bullshit."

There was a pause, then he gave me exactly what I needed to hear. "Valerie," he said, the frustration evident in his tone, "I want more. I think we should talk about—"

I thought about kicking the door down, but I wanted this to play out a certain way, so I knocked. "Who the fuck is it?"

"Trevor, from the bar? They told me where to find you."

"Just a second." I heard him shuffling across the room, and when he opened the door, he found my gun in his face. "What the—" he shouted.

"Phone check. Give it up."

His eyes widened, and he handed me the phone. I slipped the gun back into the holder at my side.

"Hello, Valerie. I was hoping we'd have a chance to talk at some point."

"I assume you would be the man who has been causing me so many problems." I wasn't sure what I expected, but her voice was soft, almost gentle. She spoke with an accent that appealed to my ear. "Killing my people, abducting my workers. Am I to assume you also took from Arianna what was mine?"

My blood began to boil. She was goading me, and I had to relax. "That would be me, yes. And yes, your *property* is safe with me."

She chuckled. "That's a very delicate way to phrase it. Do tell him I look forward to seeing him again. So, do you have a name, or shall I just call you that guy?"

"You're welcome to call me anything you want."

A heavy sigh, followed by what sounded like fingernails tapping on a hard surface. Finally, she continued. "I'm a busy woman. What can I do for you?"

"I think we should meet. We have so much to discuss."

Her laugh was delicate, like crystal chimes. "I assure you, I'm not the fool you must take me for. I know you want to kill me."

"Well, we all need a hobby."

"Can I assume that an offer of money won't deter you?"

"You can."

"Too bad, really. I could use someone like you in my organization."

"Yeah, no. I have a much better job already."

"Very well. Where and when shall we meet?"

"Really? Just like that?"

"I think we both know that this won't end until we either come to an agreement, or one of us is dead. If I don't meet with you, you'll continue attacking me, and I'll plug the holes you're creating, but you'll find new weaknesses to exploit. And I'm a woman who doesn't like loose ends or not having control of a situation. Besides, you've left me few options. Despite my network, I've not been able to find anything about you, because if I had, I assure you that you'd be dead. Now, where should we meet?"

Valerie was many things, but she definitely had style. Despite my better intentions, I found myself regretting this would soon be over. "Your choice. I figure you should have the home court advantage."

"That's very gentlemanly of you."

She rattled off an address somewhere in Texas that I committed to memory, then said, "How about two weeks from today? I'll be there, and you and I can conclude our business."

"You're not going to tell me to come alone or any of the other clichés?"

She laughed again. "I would never. I'm going to have my people there, and there will be a five hundred thousand dollar bounty to anyone who brings you to me, dead or alive."

"And how will you know it's me?"

"Because no one else would be foolish enough to set foot into my building. So I take it we've reached an agreement?"

"That would be fine. Would you like me to give the phone back to Herman?"

"I assume he's not going to be of much use to me after tonight."

"You would be correct."

She sighed. "He was good in bed, but he isn't irreplaceable."

There was no doubt about it, she was a cold-hearted bitch. I held out the phone and Herman took it in his trembling hand. "Hello?" He was quiet for a minute. "Who the hell is he?" There was a long pause before he finally said, "Oh, okay. I understand. Sure, I'll call you back."

He hung up and stepped aside to let me into the place. I wondered what it was Valerie had told him. She knew he was about to die, so why not warn him? She'd already used one man against me, so it made no sense that she wouldn't give Herman the opportunity should it arise. Or perhaps she did warn him, and he was thinking he could get to me easier inside his apartment.

"Did you want a drink?" he asked.

I watched as he moved around to the bar. The place had obviously been renovated, and the decor was definitely out of place in a building like this. Deep gold carpet in the living room gave way to a dark hardwood floor that filled the rest of the open space.

"No, thanks. Nice digs you've got here."

"Thanks."

He poured himself a generous portion of a very nice quality brandy, something Kelly probably stocked at the house. There was no doubt that Herman had a liking for the finer things in life. He sat on one of the plush leather armchairs with his legs spread wide and made a motion that I took to mean I should sit in the other one. Being the compliant guest, I sat. This was all too surreal for me.

"I have to ask, do you know why I'm here?"

"Yeah, Valerie said something about you were in town to scope us out, and that I was to show you the utmost respect. I figured she finally intended to pull me in like she promised, and you were here to take over the area."

Fuck. The woman served him up on a platter to me. I almost felt sorry for him, but then I remembered Alex James and my heart steeled, ready for what I was about to do.

"I'm going to be honest with you, that isn't why I'm here. We're going to play a game, you and I. If you win, I walk out of here and you go on breathing. If you lose, I still walk out, but Valerie will be finding a new bed warmer."

Herman jerked upright and tried to reach beneath the cushion of the chair, but I was faster. "Now it's not nice to try to move to the end of the game before we've even set the rules." I flicked the gun in his direction. "Sit down." He hesitated a moment, then collapsed back onto the chair. I reached under the cushion and came up with a long-barreled .44 Magnum.

"Seriously? How fucking Dirty Harry," I sniped. "Next time go for something less pretentious. Unless, you know, you're making up for any...shortcomings."

He glared at me, and I returned it with a grin. Enough play, I wanted to get on with my job. For what we were about to do, I needed to ensure he stayed where he was, so I grabbed a length of rope out of my bag and tied him to the chair, looping the rope around his waist, and tying it off to the chair. He tested the ropes, while I checked for other weapons. I made sure he had range of motion. Given time he would be able to get loose, but for now he had no choice but to sit there, which worked for what I had in mind. After all, it wouldn't do for the game to end because the player decided to try and get away.

His gaze tightened. "What the fuck is this?" he growled.

"We're going to play *This Is Your Life*, but it's not your life we're going to be talking about. Let's see if you can figure it out. I'll give you ten clues, and if you can guess the name of the person I'm talking about, I'll walk out that door and leave you sitting here. As each round progresses, if you can't come up with a name, there will be additional punishments. Are you ready?"

"This is crazy. I'm not doing this."

"Then I shoot you and head back home. It won't bother me any. So, what do you say, sport? Play and take a chance to live, or refuse and die right now? Honestly, it doesn't make a damn bit of difference to me either way."

I could see him sweating. His shirt clung to his chest, and the arrogance he'd shown had melted away. Resignation in his lowered gaze told me that the game was already in full swing.

"Okay, question one: I'm a sixteen year old boy. Who am I?"

His head snapped up and he sneered. "What the hell? How am I supposed to know?"

"Ooh, wrong answer." I pointed the gun at his foot and pulled the trigger. Herman cried out. "What a baby. This is only a pellet gun. It's got a sting to it, but that's all. Like I said, the higher rounds have additional penalties. Let's move on to round two."

He glared at me, a defiant expression I found myself somewhat impressed by.

"I loved my sister Teresa. Who am I?"

"I don't fucking know," he snapped.

I lifted the air pistol to his stomach and pulled the trigger. He grunted and gnashed his teeth. The man would not give me what I wanted, though.

189

"Isn't this a fun game?" I asked. "And only eight rounds to go."

His dark eyes met mine, and through gritted teeth, he growled, "Fuck you."

The next three questions played out the same way. I'd ask, but he couldn't answer. Each one got him another pellet to an extremity, and each one tore the attitude out of him more and more. For the sixth question, I put the toy back into my bag and drew out a .22 pistol. If he thought the air gun hurt, he was in for a very rude awakening.

"So after five rounds, you don't have an answer. Not even a guess. It's time we up the stakes a little. For the next five rounds, the punishment value doubles. If you don't come up with a name by then, well…for your sake, I hope you come up with something."

And the game was ready to move into sudden death.

CHAPTER TWENTY-THREE

"You're crazy." Herman moaned, rubbing at the body parts I'd shot.

"Been called worse, and it didn't change anything then either," I assured him. "Now let's continue. Question number six: When I grew up, I wanted to be a professional soccer player. I was light on my feet and could have been on the varsity team at school. Who am I?"

He scrubbed a hand through his hair. "I don't fucking know, okay? Is that what you wanted to hear? I don't fucking know who you're talking about. What kind of sick bastard are you?"

"The kind who gets paid a lot of money to deal with pieces of shit like you. But you're getting off track. We're almost done with the game, and I know you're...ahem...dying to know how it's going to end. And in case you think I forgot the punishment for this round, you're wrong."

I lifted the gun and blew off his kneecap. Now *that* elicited a scream from him. Suddenly the game became a lot more fun. Well, for me.

"I like the neighborhood you're in," I said soothingly. "It's filled with people who won't get involved, so if I wanted to, we could go at this all night. But I've got someone at home waiting for me, and if I don't get back soon, I probably won't be able to sit down for a week, not that I'd complain. So let's move on, shall we?"

He continued to cry in agony, and I found any sympathy I might have had for him vanished as the last few minutes of Alex's life played through my mind.

"Question seven," I said, my voice weary even to my own ear. "I planned to buy my parents nice things when I got my new job. Who am I?"

"Please, I don't know. Stop this."

"Ooh, sorry. Wrong answer, Herman."

"No, please don't."

I took aim at his other foot and pulled the trigger. Bones splintered and blood splashed from the wound. Herman's face went ashen as he screamed and strained against the ropes, his pale skin showing the abraded areas where the ropes dug into his chest.

"Don't worry, the game is almost over. You still have a chance to pull out a victory. Question eight: my boss supplied me with cut-rate shit designed to keep me pliable and under his thumb. Who am I?"

By now he was blubbering and tears streaked his cheeks. This made me angrier, because he was sitting here, living high off the lives of the people he'd crushed beneath his alligator skin boots. He thought his pain was unbearable, but he never gave a second thought to those whose lives he'd destroyed.

"No answer is the same as being wrong," I told him, though I doubt he heard me as his cries and pleading grew louder. I took aim and shot him in the stomach. Whatever pain he'd felt from the last few shots was nothing compared to this.

"Question nine: My life ended on June 30, 2014. Who am I?"

"You're a sick fuck," he screamed.

"*Buzz*. Wrong again. Another shot to the stomach, almost on top of the one from before. His eyes rolled back in his head, and for a moment I thought he was going to pass out, but he stayed with me. He sat on the chair, shaking his head side to side, moaning over and over, begging me to stop. That wasn't about to happen, especially now that we were on the final round.

"Last question, Herman. Last chance. Get it right, and I'll call an ambulance for you. Chances are you'd live. Get it wrong, and you'll die. It's exciting, isn't it? There's nothing quite like high stakes, am I right? For our final question, and your last chance to live: Who is Alex James?"

"I-I-I don't kn-n-now."

I grabbed his hair and yanked it back, forcing him to look me in the eye. "And that's the problem. He worked for you and you don't have a clue who he is or what role you played in the last day of his life."

"I didn't k-k-kill anyone, I swear."

"Not directly, no. But you provided him with the drugs that got him so high he set his house on fire while he was on a bad trip. The house was engulfed and the fire spread quickly. Before the fire department got there, it was already a loss, but they did their best to save something, anything for the family. In the end it didn't matter. They found the bodies of the mother, father, and daughter inside. Coroner said they died of smoke inhalation before they burned."

"But y-y-you said Alex died."

"No, I said his life ended. And it did. He lost everything in one blaze. No family, no home. He suffered burns over sixty percent of his body. The doctors said he should have died. It probably would have been more merciful for him if he had, but he was a tough little snot. He lived, even though he'll be in constant agony for the rest of his life. That, my dear Herman, is how you ended the life of a sixteen-year-old boy, and that's what you're about to pay for now."

I put my gun away and pulled a flask out of the pouch in my bag. As soon as the cap came off, you could smell the acetone. I began spreading it around the room, making sure to douse Herman liberally. His eyes widened in terror, and I think it finally dawned on him what was about to happen.

"Please, don't. Valerie said I should—"

I kept my voice even. "You should have said no. Simple enough. One word and we never would have met. You'd have survived this. Now?" I shrugged. I tossed the bottle onto the floor, the strong smell assailing my nostrils. A spark from the lighter was more than enough to start the blue flame scorching along the carpet. I turned around, ignoring his screams, and stepped out. As I made my way down the stairs, I pulled the fire alarm. By the time the fire department got there, the building would be engulfed, but anyone that was inside might not be guilty and shouldn't be judged against Herman.

As I stepped through the door into the cool night air, an explosion rocked the building and shattered windows. I smiled to myself and gathered the remainder of my stuff before I headed home, humming "Light My Fire" by the Doors. I had the strangest craving for marshmallows. I wondered if Sammy had ordered hot cocoa.

~

"You're not a nice person," Sammy purred as he slid in and out of me for the second time that night. I was going to be sore come morning, but it was going to be so fucking worth it. I'd gotten home and found no cocoa, but I did get a hell of a welcome back blow job to take the edge off, before Sammy pushed me into the bedroom and ordered me to strip.

"Nope, not nice at all," I groaned, twisting my fingers into the sheets, panting heavily. It was fucking heaven and I needed him in the worst way. No matter how shitty things were, Sammy made it better.

"Tomorrow we're going to talk all about it, but tonight I need you. It was two weeks, and I was going out of my mind."

I grunted as he shoved in hard, his balls resting against my ass.

"God, I missed this," he whispered, moving again slowly, stroking his hands down my sides. "You were made for me, you know."

I did, and he proved it to me every day. He clutched my hips and began slamming into me, his breath ragged gasps. "May never let you leave again. Come for me," he shouted, pegging my prostate several times. I shot hard, my ass clenching tight, and Sammy groaned before he dropped a second load in me before collapsing on my back.

We lay there for a few moments as our breathing returned to normal. Sammy eased out of me, but I still winced when he'd withdrawn totally. He rolled me over and lay atop my chest, his fingers drawing circles around my nipple, occasionally stopping to give it a light tug.

"We should shower," he said, even though he made no move to get up.

"Mm-hmm," I hummed, wrapping my arms around him and holding him against me. He nuzzled the crook of my neck, laving the area with his tongue. It wasn't sexy as much as it was soothing.

Sammy was right. I didn't want to leave home again, but in a few weeks, this would all be over. Valerie's organization would crumble without strong leadership, and I knew there wasn't a chance of that happening. Once I killed her, Rook would have his people sweep in and dismantle everything. It would take weeks to tear apart something she'd spent nearly two decades building. I prayed that Sammy would still be here when it was over.

"Love you," he said sleepily, threading his fingers into my hair.

"Love you more," I replied.

We fell asleep like that, both sated for the moment, and each of us grateful for the other as we reconnected. I needed this man more than I'd ever needed anything, and I would move heaven and earth to ensure I was by his side for the rest of our lives.

~

While it might have seemed romantic to fall asleep nestled against one another, the morning proved otherwise when the cum on my stomach glued us together. I don't even want to think about how much hair Sammy pulled out when he lifted himself off me, laughing all the while.

I was about to suggest a shower again when Kelly rapped on the door, reminding me that I had a debriefing with Rook in ten minutes. Sammy dragged me off to the shower where we took turns washing one another. As Sammy's fingers scratched at my scalp, working the shampoo in deep, I groaned and leaned back against him, allowing him to take care of me. The man surprised me with a combination of possessiveness and gentle demeanor. I'd given up worrying about labeling our relationship, and merely decided to enjoy it. Sammy had claimed me, many times, and that was enough for me.

It was almost an hour later when we made it into the debriefing. Kelly quirked an eyebrow and grinned when we entered, which turned into a full out laugh as I sat gingerly on the sofa. I scowled at him, which only had him laughing harder. Rook, of course, being the consummate professional, ignored the high jinks and began the rundown of my mission.

"Firemen pulled Herman's corpse out of the wreckage. My people flashed ID to the fire marshal and took possession of it. His body was disposed of in the standard way."

Sammy glanced over and opened his mouth. I shook my head and whispered, "Don't ask. You really don't want to know."

Rook continued; his voice was flat, no emotion showing at all. When it came to things like this, he was damned clinical, but it was that detachment that helped keep the nightmares at bay. An arm slid around my waist and I glanced down at Sammy, who was beaming at me, and I had to admit, Sammy had a lot to do with it, too.

"The explosion you heard was chemicals that Herman kept on property. We spun the story that he was cooking up drugs in the apartment, and we were DEA agents who had been tracking his movements, waiting to take him down.

"I figured he was doing something in the house. I got the impression he wasn't satisfied with Valerie keeping him out of the big deals and was starting to try things on his own. That would explain why she wasn't heartbroken that I was going to kill him. She'd probably planned on doing the same thing, so she got me to do her dirty work."

"Probably saved her a ton of money, too, since you took out her *enforcer*."

The thought of Lanny had me smiling at the memory of his eyes going wide when he realized his death was imminent. All those kids could begin to rest in peace now, and even though they would never know it, I liked to think I'd brought a little healing to the family, too.

"Haven?"

Kelly nudged me with his shoulder and pulled me out of my thoughts. Dangerous to let myself get distracted like that.

"I got to talk to her," I told them. "We agreed to a meeting in two weeks."

"You're kidding," Sammy snapped. "You know it's a trap."

I shrugged. "Of course. I also know there's a strong possibility she may not show, but if there's even a chance, I have to take it."

"No," Sammy argued, his mouth set in a hard line. "You're not doing this."

Kelly touched Sammy on the arm, which earned him a glare. "You were the one who told us he knew what he was doing. And you were right, but now you've got to believe in him to see this through. He's the only one who can do it. And he needs to know that you're in his corner."

"She had my father and Tim killed. She almost took Haven once. I…I can't live without him." The crack in Sammy's voice would have melted the coldest heart.

He threw himself into my arms and held tight. I gathered him up and clutched him to my chest. Kelly pushed the speaker button, disconnecting Rook, and quietly left the room, closing the door behind him.

"Hey," I whispered, "what's wrong?"

"If you kill her, it will tear you apart," he replied. "You think you'll be able to handle it, but you can't."

"I've killed before, you know that. I can give you a list of references if you'd like." My joke didn't even crack his facade.

"You don't understand," he moaned, pressing against me harder than before, like he wanted to crawl inside me.

196

"Then explain it to me. Make me understand how this is different than any other assignment I've taken. We've talked about this. I can do this assignment, because it has to be done. If you're having second thoughts about—"

"No, it's not that. I have no feelings for her at all. She's caused too much pain and she needs to be put down. I get that, but it can't be you."

"You have to tell me why," I begged. He was almost to the point of panic, clawing at my back, and I didn't have a clue what was going on in his head. "If you know it has to be done, why are you saying I can't be the one to do it?"

"Because once it's done, everything changes."

"Sammy, you need to breathe. Calm down and talk to me." I rubbed a hand over his back in slow circles, and eventually he relaxed into my arms. He sniffled and tried to draw away, but I held him tight. "Now, let's talk. Valerie is no different from anyone else. I took the assignment, and I'll finish it. And once I'm done, you and I will decide if I take any more, or if we run away together. We could live in Hawaii, if you want. Hell, we could live anywhere you want. Now tell me why she's different. She's a target. I've got a bullet with her name on it, and it won't hurt me at all to look her in the face when she dies. It's nothing personal."

"You killed people you didn't know. You saw them, but they were faceless to you. Not my mother. She has a face and a name. And she's never going to be anonymous. Every time you look at me, it'll make you remember."

"If there were another way, I'd be all for it, but there isn't. She's got too many people in her pocket. She'll get away with it forever. I promise, nothing will change between us."

"You can't know that," he insisted, and I knew there was something he'd been keeping from me. Something he was certain would make me hate him.

I cupped his face in my hands and made him look me in the eye. "Talk to me, please."

He was quiet for several moments, gulping breaths of air, before he finally spit it out. "I look like her."

CHAPTER TWENTY-FOUR

I stepped back and looked down at Sammy. "What the hell do you mean?"

He averted his gaze, and his shoulders slumped. "My dad used to tell me I favored her. Our eyes were the same green, our hair the same brown. Even after she left, he kept pictures of her. He loved her, and he always figured one day she'd get it out of her system and come back. As I grew up, people would comment on how much I looked like her, and even though I think it made him sad, my dad still loved me.

"And that's the thing. When you find her, and you look into her eyes, it won't be Valerie you see. It'll be me. The bullet you use isn't going to be killing her, in your heart, you'll see my lifeless body there, blood seeping out. The eyes that will be open and staring will be the ones you have to look into every night.

"Will you be able to do that? Can you kill her without guilt each time you see me? I don't think you can. You've gotten stronger since we met, but your heart still isn't fully vested in your job. I don't want you to do this, then find you can't stand to look at me, because you'll see her. Or worse, be so disgusted by what you're looking at, you won't touch me."

The scenario played out in my head. Valerie pleading with me not to kill her, and Sammy's face staring up at me. My stomach clenched violently at the thought of killing my lover. Slender arms wrapped around my waist.

"This is what I mean," he said. "You need to understand what you're getting into. There has to be another way."

When I turned to face him, he peered up at me, and I could tell he was anxious. I gave him a smile, and he returned it.

"Those aren't quite so scary now," he admitted.

"Sit down," I said as I gestured toward one of the high-back chairs in the room. He sat, then I took a chair opposite him. A frown marred his features, until he got up and moved over to me and took up a spot in my lap with his arms wrapped around my neck. "I'm going to be immodest here, so save the eye rolls for later, okay? The reason I got this job is because I'm the best at what I do. I have a skill set that others in our organization don't. I've never failed to complete a mission, and no matter what happens, I will see this one through.

"You asked if I could kill you. The short answer is yes. It's what I do. If you were someone who'd done some really fucked up shit, yes, I would kill you without hesitation. But you're not, and Valerie is. So you say you look like her, that doesn't mean I won't see the job through."

"Yeah, but at what cost?" he grumbled, his lips vibrating against my neck.

"I told you before, killing someone will always cost you. It's never like they show on television. You don't take a life, then walk away. It will always haunt you, unless you're a psychopath. I told you there are certain targets I like to take up close. It's not just for them, though. I do it for me, too. Believe it or not, it's a reminder of my humanity. It's important that I feel, that I look inside myself and see there is a tiny shred of a heart left. I cling to that. It might seem weird, but I have to have that little piece of me."

"Doesn't sound strange at all. Wanna know what I see? When you think I'm not watching, you'll stare at me. For a while, I wasn't sure why. At first I figured you were trying to understand your attraction to me." He brushed his fingertips over my cheek. "You blush, did you know that?"

I scowled. "No, I don't."

He laughed, and it was sweet. "You do. Your whole face pinks, but your cheeks get red here and here," he said, touching my cheekbones. "I love that I'm the one who can make you do it. Even when Kelly teases you, you've never blushed, but around me, it's your constant state."

"I thought that was arousal," I ground out.

"Yes, I suppose there's some of that in there, too." He grinned at me, and my cheeks flamed all over. "Anyway, it wasn't that simple. I think now you watch me to be sure I'm not going to go away. You've pinned a lot of hopes on me."

He was right. I had. Foolishly I'd planned a future with him, allowing him to worm his way into my heart and set up shop. It had taken me months to believe him when he said he wasn't going anywhere, and now I'd come to depend on him in ways I hadn't counted on anyone since I joined the military. "Yeah, I do."

"Good. I'm glad." He leaned forward and kissed me.

"It doesn't change the fact that I'm the only one who can do this job," I reminded him.

He snuggled against me, laying his head in the crook of my neck.

"I hate it," he said quietly. "I want to forbid you to go, but Kelly was right. I can't stop you from doing your job. And I need to trust that you're going to keep safe what belongs to me."

I shuddered at his words. It was weird the rush I got each time he claimed me as his. His territorial attitude warmed me, made me feel safe, even when I was in a dangerous situation. Sammy was the rock I clung to when the swirls and eddies of life tried to pull me down, because despite everything else, I knew he'd always be there for me, and that gave me hope that come tomorrow and each day after, I'd be there for him.

We didn't say much else. Sammy took me to our bedroom and, needing to express his feelings and understanding my own, very slowly and gently made love to me. When we were rung out, he cradled me to him and we fell asleep.

~

"I've had people check out the building," Rook told us. "It's a factory that was scheduled to be converted to lofts about six years ago. Work had started, but then been abandoned when the company ran out of money. The designs of the original building and what the renovated sections should be are in your briefing folder. My people say the building is owned by Tributal Holdings, but as far as I can tell, it's one of about two dozen shell companies she's funneled money through. This woman is...incredible."

The awe in Rook's voice was evident, and he wasn't wrong. For everything she'd done, Valerie had risen up to the top of an empire and shown she could rule it with an iron fist. The things she had to do to stay there were stomach turning, though. She definitely proved the adage that if a woman wanted to be seen as an equal to a man, she had to be twice as tough. And Valerie was that in spades.

"This woman is a sadistic bitch who gave her son to be used by men. Who murdered her husband, and a man whose only crime was wanting to protect the kid. God knows how many other people she's had killed, or allowed her people to *play* with until they broke their toys and had to be given new ones. Don't ever think she's impressive, because she's not."

Sammy's voice was hard, and it matched his expression. I took him in my arms, but he pushed away from me.

"Samuel, I didn't mean—"

"Of course you didn't, but you can't help that you're impressed by her. She's like a serial killer, people are sickened but fascinated. Not me, though. I *lived* through it. I saw her handiwork up close and personal, and let me tell you, there is not one goddamn thing there that should earn even an iota of adoration."

"That's enough," Rook roared. "I have had it up to here with you. Do you think any of our lives have been easy? Do you even know the horrors that we have all lived through? You've heard about them from Haven, but try seeing it up close and personal. You saw a young boy killed? Haven's seen dozens of bodies piled one on top of the other, left to be picked clean by scavengers. And, God help me, they were some of the lucky ones. There were some that they left alive, but damaged so badly they will spend the rest of their lives wishing they had died, because almost anything is better than the pain they'll have to experience every day.

"You did something none of them will ever be able to do. You not only survived, you prospered. You found love. Yes, you're going to have to bear the scars for the rest of your days, but you *have* a life. You could walk away now and settle down, have a nine-to-five job, a family, whatever you want. We don't have that luxury anymore. Haven has said he wants to walk away after this job, and I hope to hell he's able to do it. I've tried, but there's a never-ending supply of people out there who will use whatever means they think is necessary to get what they want.

"So you'll excuse me if there is a morbid fascination with your mother. I promise you, it's not adoration. For me, it's more along the lines of being sickened by the fact she's gotten away with what she has for so many years. No government agency has stopped her, so I need to know who she's paying off, because I swear to you, I will see that bitch taken down, her organization dismantled, and help will be found for those who aren't beyond it. Because that, Samuel, is what *we* dedicated our lives to doing."

Sammy bit his lip, and I had to wonder what he was going to say. Would he tell Rook to fuck off? It certainly wouldn't be the first time. Rook had never spoken like that to Sammy before, and I wanted desperately to say something, but Kelly glared at me and shook his head.

"I'm sorry," Sammy said, though his tone belied that. "When I was growing up, I loved comic books. I used to have a huge collection of them. You'd see a bad guy do something, and you'd say 'damn, he's evil,' but it's never real until experienced firsthand. Valerie is evil, and to listen to people talk about her like she's done something impressive pisses me off."

"I'm sorry, too," Rook replied. "I can't tell you how much I wish I could place a call to the police or FBI and tell them they need to do something. They won't, though. She's not even on their radar, and they won't invest the manpower without proof. What we have is, at best, flimsy. There isn't any way to connect the dots. What we do is something no one else can or will. It's a huge leap of faith for us to take what we have and sign someone's death warrant. I'm glad to say we've never made a mistake, because the type of people we deal with are guilty of things we probably will never know about.

"Your mother...no, *Valerie*," he stressed, "has kept her hands clean. She hires out hits to people who probably don't even know they're working for her. Even people in her organization report to her underlings, and never realize they're not working for a boss. For the hits she's probably done on her own, she's got ways to point the finger at others. So whatever you do, don't confuse respect for her skills to mean we approve of or condone her actions in any way. If anything, we'll use it as a training tool, to ensure we're better prepared for the next time we give Haven an assignment. Assuming he's still around."

My jaw was clenched so tight I worried that my teeth would crack. If Sammy told them he couldn't do it, that he'd leave, I would go with him, even if I had to abandon this job. I could see those kids' faces in my mind. I knew their stories. While Valerie might not be directly responsible, she was most certainly culpable in their deaths, and however many more we weren't aware of. Then my sister's face flashed so bright I might have whimpered. I hated myself, because this time I wasn't sure how I could choose between Sammy and my job.

"Sammy, I—"

"Need to do your job," he whispered as he turned toward the door. "I understand. It's about more than me, or even you. It doesn't mean I have to like it. Go ahead and do what you need."

He took a few more steps toward the door and panic gripped me. I rushed toward him and grabbed his arm. He turned to me and gave a weak smile. "I'll be here when you get back," he promised. He pulled me close and said softly, "I can't be around here right now. I'm going to go for a drive."

"No, you can't. It's—"

"Something I need to do. I promise I won't go far and I'll even go slow, and I'll be back in less than an hour. I just need to clear my head."

"At least take Kelly with you," I pleaded, knowing Sammy still didn't have his license.

He shook his head. "You need him here. He's going to help you come back to me. Please, if you ever promised me anything, swear to me that this won't change how you feel about me."

"How could it? You aren't her. She could be your twin brother, and it wouldn't matter to me. All I've ever gotten from you is love. You haven't hurt anyone. No one died because of you."

He opened his mouth and I put a hand over it.

"Tim's death wasn't your fault. He was a good man, and he did what he could to protect you. It wasn't enough, but you are not responsible. I want so desperately to tell you I know another way. What I see in your eyes scares me, and that's something I'm not used to. You want me to swear my feelings for you won't change, but right now I think yours have. You don't want to admit it, but I think at the moment, you might hate me."

"What? Oh hell no." He grabbed my ears and pulled me down for a kiss. "I hate what she's making you do, because despite what you're telling me, you won't be unaffected by her death. I know this as surely as I know your name. But I can't put my happiness in front of the lives of other people."

"What about your happiness? That means more to me than anyone else's. If you said you were going to walk away, to leave, I would have no choice but to come with you, even though I know I have to do this. You have been the only bright spot in my life since...well, since my sister. After she died, I knew I could never again let someone in, because when they left it hurt too much. I can't let you walk out on me."

"I told you when we got together, you weren't going to get rid of me." He placed his hand over my heart. "This is my home now, and it's one I will never move from."

"You know how sappy that sounds, right?" I teased, hoping for a genuine smile.

"It's only sappy in romance novels. In real life, it's the one truth you can pin your every hope and dream on."

I took his head in my hands, tilted it upward, and kissed him with everything I had. I needed him to feel my love. To make sure he knew it was real. When he broke the kiss, he stepped back and smiled at me.

"I'll be back soon, I promise."

There was such sadness in his voice, and I didn't know what to do. You wanted me to kill someone? Point me in their direction. You wanted me to understand feelings and emotions? I was learning, but my teacher was the one who needed comfort I couldn't provide. Sammy turned and rushed out the door. I wanted to go after him, but I knew the sooner I got this job done, the faster I'd be back in his arms.

Assuming they were going to be open for me.

~

When the meeting ended, and we had the beginnings of a plan, I hurried upstairs, hoping that Sammy would have returned. He wasn't in the house, and the Mustang was still gone. I looked at the clock. He had said an hour, but four had already passed. Panic gripped me, and I shouted for Kelly.

"He's not here, the car is gone, and it's been four hours," I babbled.

"Sammy needs space," he said. "I can't even begin to imagine what's going on in his head right now."

"Fuck space," I grunted. "He said an hour; it's been four. Check with Rook. I want to know where he is, and I want to know right fucking now."

CHAPTER TWENTY-FIVE

S even hours had gone by, each tick of the clock had my heart seizing that much more. There was no answer on his phone, and I had no idea what to do. There were no friends he would go to see. No one he could talk to. It made me realize how sheltered he was, and how little any of us had done to break him out of that cycle.

I stalked through the living room and noticed the computer he usually turned off was on. I hit the keyboard and the screen lit up. A letter appeared, and though I dreaded reading it, I couldn't help myself.

Michael,

I know right now you're probably scared out of your mind. I realize I'm not being fair to you. I should be man enough to stand up and tell you what's going on in my head, but there is no way I can explain it to you, when I'm not sure I understand it myself.

I can't be around you right now. I swear to God, it's nothing to do with you. You are the most amazing man to walk the planet, but it hurts knowing what's going to happen. I know you said nothing will change, and I pray you're right, but it will. Change is inevitable, and I'm not ready for it.

Yes, I'm a coward. When the going gets tough, I run away. Maybe it's better this way, I don't know. When I feel right with myself, I'll be back. I promise you, and I hope you'll believe me. What I need you to do is finish your job. Then, when it's over, I can look you in the eyes and see if the love that I hope to find will be there.

Until that time, please keep yourself safe.

All my love,

Sammy

I grabbed the monitor and hurled it across the room, smashing it into a hutch that Sammy had bought and filled with some kind of dragon knickknacks he claimed were protectors of the hearth. They did a pretty piss poor job, in my mind. They shattered, falling to the floor in jagged bits. I rushed over and pulled the cabinet on top of the mess. My stomach knotted in anger and my muscles screamed in agony as I rampaged through the house, destroying everything that reminded me of him. Finally I collapsed on the floor, my breathing ragged.

"Feel better now?" Kelly asked from the doorway.

"He fucking walked away," I bellowed.

"I was afraid he would. You need to understand—"

I pushed to my feet and grabbed Kelly by the shoulders, pinning him to the wall with a resounding thump. I got close to his face and snarled, "I don't need to fucking understand a goddamn thing. I need Sammy. Now."

"And you think this is the way to get him to come back?"

I hated Kelly and his goddamn sanctimonious attitude. He knew I wouldn't hurt him, and it irked the hell out of me, because right now I wanted someone to be afraid of me, to tremble when I came near them. And no one in this fucking house was going to do it. I turned loose of his shoulders and grabbed a set of keys from the hook near the garage.

"I'm going out," I told him. "I don't know when—if—I'll be back."

"Be careful," Kelly said. "And don't do anything you'll regret."

Right now there was nothing I would regret. What did I have to live for anyway?

~

The wind blew through my hair as the car hit one twenty-five. A thick cloud of dust trailed behind me and I pressed harder on the gas. I had thought about going to the club, but the idea of someone putting their hands on me turned me off completely. Sammy had ruined me for anyone else, and if he didn't come back, I doubted if I could ever see myself with another person.

When I realized where I'd ended up, I slammed on the brakes. It seemed a weird place to be, but it made sense, too. I walked through the gate, made my way over to a familiar spot, and sat on the grass.

"Hey, Chrissy. Figures it would be you I turn to when I don't know what else to do. Seems I only show up when I'm in trouble. And I'm in deep this time. I love him like I never thought I would love anyone and he walked away. How could he do that? And how am I supposed to go on? It feels like you're gone again. My heart is empty, and I don't know what the hell I'm going to do. Didn't he realize what this would do to me?"

There was no answer coming, of course. The breeze through the desert foliage and some animal sounds were the only things I heard. I lay back, my head near her gravestone, and closed my eyes. We used to talk like this when we were kids, telling each other our hopes and dreams. I needed that now, more than I realized.

"Do you remember when I said I wanted a big family? Kids, lots of them, running around in our yard, playing with the dog, and me sitting on the porch watching them? I wanted it because I knew I could show them what a family was, not that mess we lived in. As Sammy wormed his way into my heart, the desire for a family came back to me. I know I'm never going to be a good father, though. I'm too screwed up in the head now to be responsible for someone.

"But he made me *remember* when I had dreams. And he made me want things again. Not kids, but maybe a dog. I think I could love a dog as long as it's not one of those yappy little monsters that nip at your ankles. But goddamn it, he left me, and now I'm angry and worried and... I'm scared, Sis. What do I do if he never comes back? I mean I could track him down, but it's not like I can force him to come home."

The word hit me hard and a dull ache settled in my chest. He'd called my heart his home, but he walked away from it, after swearing to me he wouldn't.

"Maybe I'm meant to be alone," I whispered. "It's probable that I'm not supposed to be loved."

The truth in those words hurt, and I hated it. For a brief minute I knew what it meant to be in love, and now I was back to the emptiness that filled my life for the longest time. I was numb. I felt nothing. I stood up and kissed the gravestone, then looked over at the plot that was going to be mine.

"Guess I'll be seeing you soon, Sis," I whispered and trudged back to the car.

The drive home flew by as a plan formed in my mind. Regardless of Sammy walking out on me, I would make sure he was safe. I'd take down the bitch who had hurt him so badly and made him incapable of returning my love.

I stormed into the house and began gathering my gear. I'd go to Texas early, and find Valerie. Then I'd kill her. If I was lucky, we'd kill each other, and all the pain and rage that were building inside me would be a distant memory.

"Don't do this," Kelly begged.

"Fuck off," I growled.

"You know better than to go in angry."

I threw down the gun in my hand, spun around, and glared at him. "I'm going to be pissed off no matter if it's today or next week. We're a week out and she's already got men there, so there's no doubt it's a trap. She's going to do her best to take me out before I get to her, and it's not going to happen. If she's not there, her men will tell me what I need to know. She and I are going to meet face to face, and when she dies, I'm going to spit on her corpse."

I threw my knives, two guns with as many extra clips of ammunition as I could safely carry, my graphene vest, binoculars, and randomly tossed in things I thought might come in handy.

"You're not going to war," Kelly whispered.

I stopped, placed my hands flat on the bed, and ground out, "Yeah, I am. And I'm going to win this one."

After slinging the bag over my shoulder, I headed for the garage, then stopped. I walked over to Kelly and wrapped him in my arms. "Thank you for…everything."

I kissed him on the cheek and he grabbed me around the waist. "Haven, please…"

"I'm not Haven anymore. My name is Michael. Haven is already dead and buried. It's Michael's turn now."

I extricated myself from his grip and got into the car. As I pulled out of the drive, I tossed a glance back and smiled. It had been home for a while, and I found I already missed it. Maybe the next person to live here would be able to make it theirs, too.

~

A long drive would normally calm my nerves, but each mile that flew by had me cursing Sammy, Rook, and Kelly in turn. If Rook had never brought me into the organization, if he had just left me where I was, it was more likely I would have had a normal life. I might have met a

208

man after I got out of the military, and we could be living my dreams right now. If Kelly hadn't kept my sister's death from me, I might have realized years ago that I could let go of my need to fix the world's problems for her. And if Sammy... I swallowed hard. If I hadn't met Sammy, I would still be falling apart. I would have swallowed my gun by now, because that was where I was headed.

As much as I hated to admit it, I needed Sammy. I loved him desperately, and my insides were being torn apart knowing that when...if I got back, I wouldn't have him there to hold me together. I pulled out my phone and thumbed through my pictures, until I got to the one Kelly had sent me. His message was more important now than it ever was. *Focus on this mission, and don't let him or anything else distract me.* I could do this, because it had to be done.

In my training, I had learned breathing techniques. Things I used to keep me calm in situations that required it. I pulled in air through my nose and blew it out slowly through my mouth. I focused on my place of Zen—the koi pond—and let the images of sitting there and watching the fish relax me.

When the phone rang for the hundredth time, I continued to ignore it. I had no desire to speak to anyone. If it was Rook or Kelly, they'd try to get me to stop. If it was Sammy... I wasn't sure I could face talking to him. If he asked me to come back, I'd probably abandon what I was doing, turn around, and floor it until I got home, and never want to leave again. But she'd made a threat against him, and even if he no longer wanted to be with me, I would ensure he was safe, and she was dead.

For the remainder of the trip, I did my best to focus on my breathing and achieving my equilibrium. Kelly had been right about going in angry. It would make me stupid, and I couldn't afford to make a mistake, like underestimating Valerie. It would serve me well to remember she was probably every bit as dangerous as me. More so in the fact that she had men at her disposal, and I would be going in alone. Not that it would help her, of course.

The building was more or less exactly like the pictures, an abandoned four story factory in a relatively rundown neighborhood. According to the files Rook had provided, the city thought they could sell it off to the developers, who would rebuild the place, and attract more upscale citizens instead of making housing affordable for those who'd lived there in the first place. I could see where it appeared they'd begun work to restore it and refurbish it into lofts, but it wasn't much. Patchwork covered various sized holes and dents in the walls, a bit of whitewash, but little else had been done in the room I looked at. In fact, it appeared as though they'd come in, realized what a clusterfuck the place was, and walked away from a money pit.

At first glance, I could see the place was still a mess, but there was something odd about it. There was a symmetry to the way things were laid out. The holes were spaced too evenly, a bit of graffiti, but not like most buildings left to the mercies of bored kids. I had the feeling there was a lot more going on here than we thought. Seemed like Valerie was actually prepping the place for use. Maybe she was confident in her men, and since she had the home court advantage, it would be better to play on her terms. I checked my gear once more, then found a place to stay for the night where I'd be able to keep an eye on the building. I wanted to go in, guns blazing, but if I wasn't able to kill Valerie, then this whole thing would have been wasted.

I noticed lights flashed inside at regular intervals, giving the impression of a security sweep. I jotted down the times between passes, then went back to watching. It was weird, because I didn't see anyone venturing outside. No traffic, no people coming and going. We knew she was waiting, but could she possibly be this prepared? I got a sick knot in my stomach when I realized she'd outmaneuvered me. She was prepared in a way I wasn't. The one saving grace for me was, hopefully, they weren't expecting me yet, but that was unlikely.

I continued to watch the next day, and still no one entered or left the building. I couldn't figure out what she was doing. It both excited and unnerved me to know that Valerie could take me down. I'd never had a challenge like this before, and I was like a moth to the flame. I was going to get burned, but I couldn't keep away.

As evening fell, the lights inside kept to almost the same schedule. I made my move about twenty minutes prior to the next noted time. I went up and over the fence, then made my way inside, keeping to the darkened hallways as much as possible. Right on schedule, a beam of light flickered, then went out as someone entered one of the rooms, with me right behind him.

210

I found him rooting through one of the unfinished rooms. His back was to me, but as I stepped forward and closed the door, he spun and sneered. He brandished a knife with a wicked curved blade, holding it in front of him like a sword, despite the fact from pommel to blade it was no more than eight inches. I rolled my eyes, pulled out my gun, and put a bullet into his chest. He lay on the ground, gasping for air. Tossing my bag aside, I ripped open his shirt, not surprised to find he wore a Kevlar vest, and it had saved his life. Too bad for him.

"Now I have to be honest with you. I don't care if you live or die. I'm going to ask a few simple questions. If you answer them right, you're going to need a new job, but you'll live. Answer them wrong, and you'll either be eating your food through a tube in your stomach, or just flat out dead, which will really fuck up your need to eat. Be warned, lie to me and you'll really wish you hadn't. Do you understand, Sparky?"

His eyes were wide, and his lips trembled, but he nodded. "The only thing I want is Valerie. Is she here?" He nodded. I patted him on the cheek. "Good boy. Can you tell me where she is?"

"She'll kill me," he whimpered.

I gave him a smile. "Oh, buttercup, there are a lot worse things than death. Let me give you an example. Are you a lefty or righty. I mean which hand do you masturbate with?"

He didn't answer, but he made fists and drew back his left hand. I lifted it gently and cradled it. It was finely muscled. "You must make yourself pretty happy with this hand. I can see it gets a lot of use."

He gave a gasp, which I assumed, wrongly I'm sure, was meant to be a chuckle. I gripped his little finger and pulled it away from his palm. "Now, one more time. Where is Valerie?"

Tears flowed down his cheeks as he swore to me he didn't know. The anger I'd tried to bury returned. This little pissant stood between me and taking down Valerie. He held Sammy's life in his hands, and I couldn't have that. In that moment, I wanted to hear his pain. To know if it matched the one in my heart. I took the finger I held, and with one quick snap, his finger was touching the back of his hand. He clenched his jaws tight, and I knew it was to keep from crying out.

"Please, I don't know where she is, I swear."

211

I stared him in the eyes, and he averted his gaze. "Wrong answer, bubba," I replied, taking hold of the next finger. This one I drew back slowly, hearing the bones protest, and he screamed long and loud as they shattered.

"Now, if you answer me, you won't lose out on your whole sex life," I told him. I gripped his fuck you finger and plucked at the nail. "You know, if I had brought my pliers, I would rip these off. You haven't known pain until the nail and skin are torn off. But I don't have the luxury of time. I'm going to ask once more. If you don't answer, I'm gonna have to break the remainder of your little pork sausages. Shall I ask again?"

"No, please," he whispered, as I took his index finger in my fist and yanked it back, leaving his hand a misshapen mass.

At that moment, the sharp bite of something hit me in the neck. Sparky's screams must have covered the sound of the door opening, because I'd never heard it. I tried to turn, but my limbs were already growing heavy, my muscles betraying me as I tried to reach up to remove the dart. As I fell to the floor, there was the sound of a gunshot and something warm splattered against my face. In my head, I heard Kelly's voice remind me not to go in angry, and I'd screwed that up big time. "Fuck you, Kelly," I muttered. Then everything went dark.

CHAPTER TWENTY-SIX

Fingers slid through my hair and down the side of my face. I jerked my head away and opened my eyes. Big mistake. The bright light seared into my head, bringing nausea with it. It took everything I could muster not to puke.

"You are a pretty one," came a soft voice.

Blinking furiously to clear my head, I found I was in the same room, tied to a chair. Sparky's dead body lay a few feet away from me. A single gunshot to the head at close range had obliterated what had been a fairly handsome face.

"Another death you're responsible for," she said, stepping into the light where I could see her. Even if the voice wasn't a tipoff, I would know this woman. Sammy hadn't been wrong about their similarities. Except her eyes weren't as bright as his, and her hair was streaked with silver. I wouldn't say she wasn't attractive, but she paled in comparison to my man. The black business suit she wore accentuated her figure, leaving you to think she'd be an easy mark. One look into her eyes, though, would remove any doubt that she'd be the one in charge.

"Really?" I croaked. "How so?"

She gave a Cheshire smile and walked around me, letting her hand trail over my shoulders. I shook with revulsion and anger. I hadn't been this careless since I'd started my training, and this woman got the drop on me, which was even more mortifying. Not because she was a woman, of course. When I was in the military, there were some amazingly strong gals who had the good old boys laughing out of the other side of their mouths when they showed off their combat skills.

She sighed. "Poor Dwight. I told him if he helped me with you, I'd reward him. I even warned him about how dangerous you were, but he was eager to prove himself. After seeing what you did to him, I realized it was easier to find a new employee than pay this one's medical bills. You really do need to work on your temper."

My face grew hot. The fact she was schooling me on how to better myself rankled me, but she wasn't wrong.

"So now I need to figure out what I'm going to do with you. Dwight's job is open, if you're interested."

I pretended to mull it over for a moment, before I replied, "Nah, the retirement plan is a little harsh for my tastes."

She gave that soft laugh and worms squirmed in my belly. I could see why people might be attracted to her, but beyond the surface, there lay an incredible amount of ugly.

"I figured you'd say that," she admitted. She leaned down and brushed a kiss over my lips. "Isn't there anything I could say to change your mind?"

"Do you honestly think the ingénue suits you?" I asked.

Her expression hardened, and I got a glimpse of what the pretty shell held.

"For most men, yes. Dwight thought he'd get laid if he helped me out. Guys are so easy to twist around when sex is involved. But you're different, aren't you?" Then the side of her mouth quirked up. "You're fucking the kid, aren't you? I hear he's a great lay."

I strained against the ropes, but they didn't budge.

"Found your soft spot, didn't I?" she purred. "How about we make a deal? You leave me and my organization alone, and I'll stop looking for him. He won't end up like his father."

"I don't make deals," I said through clenched teeth.

"No, I suppose not. It was worth a try, though. Between us? I wouldn't have given up on him anyway. I should have killed him after I left, but Arianna convinced me he'd make me a lot of money. Young boys like that were in demand from her."

It would do me no good to allow her to continue to bait me, but damned if she wasn't good at what she was doing.

"He had always gotten on my nerves," she said, as she began to pace. "Between him and his father, they were constantly needy. Always wanting time. Attention. When Eric offered me a job as his secretary, I jumped at the chance to get away from them. It was wonderful. He offered excitement, opportunity—"

"Hot sex," I filled in.

She stopped and glared at me. "Yes, that, too. You don't know what it was like. I never wanted Samuel. He was my own personal albatross. I'd met his father in college. I thought we were in love, but it turned out he was, I wasn't. Then I found out I was pregnant, and all my plans were crushed. James, Samuel's father, told me it would be okay. He'd had a good job by then, so he'd earn the money, and I would stay home and take care of the snot factory. It seemed okay at first, but the grind wore on me. Every day I grew to resent them both more.

"Then by chance I met Eric at the grocery store. He was everything James wasn't. He was powerful and virile. My heart fluttered in a way it never had before. I dropped a bag of apples I'd bought, and he knelt in front of me to pick them up. When he stood, I couldn't catch my breath. I thought he had to be the most handsome man on the planet. When he smiled at me, I was lost.

"He invited me to dinner one night. I never told him about my family. The restaurant he took me to was one of the best in Houston. We had caviar as a starter, then lobster and steak. He had the waiter bring an expensive bottle of wine. It was heaven. When he told me he owned the place, I knew I was head over heels in love."

"With his money. Always important to give all the details in a story."

Her hand flashed out and caught me across the face, her nails raking against my skin. There were trickles of blood dripping from the wounds, but nothing worse than I got when I nicked myself shaving.

She ran her hands down her jacket and slacks, then chided me. "Don't interrupt. It's rude."

I glanced over at Sparky's body and shook my head.

"He took me back to his place that night, and made love to me like I'd never experienced with James. There were multiple orgasms on both our parts. The man took me in every possible way, and I loved it."

"You pretended to love it," I corrected her.

She snarled at me and raised a hand again. I smiled and turned my cheek to give her easier access. She huffed out a breath and stepped back.

"You don't want to get on my bad side. I still haven't figured out what I'm going to do with you."

"I think we both know how the story goes," I said. "He made love to you, and you were in love with something, but it wasn't him. Maybe it was his money, or the fact people kowtowed to him. You wanted to be part of that life."

She shrugged one shoulder. "You're not wrong," she admitted. "His people damn near worshiped him. Whatever he wanted, they got for him. Then one night I'd arranged for a sitter for Samuel and went to Eric's apartment to surprise him."

"And found him banging another chick."

"Don't be crude," she snapped. "He loved me and would never do something like that. No, it turned out that Eric was more than just a restaurant owner. He was actually the head of an organization, not unlike the mob. He shook people down for money, did some loan shark deals, stuff like that." She waved a dismissive hand as if it were no big deal. "The night I went to his house, I found him and two of his men beating another one who had welched on his debts. Eric tried to shield me from it, but I stepped around him and looked the man in the eye. He pleaded for help, swore all he needed was more time. I kicked him in the balls, and he screamed long and loud.

"After Eric's men dumped the guy in the gutter, Eric took me into the bedroom and it was amazing. Raw and animalistic. He had me crying out his name as he took me over and over again. He told me he loved me and wanted me to stay with him. I went home that night and told James we were through. I packed a bag and went back to Eric's place, and that was where I stayed."

Her eyes glazed over as if reliving a cherished memory. I snorted, because her happy memory had been what pushed Sammy into his nightmare. The sound jerked her out of her thoughts and she went on with the story.

"Over time, though, I wanted more. His men saw me as eye candy, someone pretty who hung on Eric's arm, and he never dissuaded them of that notion. It bothered me on so many levels. I began to assert myself, telling him what I wanted, and he gave it to me. I would ask for money, and he'd pull out his wallet, giving me whatever he had. I stored it away for a rainy day. Then I asked if he'd put my name on a checking account. He added me to his. I'd never seen that many zeroes in my life. But I wasn't about to tip my hand yet. I needed more.

"Eric had a company that manufactured kid's toys as his cover. Nothing big or fancy, but it netted him some cash and respectability. I asked if I could become his secretary. He loved the idea, because then he could bend me over the desk whenever he wanted. And I was good with that, because the sex was still incredibly hot.

"Finally, about three years after we were together, I had my name on the business, most of his assets, and realized I didn't need him anymore. Eric had given me a bodyguard, I don't remember his name, but he would leer at me when he thought I wasn't looking. When we went places, I would wear my tightest jeans and my sheerest tops. He practically walked around with an erection whenever we were together.

"One day I kissed him. It was an innocent peck on the lips, telling him how much I needed a big, strong man to watch over me. He put his hands on me, and I pushed him away, telling him I couldn't do that to Eric, thereby laying the groundwork for him to do my dirty work."

I sat quietly, listening as she spilled her guts, but while she talked, I assessed my options. The ropes were tight, and my movement was limited, but if she thought I was helpless, she'd made a bad mistake. The chair I was tied to was like one you'd find in a dining room set. It had a spindle back that the ropes were looped through. Instead of focusing on the ropes, I fiddled with the chair, trying to see if any of the slats could be loosened. They seemed to be pretty sturdy, but my chances were better with them than trying to untie myself.

"We went out to dinner one night, and I kept smiling at the bodyguard. When Eric went to the kitchen to talk with the chef, I brushed my leg against... Damn, what was his name? It really isn't fair that I don't remember it, considering what he did for me. It was Brenton, Brighton, or something like that. Anyway, I slid my leg along his, and he reached under the table, his thick digits caressing my thigh, then they slid up my skirt, finally tapping at my legs. I opened them for him, and he sank one into me, sliding it in and out. It was hot, being in a public place and getting fingered by Eric's employee. When we saw Eric coming back, Brenton took his finger out and wiped it on his napkin. Throughout the meal, he kept bringing it to his mouth, and I found that sexy."

She seemed to be lost in the memory. Her eyes glazed over and her voice went husky.

"Eric told us there had been a problem in the kitchen, and he would have to stay late to fix it, but that Brenton should ensure I made it home safely. And he did. Before we were even in the apartment, he had his hands under my shirt, playing with my nipples. I opened his zipper and reached inside. I'd never felt anything so thick before, and I ached to have him sink it inside me. When I got the door open, he picked me up and carried me to the couch, where he tossed me down. He never even took off his clothes, simply pulled out his dick and held it to my lips. I let him slide it inside my mouth and do what he wanted. He grabbed my hair and forced me to take him deep, but there was no way I could get it all the way down. Eventually he realized this, hiked my skirt up, and plunged into me. He was a bull of a man, let me tell you, and had the stamina of one to boot.

"I heard the key turn in the lock and started crying. When Eric opened the door, he saw Brenton on top of me, pumping hard. Eric grabbed him by the hair and yanked him off. Brenton's eyes went wide, and he began apologizing, telling Eric how sorry he was and it was a mistake. Eric pulled a gun and held it up to Brenton's face, but I pushed it aside, and begged him not to kill my bodyguard. When Eric hesitated, Brenton hit him, knocking him to the ground. He grabbed the gun and held it on Eric, uncertain what to do. I wrapped an arm around his waist, leaned my head against his shoulder, and urged him to pull the trigger."

Her smile sent chills down my spine. She enjoyed this way too much.

"Eric's eyes went wide for about a second, before the bullet tore through his chest, spattering blood everywhere. Brenton dropped the gun and stumbled back, and I could see the shock in his eyes. I picked up the gun and smiled at him, then shot him in the same spot he'd shot Eric. When the police came, I told them that Brenton had gone insane and was raping me when Eric came home. Brenton had shot him, and I'd defended myself the only way I could. They did tests that corroborated the fact we'd had sex, plus they found gunpowder residue on Brenton's hand, which my lawyer told them proved my story. The police couldn't find evidence of me having done anything wrong.

"So Eric was dead, Brenton was dead, and the only people who stood between me and getting what I wanted were my husband and kid. The first thing I did as the head of Eric's group was expand our territory. The men came to respect me. Those that didn't were shown the error of their ways by the ones who did. Not long after that, I found Lanny. He asked for so little in return for doing so much for me. He killed James and, even though he wanted Samuel for himself, agreed to do jobs for me in exchange for future considerations."

I tugged harder at the ropes, desperate to get my hands on this woman who had reduced Sammy to a commodity. I wanted to grab her by throat and squeeze until her face turned blue and her eyes bugged out. There had never been a job so personal to me, not even Chrissy's death had affected me like this. It took me a moment to realize when I thought about my job, it wasn't Chrissy I was doing it for anymore. Sammy had become my reason for fighting. He became the innocent in my eyes, even with all the hell this bitch had put him through.

"So at his going rate, multiplied by the time he's been…out of service, I'm guessing you owe me about fifteen thousand dollars."

The number was staggering, and she must have seen it in my expression.

"He was aging out, of course, but back when Arianna first got him, he pulled in at least a thousand a week. She was right to talk me into keeping him, because I have to tell you, over the years, he's more than made up for everything he cost me."

Pushing up, I stood, still tied to the chair. She laughed then kicked out, knocking me to the floor. The chair hadn't broken, and now I found myself on my side, my wrists throbbing from the tight ropes. She knelt next to me and whispered in my ear, "Don't fall in love with him. If…*when* I find him, I'm going to finish what I started. Lanny may not be here anymore, thanks to you, but after we get done, you'll tell me everything I want to know, and even some stuff I don't.

She reached into the pocket of her jacket and extracted a box cutter, pushing the tab to release a wicked blade, which she used to begin slicing off my shirt, followed by the straps of my vest, which she pulled off and tossed across the room.

"Mmm," she hummed, "I do like hairy men."

She ran her fingers through the mat on my chest, tweaking my nipples.

"So you're going to get your boys to rough me up?"

This brought a laugh, nasty and cruel. "I don't need a man to do my job. Dwight was the only one here, besides me. He only needed to get you here. I planned on taking care of the rest."

"And what would you have done if he'd killed me?"

She gave me a look of incredulity. "If he had killed you with that little pigsticker I gave him, then I would have known you weren't the man who'd taken down members of my organization."

"So he was a sacrifice from the beginning?"

She shrugged one slender shoulder. "Naturally. Your death is mine, and I won't share it with anyone. You've cost me time, money, and people I have to find replacements for."

"I'm heartbroken," I told her.

"Not yet," she said enigmatically, bringing the blade to bear over my chest. She sliced downward, drawing up a thin stream of blood. I flinched, but didn't cry out at the pain. I'd endured worse.

"Delightful," she purred. "It looks like this might go all night long."

Then she slashed me in the stomach, the razor-sharp edge tearing through my skin. I hunched involuntarily from the pain.

"We can make this easy, you know. Tell me everything I want to know, and I'll slice your throat and leave you here to bleed out. It won't hurt too badly. You'll simply fall asleep."

I glared at her, and she sighed.

"You want to be difficult? That's okay. I actually enjoy this part."

Her words triggered thoughts and memories. I'd uttered similar lines in the past to people I'd taken down, especially back in my younger days. To have them thrown in my face pissed me off. She and I were nothing alike. She'd murdered the innocent in cold blood, given her son away, had her husband killed. I'd only ever done what I could to protect people from psychos like her. If there were similarities between us, they were far outweighed by the differences.

220

"Now, I don't want you to get lost in thought when you should be paying attention to me. Right now I'm all that stands between you and the grave, so keep that in mind." She wiped the blood off the blade of the knife on her pant leg, leaving a long glistening smear on the fabric. She looked back at me and smiled. "So you know, this might sting a bit."

Then she jabbed me again.

CHAPTER TWENTY-SEVEN

O ne thing I could say for certain, she had torture down to an art form. Over the next two hours I bled from cuts, shallow and deep, along my torso, chest, arms, neck. With each slice, she demanded to know who I worked for, why was I doing this, and where was Sammy. The questions were different, but the answers were always the same. "Fuck you."

She began poking me in the stomach with the tip of the box cutter, not deep, but on top of the slices she already had there, they hurt like a bitch. From my spot on the floor, it was harder to work the chair slats, but I kept up as best as I could. The middle piece of wood rotated freely in the socket, and I nudged it back and forth, usually when she was giving me her version of tender loving care. I timed it that way so there would be a reason for me to strain, and hopefully give her less time to react if I was to get free.

"You really are an interesting man," she said, brushing her hair out of her face. She pulled a band from her pocket and tied the hair into a ponytail. "I don't know anyone who wouldn't have given me what I wanted by now. Then to give me attitude on top of it."

"Sammy said I was prickly," I told her.

"Sammy? Well, that's a fitting name, I guess. He never was man enough to carry Samuel. It was my father's name, you know. James thought we'd name one child after my father, and the next after his. When the squalling brat was born, I knew there was no way there'd ever be another. Then the little shit kept getting beaten up in school. He was too weak and effeminate and the bigger boys preyed on that. I'd hoped the beatings he got would toughen him up, but James kept telling Samuel he was better than that, and he didn't need to fight to prove it."

I hated her, and with each passing second, it consumed me. She'd given up on Sammy, yet wanted to kill him. I needed to know why. "You seem awfully hung up on a kid you didn't want."

"I don't like unfinished business," she said, affecting a bored tone. "He was never supposed to make it out of Arianna's. He wasn't requested anymore, so we were going to get rid of him. The house you found him in was supposed to be where both of you died. Arianna and Amber had set it up where the three men were going to kill you, then run into an unfortunate accident after. Of course you ruined that when you killed them first."

"And I'll go to my grave regretting their deaths," I assured her.

"Please. You left one of them alive, but he couldn't tell me anything about you. So you know, he pleaded with me not to kill him. The damage you did to his face? It was a mercy killing, honestly."

She laughed as if she'd made the world's funniest joke, then went back to sticking me in the stomach. "Did you know that if I stabbed you in the gut, the contents would pour out over your organs and you'd go into septic shock? It's a terrible way to die."

I rolled my eyes. "Been there, done that. Tell me something I don't already know."

She pushed the knife between my arm and chest, cutting deep into my side, then slashed at my underarm, and I yelped. It was a tender area and hurt like hell.

"Anyway, enough distraction. Back to the questions at hand. Why are you doing this? You're too well trained for someone trying to help *Sammy*, so I assume you've been at this for a time. The only thing I don't understand is what you're getting out of it. Is this a job for you? Are you someone with a hero complex? Or is the sex simply that amazing? He has had enough experience, I guess."

I strained against the slat and felt it give. I could only hope that I was able to get it loose before she grew bored and decided to up the damage.

"Okay, how about this?" she started, "You tell me where to find him, and I'll leave you here, but let someone know where to find you."

I laughed. "I've no doubt you would. Some gang members? Or your people who get their jollies out of having someone tied up?"

"Okay, that tells me something. You've definitely done this before. Most people in your position would do anything for a chance to live. I think we need to step it up. Maybe we need to try something more persuasive than the box cutter, though. What I really want now is to get the information I've tried to ask nicely for, then get rid of you. There were so many times you could have made this easier on yourself, but I can see that's not going to happen, and frankly, you're starting to bore me."

She grabbed my bag and opened it up. I winced and cursed myself once more for going in angry. If I had waited, done a better job of recon, then I wouldn't be in this position. But no, I had to be stupid. Didn't matter; there was nothing I could do about it. Let it go, move on, and take her down. Recriminations would wait.

She reached in and grabbed one of my knives. I flinched reflexively, knowing how sharp they were. Then she set that aside and grabbed my second gun.

"Two-fisted shooter, huh? Trying to compensate for other shortcomings?"

She took aim at my face, then lowered the gun. "I'm not going to ask again. Who are you working for? Why are you doing this?"

"Your son hired me to track you down and take you out," I growled.

A flush ran up her cheeks. "I didn't get where I am by being stupid," she yelled. "You're police or FBI or something like that. Tell me who you work for!"

She pulled back and slammed the gun against my face, rattling my teeth. It struck me she was beginning to lose patience, and hopefully that would make her sloppy, too.

"I'm a private detective. I was hired by the family of one of the kids who disappeared. They're paying me good money to find out who killed their daughter."

"Too well trained," she grumbled. "There's no way you're a detective."

"Would you believe former military?" I asked, giving her a grin.

"Bullshit," she snapped. "You'd have no reason to get involved with me. I don't know how you got your information, but there is no way you'd know about my people. Who the hell are you?"

"Okay then, how about a telepathic detective?" I taunted.

She hit me in the face again. Between the cuts and hits, I was weakening, and I knew it. It didn't help that I was lying close to Sparky's body and I swore it was beginning to smell. When she stood up and kicked me in the

224

ribs, I knew she'd finally lost her cool. This would be when she'd be most likely to make a mistake.

"You kick like a girl," I groaned.

That brought an even harder kick to the ribs.

"You think you're so damned funny, but let me tell you, I've broken bigger guys than you."

"Size queen."

The next kick she aimed at my crotch. Only a quick shift kept my jewels from being crowned. I received several kicks to the ribs, wishing I still had my vest to protect me even a little. Each was punctuated by her grunting, and me chuckling, even though they hurt like hell. But every time she did it, I tugged harder, determined to break the chair.

Finally she stopped and took several steps backward, huffing hard.

"Best you got?" I asked.

"Not even close."

She picked up my knife and sauntered over, apparently back in control again. She squatted near me and chuckled. "You're good, but I'm better." She slammed the knife into my side, pushing through the flesh and muscle. This time I screamed.

"Everyone has a breaking point," she reminded me. "Looks like I found yours."

She ripped the knife back out, but it took several tries, and each one hurt like hell.

"Who do you work for?" she asked, once again schooling her tone.

"I don't work for anyone. I found your *son* in that basement, and I swore to him I would take you down. I used to be military, it's true. They trained me to kill, and then I found some people who gave me even better skills, and when I get up off this floor, I am going to use them to end your miserable existence, and bring some peace to Sammy's life."

She smiled then, and it freaked me the hell out. It wasn't a normal smile; it was cold and predatory. "I fully plan on giving him peace. He's going to be buried next to his father, and he'll never have to worry about anything again. If you tell me where he is, I'll send him your hand as a calling card. I want him to know that I'm coming for him. And what I'm going to do once I find him? It's going to make what I did to you look like grade-school bullying."

I thrashed on the floor, shouting invectives at her, swearing to her that I would kill her before she even laid eyes on him, but I used the time to give one last go on the chair. Blood pooled beneath me, and added to the damage she'd already done, it wasn't likely either of us would be walking out of there.

"You might think you're powerful, but you're nothing compared to me. I will take you down, even if it kills me, because Sammy is my life, and I won't let you take that from me."

She knelt by me again and grabbed my hair, tugging my head back. She placed the blade of the knife against my throat, and I swallowed hard. It couldn't end like this, because I wouldn't let it. I put everything I had into one last pull on the chair. The entire back cracked, allowing the ropes to slacken. I clutched the slat I'd been holding, and swung my arms around as best as I could, plunging the piece into her chest, and hearing the satisfying shriek that came with it. She dropped the knife and scrabbled back, fingernails clawing at the floor, as I pushed to my feet. I stumbled over, picked up my gun in my trembling hand, and turned it on her.

Valerie's eyes were feral and she hissed at me. "I'll not give you the satisfaction of begging for my life," she spat, holding the slat that protruded from her shoulder.

While she glared at me, I got myself free of the rope, making sure I kept the gun trained on her at all times. She might be down, but no way would I believe she was out. "You're mistaken. I don't want you to beg for your life. I thought about taking you out at a distance. The idea held a certain appeal to me, but to tell the truth, I wanted you to see my face. To know that I'm the son-of-a-bitch who's going to kill you. For what you did to those kids, and for what you did to Sammy."

"Haven?"

I cursed myself. Again I'd allowed someone to come up behind me. Maybe some remedial training would be in my future. I twisted toward the soft voice I thought I might never hear again. Sammy.

"What are you doing here?" I snapped.

He shook his head sadly. "I don't want you to do this. Not for me."

"This isn't just for you. It's for all those kids she pushed to die. The one they found in the Dumpster. The ones who clogged the coroner's office as

John and Jane Does. The kids who'll never see home again because of what she did."

He took me by the hand and tugged me toward him. "Please. Don't do this." The pleading tone yanked on a thread in my heart. "If she's going to die, it should be me. I'm the one who should kill her," he said, his voice whisper soft.

"Hell no," I roared, stepping back a few paces, but keeping Valerie in my line of sight. No fucking way would I let her get near Sammy again. "I don't want you here. Not for this. Killing someone takes a piece out of your soul that you'll never get back. That's my job, not yours." I lowered my voice. "Call Kelly to come get you. Go back home and wait for me. Run a bath and soak in it. Sleep. When I get there, I'll wake you."

"Take me home?" he begged.

Valerie was quiet, but the smug look on her face showed me how weak Sammy had made me, how much of an impact he'd had from the moment he'd walked into my life. I couldn't kill her with Sammy in the room. I'd get him out, call Kelly to send someone for him, then come back for her and finish what I'd started. As plans went, it was awful. I knew we ran the risk of her getting away and starting over, but Sammy had to be my top priority. I put the gun inside my bag, wrapped an arm around his slender waist, and guided him toward the door. "Okay, sweetheart. We'll go home."

I never saw him move. Weak from the loss of blood, I couldn't have stopped him anyway. In a heartbeat, he had my gun in his hand, turned, and fired. The bullet snapped Valerie's head back, blood spattering on the floor. She slammed back against the wall, her jaw hanging off her face. It wasn't a clean shot, but it did what it was meant to do.

"Sammy? What did you do?"

He handed the gun back to me, his hand shaking violently as tears streamed down his cheeks. "You said that killing takes a piece of your soul. That would be okay if I had any left. What there was, she stole from me a long time ago. Can we go home now?"

The words were a lie. Sammy had more heart and soul than anyone I'd ever known. He'd done this so I wouldn't have to. He didn't want me to be his mother's killer, and this was the only way he could protect me. He pulled me close, making me lean on him, but not letting me comfort him. Even in this, he had to take care of me first.

~

Sammy insisted on driving, and I didn't have the strength to argue. I knew he shouldn't drive, that we should have called Rook or Kelly, but he manhandled me into the car, took out his phone and typed something in. A moment later, he got an answer that seemed to satisfy him. He sighed and put the key in the ignition. I wanted to know who he'd talked with, but dizziness forced me to stay still.

He drove us to a hospital only a few miles away. He helped me inside, and they took me to a cubicle right away. I told them I went nowhere without Sammy, so they allowed him to sit in a chair outside the small room. When he sat down, he curled in on himself, and my heart broke, because Sammy hadn't deserved this. He'd been a victim of Valerie one more time.

After receiving a pint of blood and getting stitched up, I discharged myself against their wishes. They'd insisted I needed to rest, so I figured we'd stay overnight at a hotel. We got back into the car and headed for one that was pretty much off the beaten path. This time I drove, even though the doctor had warned me not to do so. Sammy sat on the passenger side, slumped over, his hands covering his face, his body shaking. I recognized the signs of an adrenaline crash. I called Kelly and told him we'd be home tomorrow, where Rook would find Valerie's body, and when he tried to ask a million questions, I let him know that when the time was right, we'd hopefully both find the answers.

It was late by the time we pulled into the parking lot. It wasn't anything extravagant, but for the night, it would do. After checking in, I went back to the car and, being careful of my multiple stitches, picked Sammy up, cradling him to my chest. He tucked his head against my shoulder. Memories of doing this when we first met flashed in my mind, and I clutched him a little tighter. He whimpered and snuggled against me. I stood there for a moment, gazing down at him. He'd come so far, overcome so many obstacles, and had begun building his life over. Then he had to be noble, to protect me, and it seemed that cost him all of the advances he'd made, and pushed him back into his shell. I had no idea how to fix it, despite my desperation to do so.

He said nothing as I stripped off his clothes and carried him to the shower. He stood still as I ran the cloth over his body, wishing I could clean the memories from him as well. We went back to the bedroom, and I tucked him in. I pulled the covers back to crawl in beside him, and he whispered, "Turn off the light, please." I did as he asked.

Once the room was plunged into darkness, he moved closer, wrapping his arms around me. He shivered violently, and I pulled him close, whispering to him that it would be okay.

"I'm sorry I left," he said, his voice so low I had to strain to hear.

"Why did you go?"

He sniffled. "I wanted to do this so you wouldn't have to. I didn't want you to be torn apart by it, and I knew you would. But when I got here, I couldn't. I was afraid. I didn't know how many people were there, or even if she was. I had no idea what to do, so I sat in the car and reminded myself how useless I am."

"Shut up," I insisted. "You're everything to me, don't you understand? I realized that, without you, I wouldn't have had the strength to go on. I need you in ways I've never needed anyone else."

He burrowed in deeper and let his hands run gently over my sides, down to my hips, where he cupped my ass. He pressed closer, and I knew there would be no erection. This wasn't sexual, it was a need he finally realized he had. The desire to be comforted, to admit that he couldn't always be strong. I put a hand behind his head and dragged him over on top of me. It hurt like hell, but I didn't care. We needed one another, and I wanted to hold him. He shifted a bit, until I told him to stay still.

"You don't need to do this," he said, but stopped moving.

"I want to do this. I need to be sure you don't go anywhere. I was so afraid after you left that you'd never come home. Let me have this, please. Just stay close to me."

"I'm never going anywhere again," he swore. "It was a mistake to think I could do it in the first place. I saw you go in, but when hours went by and you didn't come back out, I had to make sure you were okay. I'm sorry if I worried you. I wanted to do it for you."

He couldn't know how his leaving had gutted me. How, after a few months of having him, I'd been afraid to be alone again. I wouldn't tell him, either. I'd come to terms with it eventually, but he'd killed his mother to protect me, and it had been an act of his love for me, not hatred for her. That told me everything I needed to know about the depth of his feelings for me. His voice drifted and I knew sleep wouldn't be far behind. I kissed him on the head and whispered, "You do everything for me," then I slept, too.

We didn't wake up until three in the afternoon. Sammy was still quiet and unwilling to leave my side. He held my hand whenever we went anywhere, and I won't deny I didn't mind at all. He needed to know he belonged with me again, and I didn't want him to move away either. We checked out and got into the car, Sammy moving as close as he could with the center console between us.

I had him call Kelly, reminding Sammy we were all worried about him. I listened as he issued a litany of apologies, terse yeses, and soft nos. When he was done, he handed me the phone.

"When Rook got his text that you were hurt, he flipped out. He told Samuel where to go, then called the hospital directly. He talked to the chief of staff and told her a VIP was heading their way, and that she needed her best people on the job." Kelly paused, then asked, "Is he really okay?"

"As well as can be expected."

"I've already called Lilah and told her he needs to be checked out when you get back. I hope that's all right."

Though he couldn't see me smile, I hoped he'd hear it in my voice. Kelly would never know how much he meant to me. To both of us. "Yes, it's fine."

I didn't realize he could hear us, but Sammy leaned closer and whispered to me, "Will you also let her know I'm ready to see someone, like she wanted. I'm ready to live again."

EPILOGUE

L ilah had checked Sammy out after the incident and given him a clean bill of health physically. Mentally was a different problem we'd had to tackle. With a list of doctors Lilah recommended, we finally found one that Sammy seemed comfortable with. Or at least one he didn't shrink away from when she talked to him.

I remembered the last time I'd tried to get him to open up about the sessions. Sammy had drawn away.

"I'm not ready to talk about it," he said wearily. "I might never be. I just—please, don't ask right now. Dr. Kiley wants me to take my time and come to terms with what happened. She said I need to be in a better state of mind before I'm ready to share. Tell me you understand."

"I do," I assured him as I wrapped him in a hug. He sighed and sank into my arms.

"I'm sorry," he murmured. "I want you to tell you everything, but I wouldn't even know where to begin. I said I was over it, but it turns out I'm not." He barked a laugh. "Can you believe it? I wanted to be strong for you. Now I find out I can't even do it for myself."

"It'll come," I promised. "Healing takes time and patience. And someone who loves you and is willing to keep you together when you think you're about to fall apart."

Sammy's eyes went wide, and he buried his face in my chest. "Thank you for not giving up on me."

"I swear, it's not ever going to happen. I'll always be here. No matter what."

It had been almost sixteen months since that day in Dallas when Sammy had shot and killed his mother, thus removing any chance she'd be able to reach him again. So much had changed between Sammy and me. We hadn't had sex, but that didn't bother me nearly as much as I thought it would. Sammy still touched me constantly during the day, keeping me grounded. At night, though, it became my turn to hold him when the dreams plagued him, and he'd wake up in a cold sweat, needing me to assure him he was okay, and that the nightmare was over.

Sammy wasn't happy with the process. He wanted to be better, and he wanted it now. The work involved, the multiple sessions, all had taken their toll. He'd lash out at a slight, no matter how small, then he'd apologize, his eyes wide with the realization of what had happened, and run to our room and lock himself away for a while. The doctor said everyone handled grief in their own way, and I needed to let Sammy find his.

Sammy grew a little bolder as time passed, adding kisses to our touching, but I could still see the shadows that haunted him. They frightened me, because this Sammy had been the one I found chained to the floor, with eyes full of fear. The nice thing, though, was I could also see when those shadows began to disappear. His smile became more genuine, his touches less urgent, and the nightmares had faded. He'd gone months without one, a fact we celebrated one night with a nice dinner and some champagne. That evening we'd gone to bed, and Sammy seemed almost giddy.

"I love you," he whispered softly into my ear that night, spooning up behind me.

"Love you, too," I replied.

"Do you think we could go to the gun range this weekend?"

We'd been going to the gun range for several months, and we both enjoyed it. At first Sammy had been nervous about holding a gun, and I think it had been the association with shooting Valerie. Soon enough, though, he gained a respect for firearms. I admit, I had been so damned proud when he hit the target near dead center for the first time and screamed, "Bull's-eye!"

"Sure. I'll set it up. Saturday good for you?"

"Yes, perfect," he replied, kissing the back of my neck.

That night, he drifted off to sleep, holding me the way he used to, and I sighed in relief.

The next morning, Sammy was up before me. He had breakfast ready and on the table and beamed at me as I came into the kitchen.

"Good morning, Haven," he said, giving me a hug.

I growled good morning and reached for the coffee.

"Oh, it's going to be one of those days, huh?" he teased.

"Need coffee if you're going to be so chipper," I grumbled. "Can't stand morning people."

Sammy clapped his hands. "Well hurry up and eat. I want to get to the range. I've got a feeling it's going to be a very good day."

Everything about him exuded confidence and happiness. It had been so long since I'd seen this side of Sammy that I worried he might be lost to me. I pushed those thoughts away. I knew the shadows might return, but I intended enjoy today.

~

"You need to focus," I told him.

"Oh, I am," he assured me, giving me a cocky grin. "You're just mad because I've got a better score than you."

Not mad, exactly. I'd been distracted as I watched Sammy. He had a…glow about him, and it drew my attention every time I even glanced in his direction. I hadn't seen him like this in so long and I wanted to bask in it as long as I could.

"Shut up. Let me go reset the targets."

He laughed as I walked away.

I hung the new targets on the bales of hay and returned to where Sammy stood, disassembling his gear and stowing it away.

"What are you doing?" I asked. "We still have the range for another hour. I paid good money to ensure we were the only ones here."

He didn't look at me as he slipped his gun into the carrying case, then placed it inside the lockbox. "I know, and I intend on putting it to good use. I want you to go into the woods and strip naked."

He said it so matter-of-factly that I couldn't be certain of what I'd heard.

"Do you have a hearing problem?" he asked, a playful grin on his lips.

"No," I whispered. "But are you sure?"

"Go into the woods, strip off your clothes, and put them on the ground. I'll be there as soon as I finish taking care of your gun."

He picked up my gear and slowly began taking things apart and packing them away. I rushed to the wooded area of the range and stripped off my clothes. My cock was harder than I ever remembered it being. I knelt on the pile of clothing, my arms crossed behind me, and waited. It wasn't long before he came into sight, and he was magnificent.

"I like seeing you like this," he admitted. "Why are you on your knees, though?"

It seemed so natural that I hadn't even thought about it. Sammy stepped closer and put his hands on the sides of my head, then tilted it back so I was looking at him.

"I'm going to ask you a question, and I hope you'll give me the answer I'm looking for. Do you like being dominated? Do you enjoy it when I tell you what to do? Make decisions for you?"

"Yes," I answered without hesitation. "But only by you. I never thought I would, but you make me feel. You take me places I've never been. With you, I believe I can fly."

He knelt next to me and ran his hands over my body, lingering on my crotch.

"I'm glad," he replied. "I need to take care of you so much. It killed me when I left, but it was the only way I thought I could do it. I knew if I told you what I was planning, you would have stopped me, and I couldn't let you do that. You're mine, Michael Patrick Phelps. Do you understand that? I decide what's best for you, for us, and you let me. I need you to tell me that it's okay with you."

My voice was strained when I answered. "Yes, please."

He leaned forward and kissed me gently.

"But I'm not calling you Sir," I added cheekily.

"No, I don't want that. I love hearing you say my name. Especially when I do this…" He tilted my head and latched his lips onto my neck, sucking hard. I whimpered as his hands stroked my chest. So many sensations rushed through my body, and I reveled in every one of them.

"I want you to suck me," he whispered in my ear. "I want you to take me all the way down and let me come in your mouth. Can you do that for me?"

"Hell yes," I practically shouted.

I pushed him down onto my clothes and fumbled with his belt. "No," he said, stilling my hands. He reached down and unzipped his pants, sliding his dick out. "Like this."

I grabbed his cock and held it in my hand. So warm, so thick. I wanted to take this slowly, to take him to the edge and keep him there, but he had other ideas. As soon as I took his cock in, he held my head in place and began thrusting deep. I had no choice but to take what he gave me, and I loved it. I loved him.

It was only a few moments, but each one was delicious. He murmured my name over and over, slamming my head down as he thrust up. When he came, he shouted, and held me tight until I'd taken his entire load and swallowed it. He finally slumped back and put his arms behind his head. I licked his cock clean, wanting just one more drop, and then lay down beside him.

"I love you," he said as if it were a universal truth.

"I know," I replied. "I feel it every time you touch me. Speaking of," I added, pushing my erection into his leg.

There was a wicked gleam in his eye when he looked over at me. "No, not right now. I want you hard and aching for me when we get home. Besides, I think I still owe you a punishment for destroying the house. So until I decide otherwise, you don't get to come. No masturbation, nothing."

It was the first time he'd said anything about it. Kelly had it all cleaned by the time we got back, but there was no way Sammy wouldn't have noticed his dragons missing. I'd gone online and went crazy with the credit card, buying all manner of dragons, large and small, to make up for what I'd done. He still never said anything.

"I'm sorry about the dragons," I told him.

"They're only things," he reminded me. "I could live my whole life without needing to buy anything, as long as I have you."

"So no food, no gas, no trip to Hawaii?"

That sparked his interest. "Hawaii?"

"I have two tickets ready for whenever you want to go."

"Seriously?" he asked, an expression of pure joy on his face.

I nodded. I'd ordered them after his first appointment, intending on giving them to him on our anniversary, which was coming—oh shit.

"Happy anniversary," I shot out. It had been a year today since we'd exchanged rings. After Valerie's death, and Sammy's tentative steps into the world, I'd asked him to marry me. He laughed and informed me he should be the one asking, but he accepted anyway.

I had been surprised, but moved, when he said he wanted to take my name instead of keeping his own, or me taking his. The reason he gave was that he didn't want to be Samuel Morin anymore. He told us all that he didn't want any ties to his old life, and becoming Samuel Phelps would give him a fresh start. Rook assured us he would make sure it happened, and we both expressed our appreciation, which paled in comparison to setting Sammy up with a completely new identity. But Rook had been only too happy to welcome a new member to our family.

We filed the paperwork, and a few days later, in the cemetery where Chrissy was buried—Sammy's idea, because he said our family should be together—he slipped a ring on my finger, promising to hold my heart forever.

The actual ceremony had been beautiful. Sammy wore a white tuxedo, while I had on a black one. Kelly had been our witness, and he cried, but swore it was only allergies. As we exchanged our vows, I noticed there was another man there, older, thickset, gray hair. Being protective of Sammy, I leaned forward and asked Kelly who he was, but he gave me a weird look and said, "Who?" When I turned back, the man was gone. I'd like to think it was Rook, come to see Sammy and I get married, but not wanting to step over the line of employee/employer. I asked him about it later, and he said he hadn't been there, but I didn't believe him.

Sammy smiled. "You remembered." He rolled me onto my back and grabbed my shaft, stroking it back to full hardness. "I wasn't going to give you an orgasm until you realized what today was," he admitted. Then without another word, he plunged his mouth, so hot and wet, down on my cock. When I reached for his head, he pulled off. "Keep your hands on the ground and don't move. If I feel your hands, I stop, and you get a case of blue balls for your trouble."

I slammed my hands down on the dirt, and he chuckled then took me back into his mouth. My head thrashed side to side, and it took everything I could muster not to thrust up or grab his head. He teased, he taunted, and he infuriated me with gentle licks and kisses. Finally he had me where he wanted me. I was a babbling mess. Then, and only when he was satisfied, did he speed up, sliding a finger into my ass and tickling my prostate. I came so hard I wasn't surprised when he choked a little bit. He backed off, a smile on his beautiful face, then leaned down and kissed me, our tongues mingling our flavors.

236

"Tonight you'll get your punishment," he promised. "For now, though, I want you to know how much I love you."

They were the sweetest words I'd ever heard, and if I could hear them from him for the rest of my life, I'd be happy. From somewhere nearby, my phone rang. I picked it up, and saw no number on the screen. I knew what it was. I flipped it open. "Hello?"

"I'm sorry to disturb you," Rook said, still sounding like Darth Vader, even on the phone.

"I'm sure you're not," I retorted.

"No, you're right, but Samuel has been insisting I work on my social skills."

I snorted and looked over at Sammy, my heart doing that familiar pitter-pat.

"We have a job, and it's not a pretty one."

"I told you—" I began, then stopped when Sammy took my hand and shook his head.

"Tell him we'll be there soon and he can fill us in."

"Are you sure?" I asked.

"Your heart belongs to me. Your body belongs to the world."

I'd never felt so loved in my entire life as when he gave me a look that promised he'd be with me every step of the way.

"We're on our way," I told Rook then hung up.

Sammy grabbed my clothes and handed them to me, watching as I dressed. He straightened his own clothes, then held out his hand. "Ready to go save the world?" he asked.

As long as he was by my side, I would be able to tackle anything. Hand in hand, we headed out into the unknown, but with the understanding we'd be doing it together.

~~The End~~

ALSO AVAILABLE

500 Miles

Mark loves Jase, but will that be enough to bring Jase back from the brink after a devastating tragedy?

Since he was fourteen, Mark knew he loved Jase, his brother Eric's best friend. As Jase and Eric leave for the Army, Jase leaves Mark something to hold onto, but when the two men are shipped to Kuwait, things change when Jase tells Mark he's met someone. Confused and hurt, Mark is left to wonder what happened. Eric returns, but with devastating news - and needing Mark's help. Can Mark help the man who broke his heart? Or will he let Jase push him away - for the second time?

Someone to Keep MeA Collars and Cuffs Novel (with K.C. Wells)

Eighteen-year-old Scott Keating knows a whole world exists beyond his parents' strict control, but until he gains access to the World Wide Web, he really has no idea what's out there. In a chat room, Scott meets "JeffUK." Jeff loves and understands him, and when he offers to bring Scott to the UK, Scott seizes his chance to escape his humdrum life and see the world. But when his plane touches down and Jeff isn't there, panic sets in.

Collars & Cuffs favorite barman and Dom-in-training, Ben Winters, drops his sister off at the airport and finds a lost, anxious Scott. Hearing Scott's story sets off alarm bells, along with his protective instincts. Taking pity on the naïve boy, Ben offers him a place to crash and invites him to Collars & Cuffs, hoping his bosses will know how to help. Scott dreams of belonging to someone, heart and soul. Ben longs for a sub of his own. And neither man sees what's right under his nose.

Mr. Average

Lucas Manetti has had sex with some very hot men, so why is it he can't get one average man out of his mind?

Lucas doesn't want attachments. He thinks life is much easier that way. Watching the way his mom suffered when his father was dying taught him that. But deep down, Lucas likes the idea of someone taking care of him, of coming home to the same person every night. Yeah, what Lucas really wants is love. So why is he settling for random quick sex in seedy bathrooms? Kyle has been taking care of Lucas's car forever. So for Lucas, it's a logical step to think of Kyle taking care of him. And he has so much that he can offer Kyle--whether Kyle wants it or not. So imagine Lucas's surprise when Kyle isn't particularly enamored of Lucas's 'proposition'. Lucas thought his money would buy him anything. And then he realizes... boy, did he get it wrong. He's so busy reeling from the shock that he almost misses what---or who---has been waiting for him all this time.

Storming Love: Bear & Travis

Is it possible to fall in love from nothing more than a few phone calls and e-mails? Dr. David 'Bear' Berickza thinks so. Despite the distance and limited contact, Bear can only think about Travis Michaels, a fellow veterinarian in the small town of Timber Creek.

When he hears that Timber Creek is directly in the path of Hurricane Lauris, Bear makes a promise. He will be there to help Travis and his daughter, the smart-mouthed Tina, to save the abandoned animals.

The road to hell is paved with good intentions, and when Lauris hits, Bear and Travis find that despite their best efforts, it's going to take more than that to save any lives, including their own.

Lost Time

Alex Jeffers and his best friend, Kurt Danvers, were always inseparable. When you found one, you would inevitably find the other. And Alex dreamed it would always be that way.

Kurt swore that when they went to different colleges, nothing would change. They'd keep in contact and would always be best friends. By the time Alex realizes it, he and Kurt have drifted apart. Years of friendship are just...gone.

Starting a new life is scary, but eventually Alex forges ahead and begins building one he's proud of. While at a dinner meeting with a student's father, Alex panics when he sees Kurt Danvers for the first time in five years. He flees the restaurant, but he can't outrun his past as Kurt finds him and lets Alex know that he's not willing to lose him again.

(Please note: This is a new version of the original story, which was a free read at GoodReads. This story has been professionally edited and expanded by 2,000 words, which includes a new ending.)

Damian's DisciplineA Collars and Cuffs Novel (with K.C. Wells)

The man who pimped Jeff may be in prison, but Jeff is still living the nightmare, selling himself to men and relying on pills to manage. Then he meets Scott, a young American man who could easily have been where Jeff is now. Scott's friends extend a helping hand to Jeff, and he grabs it.

Leo and Thomas bring Jeff to stay with Dom Damian Barnett until they can find him someplace more long-term. Still grieving from losing his sub to cancer two years before, Damian agrees to help. But when he glimpses the extent of the damage, Damian wants to do more than offer his guestroom. Jeff is not a submissive, but Damian can see he desperately needs structure in his life. It's up to Damian to find an answer.

He never expects that what he discovers will change both their lives.

Protector of the Alpha

Adopted at an early age by a wealthy family, Jake Davis has always seemed to have an easy life. Even in college he was blessed with good grades and an apparently clear path to a pro football career. Good thing his best friend keeps hanging around to keep his head from getting too swollen.

Zakiya Incekara has always been...odd. Being fluent in six languages and having a flair for international cooking should open the world to him, but those skills leave him isolated.

When Jake sees Zak for the first time, with water beading down his slender form, something inside him shifts, and it hungers for Zak. To have him. To claim him. And Jake knows that whatever it is, it won't be denied.

When they are approached by a man who claims knowledge of a secret past they share, Jake and Zak are thrust into a world they would never have believed existed. The forests of Alaska might seem an odd place to find your destiny, but these men will meet the challenges head on, as they learn that sometimes you have to make sacrifices to be Protector of the Alpha.

Scent of the Heart

Casey Scott grew up being told he'd never amount to anything, and despite the unwavering love and support from his best friend, Jake, the idea sticks in the back of Casey's mind. When he discovers he has a unique destiny in an enclave where shifters and humans live together, he seizes the chance, wanting for once in his life to be someone special.

Tsvetok Yerokhin lost his parents to the evil ruler of the enclave when he was a boy. The responsibilities of raising his two younger brothers nearly overwhelmed him and self-doubt took over. When the new Alpha and his Protector arrive in time to save his life, Sev is grateful, but he's even more shocked when he scents his mate with them.

Casey isn't prepared for the feelings that sweep over him when he meets Sev, but he refuses to act on them because he's straight. Still, there is something so alluring about Sev that Casey can't help being drawn to him.

As the two explore the edges of their new discovery, an evil returns, determined to control the enclave or destroy it. The Alpha and Protector are powerless to stop it, but Casey holds the key to victory. If he can discover what it is, he has a chance to save them all. To be the hero.

Unfortunately, the hero has to be willing to make the ultimate sacrifice, and for Casey that means losing his heart.

Dom of Ages: A Collars and Cuffs Novel (with K.C. Wells)

Eli may only be thirty, but he has had enough of pretend submissives. When he spies Jarod in a BDSM club, everything about the man screams submission. So what if Jarod is probably twenty years older than Eli. What does age matter, anyway? All he can see is what he's always wanted—a sub who wants to serve.

Jarod spent twenty-four years with his Master before Fate took him. Four years on, Jarod is still lost, so when a young Dom takes charge, Jarod rolls with it and finds himself serving again. But he keeps waiting for the other shoe to drop. Because there's going to come a point when Eli realizes he's a laughingstock in the club. Who would want to be seen with a fifty-year-old sub?

After several missteps, Eli realizes that in order to find happiness, they will need friends who will understand. At a friend's insistence, he visits Collars & Cuffs, where they are met with open arms. As they settle in to their new life, Eli begins to see things differently and he dares to think he can have it all. Until a phone call threatens to take it all away....

ABOUT THE AUTHOR

Parker Williams believes that true love exists, but it always comes with a price. No happily ever after can ever be had without work, sweat, and tears that come with melding lives together.

Living in Milwaukee, Wisconsin, Parker held his job for nearly 28 years before he decided to retire and try new things. He enjoys his new life as a stay-at-home author and also working on Pride-Promotions, an LGBT author promotion service.

Connect with Parker on:

Twitter: @ParkerWAuthor

Facebook:

https://www.facebook.com/parker.williams.75641

Or you can visit his website: ParkerWilliamsAuthor.com

TRADEMARK ACKNOWLEDGEMENTS

The author acknowledges the trademarked status and trademark owners of the following trademarks mentioned in this work of fiction:

007: Danjaq, LLC

Apple: Apple, Inc.

Beretta M9: Fabrica D'armi P. Baretta, SPA

Bose: Bose Corporation

Chevy Spark: General Motors, LLC

Chivas Regal Royal Salute: Chivas Holdings (IP) Limited

Chubby Hubby: Ben & Jerry's Homemade, Inc.

Def Leppard: Bludgeon Riffola Limited

Desert Eagle 50AE: Saeilo Enterprises, Inc.

Disney's Hunchback: Disney Enterprises, Inc.

Dom Pérignon: Moet Hennessy USA, Inc.

Dumpster: Toccoa Metal Technologies, Inc.

Facebook: Facebook, Inc.

FBI: Federal Bureau of Investigation

Ford Escort: Ford Motor Company

Girl Scout: Girl Scouts of the United States of America Corporation

iPod: Apple, Inc.

Jack Bauer (character in 24): Twentieth Century Fox Film Corporation

Johnnie Walker: Diageo Brands B.V.

Kevlar: E. I. Du Pont De Nemours

Legend of Zelda: Nintendo of America, Inc.

Maglite: Mag Instrument, Inc.

McDonald's: McDonald's Corporation

Mustang (1969 Boss 429): Ford Motor Company

Navy SEAL: The Department of the Navy

Sony: Sony Corporation

The Doors ("Light My Fire"): John Densmore, Robby Krieger, Ray Manzarek, the Estate of James Morrison, and the Estate of Pamela Courson

This is Your Life: TIYL Productions

US Army: Department of the Army

Xbox: Microsoft Corporation

www.ingramcontent.com/pod-product-compliance
Lightning Source LLC
Chambersburg PA
CBHW021959170626
46808CB00001B/215